SWORDS
ACROSS
the thames

Other novels in the Warrior Queen Series

The Forgotten Queen
1998

SWORDS
ACROSS
the thames

haley elizabeth garwood

1999
the writers block
Bruceton mills, west virginia

swords across the thames

The Writers Block/published by arrangement with the author

First Printing, April 1999

All rights reserved.

Copyright © 1999 by Haley Elizabeth Garwood

Cover concept by Mel Graham

Cover art by Tell Hicks

Graphic Design by Richard Hill and Richard Hopkins
of Pioneer Press of W. Va., Inc.

ISBN: 0-9659721-8-6
LCCN: 98-061845

THE WRITERS BLOCK
The Writers Block books are published by The Writers Block,
Laurel Run, Route One, Box 254, Bruceton Mills, WV 26525-9748
Designed by Pioneer Press of W. Va., Inc., Terra Alta, WV

Publisher's Cataloging-in-Publication
(Provided by Quality Books, Inc.)

Garwood, Haley Elizabeth
    Swords across the Thames / Haley Elizabeth Garwood. — 1st ed.
    p. cm.— (Warrior queen series)
    ISBN: 0-965972186

    1. Ethelfled, d. 918—Fiction. 2. Queens—Great
Britain—Fiction.   3. Great Britain—History—
Anglo-Saxon period, 449-1066. 4. Mercia (Kingdom)—
Fiction. 5. Vikings—England—Fiction. I. Title.
II. Series: Garwood, Haley Elizabeth. Warrior queen series

PS3557.A8417S9 1999   813'.54
                             QBI98-1742

Printed in the United States of America
10 9 8 7 6 5 4 3 2 1

Dedicated to

The clans of

Haley, Porter, Dalebout, Thomas, Stonebraker, Garwood,
and Wales

and

Linda Lee Trout Johnson
a woman warrior who has never stopped fighting
and has never stopped laughing

and

Charles, my husband, who has
never stopped supporting me.

acknowledgments

Writers always feel that they work alone. Usually they do. After agonizing months in which a title for this book eluded the author, she decided that the only way to get the novel to press was to have a contest. Thus, "Name the Novel" contest was launched through *Romantic Times Magazine*. No longer alone, but with fifty "co-authors" and others who agreed to judge the entries, the nameless novel was at last baptized. Now the presses could run. Cover art could be finished. The author could relax.

Selecting the title took longer than expected because all titles had merit in one way or another. There was a lot of e-mailing back and forth between The Writers Block and the judges. At last, we decided that we would start by asking for three best titles from each judge. That did not help, either. We narrowed the list, but had as many different title preferences as judges. The creators of the final titles are named below:

Carla jeanne Bingham
Heather Cuppett
Carol Lynn Cunningham
Angela Davidson
Mary Kennedy
Jessica Montoya
Theresa M. Norman

Patricia Pearson
Marti Phillips
Kim Richardson
Melanie Savage
Sharon Swearengen
MacKenzie Raye Van Cleef

The task continued to be daunting, but we did choose one title. However, there was a second title that was so similar we decided to have two winners and two literary walk-on parts. The title chosen, *Swords Across the Thames*, was entered by Heather Cuppett. Theresa M. Norman entered the second title, *Crossing the Thames*.

The other great entries were by:

J. H. Baker	Denise Lotz
Kathleen Babcock	Regina Maclntyre
Mariam Belowich	Colleen Martin
Pamala Bistel	Ladonna Mendel
Paulette Boucher	Emma L. Metz
Sandra Kaye Burche	Maria Morgan
Denise I. Coats	Patricia Osback
Yvonne Crocker Cook	Deborah Pace
Katherine M. Dean	Candace Peterson
Robin Dillon	Sandra Quinn
Lynn Frost	Ginger Rapsus
Florence Haas	Fran Robinson
Shirley Hailstock	Belkis Rodriguez
Sharon Hamilton	Dawn C. Smith
Michelle Calabro Hubbard	Simone Therese Tschida
Linda Kendall	Janet L. Therens
Sharon LaMasney	Noelene Thompson
Ruth Long	Rosalie Zachary
Rosemary Longworth	

Thanks to all of you who took the time to help with the book's title. We're in this together and writing isn't so lonely anymore.

Thanks also to Juliana Garnett who took time from the book tour for her newest novel, *The Scotsman*, to help.

Constance O' Banyon gave freely of her time right in the middle of her new novel, *Texas Proud*. Thank you, Constance.

All the other judges were editors and/or in the publishing business and wish to remain anonymous.

ABOUT
SWORDS ACROSS
the thames

It is difficult enough to do research about the past, but it's infinitely more difficult when the main character is a woman from history. The story takes place on the British Isles in the tenth century. That alone precludes an easy research task. The heroine's father, Aelfred the Great, kept detailed accounts of the history of his times. He dutifully recorded the births and occupations of his offspring, the wars with the Vikings, and all manner of important ideas. In spite of this, only the birth of his daughter, Aethelflaed (Lae), is recorded. Any mention of her wondrous feats is left out of the Anglo-Saxon Chronicles. Why? Was there animosity between father and daughter and their two countries? Were women not valued even though they were instrumental in changing history?

Ironically, we know of this intriguing warrior queen because her fame reached Ireland and Wales. She is known because the Irish and Welsh chronicles listed her achievements. This novel is an attempt to add another facet to our history.

about the author

Haley Elizabeth Garwood's goal to write forgotten women warriors back into history has been realized with her second novel in the Warrior Queen Series. *Swords Across the Thames* follows her successful first novel, *The Forgotten Queen.*

Dr. Garwood graduated from Purdue University with a degree in journalism/creative writing, then furthered her education at West Virginia University by obtaining a master's degree in theatre and a doctorate in education. She taught special education before becoming a high school principal.

A mountain top farm in West Virginia is home to Dr. Garwood and her family, which includes the obligatory cache of cats and dogs. Each novel has a bit part played by one of her barn cats.

main characters

Aethelflaed (Lae), daughter of Aelfred the Great, Queen of Mercia.

Aethelred (Red), husband of Lae and King of Mercia.

Aeflwyn, daughter of Lae and Red.

Eahlswith, mother of Lae and wife of Aelfred the Great.

Aelfred the Great, King of Wessex and father of Lae.

Edward, Prince of Wessex and brother of Lae.

Aethelstan (Stan), illegitimate son of Edward and nephew of Lae.

Egwinna, mother of Stan.

Elflaed, wife to Prince Edward of Wessex.

Eiric, son of Viking Chief Thorsten.

Thorsten, Viking Chief and father of Eiric.

Nissa, wife to Eiric and mother of his three sons.

Rorik, Kerby, and Hoskuld, sons of Eiric and Nissa.

Olenka, sister to Eiric and daughter of Thorsten.

King Niall, King of an Irish principality.

Heather, Irish Princess and sister to King Niall.

Melvyn, Irish Prince and brother to King Niall.

Theresa, midwife to Egwinna.

map of Britain in the tenth century

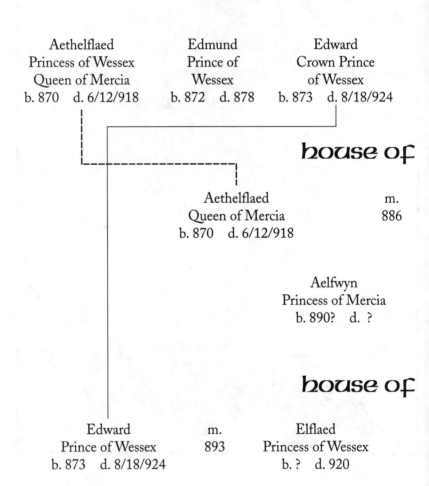

house of

Aelfred the Great   m.
King of Wessex   868
b. 848   d. 10/26/899

Aethelflaed	Edmund	Edward
Princess of Wessex	Prince of	Crown Prince
Queen of Mercia	Wessex	of Wessex
b. 870 d. 6/12/918	b. 872 d. 878	b. 873 d. 8/18/924

house of

Aethelflaed   m.
Queen of Mercia   886
b. 870   d. 6/12/918

Aelfwyn
Princess of Mercia
b. 890?   d. ?

house of

Edward	m.	Elflaed
Prince of Wessex	893	Princess of Wessex
b. 873 d. 8/18/924		b. ? d. 920

2 sons/8 daughters

wessex (aelfred the great)

Eahlswith, Princess of Mercia
Queen of Wessex
b. 850   d. 12/5/905

Aethelgifu	Aefthryth	Aethweard
Princess of Wessex	Princess of Wessex &	Prince of
Abbess of Shaftsbury	Countess of Flanders	Wessex
b. 874 d. 896	b. 876 d. 929	b 878? d. 920

mercia

Aethelred
King of Mercia
b. 854?   d. 911

wessex (edward)

Egwinna
Shepherdess and mistress to Edward
b. ?   d. 899?

Aethelstan	Aelfred	Edith
b. 891? d. 939	b. 898? d. 898?	b. 899? d. 927

chapter

Í

UN! RUN!" Lae kicked her horse in the ribs and lay against his neck holding onto her cowl with one hand. The strength of the wind against the cowl was too much trouble, and she let the head covering go. The cowl flew off like a white sail, and Lae was free of that troublesome burden. She felt her silver-blonde hair ripple behind her in the wind. Had she inherited the brown hair of her father, brothers and sisters, she would be safer at this moment. Lae's hair, however, was like her mother's, unusual enough to be the one mark of identification amongst Lae's people as well as the enemy.

Lae dropped her hand to Tanton's blowing mane and intertwined her fingers through the coarse hair. As a child whenever she had been frightened or sad, Lae had been allowed to go to the stables to visit the horses. She had drawn comfort from the strength of her father's horse. She had wrapped her arms around the horse's neck and had laced her fingers through his mane until she had felt better.

Lae's hands blistered, and she wished she had worn gloves so Tanton's mane wouldn't cut into her fingers. But, as usual, she had left her gloves behind. She hated them. Lae held the reins loosely in her free hand, giving the horse his lead and letting him choose the path back to the fortress.

An arrow whistled past her, and she flinched. Too close! She glanced over her shoulder and saw the Viking patrol riding hard behind her. The gap was closing. There were only three Vikings, but they had surprised her. The only way to keep from being killed was to race to her own territory. Now she wasn't certain that she could get to her country in time.

Blinking wind-caused tears from her eyes, Lae could see a stretch of old paving stones from the ancient Roman road ahead of her a few hundred feet. She slapped the reins against Tanton's neck and kicked him with her heels. As soon as they drew close to the old road, they would run parallel to it, heading northeast until they reached the bridge that crossed the Thames. If she could get to her border guards, she would be safe. The bridge was guarded by her men, but not by the Vikings. She had often wondered at their lack of guards. Was it because they were arrogant or foolish? They were built like oxen. Mayhap they had the brains of oxen.

The road loomed closer, and Lae felt relief. She shifted in the saddle to loosen her tunic that had twisted around her legs. In her haste to escape from the Vikings, her under-kirtle had bunched up; she had not had time to mount Tanton properly. How stupid to have let them see her! Usually the patrols were so lax that she could hear their voices drifting across the distance that separated them from her, but these men had crept up on her.

Lae should not have underestimated them. Her father had warned her about thinking of the enemy as lacking intelligence. Most of them seemed to be stupid, of course, but there were always the exceptions. Until now, her weekly spying trips had given her the excitement she craved. This was more than enough excitement, and Lae vowed that she would try to obey her husband when he told her to leave the spying to their lieutenants.

When she reached the road, she raced Tanton on the soft grass rather than on the paving stones. He was shod, but she did not want his tendons to be bruised from the grueling pace. The road rushed past her in a gray blur. She saw the bridge ahead and, farther in the distance, the wall of Lundenburh. Never had she been so happy to see the wall.

All the other times that she had slipped across the bridge, she had been able to ride back to the fortress calmly. She was less than a mile away and each hoof beat that brought her closer to her own country caused her nerves to scream louder instead of calming her as she had expected.

Lae had concentrated so hard on reaching the bridge that she heard the sound of pounding hooves too late. Horrified, she felt an arm around her waist. She kicked her feet loose from the stirrups so that she would not be dragged by Tanton, and fell with the Viking to the ground. Both of them lay unmoving. Horrified, Lae realized that she was stretched out from head to toe on the damnable Dane. She wanted to move, but had to wait for her breath to return. She thought she was going to suffocate from the fall and from the force of the thick arm that held her so tightly she could not move.

Her breath returned slowly, but her mind had been working quickly. No one knew that she had crossed into Viking territory, for she had slipped across the Thames at a ford in spite of the chilly November water. Lae took a quick inventory of her family. Her husband, Aethelred, was alone at the fortress. Her brother and her father were to have come last week to discuss the surge of new Viking settlements to the north of Lundenburh beyond the boundary of the Danelaw, but plans had changed.

Lae had spied on the Danes several times to answer the question of whether or not the Vikings were a threat to Mercia and Wessex. She had grown tired of wondering and had wanted action, and until today spying had been easy.

Lae felt the man beneath her breathing, and was sorry he still lived. Why could he not have hit his head on a rock? The sound of the other two Vikings pushed through her thoughts. She was in a great deal of trouble. Even though their two countries were not at war, the truce between the Mercians and the Vikings was an uneasy one. Her only hope was to kill all three of them. But that could cause a war and though she would like that, the time was not right.

"Who have we here?" the Dane asked. He sat up, still holding Lae tightly.

She pushed his arm from her waist, aware of the softness of his wool sleeve, pulled her under-kirtle down to her ankles, and straightened her tunic. "It is no concern of yours who I am. It matters only that I am a Mercian."

The Dane laughed and looked up at his companions. "She claims to only be a Mercian. We know that we have the Lady herself, King Aelfred's daughter and the wife of Aethelred, Lord of the Mercians."

"Why did you say that?" Lae's breath left her, for she knew he had recognized her unusual hair coloring. Should she be worried about being held for ransom? It happened to women all too often. She flexed her arm. The knife was still in its special sheath, hidden between the tight sleeve of her under-kirtle and the loose sleeve of her tunic. She might be taken, but she would kill someone first. She felt like stabbing the man whose dark eyes laughed at her.

Lae pushed herself away from the Viking and stood. She brushed off the back of her tunic while she stalled for time. The Dane stared at her with a smirk on his face, resting one arm on his knee. He was dressed in a blue wool tunic trimmed with embroidered bands of red, gold, and saffron at the cuffs, the hemline, and the neckline. The colors matched his reddish-blonde hair. A gold and silver brooch pinned his rose-colored cloak, which was thrown back over one shoulder. He wore a silver ring in the likeness of a wolf on his left hand, an indication of high birth. The other two horsemen in tunics of common, undyed wool were apparently his servants. Lae was irritated at their laughter. They would not laugh when the war started.

"You are Aethelflaed, Lady of the Mercians, are you not?" asked the man who had pulled her out of the saddle. "Allow me to introduce myself. I am Eiric, son of the chief of our village, which is known as Beamfleot in your language." He leaped up and bowed. "Forgive my rudeness, my lady. I was so enamored by your beauty that I failed to obey my good mother's teachings."

Lae gasped at this man's impertinence. "If my husband were here, he would run you through with his sword for your mocking tone of voice. You are beyond rude. You are vulgar, even for a Viking."

"I, vulgar? My lady, I was trying to be polite and follow your courtly rules. How can I help my ignorance?"

Lae glared at the handsome man whose mocking smile made him all the more intriguing. He was well built, carrying himself in the easy manner of one who knew that he was attractive to women. She would show him that this was one woman who was too intelligent to be fooled. Her husband was far superior in every way to this poor excuse for a human being.

"Viking, you are a fool. Do you know what will happen to you, to your people, if you harm me?"

"I wish no harm to you. I am here to help you." Eiric swept his arm back to include the other Vikings. "These two lads are my servants, Hroald and Yvor. They, along with me, are at your service, my lady."

"The only service you can do for me is to die."

"A nice sentiment from one we were trying to help. We thought that your horse had run away." Eiric grinned.

"I have never had difficulty riding any horse." Lae was angry with herself for feeling that she had to justify her expertise to this man. She whirled around and marched toward Tanton, who stood a few feet away.

Lae grabbed the reins and threw them across Tanton's neck. She checked the girth, put her foot in the stirrup and swung her leg across the saddle, her loose fitting riding tunic falling into place. Listening for any sudden movement behind her, Lae settled herself, she hoped, without showing any signs of fear. She wondered if she were about to be snatched off the horse again by the leader of this small band of Danes. She turned and looked at the Viking over her shoulder. "Are you not far from your village?"

"Not for a Dane set on adventure," Eiric said.

Lae urged Tanton forward and started toward Lundenburh. She remembered the arrow that had whizzed past her, and she could not ride away. She reined Tanton around and rode back to the Viking, stopping inches from Eiric's smirking countenance. "I find your actions despicable. You shot an arrow at me. You are a coward, for the arrow was aimed at my back. I had always suspected the Vikings were beset by weakness, but I thought it was in their brains."

"You are indeed the fiery Lady of the Mercians. Your reputation precedes you. Had your hair not given you away, your imperial attitude would have." Eiric was still smiling.

"You are still a coward. The arrow was intended for me." Lae's voice was hard and cold. "When we fight you again, I know we will be the victors."

Eiric stopped smiling. Grabbing Tanton's bridle he said, "Had I wanted to kill you, the arrow would have struck you in the heart — from the front. I have been watching you since you forded the Thames crossing from your country to mine. You should send a man to do a man's job."

Lae pulled the reins taut. Tanton reared and pawed the air, his hooves nearly slicing through the Dane's tunic. She loosened the reins, and the horse dropped down. If she had not been so angry, she would have laughed at the look on his face. "There is no such thing as a man's job when it comes to fighting. I will be on the front lines of battle the same as any man. That is the way my father, my brother, and my husband have taught me. Thus has it always been among the Anglo-Saxons. They value their women."

"Women are to be kept out of the army's camps." Eiric's upper lip curled in contempt. "Women do not have the brains to wage war. Women are only good for sport and to make sons."

"If Vikings were real men, you would allow your women to fight, too. Or are you afraid to let them see you fight? You are a pathetic race."

"Our women have our sons yearly. You, I understand, have married an old man and have only one daughter to show for your years. Is your husband too old to bring you the joys of the marriage bed?"

"An impertinent question from a boorish man. You Vikings breed like cats and think that proves you manly. You do not look like either a lover or a warrior. If we meet again, may it be on the field of battle. I pray to God that I will have the pleasure of killing you myself."

Eiric stared at Lae. "You misunderstand us. We do not want to fight the Anglo-Saxons. We want only to live in peace on our side of the border. We are farmers by trade and want to till the soil, raise our families, and explore the lands beyond the sea."

"You want to have so many sons that your land will be too crowded for farming. You think that you can take our land and give it to all the brats you father. I wish all Danes would return to their homelands across the Narrow Sea."

"This is my homeland and the homeland of my father and grandfather before me," Eiric said. "My sons were born here. This country is as much mine as it is yours. Hroald and Yvor were born on this island. They have no other home."

Lae leaned down and glared at Eiric. She remembered the Danish villages she had seen where the armorer made chain-mail and the blacksmith pounded out Viking swords. It did not look as if any farm tools were being made in those villages. "There is not room enough for both our peoples. You stole the land you hold from the Anglo-Saxons. You pillaged Anglo-Saxon villages, killed our men, stole our children, and raped our women. The Anglo-Saxons are my ancestors. We do not forget the enemy of our ancestors. When the sun sets on your people, it will not be on

British soil. I will personally help remove you from this island if it takes the rest of my life."

Lae pulled Tanton around and nudged him in the ribs. His muscles bunched, then lengthened as he lunged forward. She looked back once as Eiric shouted to her. She thought he said that they would meet again.

Tanton's hooves clattered across the wooden bridge. Lae rode so fast that the Thames was a blur of silver-blue, like a ribbon woven between the velvet grasslands of the marsh. The guards seemed surprised as Lae rode past them through the gate in the old Roman wall that surrounded the town of Lundenburh. A mere half-dozen years ago, her father and her husband had led their combined armies against the Vikings and had recaptured the town for Mercia. She had been married just after the battle.

Lae smiled at the memory of her joyous wedding and the handsome warrior who had become her groom. She had first met Red when she was ten and had loved him instantly. To her youthful dismay, he had thought of her as a mere child. Lae had seen him often during the next six years before their wedding, since Red had fought with her father against the Danes. Lae remembered the thrill of learning that her father and Red had decided that their two countries – Wessex and Mercia – would be stronger if bound by marriage. Since she was King Aelfred's eldest daughter, she was the logical choice. It would have been terrible if Red had married someone else, but he had waited for her. She, in the meantime, had been trained by her father to be a leader of men and by her mother to be a leader in the household. Lae found that both jobs had suited her. They seemed to have given her a way to spend some of her enormous store of energy.

During the six years of their betrothal, Lae and Red had never talked of love. Instead, they had talked of battles, always battles, and always in the presence of her father. The two men had taught her strategies and had told her how to trick the Vikings. They had taught her to use a bow and arrow, a battle-ax, a sword, and to ride a horse. Never had she been alone with Red until her wedding night, and never had she talked of love with him until the day their daughter was born. He was a fierce warrior, but had been afraid to talk of love. Lae smiled at the memory of his shyness on their wedding night.

Red would not be shy about scolding her for this mistake. He needed to know what she had observed in the Viking village from the top of the hill, but she could not tell him about her encounter with the Danes. He was as protective of her as she was of him. Red would be livid if he thought there had been any threat from a Dane. If Red had encountered the Vikings, his response would be to invade their country immediately because of the insult.

The fortress that was home lay ahead. It was adequate, but Lae missed her home in Wessex. In comparison to her father's stronghold, this fortress was rough, its stonework only waist high and the rest timber. The second floor was basically a tower for the nursery.

Lae planned for the day when she could move to Tamoworthig to the north. It was, unfortunately, behind the Danelaw boundary. Red had promised her that they would retrieve the land that had been Mercian. It was colder than Lundenburh, but she would not mind. One had to expect that when living north. The crisp winter air and the biting wind made her feel alive.

The guard recognized her and opened the gate to the palisade. Lae rode across the keep to the stables and dismounted as the groom rushed over to hold her horse. She handed him the reins and, glancing toward the stables, noted that her husband's horse was in his stall, nosing and snuffing at the feed box.

"Is my husband in the great hall?" Lae asked.

"Yes, my lady."

"Thank you." Lae walked quickly across the keep toward the great hall. She was anxious to see her daughter, Aelfwyn, as well as Red. Lae glanced up at the sky and was surprised to see that it was dark already. Her encounter with the Vikings had taken longer than she had thought. She crossed herself and said a small prayer to the Virgin Mary. Lae hoped that she would not go to hell for lying, but she was not really going to lie, she told herself. Just leave out a fact or two about her weekly rides across the border.

She pushed her hair away from her face. The cowl! She had forgotten to ride back and retrieve it. Mayhap Red would not be offended by her hair showing. It was not as if it were the first time she had gone without a head covering, but, from the time she could remember, her mother had always chided her for not wearing her cowl. Lae hated having all that material on her head, flowing down her back. It seemed to slow her down. When she had told that to her mother, Eahlswith, she had laughed at Lae and said that young ladies, especially royalty, were not supposed to be running everywhere or riding as fast as men.

Lae put her hand out to push open the heavy plank door to the great hall, but one of the servants pulled it open for her. Heat rushed out to meet her as she stepped into the room. The old man shut the door with a thud. Across the great room next to the firepit, Red sat at a table, a vellum map spread out in front of him.

He was as handsome, lean, and strong as the day Lae had married him seven years ago. His red hair had given him his name, and she loved the way it shone in the light from the fire. He was older than she by sixteen years, but that did not matter to her. She loved the lines around his eyes that crinkled when he laughed, the deepness of his voice, and the way he looked at her in the mornings when they first awakened.

"Lae, come here and tell me what you think of this plan." Red's voice boomed across the room. "I need the advice of an intelligent person. Not that your father and your brother are not intelligent, but we have been arguing all afternoon. They just left to visit the blacksmith in the outer bailey. They should return in an hour."

"Father is here? When did he come? Edward, too? What has happened that they should make the long trip here? Lae leaned against the door, feeling the need to have the thick planks behind her.

Red chuckled. "You should have stayed home today."

"They sent no word they were coming!" Lae moved away from the door, putting her hands on her hips. "Why did they not? Had I known they were coming, I would have waited for them."

"It was better that they travel in secret in these difficult times. No message is safe with the Vikings everywhere. They are an untrustworthy mix of barbarians. Remember, your father had to ask for Danish hostages from East Anglia so that peace could be kept between our countries. I do not see any hope for peace with the Danes even if we do have hostages."

"The Danes would not know how to leave without a fight." Lae unpinned the brooch that held her cape in place. "I am ready to run them out of our country. I am ready now." She repinned the brooch to the woolen cape, being careful not to damage the precious fur skins that lined the cloak, and tossed the garment across the back of a chair.

"Red, why are they going to our blacksmith and not their own?"

"Because, my dearest, you stole the best blacksmith in four countries away from your father."

"I did not. So why do they need a blacksmith?"

"They are checking to see how long it would take to make a few more swords. I believe your brother, Edward, wants a new helmet as well."

Lae smiled, glad that her suspicions had been confirmed. "I hope we go to war soon." She walked briskly across the room, stepped behind her husband, and wrapped her arms around his neck. She laid her cheek against his and stared down at the map spread in front of him. "You know maps have always fascinated me."

He patted her other cheek and chuckled. "You like maps because the only time we look at them is to plan a battle. I have never seen anyone who wanted the Vikings off the island more than you, my dear." Red took Lae's hand. "Your hand is cold. Have you been riding without your gloves again?"

"I confess that I have. I seem to forget to clothe myself properly in my excitement to get outside and ride." Lae smiled as Red kissed her fingertips. "Have you seen our daughter this afternoon? She usually comes to greet me when I come in."

"The nurse said that she had another screaming fit. I do not know why. Our Wyn kicked the nurse so hard that we thought she had broken the poor old woman's leg. It took two women to get her to her nursery. Wyn kicked and screamed until she was exhausted, then was put to bed." Red sighed. "Ella is the kindest nurse I have ever known. She would do nothing to Wyn to cause her to behave this way."

"It seems that Wyn cannot tolerate my old nurse. I do not understand the problem. I have loved Ella for as long as I can remember. I suppose I will have to find a younger nurse, so I will ask Ella to train someone else. I will have to think of something to tell her so that her feelings will not be hurt. I remember the one nurse that we had who used to think that Wyn could be beaten into behaving." Lae winced at the memory of the little girl covered with welts from a willow switch, the defiance stronger in her. Lae had ordered that nurse from the fortress with a mixture of anger at the woman and anger at herself for failing to detect her daughter's pain brought on by harsh treatment. The child was strong in spite of that nurse, but now she was too difficult for Ella.

Lae moved around her husband and sat on the bench next to him. "Why were you studying the map when I came in?"

"There seems to be some activity along the borders between Lundenburh and Tamoworthig. Of course, the Danes keep their main camp at Beamfleot. I wish I knew what they were doing."

Lae's heart skipped a beat at the mention of the town on which she had been spying, but she could only mumble a noncommittal response.

Red unfurled the right side of the map and sat quietly while Lae studied it. She ran her hand across the vellum, marveling at the smoothness of the lambskin. Only many hours of rubbing the skin with pumice could have made it so fine. The map maker who had drawn this map had done an excellent job. The inks were vibrant and the lines clear. Lae hoped they were true.

She held the edge of the map down with her right hand and looked at the Roman road on which she had been riding less than an hour ago. Beamfleot was located on a small finger bay that jutted inland from a larger bay off the Narrow Sea. That much was correct, but the map maker did not know all the things she had seen in the Viking towns over the last month. Beamfleot was bigger now that new settlers from across the Narrow Sea had built more and more huts.

"Red, Beamfleot is situated in a perfect place to receive materials from the Viking homelands."

"Why would they want to bring in materials when they can get them here?"

"What if they do not want us to know what they are buying?" Lae traced the line where land met sea. She did not want to confess her escapades to Red unless she had to. He would worry so.

Red tapped the Roman road from Lundenburh northeast, then ran his finger due east until it came to Beamfleot, where he let it rest against Lae's finger. "The Vikings are too close."

"If they wanted to attack us, it would not take much effort," Lae said. "We would not be ready for a major attack from the Vikings who live in Danelaw and those who could come from their homeland."

"That is the very thing your father, brother and I have been discussing in the last few months." Red rubbed his eyes. "I am opposed to going into the Vikings' territory unless we are prepared to win. We need to know how strong they are at this moment." Red put his hand on Lae's. "I know you want to fight, but to fight to win is most important."

Lae remembered the humiliation of the flight from the Danes when she was a child. She nodded. "When we fight, it will be to win." Lae had hated the Danes ever since they had forced her family to flee to Somerset. She remembered the anger and the humiliation of watching her father give the orders to retreat as the Vikings poured over the land — Anglo-Saxon land — and rushed toward the fort. The most horrible memory for her was not the blood of the injured or the dead or the fear, but the deafening noise of the Vikings as they shook the earth with their pounding feet and cut the air with their victory yells.

Underscoring the screams of the enemy were the screams of Lae's infant sister whom she held in her arms. Her mother had carried little Edmund, a frail child of five summers who did not live past his sixth summer. Lae had always blamed the death of this elf-like child on the Vikings. He seemed unable to survive in the violent world into which he had been thrust. Edmund was the gentle child, always smiling, always terrified by noise, but always ready to give love. For Edmund, she would hate the Vikings. He would not have been able to, for it was against his nature to hate or to fight.

Lae's cheeks flushed from the memory of the flight to Somerset. She had vowed then, as a child of eight years, that she would one day ride beside her father and lead men into battle against these Vikings until every last one of them was dead.

"Lae, did you hear me? You seem to be asleep with your eyes open," Red said.

"I was remembering the Somerset raid."

"That was the last battle King Aelfred lost." Red patted Lae's hand. "You have hated the Vikings for many years."

"With good cause, dear husband." A picture of the three laughing Danes Lae had just encountered made her resolve that she would be the one laughing when she ran them through with a sword. After spearing Eiric like a fish, she would go after the fat one with the brown hair and the half-witted, thin-lipped smile.

"We should send out a few men to look at the activity in Beamfleot." Red tapped the spot where Beamfleot was marked on the map. "I am as weary of the Danes as you are, but my motives are different. You want to avenge a wrong. I want to rid ourselves of a potential problem for our people. It is time to reclaim the land of the Anglo-Saxons from the invaders."

"Yes, yes, yes!" Was the time right to let Red know about her adventures in spying? Lae would have to lead into the conversation delicately, making the information appear so valuable that the method of obtaining it would be overlooked. "The Vikings seem to be preparing for a war."

"It is odd that you should say that." Red pointed to the lower right hand corner of the map. "Your father has reports from an excellent source that the Vikings have established new forts at Apuldre and Middeltun. They have two hundred and fifty ships strung out from Rye Bay all the way up the Canal. At Middeltun, they have another eighty ships on Swale Bay."

"That many?" Lae looked at the map, following her husband's finger as he traced the location of the Viking fleet. "It makes me feel uncomfortable to have them behind us and alongside my father's country." Lae moved her hand north to Beamfleot, then traced an imaginary line down the map to Apuldre and Middeltun. "If we allow them time to gain strength, they will sweep across our lands from east to west, destroying both our country and my father's." Chills raced up and down her spine. Would she be here to celebrate her next birthday at the beginning of summer?

Red wrapped his fingers around Lae's. "You look pensive."

"I have waited a long time to avenge the many wrongs thrust upon the countries of Wessex and Mercia." The chills slowly dissipated, replaced by calmness that she had known every time she had gone into battle with her menfolk. Lae thought it odd that calmness had come before there was a battle, and she wondered if she had found her reason for being. Had God given her the talents for this purpose?

"We need to know what is happening at Beamfleot before we declare war on the Danes, Lae. Do not frown at me. You know I am right. Beamfleot is their main city, and all battle plans will come from there. We will have to send out spies over the next several weeks to see what is happening."

"I do not think that will be necessary." Lae used the calmness that had swept over her to force back the excitement she felt. She had learned a long time ago that Red would listen to a calm discussion of facts before he listened to a plea for revenge.

She was forming the proper words in her mind to sway her husband when her thoughts were interrupted by stamping and banging. Lae turned toward the dreaded sound she remembered from childhood. Reason told her that it was not the Vikings pounding at her front door, but her throat constricted just the same. When the door opened, it took her a moment to realize that her father and brother had returned.

She stood, along with Red, as was expected when a king entered the room. Her father was a head taller than any of his vassals. His hair was the color of oak leaves in winter. His handsome face and rosy cheeks were framed by a neatly trimmed beard. Dark eyebrows gave expression to deep gray eyes that reflected King Aelfred's vast intellect. He carried a rolled stack of vellum, and Lae wondered what his latest writing would contain. It was probably an addition to his chronicles. She would have to beg him to let her see his latest work that recorded Wessex's history, but she would be allowed. Lae felt the pride that always came when she saw her father's powerful figure; he was still as strong a warrior as her brother.

Edward, not quite as tall as his father, was still able to look down on the men in his army. His hair and beard were as brown as his father's, and he was as strong, but there the similarity ended. Edward viewed the world as an easy place to live, and the wars never seemed to bother him. He seemed to think, Lae believed, that life was just for sport, and his laughter was easy.

Lae felt a rush of love for her younger brother, and memories of their childhood together danced through her mind. She hardly saw Edward anymore; he lived in Wessex near their father, and she missed them both.

Lae moved away from the table and curtsied. She bobbed up before her father acknowledged her and rushed toward the two men, throwing her arms around both of them. "Father and Edward! How long has it been?"

"Only from one full moon to another, Daughter. You have never had patience with time." King Aelfred returned Lae's hug, then pulled off his fur cloak and handed it to her. "I have come to discuss the Vikings with you and Red."

"I will get something to eat and drink for us while we talk." Lae rubbed her cheek against the soft fox fur, then hung the cloak on a peg next to the door. "Edward, why do you not give me your cape as well? Why are you staring at me that way? Have I grown a third eye?"

"It seems you have." Edward frowned.

"Your allusion escapes me." Lae took the cape that Edward held out to her and placed it on a peg next to her father's cloak. "I shall return, and then we will discuss your mysterious mood. Rarely have I seen you frown so." Lae turned away from her brother and his angry face. She dismissed his strange mood as something she could deal with later.

Lae crossed the great hall to the kitchen where the activity was almost too much for her to comprehend. The spicy smells from the kitchen reminded Lae that she had not eaten since the morning meal. Her stomach growled, but no one would hear it over the clattering of pans and pots. The cooks were frantic and their helpers rushed about the kitchen under the commands of Lae's chief cook, Bordy. His face was as red as the coals in the middle of the hearth. A servant tended three steaming cauldrons set inside the huge firepit.

One of the kitchen helpers was standing at a long table, slicing pieces of meat from a side of roast beef. Bordy's assistant ran back and forth from the table to the cauldron, carrying meat on slabs of stale bread, then dumping the meat into boiling water. The young boy wiped his greasy hands on his tunic, then laid more meat on the bread.

Lae watched him run back and forth a few more times before her attention was drawn to Bordy, who moved from person to person, checking the ducks and geese cooking on the spits, the baker at the ovens, and even taking time to check on the servant who was drawing water from the well. Lae thought that she had not been noticed by Bordy until he swept past, bowed, and asked in a booming voice, "May I serve my lady?"

"King Aelfred and Prince Edward have arrived from Wessex. They are as hungry as your lord." Lae smiled. "Your good meals should put some fat on their lean frames."

"What is your desire, my lady?" Bordy asked.

"See to the butler. I want the mead and wine to be perfect." Lae surveyed the kitchen once again. "I trust your judgment, and you seem to have everything well in hand. See to the pastry cook, too. King Aelfred loves his sweets." Lae patted Bordy's arm. "You do have a talent in the kitchen. I will be in the great hall. Dinner should be served immediately."

"Yes, my lady." Bordy bowed again.

"Dispense with all the normal ceremony for laying of the table. Tonight we talk of important things and cannot be bothered."

Lae left the kitchen as Bordy shouted instructions to his staff. Bordy always had a superb meal prepared for her father in spite of low winter supplies. It seemed that King Aelfred brought out the best in the servants, and though Lae tried to imitate her father, sometimes it was difficult for her because some of the servants did not seem to be very intelligent. She always had trouble with people who could not think.

As Lae crossed the great hall toward the trestle table, she looked at the three men seated together, heads nearly touching as they studied the map, her husband's copper-colored hair between the darker heads of the other men she loved. If her mother could have been there as well as Lae's other siblings, it would have been perfect.

Lae slid down the bench until she was sitting next to Red. She watched his slender fingers as they pointed out the Viking settlements. The light from the firepit made the gold ring on his finger shine like the sun, and Lae remembered that, as a child, she had been fascinated by the ring that was the mark of a king. She used to think that the sun had been captured by Red and made into a ring. She tried to remember if he had told her a tale about it or if it were only the work of her overactive imagination.

Lae leaned over the map, straining to see the marks that seemed to interest her father.

"Here and here," King Aelfred said. "These are their weak points, but even at their worst, we must respect them. They fight well from ship or horse. If I only knew what was happening at Beamfleot, then we could make a decision about invading."

Edward glanced up from the map and stared at Lae, his eyes never wavering. "Father, mayhap you should ask Lae what is happening in Danelaw."

"Lae?" King Aelfred looked from his daughter to his son. "Why say you such things, Edward?"

Lae was exasperated to find Edward smiling the same smile he had worn as a child whenever he had tattled on her. Not now, Edward, she thought, please do not tell now. Lae knew what he was going to say, and she waited for the damning words.

"My sister has been spying on the Danes weekly for the past month. She rides out of the keep, crosses the Thames into Viking territory, and follows the Roman road for a half-mile before heading east. Ask her what kind of trouble she got her into today."

Lae felt her cheeks burning, but she refused to look away from Edward. Her thoughts flew swiftly, and she struggled to sort them out. He could not have seen her since he had been with her father in Wessex. That meant that he had stationed spies to keep a watch on her or mayhap the Danes. There would be no reason to watch her, so Lae guessed that Edward was spying on the Danes. She pursued this idea, so that she would appear more knowledgeable than she was. "If you mean that the spies you have sent out have seen me, then that is of no consequence. I have been perfectly safe," she said. "Most of the Vikings do not have the brains of a goat."

Edward returned her stare. His jaw was set. "You were not so safe this afternoon when . . ."

Lae gave her brother the look that they had often exchanged as children when they wanted to keep secrets from the grownups. Holding her breath, she hoped he would remember their secret signal.

Edward looked away from Lae and stared at the hearth. "You should not have been riding around in the Danelaw."

"Is it true that your rides have been into enemy territory?" Red's voice revealed his astonishment. "Lae, you have taken a risk that could have put Wessex and Mercia at war against the Danes before we were ready. What if the Danes had captured you? They could have . . . You know how they are with women."

Red's fear for her made his voice quiver. Lae swallowed a lump that rose in her throat. She had not wanted to injure him. She glanced down at her fingers, pulling at a hangnail, then looked into her husband's eyes. "I have been into the Danelaw many times. They are lax. I was able to learn a great deal."

King Aelfred cleared his throat. "Red, she is your wife first, my daughter second. I leave it to you to try and contain her childish enthusiasm for this war."

Feeling her face flush, Lae fought to hold back the torrent of anger. She looked at the churlish face of Edward, the astonished face of her father, and the concerned look of her husband, and she no longer cared to hold back the fury that boiled within her. Would they never let her be the warrior that she knew she could be? She was no longer the young girl who needed to be coached, but a grown woman with the skills to fight.

Lae slapped her hand on the planked table, sending vibrations through the thick boards. She stood and spoke to her father. Her calm voice belied her inner turmoil. "You, Father, leave it to my husband to try to contain me? I do not care if you are the King of Wessex. I am a ruler in my own right, for, if you would be so kind as to remember, I rule equally with Red. I take the risks on the battlefield as he does, as you do, and as Edward does. I will not relinquish the danger of being a ruler, for to do so destroys my respect among my subjects. Worse, if I play the fearful one, I lose respect for myself as a leader." Lae clamped her lips shut to stop the flow of words that had rushed forward. She felt a certain glee at the stunned looks on the faces of her menfolk. "If you would like to know what I have found out at Beamfleot. . . ."

"Beamfleot!" Red shouted. "You have been to Beamfleot? You have been that far behind the lines?"

"I did no more than you would have done, Husband."

Red threw up his hands. "I would not have been so . . ."

Lae turned and glared at Red. "If you so much as utter the word 'foolish' . . ."

"Brave. I would not have been so brave."

The sound of chuckling broke through Lae's consciousness slowly. It had started like the low growl of an animal, then grew in volume until Lae recognized the rare laughter of her father. Her head snapped around and she glared at him as she had done Red. It was a look that she had always wanted to give him, but as a child she could not. As the Lady of Mercia, she could glower all she wanted. She was not his daughter at this moment, but the ruler of a neighboring country and his equal. Lae continued to scowl at King Aelfred. "Dare you laugh at the Lady of Mercia?"

"I laugh at the Lord of Mercia who has discovered that the weakness of men is that they never understand the strength of their women. I see myself in Red's confused countenance. I see the look that every woman puts on the faces of the men in her life." King Aelfred wiped the tears of laughter from his eyes. "Please, Lae, tell us what you found in Beamfleot. I am certain that your observations have been astute."

Edward cleared his throat. "Red, I think you should know the danger of Lae's rides into . . ." Edward tried to suppress a moan as Lae's foot connected with his shin.

"Dear brother. What ails you? Does your stomach growl from hunger? I have food coming presently." Lae smiled at Edward. "Or does your leg pain you from an injury mayhap inflicted during a battle?"

"My sister pains me."

"The selfsame sister who taught you to ride? To hunt? To shoot an arrow straight? The sister who showed you the tricks with the two-handed battle-ax? Would this sister hurt you?"

"Yes." Edward reached down and rubbed his shin. "There is not armor strong enough to withstand the wrath of a sister."

King Aelfred, still chuckling, clapped Edward on the back. "It is not just sisters who can inflict pain on us helpless men at their will, but wives and mothers as well. Any woman is dangerous when she is angry."

Lae looked at each man in turn. "Mayhap you should take pains not to anger this woman."

"Well said, Lae." Red took her hand. "Forgive me in my concern for you. Be you woman or man, my concern would be the same. Tell us what you found in Beamfleot."

"Notice the bay on which Beamfleot is located." Lae sat and pointed to the blue coloring that represented the bay on the map. "It is easy for the Vikings to get the materials they need for making swords and chain-mail without our knowledge."

"What did you see in Beamfleot?" Edward asked.

"At first I noticed nothing. It seemed to be one of their normal villages with farms lying on the outskirts, ships coming in and out of port with goods, and marketing in the center of town. On my second trip, I noticed more ships in the harbor. I thought that was odd for such a small village, so I rode closer and was fortunate enough to see the ships being unloaded. There were the things you expect to find at a farming village. But then some heavy chests were carried off the ships."

"How do you know they were heavy?" King Aelfred asked.

"Two strong men struggled with each chest. I watched for as long as I dared. I saw the chests placed on a wagon and taken to the blacksmith's. I had to leave before I saw what was hidden inside."

"I am sure that you found out what the blacksmith was making. You were always curious about things that you were not supposed to know about. You practiced spying on me when we were children," Edward said.

"Oh, Edward. You needed looking after."

"Even if I did not, you looked after me," Edward said.

"So tell us, how many trips did it take you to find out what the Vikings were doing?"

"I found out the next time, but I kept going back to make certain. They were importing swords and metal to make chain-mail." Lae leaned forward and tapped the map. "We should uncover what is happening in Apuldre. It, too, is on a bay, and we know that they have more ships than they need for peacetime."

"Daughter, we have men checking Apuldre at this time. I am as concerned as you are about the increase in Viking activity. It seems that their population has grown fast — too fast." King Aelfred pulled on his beard and studied the map, then sat back and nodded to Lae. "Continue."

"The Danes in Beamfleot were making swords and chain-mail. They were not making farm implements, as they would like us to believe. It is impossible for me to return to Beamfleot to find out the numbers the Vikings are trying to equip. I may have been seen." Lae pointed to the map and rushed on before Edward told King Aelfred and Red about her narrow escape. "If the Vikings plan to attack, they will do so in the spring or early summer. They want to surprise us, but we can turn the battle in our favor."

"Given what our spies have told us about the other Viking settlements, your conjecture makes sense." King Aelfred nodded. "The Vikings are preparing to attack. See? If they attack from Beamfleot, Apuldre, and Middeltun, they can move from east to west in one large wave and wipe out both our kingdoms simultaneously."

Red rubbed his forehead with his hand. "The thought is astonishing. The Vikings have grand plans, but do they have enough warriors? It would take a great number to do damage to both our countries at the same time."

"Lae says that they are preparing for war," Edward said. "Even though she has been anxious to send the Vikings back across the Narrow Sea for years, I trust her judgment. If she says the Vikings are making armor and swords, then the time has come to rid ourselves of this menace that has plagued our country for generations."

"I agree with you, Edward." Red folded his hands together, looking like a monk in prayer.

"The question is whether or not we attack or wait for them." King Aelfred ran his thumbnail under a sliver of wood and peeled it from the edge of the table, then rolled the splinter between his thumb and forefinger. "If we wait, they will not realize that we know about their plans. We have taken away the advantage of surprise."

"We will have to guess where they are most likely to attack us." Lae spoke softly, almost to herself. "I want to kill every Viking in Britain, and I want to do it now. However, if we wait, we will know the site of their attack. We can have several armies ready for counterattacks in strategic places. I vote that we wait."

Edward nodded. "For once, I agree with Lae, Father. We should wait and see where the Danes plan to attack us."

"Where will they attack?" Red, his hands still folded, leaned over and stared at the map.

King Aelfred stabbed at the map with the splinter. "It has to be south and east of the Danelaw. Lundenburh is too well fortified and would offer them no advantage, even if they did take it."

Red traced his finger along a thin, blue line. "They probably will come up the rivers in their ships. Do you not think so, Edward?"

"That is their strength." Edward unfurled the edge of the map with his left hand and held it down. "They can come up many of our rivers. We can watch them to see what they are doing, but in order to know where they will attack, we would have to be privy to their plans."

"An impossible task," King Aelfred said.

"Not necessarily," Lae said.

"No!"

The collective voices of the three men startled Lae. She glanced from one face to another noticing that Edward scowled, her father's face was noncommittal, and Red looked pained. Lae almost laughed at them, for they seemed to think that she would ride at will in and out of Danelaw. They had less common sense than she had. She wondered how they viewed her. Mayhap it was difficult for her father and her husband to realize that she was no longer a child but a woman who had seen almost twenty-three summers. Even Edward, who was two years younger, tended to see himself as more powerful than she.

Lae did not know how she would change the way they saw her, but she knew she would make certain that they would see her as a woman of fortitude and intelligence. She had been placed on the throne of Mercia to rule by the fact of her birth, but she would prove herself worthy of the task.

"Father, I did not mean that I should go into their towns. It is known that they keep women away from their council. I would be no use as a spy in close quarters."

"Of course." King Aelfred leaned away from the map and let it roll up. "I have an important matter to discuss with Edward, but it concerns you, too, Lae. Red and I have discussed this plan, and we feel that it is in the best interest of both our countries."

Lae was intrigued by her father. His demeanor did nothing to tell her what had been discussed with her husband. She looked at Edward, who seemed as puzzled as she.

"For the next few years, not only will we be under attack, but we will be the aggressors, as well." King Aelfred looked at Edward. "Wessex and Mercia must always remain allies and under strong leadership so that the effort we put into forging two strong nations will not come undone. Edward, you have a frail wife who has had no male issue, save young Prince Aelfred who died before he was six months old. The two children born since have been sickly girls. They will not live past three or four summers."

"That is true, Father," Edward said. "I have always dreamt of a son who would ride with me. A son to carry on the seed of the House of Wessex. A son to fill father and grandfather with pride. Alas, I have no heirs with the vigor to survive or lead a country."

"Save for one youngster — a bastard." King Aelfred cocked an eyebrow and scrutinized Edward.

Lae was shocked. What did her father mean? Edward with a child that she did not know about? Lae leaned forward and studied her father's expression. As usual, he revealed nothing of his thoughts. Edward, on the other hand, was flustered, and he blushed like a young girl! This was almost as interesting as talking about war.

"One youngster, Father?" Edward asked.

"The strong son of a shepherdess has been receiving money from you for his care. He was named in the royal fashion, I believe, so I assume you have acknowledged him."

"I have acknowledged the child. It was a foolish boy's lust and not the fault of the infant that he was born out of wedlock." Edward stared at his hands in his lap. "I confessed to my priest. My penance was severe, for the priest knew the . . . the infant's mother. He said that she was not an ordinary shepherd's daughter."

Lae could contain her curiosity no longer, and she blurted out, "Who is this child? Who is the mother?" Lae felt Red's hand on her arm, reminding her not to interrupt the king. She bit her lip to keep from speaking out again.

King Aelfred continued as if Lae had not spoken. "I have had the young lad investigated. He is strong, intelligent, and healthy. I have decided that he is to be your heir."

Lae could not help but gasp. "Father, the impropriety of a bastard son becoming heir to the throne is unheard of!"

"You speak when it is not your concern, Lae."

"I am sorry, Father. It is just that I have been shocked by the knowledge of a child I did not know existed."

"I will forgive you, for I understand your surprise. I want the youngster to be reared under your guardianship and trained to assume leadership as Edward's rightful heir."

Edward's facial expression had changed from chagrin to anger. "I cannot allow a bastard to succeed me! What if I have other sons? I will have other sons."

"You may have nothing but sickly daughters, Edward. I want to know now that my kingdom and Mercia will be as one. This child can be that future. He is about the same age as Lae's daughter, and the two of them would make a good marriage."

"Father!" Lae felt weak. Had her father gone mad? Did he have a fever that she knew nothing about? "I cannot let my daughter marry a bastard."

"He will not be a bastard. I will declare him legitimate." King Aelfred folded his arms across his chest and glared at Edward and Lae in turn. "I have studied the histories of countries older than ours. There have been bastards in positions of power before, and the countries have done well. Mayhap it is that the poor bastard, being an outcast, feels he must prove something to himself and others. There will be no debate. The young man will be reared in this court. Red has agreed to see to his military training. You, Lae, will see that he learns the manners expected of a future king, bastard or no."

"Yes, Father," Lae said.

"I still protest," Edward said. "What of my wife? She will not take kindly to a bastard taking away the rights of her unborn sons."

"I have thought of your wife, hence the child will be reared in this court. I have also observed your wife on many occasions. When the boy is grown, she will have been a long time in the grave." King Aelfred clapped his hands together. "So, Edward, you and Lae will fetch the child and attend to his needs. Pay whatever his mother requires to release him. She has no choice, but I prefer to be civil."

King Aelfred's attention was drawn to a parade of servants coming toward them from the kitchen. He smiled at Lae. "The food smells delicious. I did not realize I was so hungry."

Lae knew that there would be no arguing with the king. Edward and she would have to obey. Lae decided to accept the dictate in good humor. She would sort out the problems later, so she smiled at the king. "Father, I swear you come to visit the cook instead of me. I have never seen anyone who is as concerned about the quality of food as you are. My first memory of you is in the kitchen, peering into the cooking pots. Mother always thought you were deranged when it came to food. She used to tell me she wondered if you had been starved as a child."

Lae motioned to the servants to put the meat platter in front of her father. She checked the slices of meat and nodded to the servant who had waited for her approval. She had been told by her handmaiden that she was demanding but not mean. Lae wondered what that meant, but she had never worried about it. She had been trained by her mother to always check details. If that meant she was demanding, then she did not care.

Lae sniffed the plate of turnips. They did not smell as if they had come from the bottom of the pile where they could be moldy. It was only November, and she was already tired of turnips. There were cooked carrots, too, but fewer in number. The dark, coarse bread was good when dipped into the mutton broth and lentil soup. The wine was excellent this year, but mead was her father's favorite drink, and so it was served.

In winter, food was sparse even for the tables of kings. During times of war, when the farmers and servants followed their masters to battle, the fields lay fallow. War brought sacrifice to everyone, especially the peasants.

Lae watched the men take eating knives from their belts. Without ceremony, they began to eat. Lae caught movement from the corner of her eye as she took her eating knife from its sheath and stabbed a piece of meat. Dropping the meat on the trencher that had been placed before her to hold her food, she waved her knife at the dogs that had sneaked away from the corner of the room to sit by the table. "Away! You belong in the stables." Lae turned to Red. "You have let in those animals again."

"Only so they can warm themselves. They did a fine job of . . . of hunting today."

"The only thing those worthless dogs hunted today was a warm place to sleep." Lae waved her knife at them again. "Get away from the table." She heard the men laugh as the dogs tucked their tails between their legs and scurried back to the corner of the great hall.

"Were the Vikings so well trained, Lae, we could turn you loose on them." King Aelfred's laughter was as low as the rumble of thunder.

Lae waved her knife under her father's nose. "If you do not stop with your fun at my expense, I shall pretend you are a Viking or a dog, which are one and the same, and send you to a corner."

King Aelfred threw up his hands in resignation. "I surrender to you."

"Good. Next, it is the Vikings who need to surrender."

Lae stabbed a turnip, cutting it in half. She cut it again and again. When the pieces were bite sized, she pushed them to the side of her plate. "We will not be able to spy on the Danes, so we will have to figure out what they are doing by their actions." Lae looked from one man to another. "I know the Vikings will attack us. We should be alert and ready. I, for one, will have our blacksmith begin to make our armor and swords. However, in order to keep that activity secret from the Danes, I will double the guards. Red, is that a sound plan?"

"I believe it to be so." Red leaned on his elbows and looked at Edward. "Do you believe the Vikings will attack in the spring?"

Edward nodded and wiped his mouth with a cloth. "I do. If we are to survive, it will have to be as an alliance between Mercia and Wessex. I believe that if we present what we know to the Welsh, they will fight with us. We need their strength, undisciplined though it be."

King Aelfred put down his soup bowl. "Both my children give me pride with their strategies on war. Mercia and Wessex can but grow stronger under their tutelage. Through them, my dream of having the entire island for our people will come true. There is not room enough for the Vikings, with their passion for raids, and the Anglo-Saxons, who prefer peace, to live in the same area."

"Then let me propose a toast." Lae stood, holding a bowl of mead above her head. As she looked at the trio of men seated at the table, she felt proud that the three strongest men in this land belonged to her. Her voice was forceful and her arm steady as she said, "Let us swear that we will fight to the death to free our people and our land from the invaders."

King Aelfred, Prince Edward, and King Athelred stood and held their bowls high. Together all four drank to the future.

chapter

II

COLLECTION OF THATCHED HUTS squatted in a circle at the base of a low hill. Smoke rose from the smoke holes and hovered in a cloud above the tiny village. An inch of snow lay atop the straw roofs save for a circle next to the holes where heat had melted it leaving the thatching naked to the sky. Icicles hung down from the corners of the roofs, shining in the bright sun like newly polished swords.

Lae shifted in her saddle and frowning, stared at the surrounding countryside. "Edward, were we not here at one time? Is this not where we fought the Danes in a small skirmish?"

Edward sat quietly on his horse with no expression on his face. "We have been here before."

"I remember." Lae leaned over and touched Edward on the arm. "You were just at the beginning of your manhood. Father had sent the two of us out with his most trusted men to test our ability in war."

"Lae, you were riding to my left, but dropped back to let me have my first kill. Then, smeared with the blood of a Viking soldier, I rode down the hill and stopped at this village to bathe in the creek. I was feeling powerful because I knew that Father would be proud of me."

"It was expected that you would feel proud. I was pleased to see you ride into a fight without fear. I remember the sunlight glinting off your sword as you swung at the hapless Dane."

"That was not the only conquest I made that day." Edward looked away from Lae's stare.

"Pray tell, Edward." Lae was ashamed that her curiosity had overcome her mother's careful instructions in propriety. However, she pushed aside those thoughts. "Edward, I should have some knowledge of this boy's background."

"I see no reason." Edward's face was flushed.

"Are you too embarrassed to tell me?"

"I am embarrassed that you have the audacity to ask such a personal question."

"Edward! I would not ask if I did not think it important to the understanding of the child. I am to take on a large responsibility at Father's orders. My own daughter has been betrothed to this boy by our father. I have some right to the knowledge of his parentage." Lae felt like crossing herself to offset any hint of her meddlesome nature when it came to Edward's son. However, she knew it would be inappropriate, and the saints in heaven would probably be more irritated with her than they already were. She had always been too curious about people's private lives, especially if it bordered on the base. She promised that she would pray for her sins later.

"Is the shepherdess a pretty girl?"

Edward shrugged his shoulders and stared at a hut that was nearest the creek. "Close by the creek where I had turned the water pink with the enemy's blood was a wattle and daub hut to which I paid no attention until I saw a pretty girl peering at me from the doorway. She looked so pure, so innocent. She smiled at me. I called out and asked her if the Danes had harmed her or her family. I was feeling omnipotent. I had probably saved this young girl from a terrible fate." Edward fell silent.

"Why do you not finish the tale, Edward?" Lae's curiosity was so inflamed that she pushed her mother's teachings completely to the back of her mind.

"Do not make me tell you what I did."

"You did not force her, did you?" Lae could not keep the horror from her voice.

"No, I would not do that to one of our own, but I went against the teaching of the Church. I may die in hell for this sin, although I am still doing penance." Edward rushed on. "I could not resist her, standing in the doorway admiring me, so I went to her. Her father and mother were standing behind her. I could see the greed in the father's eyes, so I offered him a gold piece for her."

"So with one piece of gold you made a whore out of a simple shepherdess. I am ashamed of you, Edward. We are supposed to be Christians. If we do not uphold the laws of God, how can we expect our subjects to do so?"

"It is easy for you to preach perfection. It is easy for you not to be tempted. Have you ever broken a commandment?" Edward sat astride his horse, eyes cast downward.

"I am sorry, Edward. I forget that you are no longer the younger brother that I must scold. If you do not wish to continue, I will understand."

"Her mother was horrified and clucked her disapproval, but the father jerked the old woman out the door slamming it behind him."

Lae felt her face turn red, and she held her hand up to ward off more words. "Stop, I want to hear no more of your escapades. I am not a priest, therefore I am not your confessor."

"I treated the shepherdess like a whore. To me, she was another battle won, another conquest. She was the better person, for she treated me like a prince. I paid her mother for each visit with two pieces of silver, one of which was slyly tucked away in the old woman's clothing, and one she gave her husband."

"You need not go on, Edward." Lae took off her gloves and held her cold hands to her cheeks to cool the fire that her embarrassment had caused.

"The girl sent word that she had given birth to my son. My only thought was how surprised I was that she could write. I had had no desire to see my son mayhap because of the anger it had caused my new wife, Elflaed, but I did feel duty bound to provide for his support. I should amend this lie. Actually, our younger sister, Aethelgifu, pious even then, begged me to give money to the family to help rear the boy."

"Do not be so harsh with yourself. You were but a boy those four summers ago. Now you are a man, and as a man, you can correct the damage."

"My wife will not take kindly to an heir to replace the child she carries at this moment. She still cries for little Aelfred." Edward patted his horse's neck. "I named him for Father, hoping to give him stamina, but he was always frail. He died as he had lived;

quietly and without a fuss. It was a poor ending for a boy who would be king."

"It was sad for us all to lose an heir," Lae said.

"I tried to like the boy and match my wife's grief, but he had been so sickly that most of his six months of life had been spent under the care of women. I would never have been allowed to teach him to hunt and to fight. I was an outsider and destined to never know my first legitimate son."

"A fate that is difficult to fathom." Lae was startled to hear her brother speak thusly. His tenderness of voice should have seemed unmanly to her, but it did not. It was a surprise to her to hear a man talk of the loss of a child. Elflaed was getting weaker with each pregnancy, having lost two babies, although she had carried her last pregnancy almost to term. There seemed to be no hope that Edward would ever have a healthy boy by his wife. Lae had to agree with her father that it would be better to have a healthy boy, even an illegitimate one, to continue Edward's line.

"Come, Lae. It is time." Edward motioned for his companions to wait for him by the wagon.

Lae followed her brother as he moved his horse down the hill on an angle so that their arrival would not be seen by the shepherdess. "What countenance does this shepherdess have that she ruled a prince?"

"I only remember that her hair was dark red and that it curled from crown to the ends. Her skin was smooth, but then she had been still young enough that the hard peasant life had not made her old yet."

"See, Edward, faces peer at you from the doorway of each hut as we pass."

Edward said nothing as they made their way to the cottage closest to the creek. They stopped in front of the lowly dwelling. "I feel as if this hut comes to me from a fairy tale, another life, mayhap a dream." Edward dismounted and dropped the reins to the ground, before helping Lae to dismount.

Edward raised his hand to knock, but the door opened before knuckle touched wood. Lae stared at the girl in front of her, holding the hand of a boy with silver-blonde hair as fine as spider webs. It was hair the color of Lea and her mother. Lae looked into the boy's blue eyes and was startled when the child smiled at her. She watched as Edward scanned the child, noting as he must, that the boy's arms and legs were straight and sturdy. He was not scarred from the pox, and his eyes were bright. Apparently the child was not timid, for he was appraising Edward with a solemn face that was plump and rosy. At least, thought Lae, his mother had made good use of the money Edward had sent.

Lae was startled at the curtsy. She would have to inquire as to where this simple girl had learned her manners.

"Come in, please." The boy's mother stepped aside and gestured toward the small firepit. "Please warm yourselves by my humble fire."

Edward stepped aside for Lae, taking her arm to help her down two wooden steps and ducking as he entered the low doorway. They crossed to the firepit. Lae held her hands toward the fire, noticing that the entire room was warm. She glanced around the hut. The wattle and daub walls were without the cracks that most peasant huts had. No chilling gusts of wind cut across the room to stir the fire.

"Why have you returned after all these years?" The girl had moved like a shadow to stand beside Edward. She reached out and held the hand of the child so tightly that, even though he tried to pull free, he could not.

The boy stared at Edward. Lae wanted to swoop him up and hold him, but she refrained. Lae thought mayhap the boy would be afraid. Besides, it did not seem appropriate. They were here, after all, to take him from his mother, and it was obvious that she treasured him.

"Why have you come now?" Her voice quivered. "What is it that you want from me?"

Edward looked from his son's face to the girl's face. He seemed surprised to see tears flowing down her cheeks. Lae knew why she was crying even though it was obvious that Edward did not. "Edward, would you tell me this girl's name?"

Edward's chin jutted outward. "I have no use for names of those who are from my past." Edward behaved as he did when he was a child. Lae knew that he had always used arrogance to cover chagrin. She smiled at the tearful girl. "Would you tell me your name?"

"I am called Egwinna."

"Why do you cry?"

"My lady and my lord have come to take my son. You have no other reason to be here." She looked down at the boy and pulled him to her. She wrapped her arms around him, holding him against her. "My lord gave me a gift, and now the gift is too valuable for a poor shepherdess."

Edward glared at Egwinna. "How do you know that?"

"I know that your other children are sickly. I know your wife has trouble with her pregnancies, and I know that you need an heir who is strong. My son is strong. He has never been sick. I nursed him whenever he wanted my breast. I kept him away from sick children. I kept him clean, and I kept this hut clean. The gold you sent was used to feed him the best food I could get and to repair the hut so that he would not be cold. I spun the best woolen blankets for this child and the best tunics.

"I refused marriage. I even refused to let other men sleep with me so that there would be no other children to share the gold. I have brought him up as a king's grandson should be brought up. He was never baptized because of his parentage, but he attends mass regularly. I have made arrangements for him to be taught letters by the priest."

"You have done well for an unlearned peasant girl," Edward said.

"I am not stupid. I have not the advantages of the nobility, but I am not stupid."

"No, you have made me proud." Edward stamped out a spark that had flown from the firepit and had landed on the rush-covered floor. "You know why I have come for the boy."

Lae watched as Egwinna held the boy tighter. Much tighter and all of life's breath would be driven from the child. She was angry with Edward for blurting out the truth. He had no common sense when it came to women. He should have been able to see that Egwinna was heartbroken and desperate. Desperate women did strange things. "Edward, mayhap you should refrain a bit."

Edward seemed not to hear. "This boy has come to the attention of King Aelfred. I am here to obey my father and become father to my son."

"I cannot let him go. He is my life. He is the only reason I arise in the morning singing and wanting to savor each day. Since his birth and the gold that you have sent, I have been able to prevent my father from beating my mother, from beating my sisters, and from beating me." She brushed a lock of hair from her face and looked Edward straight in the eye. "I have learned pride in myself for bearing a healthy son of a prince and in caring for him. You have come to take the reason for my pride from me."

"I see that you have done a fine job with the boy, but do you not see that you cannot give him the education that he needs or the guidance? Who in your family can teach this boy to wield a sword, to ride a horse, to use a bow and arrow? You cannot prepare him to be a ruler."

Lae heard Egwinna's breath suck in, and she knew that Edward had struck the shepherdess in a most vulnerable area. Lae hoped to ease the pain. "Egwinna, your son would have a fine life as the son of a prince. We could give him everything."

"Would you give him a mother's kisses when he cries?"

Edward snorted. "He is to be reared as a warrior, not a cleric. We are here under orders of King Aelfred. No matter your arguments, the boy is to come with us. Now. Today."

From the look on Edward's face, Lae knew that his patience was gone. She hated to see him wrench Egwinna's child away from her, but it had to be done.

Edward turned away from the tears that flowed afresh down Egwinna's cheeks and scuffed the floor with the toe of his boot. "Why do you cry?"

"If you have to ask, then you do not understand a mother's love for her bearn. I used to imagine being married to you. I used to think that I could be a princess. My mother kept telling me that the daughter of a shepherd was only good for one thing where princes were concerned. I did not believe her for a long time, but then you did not come back to see me or your son."

"I sent gold."

"I thank you for that, but what I desired was to be a princess. It does not matter anymore, for I have grown from a girl to a woman, and my heart has changed because of that." Egwinna ran her hand through her son's silky hair. "You gave me a child who is more precious than gold. Please do not take him." Her voice caught, and she turned away from Edward, placing herself between him and her son.

"What name did you give the boy?" Edward said.

"He is called Aethelstan after the House of Wessex."

"That is a fine name for a king." Edward touched her arm.

Egwinna shivered as Edward touched her. Mayhap the love for him was not gone. Edward was clever for trying softness instead of threats with this woman. Lae watched the interplay between the former lovers with much interest.

"He can be a king if you allow him to be. You alone control the fate of this child. You could be the mother of a king, if you choose."

"You play me like an instrument. You know which strings to pluck to make my heart break. I would prefer that you take my son by force so I do not have to give him away."

"Do you think that I am so harsh that I would do that? I do not wish to have the reputation of being a villain. Someday I will rule Wessex. I prefer to be as kind as is my father. You have the chance to do a kindness for your son."

"Stop! You torture me. I know what I have to do, but I cannot bear to say it. Do not make me put the words into my mouth so soon." Egwinna stooped down and wrapped her arms about Aethelstan. She kissed his cheek, then stood and faced Edward. "You do not know this child. How are you to care for him?"

Edward dismissed her concern with a wave of his hand. "I have nurses who will care for him. However, since my wife is not well enough to rear him in the ways of the court, I intend to allow your lady who rules Mercia to rear him in her court."

Lae saw the look of surprise on Egwinna's face. "I have a daughter nearly the same age. They will become good playmates."

"He will be too far away. I had imagined Stan in the same country. Mercia will be beyond my reach. I will grow old wondering how my son fares. Can he not stay in Wessex where with one day's journey I can gaze on the fortress walls and know that my son is there?"

"That is not advisable. Wives generally dislike the bastard children of their husbands. My wife is not the forgiving kind. She would not care to see the oldest heir to the throne on a daily basis to remind her that her own children will not reign."

"Are you telling me that our son will be in danger from your wife? How can you take him from a safe place to one of danger?"

Egwinna reached behind her and put her hand on the boy. "He will be safer here."

"By the saints!" Lae was tired of the arguing. "How long will it be before someone finds him? How would you protect him from the people who would not want him to rule? How would you protect him if the Danes set upon this village?" Egwinna's gasp told Lae that she had found another weakness in her. "The Danes would not hesitate to kidnap this child or to kill him." Lae watched Egwinna's face as she paled. "The Vikings are particularly vicious when it comes to children."

Egwinna's lower lip quivered. "Would you not take me, too, as a nurse to Stan? Who better to serve him than I, who have protected him these four years?"

Edward shook his head. "No. A complete break with the past would be best for the child." Edward turned away from Egwinna's pleading expression.

Egwinna grabbed Edward by the arm and jerked him around. "I refuse to be a mother to a king if I cannot help to rear him, to protect him. I am not an ordinary peasant! I have worked to educate myself so that I could make Stan proud of his mother. I have used part of the gold you gave us to pay the priest to teach me the proper way to speak, the correct way to act with a king, to read and to write. I began to fill my brain as our son filled my belly. I have become more than a peasant girl. I refuse to become nothing in life. I refuse to allow my son to forget me."

Lae felt anger rising up within her. How dare this lowly girl refuse Edward's offer! He did not have to discuss the matter with her. He was of the royal family and could do what he wanted. "If Edward chooses to take Stan by force, then he will."

Egwinna glared at Lae, then at Edward, her eyes flashing and her lips clamped shut. She held the boy behind her, and stepped back, pushing him further away from Edward. "You may abuse your power if you want, but let me warn you. I will see the boy dead before he is reared by strangers."

Lae had to admire Egwinna's mettle, even if it went against good sense. "Do not do anything to frighten the boy."

Edward took a step toward Egwinna who moved farther away from him. "Do not be stupid. What real mother would kill her own son?"

"What real father would take a son from his true mother?" Egwinna reached under her kirtle and grabbed a knife, holding it in front of her. "Do not come near me."

Lae moved to her left in order to look into Egwinna's eyes as she had been taught to do when confronting the enemy. Egwinna was calm, her eyes never wavering. That was not a good sign, for Lae knew that she meant to do whatever she decided. "There is no cause for knives. Neither Edward nor I will harm you."

Egwinna stepped behind the child, still wielding the knife. "Stan, do not be afraid. Do not cry out. Remember the game of silence that we have often played?" She waited for the child to nod. "We are going to play the game of silence now. No matter what happens, you are not to cry out, even if you have pain."

Egwinna placed the blade of the knife against her son's neck. "I will kill him and then myself. If my son and I are to be separated on earth, then we shall dwell together in heaven."

"Dear God help us," Lae said. "Edward, do nothing rash." Lae measured the distance between Edward and Egwinna. It would be possible to wrench the knife from her grasp, but could it be done before she sliced the boy's throat? As if she were reading Lae's thoughts, Egwinna stepped back, dragging the boy with her.

"Egwinna, I do not want harm to come to the boy," Edward said.

"I do not want to be separated from my child. I repeat, who better to care and protect Stan than one who loves him?" Egwinna moved another step back into the shadows of the hut.

Lae's surprise was slowly changing to one of awe. Egwinna was right. She was no ordinary peasant. She would make a fine nurse for Edward's son. She might also be a nurse for her own daughter, who had driven her old nurse to desperation. "Do you think you could travel to Lundenburh? Could you leave your parents, your sisters, your village?"

"In a moment. There is no way for me to better myself here. I have chosen to learn, and in so doing, I have alienated myself from the people here." Egwinna continued to hold the knife to her son's throat. "Do not give me hope in order to trick me."

"How is it that the priest taught a peasant girl to read? It is most unusual," Edward asked.

"The priest said that he had had a vision, and that it was God's will." Egwinna shrugged. "I never understood him. My will to read was strong and so is my will to be with my son. I fear neither God nor death. Our blood will be on your soul if you come closer."

"Edward, move away." Lae was helpless to stop either Edward or Egwinna. "We will not trick you, Egwinna. Move away, Edward." Edward's impetuous behavior could cause trouble for all of them. "Edward!"

Edward glanced toward Lae. "I know that Egwinna will do whatever she thinks she has to do. I do not wish to have the blood of my son on my hands."

"Then step aside before something happens to the boy." Lae gritted her teeth. This was no time for Edward to go deaf.

Edward turned toward Egwinna. "I have told you that Stan is to be king after me. It is what my father has ordered."

Watching Egwinna's hand that held the knife, Lae saw it waver the same time that she knew Edward did. Fearing the worst, Lae called out, "No!"

Edward lunged forward, pushing the boy out of the way as he grabbed Egwinna's arm. Lae saw a spot of blood on the boy's neck as the child fell to the floor. She watched, horrified as Edward and Egwinna staggered against the wooden cot that was next to the wall. Edward held Egwinna down with his body until he had control of her flailing arms and kicking legs and wrested the knife from her.

"I will kill you, prince or not. I will kill you!" Egwinna lunged at Edward and bit his bearded chin.

Edward tried to stifle a yelp. "You may bite like a wounded wolf, but I will not let go. If I have to tie you like a pig for market, then I will do so. I have decided that no one could protect my son better than you. Get yourself ready for a journey to Lundenburh."

Egwinna glared at him. "You have a peculiar way of showing agreement with my plan. I do not trust you."

"You have no choice. I have control over you. I also have men outside who are ready to come when I call. The lady who has come with me is as capable of killing you if necessary. The boy will be reared by the Lady of the Mercians, whether or not you or I live." Edward held her wrists.

"You did not care whether I would have grieved for a son lost. You would have taken him from me."

"That is true, but now I am offering to honor your request. It suits my plans." Edward did not loosen his grip as he turned to look at Lae. "How fares my son?"

Lae was startled by the question, having become so involved with the drama before her. "He sits quietly, watching both of you, a trickle of blood running down his neck and spotting his tunic. He is brave. The cut does not bother him."

"I have taught him to be a king," Egwinna said.

"You have done well." Lae wondered if the lower classes had very many of these feisty women.

"If I let you go, will you pack your belongings for the journey to Lundenburh?" Edward asked.

"Will you guarantee that I will arrive in Lundenburh?"

"You exasperate me, girl! Do you not take my word as safe passage?"

"You swear on the blood of your son?"

Edward released her, rose from the bed and picked up his son. Running his fingers across the cut, he held his hand up. "I swear on the blood of Athelstan that no harm shall come to him or to his mother from me. The Lady of Mercia and I will protect both of you as we protect ourselves and our children."

"What other duties will I have besides caring for my son?" Egwinna's voice was accusatory.

Edward's face flamed from embarrassment. "You will be in Mercia, and I will be in Wessex. We will hardly meet. I ask nothing more of you than what you already do."

"I have a request," Lae said. "I would like for you to be nurse to my daughter."

Egwinna nodded and moved from the cot without a word. She gathered neatly folded tunics from shelves and placed them in the center of the woolen cover on the cot. When she had her possessions, she tied the four corners of the blanket together. Gesturing toward the pile, she said, "Make your men useful. They may carry that." She took a linen cloth and placed a round of cheese in the center along with half a loaf of bread, and tied the corners. Egwinna picked up a flagon that sat on the table, shook it, and, satisfied that it contained enough drink, handed it to Edward. "Am I to be your handmaiden?" Edward looked down at the flagon in one hand and the food in the other.

Lae laughed at the exchange between the two. It was too bad that life had given Edward a weak but royal wife instead of Egwinna.

"It would not hurt you to learn to serve," Egwinna said.

"How true, but my brother is a reluctant student, I fear," Lae said.

Egwinna grinned as she took her cloak from a peg and pinned it with a silver brooch.

Edward touched the silver braid wrapped around an oval piece of tortoise shell. "Where did you get this?"

Egwinna laughed. "The first time we . . . were together you gave it to me. I thought it was the most wonderful gift."

"And now?"

"Now I am older, and I see it for what it is. I am certain that you had taken it from a Viking that same day. It was payment for pleasure. I may be the mother of a king, but I am still a prostitute." Egwinna dipped a cloth into a wooden bucket that sat by the firepit. She wiped blood from Stan's neck, wrapped a fur about him, and held him as she looked around the hut. "My mother may miss the child, but neither of my parents will miss me as much as they will miss the gold. Would you continue to send them a little pension for their old age?"

Lae was surprised at the request, but was pleased at Egwinna's generosity. Mayhap some of these good qualities could be taught to her daughter, Wyn.

"I will." Edward opened the door to the hut and motioned for his men. "Take this bundle from the bed and place it in the wagon." Edward escorted Lae and Egwinna out the door. "Do you ride?" He motioned toward the horses.

"No. You forget that peasants have no money for horses." Egwinna put Stan in the bed of the wagon, and while he burrowed into place, she pulled her kirtle up and climbed the spokes of the wheel to sit beside him in the hay. She looked down at Edward. "Does the Lady of the Mercians ride all the way on a horse?"

"I do. From now on, Egwinna, you may address me directly. It would please me." Lae had to cover her mouth with a gloved hand to hide a smile.

"My lord, do you ride with us to Lundenburh?"

"Yes. I have promised to protect you. The Vikings have started to pretend to be strong again and may rush in to attack us." Edward laughed at Egwinna's shudder. "I thought you were a brave one. After all, you did attack me."

"You are not a Dane." Egwinna arranged her cloak so that it covered her son. Her breath plumed outward in feathered shapes, then dissipated as the wind carried it away. Egwinna shivered. "I may have to crawl under the hay soon. It will make a warm place to sleep. Are you going to drive?"

"I will for awhile to give my horse a rest." Edward placed the food and drink in the back of the wagon, then heaved himself up. Taking up the reins, he slapped the backs of the oxen. The wagon lurched forward, its wheels squeaking against the thin layer of snow that covered the ground. "We will stay at a church tonight along the old Roman road. It is too late to make Lundenburh in one day." Edward looked at Lae. "How fares my sister?"

"I will be more comfortable on this horse than you will be in that bone-jolting wagon. However, I do envy Egwinna the hay on this cold day."

"I wish that you had come for us on a warmer day," Egwinna said.

"With the Danes pushing into our countries, it would have been dangerous to wait," Edward said. "Does Stan ever speak?"

"Of course, but I have asked that he remain silent. Do you not remember?" Egwinna leaned down and whispered to Stan.

The boy smiled at Edward and said, "Are you my father?"

Lae giggled. This child could make her life quite lively. "Answer him in truth, Edward."

Edward cleared his throat. "He has the bluntness of a dull ax. Yes, I am your father. Do you find that strange?"

"Are you a king? Mother said that my father was a king, and I must always be brave because the sons of kings should be strong." Stan's earnest face studied Edward.

"I am not a king, yet. My father, Aelfred, is king. I am to be king one day. If you learn to wield a sword and fight bravely, then some day you will be King of Wessex."

"Will I have a fine horse?" Stan asked.

"The finest of horses shall be yours. You will have to earn a horse by learning to ride. Nothing will be given you because you are a prince. A true prince must work hard for everything he gets."

Lae was in awe of the tiny person that Edward had acknowledged as his son. It seemed that he was an intelligent child. Egwinna had done well by him. Mayhap Egwinna was just what Lae's daughter needed to keep her from screaming and raving most of her waking hours. Lae felt a sense of duty toward this boy that went beyond wanting to preserve King Aelfred's lineage. With pride, Lae realized that Edward and she could teach this child easily. Edward seemed to be as enchanted as she was by the boy.

"He pleases you, does he not?" Egwinna kissed her son on top of his head.

"Yes, he pleases me," Edward said. "Are you by chance the offspring of some royal house?"

"What kind of a question is that?" Egwinna asked.

"You are very beautiful. You have kept yourself clean and the child clean." Edward took her hand from beneath her cloak. "Even your hand is soft and white. It is not like the hand of a shepherd's daughter."

"What do you know about the hand of a shepherd's daughter? What do you know about who washes and who does not? What do you know about common folk?"

Lae chuckled. "Egwinna, your frown would stop the Vikings in the middle of an invasion."

"Do you think that peasants are dirty just because they are peasants? I used to think that all royalty were . . . were haughty. Now I find royalty merely ignorant." Egwinna turned from Edward, muttering under her breath. "I cannot imagine anyone being surprised at a peasant being clean. I was taught that cleanliness was next to Godliness."

Edward's confusion was evident. It must be a shock for a prince to have his attempt at flattery fail so miserably. Lae loved her brother, but sometimes his arrogance annoyed her. Mayhap he had met his match. She would have to make certain that Egwinna would not overstep her role as a servant. The girl had spirit, but it must be tempered or the other servants would think they could be the same way. Edward could have hit her for her impertinence, but King

Aelfred frowned on brutality to servants. He often quoted scripture to prove his point.

What problems could this servant cause her? After all, Lae was taking most of the burden in this situation. Even with her scowling face, she was beautiful.

Edward pulled his cloak tighter about him. "I do not know what to say to you."

"Say nothing." Egwinna pulled her cloak and kirtle above her ankles and crawled across the wagon to join her son. She burrowed down in the hay and pulled Stan to her, wrapping him in her cloak. She crooned to him until he fell asleep.

Lae watched mother and child drift off to sleep from her vantage point on her horse. She wished that Edward had taken the time in his youth to know the girl before she had been thrown into their lives. Was it God's plan that one person be born in a royal house and another in the shack of a peasant, or was it just by chance, like the game of knuckles and bones, that decided where one was born? Her father loved to ask his children philosophical questions that would puzzle a priest. No, a priest would call it God's plan, but Lae had always rebelled at the thought of a plan for her life. She wanted to control her own destiny.

Her father had taught all of his children to question everything, much to the horror of her mother. Lae wanted to be as learned as was her father, but that would be difficult; he never stopped reading the ancients or stopped writing his chronicles.

Edward slapped the reins against the backs of the team of oxen. They jumped forward, then settled into the same slow pace crossing the snow-covered grasslands following the trail of other wagons toward the old Roman road that would take them to Lundenburh.

chapter
ÍÍÍ

DWARD TRIED TO SLEEP before the firepit in the room usually occupied by the local parish priest. He rolled over carefully to avoid the stone slab that jutted out from the hearth. The heavy sheepskin did not provide much protection from the hardpacked earthen floor. His back was warm from the fire, but the other side felt chilled from the draft that flowed under the door like water under a bridge. Edward pulled his woolen cloak tighter around his chin and shivered. He would never get used to the cold weather that plagued his country.

Lae was asleep in a small room usually reserved for visiting dignitaries. At her insistence, Edward had given the only remaining cot to Egwinna and Stan, both of whom slept near by, much to Egwinna's amusement and the chagrin of the priest who muttered prayers under his breath. Edward's attempted act of compassion had not produced the effect he thought it would. He was angry at Egwinna's lack of reverence for the sacrifice he was making for her. Egwinna had given the priest an angry look when he hovered around them trying to keep man and woman separated. The priest had gone away, finally, grumbling about the perils of adultery. It seemed that Egwinna had no regard for any man, be he priest or prince.

Edward was in the deepest stages of sleep where dreams are forgotten, but a warrior part of him was always awake, and he knew when the door opened. He wrapped his hand around the handle of his knife. The bothersome priest rushed in and knelt beside Edward, shaking him much too hard. "Sir, you must wake up."

Edward opened his eyes. In the firelight, he saw the gnarled hand of the priest on his shoulder. It was brown from years of working in the sunny garden, tending a tiny flock of sheep, and keeping the small church in repair. This was a working priest and not one who said mass and spent the rest of the time thinking profound thoughts. "What is it, Father?"

"Your night watch has reported unusual activity across the field from here."

Edward sat up, pushing his cloak over his shoulders as he stood. "What time is it?"

"Nearly sunrise; although there will be no sun today. My old bones tell me that we get snow. The darkness lingers under clouds."

"Wake the rest of the men who sleep in the chapel." Edward watched the priest leave, grabbed his sword and buckled it in place. As always he thanked the blacksmith who had forged such a fine weapon. The gold buckle that held both ends of the leather belt together was crafted to represent a sea serpent. When the belt was buckled, both ends of the serpent closed so that it looked as if the snake were swallowing its own tail. The golden beast's garnet eyes glowed red in the firelight as Edward pulled his cloak about himself. He turned and saw Egwinna propped up on an elbow staring at him.

"There may be some trouble. Warn your lady immediately. I shall return for you, so make yourself and the boy ready for travel." Edward opened the door, turned back and looked at the sleeping child. "If you need to protect yourself, there is a dagger in my pack." Without waiting for an answer, Edward closed the door behind him and crossed to the chapel toward the soldiers who waited for him. "Where are the night watch, and what do they report?"

"They are watching the east. Their horses were nervous. Suspecting wolves, the men were about to light a torch to hold off the beasts when they saw movement across the field from east to southeast. They dismounted and crept within a few yards of a small band of Danes."

Edward grunted. It was not unusual to have the Danes skulking around. "How did the guards know the men were Danes?"

"From their manner of dress. The moon came out briefly while the guards were close to them. There are only three."

"Thank you, Adair." Edward nodded to the older man who had told the story. Light from the torches showed how much silver hair was mixed with the black. Time had flown by without notice, and the man who had been with him since Edward could ride was aging. Edward clapped Adair on the shoulder. "Would you do me the great favor of staying here to guard the Lady of the Mercians, the peasant woman, and my son? I would not want harm to come to them." He handed Adair his cloak and adjusted his sword.

Adair bowed. "With great honor, sir."

"Our lady knows the ways of fighting. Egwinna has a dagger, and she is afraid of no one. Be careful that you do not surprise either of them." Edward smiled at the memory of Egwinna as she had stood between him and their son.

The sky was lighter in the east, and Edward could see the three figures more easily. They moved from the clearing to the wooded area, slipping from tree to tree. He and six of his men watched.

"You two," Edward whispered. "Get the guards and go around to the left. The rest of us will come from the right. Capture them alive. We need to know why they are here. Hurry, too, before daylight reveals us."

Keeping low against the ground, Edward sneaked around a small hill toward the figures who, hunched down, were skulking along from tree to tree. He was within three arm's length of the last one. Holding his sword still against his body, he walked quietly toward the enemy. If he got too close, the sword would be no good. He should have brought the dagger.

Edward almost stopped breathing, he was so close to the last man. His concentration blocked any awareness of the men who had come with him. He moved faster, pacing his footsteps to match the Vikings' so that they would not hear him. One man stopped and listened, his head cocked toward his left, toward the men Edward had sent to come in the opposite way.

The leader of the Danes stopped and raised his hand. Edward wanted to deal with him. The Viking disappeared behind a tree. Had he waited too long to make a clean attack? Edward moved behind another tree and waited. The sky was lighter, but the tall trees blocked the daylight. Had it been summer, the leaves would have made it darker.

He saw the figures again, but this time the leader was beside him. Edward was so shocked that he nearly missed his chance to attack. Holding his sword in place, he leaped forward, flung his arm under the Viking's chin, and pulled back until he heard the Viking gasp. The Viking reached around and ran his fingers into Edward's left eye. Clenching his teeth, Edward ignored the pain and concentrated on felling his opponent before he himself was downed. He wrestled the Viking to the ground and pinned him after rolling two or three times. Edward was aware of other skirmishes around him.

The sound of pounding hooves caused his head to snap up. Laughter from the Viking on the ground confirmed his fears. These few men were merely the scouts for a horde of Vikings who were, no doubt, planning to raid the church.

Edward kneed the man in the groin, gave him an uppercut to the chin, and, certain that he was knocked out, left him. Edward's pride did not allow him to stab an unconscious man. "Draw your swords, men, and take a stand in the meadow. Do not let the Vikings get to the church! They think nothing of killing priests!"

Edward grabbed his sword and heard the familiar sound of metal against lamb's wool lining of the scabbard as he pulled out his weapon. That sound always prepared him for a fight. He had named the sword Caelan after an old friend. In Gaelic it meant powerful in battle. Edward hoped that, since he and his men were outnumbered, the sword would live up to its name. It would be a waste if his son were to be killed when Edward had just decided to rear him as a prince.

Edward met the first Viking as they both emerged from the woods, swords drawn. Edward swung his sword up and across in front of him, effectively blocking the thrust meant for his stomach. Another swing and he caught the man in the side of his neck, felling him like a large tree. Edward did not stay to watch the Viking's life's blood flow into the ground. He knew the blow had been fatal.

Edward surveyed the fight that had been behind him and ran to help two of his men who held off five Vikings, but were overburdened. As Edward came up behind one of the Vikings, that enemy was run through by one of Edward's own Wessex guards. Another

Viking turned to face him. Edward glanced at his opponent's armor and sword, noting that the equipment seemed expensive and well made. It would be more difficult to bring down this Dane.

Edward waited a fraction of a second to see how the man would fight. The Viking was quick, but his swing was short and choppy. Edward raised his sword, stepped into the enemy's swing and deflected the blow. The Dane brought his sword up a second time, and again Edward was able to divert the blade. Edward noted that the swordsman was inexperienced, and it would be only a matter of time before he made a fatal mistake.

Edward maneuvered his opponent away from the other Vikings so that his men could deal with them more easily. The Viking did not realize he was being led, another indication to Edward that he was youthful. They parried for five more strokes before the Viking, obviously frustrated, raised his sword above his head for a fatal blow to Edward, leaving his own stomach exposed. Edward took the opportunity and ran the Viking through. As he pulled his sword free from the falling man, Edward could not help but see the look of surprise in the eyes of his dying enemy. Edward refused to feel any sympathy for a youth who thought he was ready for pillaging and killing when he was not.

Turning quickly, Edward saw that the fight had moved away from him toward the church. He ran toward the sound of metal clanking against metal. He thought of Lae, Egwinna, and Adair guarding Stan. If the Vikings broke through their thin line of defense, his old soldier, Adair, would not be able to make much of a stand in the church to hold them off. Edward was angry with himself for assuming that there were only three Vikings. He should have known there would be more.

The light was good now; daylight having burst forth in spite of the absence of the sun. Edward saw too many of the Vikings between him and the church. He ran toward the closest of the enemy, and as the man turned and swung his sword, Edward, never slowing, down, ran him through. Edward kept running, although it was difficult. Two Vikings turned on him as he neared the knot of men brandishing swords. He held them off the first time they both ran at him, but he could not fight these two easily. They were experienced and their timing was well coordinated. Edward was tired and his right arm hurt from holding the heavy sword. One of his men came over to even up the fight, and Edward smiled his thanks. They dispatched the two Vikings to Valhalla quickly, although Edward's fellow soldier was cut on his sword arm.

"Go and have your wound tended. You would be no good to me dead. You can help keep my son safe. Do not stand there wasting my time! Go!" Edward did not wait for the soldier to argue, but advanced toward another fight. As he drew close, he heard the Viking leader shout and the Vikings ran back toward the woods. When Edward's men started to follow, he yelled, "Let them go. It is not worth our time. Let it be enough that we killed some and sent the other cowards running. Come, we need to see to my sister and my son."

Edward ran to the chapel, stopping at its open door. "May God have mercy." The priest lay dead in front of the altar. Blood, like dark wine, flowed across the floor, making its way into channels between the flagstones and streaming in neat rows down the aisle. The work-worn hands of the priest still clutched the altar cloth that he had grabbed as he fell.

The priest was beyond Edward's help, but mayhap Stan was not. Edward stepped over the body and moved quickly to the room where Lae had been sleeping. He heard sobbing through the open door and expected the worst as he lunged through the doorway. It took a moment for his mind to understand what his eyes saw. Lae, a clean dagger in her hand, stood across the room from Egwinna. With her mouth agape, she stared at Egwinna who stood by the cot, Adair's sword in her hand. Egwinna was covered with blood, her hair was flying about her face in wild disarray, and two bodies lay at her feet. One was Adair and the other a Viking. Edward knelt by his old soldier, crossed himself as he said a prayer for his soul, and closed the man's lifeless eyes. He had thought keeping Adair with the women would ensure the old man's safety. How wrong he had been.

The Viking was a few feet away, his right arm nearly severed, but even in death still clutching his sword. Edward stood and faced his sister.

"What happened?"

Lae's eyebrows raised. "I heard terrible screams and came running from the chapel where I had watched the fighting. I thought I should stay here in case there were more Vikings. By the time I opened the door, everything was quiet. I know no more than that."

"For God's sake, Egwinna, tell me what happened!"

Egwinna shook her head, still sobbing.

"The boy!" Edward stepped across the two bodies and threw back the covers on the cot. Stan was not there. "Where is my son?"

"He is my son more than he is yours." Egwinna stopped crying and wiped her eyes with her left hand, her right hand still holding the sword.

"Do not play games with me! Is he dead?" Edward had not wanted to say the words, but he needed to know.

"He is safe. He plays the game of silence well." Egwinna pointed to a stand that held a wash basin and pitcher. "Come out, Stan, it is safe. Your father is here."

Edward watched with awe as the small doors in the lower cabinet portion of the washstand opened, and Stan crawled out. The boy looked at the bodies in front of him and, with chin quivering, ran to his mother. Egwinna dropped the sword with a clang against the stone floor and scooped the child into her arms. She hugged and kissed him, being careful, Edward noticed, to keep his eyes away from the terrible scene in front of her.

Edward grabbed the legs of the dead Viking and dragged him out the door. He came back for Adair and carried the knight into the passageway that led to the chapel. He saw two of his men standing by the priest.

"Get some men to bury the dead. Bury the Vikings in one grave. They deserve no better. One of you should ride to find someone who will care for the priest and say prayers for the dead." Edward looked down at Adair. "Our comrade would not mind being buried here. Put him in the church graveyard and mark his resting place well. I will send a stone mason later to carve a marker for him."

Edward returned to the room and closed the door. A path of blood where he had dragged out the dead Dane had already started to dry. Splattered and smeared and sticky, the smell of iron assaulted Edward.

"I am most sorry about Adair," Lae said. "I have known him all my life. He was your special protector."

"That he was. He would have not wanted a quiet death, but one like this, full of honor."

"I will tend to the wounded." Lae touched Edward's arm as she left the room and closed the door.

Edward surveyed the room. Egwinna sat on the bed with the boy, combing his hair and singing to him. Edward wanted to put his arms around her to tell her that he was pleased, but she seemed unwilling to look at him. "Can you tell me how Adair and the Viking were killed?"

Egwinna shook her head and frowned. "I do not want to think about it."

Edward watched her comb the boy's hair until he thought the child would go bald. Her hands trembled. Edward knew the reason most soldiers bragged about their escapades was to allay the fears that came with battles. When a soldier saw a man die for the first time in the field, it showed him his own tenuous hold on life. Egwinna was like a soldier who has killed for the first time. She could not deal with death or her own mortality unless she talked to someone. "I need to know how Adair died so that I may tell his widow, his children, and his grandchildren."

Egwinna looked at him, blinking to hold back tears. "I did not know him, yet he gave his life for my son."

"And for you, Egwinna. He gave his life for you." Edward took the comb from her hand and laid it aside. He sat on the bed and held her hand. Stan stared at him from his mother's lap. "Tell me."

"We heard a noise in the chapel and an awful scream from the priest. The priest yelled that he had been run through. Your man, his name was Adair?"

Edward nodded.

"Adair, who was by the door, ran out. I knew that Stan had to be hidden. I hoped that the Vikings did not know he was with us or who he was. I spied the washstand and shoved him in there just as Adair backed into the room wielding his sword. I was terrified when I saw that big Viking come at Adair. They fought, but the space was so small that Adair could not get a good swing. After what seemed like a long, long time, Adair faltered and the . . . the Viking killed him." Egwinna turned her face away from Edward.

"How did the Viking get the gash in his arm?"

"I picked up Adair's sword. I swung before I really thought. I just took it in both hands and whirled around with all the strength I had. The Viking saw me too late, but he had time to turn away. I hit him in the arm." Egwinna shuddered. "Oh, Edward, his scream was so terrible," she whispered.

Edward put his arm around her shoulders, surprised that he felt an overwhelming urge to protect her. He had noticed that she called him by name for the first time. "Tell me the rest."

"He fell to the floor, swore at me, then called on the gods to forgive him for having been killed by a woman." Egwinna's eyes opened wide. "Whatever did he mean by that?"

"The Vikings do not hold their women in high esteem. They do not believe women should have any power except to bear children. It was an insult to him to be killed by a woman." Edward almost laughed at the look she gave him.

"If I had known that, I would have gloated over him as he died. What an absurd way of thinking. Why, if they taught their women to do more than have children, think of the power they would have in sheer numbers alone. I hope he goes to his place for eternal punishment." Egwinna leaned into Edward. "He scared me. He reached for me with his good arm, and I had to jump on the cot to keep him from touching my kirtle."

"You are safe with me."

Egwinna pushed Edward away from her. "Safe with you! Had I stayed in my own cottage, I would never have had to kill a Viking. We never had anyone raid our village since the time you chased the Vikings toward us. We never had a priest killed. I am not safe with you!"

"Egwinna, do not play the goose. It is only a matter of time before the Vikings come into your village. I can protect you, and I will."

"If this is your idea of protection, then I do not want it. I cannot endure the danger. I have a son to think about." Egwinna shook her head. "Do not look at me so. I want to go back to my village. I will go if I have to walk."

"You may as well forget about walking to your village. In the first place, the Vikings that we chased away came from the direction of your village. Mayhap they had already been there." Edward heard Egwinna's gasp, and he knew he had to convince her now, or she would try to run away and take his son with her.

"My sister has seen the Vikings amass great numbers of men. The enemy is bringing over many ships, swords, and chain-mail.

The Vikings have decided to expand from behind the Danelaw into our two countries. No village will be safe, but you will be within the fortress at the Mercian court. You will be under guard at all times. There will be no more Vikings to invade your sleeping quarters and put our child at risk. There will be no more bloody bodies on the floor for Stan to see. It will be better for our son if he is trained to fight so he can protect himself. He will have a better life than that of a sheep herder." Edward watched her face. He could see the doubt that was there. "I deserve a son to be king."

Egwinna looked at Stan, who sat quietly on her lap. She kissed his rosy cheek. "All right. We go to Lundenburh. I owe him a royal life, for he is royalty."

"You deserve a good life, too, Egwinna. You fought as bravely as any soldier trained in battle. Mayhap you were braver, for the lack of training did not stop you from protecting our son. I want the woman who rears Stan to have courage. It is only fitting for a king that his mother show him how to be bold. You remind me of my sister." Edward kissed Egwinna on the forehead. "Ready yourself for the ride to Lundenburh. I need to attend to the burials."

The trip to Lundenburh went easily but with a certain amount of trepidation and sadness for everyone. The body of Adair had been buried in the corner of the churchyard next to a grove of ash trees where it would be easy for his family to find it.

Edward taught Egwinna to drive the wagon to give her something to do. He rode along beside her for part of the way, marveling at how quickly she learned. The rest of the time he talked with the men while Lae and Egwinna discussed whatever it was that women talked about. His men were still shaken by the death of Adair. He had been their friend, their advisor, their father, and his death made them resolve to avenge it.

The gates of Lundenburh opened up to them as soon as the guards recognized Lae. Edward watched her gallop ahead toward the main doorway where her husband waited with their only offspring. The rest of the entourage moved toward the fortress palisades at a less reckless pace.

Once inside the fortress walls Edward felt relieved, and he was surprised at this. He must have been more concerned about meeting the Vikings again than he had realized. It was not for fear of his own safety, he told himself, but for the safety of Lae, Stan, and Egwinna. Having a family certainly changed one's perspective.

Of course, he already had a family, but Egwinna was different from his wife. His wife had never combed the hair of their son, nor had she sung songs to him. She had made certain that other women tended the boy. Did the child die because he had no love? Edward shook himself. Stupid thoughts about love could never be answered.

His sister had dismounted and stood by her husband at the main doors, holding tightly to the hand of her daughter, Aelfwyn, who tried to pull away. The girl's face was red from screaming. She always seemed to be screaming, and Edward had a sudden impulse to turn back and let his father's court protect Stan. Edward knew that his mother, Eahlswith, would not allow him to bring his mistress and illegitimate son into the same household with his wife. That would be too cruel, even for a wife who seemed not to have the heart to bear healthy children. His marriage to Elflaed was a union of politics, nothing more. Had Elflaed some wit or kindness to go with her beauty, Edward could have tolerated her better. Ah, well. It was for heirs that men married.

Edward's sister motioned for them, and he saw Lae grimace as her daughter kicked her shins to get away. Aelfwyn was only tolerable when she was asleep. Edward could not understand how a child could get so spoiled. Her beautiful black hair, so unlike her mother's or her father's was the only thing that Edward admired about the child.

Egwinna leaned out the wagon to whisper to Edward. "Edward, who is that horrid child held tightly by my lady?"

Edward chuckled. "That is the darling daughter of my sister. This is the child you will tend. Her name is Aelfwyn."

"No! Whatever is wrong with her? Am I to be nurse to that? Poor Stan! He has been brought up to be gentle. I have changed my mind about this arrangement, Edward. Please turn this wagon around and take me home!"

"I cannot do that. You are here to stay." Edward did not blame Egwinna for wanting to leave. He could hear the screams of the girl as they pulled up next to Lae.

"Brother-in-law, it is wonderful to see you, again," Red shouted. "It seems that you had an adventure. I wish that I had been there to run a few of the Vikings through myself."

Dismounting quickly, Edward grabbed Red in a huge bear hug, deftly side-stepping the kicking child. "It is good to be with you once more. We have to discuss the Vikings. They are causing more trouble than we anticipated."

"Mayhap we should send them our most horrible weapon." Red nodded toward his daughter.

"Red! What a terrible thing to say about Wyn." Lae pushed the child through the door toward a woman who seemed to have wrinkles on wrinkles. "Take her to her chambers. See that the door to the nursery is closed, so that Wyn will not embarrass herself." Lae took Red's hand and pulled him to the wagon. "Come, I want to show you Edward's son." She peered into the back of the wagon where Stan sat on a small mound of hay. "He has the hair of my mother."

"So this is Edward's son. He is a fine looking boy," Red said. He scrutinized Egwinna. "You are the one who has come as a nurse. Do I dare hope that you have come to care for the boy as well as my daughter?"

"I do not know if I am capable enough for the . . . the honor of tending your daughter, my lord." Egwinna put her hand over one ear as a screeching sound came from inside the great hall.

Edward chuckled. "I am afraid that Egwinna might want to do away with that raging animal, as I feel like doing. Why did you let her get so spoiled?"

"I do not think the nurse spoiled her, Edward," Lae said. "I swear she was born this way. I will give her new nurse the freedom to make this child human. I have tried everything the priests have suggested, but they know absolutely nothing of life and nothing of children."

"That is true, my lady. I have little use for priests who try to tell us about life and love without having seen enough of it for themselves." Egwinna clapped her hand over her mouth.

Lae frowned. "It is unseemly to discuss priests as we do." Her face softened. "However, never fear about insulting me when you talk of priests. I have made similar statements."

Red cleared his throat. "Lae, are you going to let everyone stay outside in the cold? You must be in great need of food and drink. I want to hear about the skirmish with the Vikings."

"Red, you will be happy to know that Egwinna killed her first Viking." Edward gestured to Egwinna. "This is the mother of my son."

"She killed a Viking? Mayhap you will be able to control our daughter as easily as you did the Dane. Edward, do help her down, and we will celebrate." Red chuckled. "Come in, Egwinna. You and your son have a home here fit for the future king of Wessex. I do hope these two children can get along together for the sake of both our countries. Wyn, being our only child, will be the ruler of Mercia after her mother and I are dead."

Edward swung down off his horse and glanced at his son. "I hope for the sake of my country that Wyn never becomes angry with us. Is there some way we can use her against the Vikings?"

"Edward! She is not always this bad. Sometimes she is very quiet," Lae said.

Edward helped Egwinna from the wagon and handed Stan to her. He led them into the great hall, then watched as Lae ran her fingers through Stan's hair, cooed over him, and kissed his cheek. Lae chuckled when Stan buried his face in his mother's shoulder.

"He is beautifully behaved, Edward. I am certain that he will give this old place much joy. Egwinna, how pleased I am to have you here." Lae waved her hand toward the firepit. "Let us move to where it is warmer."

"I want Egwinna to tell all the horrible details of her first Viking kill," Red said.

Egwinna blushed. "I am not a good story teller, having never told one before."

"Just tell us as best you remember it," Lae said. "The excitement of the memory will carry your tale to us. I, too, shall be glad to hear the details while we wait for our food."

Edward watched Egwinna as she began her story, staring at her hands, her voice quiet. She was enchanting, the shyness adding to her comeliness. Edward felt content. He would visit Mercia more often now that Egwinna and Stan were to live here.

chapter

ÍV

HE SCREAMING STOPPED. Lae met her father's gaze, and shrugged. "I am afraid to hope for much. Wyn has been screaming since Egwinna arrived."

"How does she get along with Stan?" King Aelfred pulled his chair closer to the fire and stretched his feet toward the flames.

"She kicked him so hard that his legs have bumps covered by bruises. Egwinna has tried to keep him away from my daughter, but to no avail."

"Wyn has the worst disposition of any child I have ever seen. You have spoiled her."

"Father! Had you been around her when she was an infant, you would have seen how unhappy she was." Lae felt uncomfortable arguing with her father, but he knew little of rearing children. He had always left that to her mother. "Wyn cannot help how she is."

"Your daughter will make a miserable wife for Stan."

"It was your idea to remove him from his village and groom him to be king after Edward. It is not my fault that you arranged his future." Lae tapped her finger against the arm of her chair.

"You are angry with me."

"I am not." Lae twisted the sleeve of her tunic around her finger.

"I can always tell when you are angry. First you tap your fingers, then you twist your tunic." King Aelfred smiled. "I know you better than you think I do."

"I am angry." Lae let go of her sleeve and watched the woolen material settle back into place. "Most Christians would never acknowledge a bastard child. Why is it that you not only acknowledged Stan, but have planned for his future?"

"I have never believed that a child should pay all his life for the mistake his parents made. I know, as you do, that there are priests who have had children. God has not struck them dead, so I have decided that God is more forgiving than man. If God can forgive, so can I."

"I have trouble following your generous nature. Mayhap it is because you have betrothed my only child to a bastard. I am not certain I can follow your dictate." Lae stared at the floor. She could not meet her father's piercing gaze.

King Aelfred picked up a stack of vellum sheets and glanced over them. "Then I suggest you pray for help."

"I have prayed for help. I have tried to see Stan as a king for Wessex and as a husband for Wyn. I find myself unable to agree with you, Father."

"Since I am only your father and no longer your king, you have presented me with a problem." King Aelfred waved a sheet of vellum at Lae. "Here is the latest section of the chronicles that I have penned. Allow me to paint you a picture of the future as it could be written. Edward's children are sickly and all have died. Edward has no heir, so Mercia has agreed to oversee the country until another king is elected. There is civil war in Wessex, and one of our weaker neighbors tries to take part of Wessex, but is stopped by the Vikings who have invaded my poor country. The Vikings take Wessex, then march toward Mercia. Your daughter is unable to stop the murderous Danes, and they take your country, too. What think you of my story so far?"

"I have heard nicer tales." Lae shifted in her chair. "If you had not been king and a writer of history, you could have been the court storyteller."

"It may be a story to you, Daughter, but it is a nightmare for me. I am looking at the future. I suppose I am a selfish man to ask that you rear a bastard for Wessex, and that you give your daughter to him in marriage."

"I would not have chosen the word selfish." Lae looked up from the floor and scrutinized her father.

"You would have called me stubborn?"

Lae grinned. "I would have called you stone-headed, for you did not take the time to ask me what I wanted for my daughter's future and the future of Mercia. You are right in one thing. You may be my father, but you are not my king. My husband is my king."

"Your husband agrees with me."

"My husband is your friend and has been for longer than I have been alive." Lae pulled a piece of lint from the end of her braid. "I will try harder to befriend little Stan. It will not be easy for me."

"Nothing in your life has been easy, Lae. We have been beset by the Vikings all your life. Before that, our ancestors were attacked by others. The only hope we have is to become one strong country. Until we control this island, our people will not be secure. When we are one nation, we will be forever invincible."

"You tell me this so that I can see the greater need is for me to put aside the prejudices that I hold. I will try. If you will excuse me, I want to see to Wyn. She has been quiet far longer than is normal. I am curious about the silence."

"You may go, Lae, with my blessing. I am to meet with your armorer this afternoon. He is a genius at sword-making. He has promised to make a new sword for me."

"As my father, you have more of my heart than if you were my king still." Lae rose, curtsied, and left the great hall. As she climbed the long stairway to the tower, she willed herself to follow the commands of her father. Even though her heart was against rearing Stan, Lae's mind told her that her father was right.

Lae pushed open the door to the tower room. The quiet was disconcerting. She glanced around the room as she had been taught to do when confronting a dangerous situation, then realized how silly her fears were. Wyn was on the floor, her hair a tangled mass of raven curls. Her feet were against a chest and from the marks on it, Lae could tell the child had been kicking it for a long time. She hoped that Wyn had not hurt herself.

Egwinna leaped to her feet, scattering sewing across the floor. She curtsied. "My lady. I did not expect a visit from you. I thought I was supposed to bring Wyn to you in the afternoon."

Lae looked at Wyn from the corner of her eye. Her daughter was too quiet. "What have you done to her? Do you have potions that I do not know about?"

"I have nothing, my lady. I have not touched her. I have given her no potions. What would you have me do that I have not done?"

"Why did her screams stop?"

"I will not talk to her when she screams."

"I do not understand what you mean. Why will you not talk to her?"

Egwinna's face turned red, and she stared at the tips of her shoes. "I will not feed her or let her go anywhere as long as she screams."

"You are starving her?"

"Oh no, my lady!" Egwinna's head snapped up. "She has not screamed continuously these last three days, although it seems like it."

"My daughter is a princess and should be treated like one though it is difficult. Pray, do not treat her harshly as did her old nurse. I fear the results." Egwinna had such a charming child, and Wyn was such a defiant one. "Where is Stan?"

"He spends much of his time in the stables. He smells more like a horse than the horses do."

"Just like Edward." Lae smiled to herself at the memory of her younger brother tumbling through the legs of the horses in his excitement.

"Really? Edward liked horses?"

"You ask a lot of questions."

Egwinna clapped her hand across her mouth, and spoke through her fingers. "I am sorry for the disrespect, my lady. I do not mean to be worrisome. It has always been my worst fault. If allowed, I tend to prattle on."

"Indeed, you do." Lae wanted to laugh at the simple girl who was so winsome, but she refrained. She did not want to span the breach she was trying to create. Egwinna would not be a proper wife to her brother and would probably never have a chance to become one.

"What is that web of color at your feet?"

"Embroidery, my lady." Egwinna dropped her hand to her side.

Lae stared at the woman. "Embroidery? Whence came you by that knowledge?"

"My mother taught me."

"Your mother? Learning to embroider is usually reserved for nobility. I do not understand."

"Neither do I. I thought everyone knew the art, so it was not until I was older that I realized this was not so. I often asked my mother how she learned to embroider, but she always pretended that she had not heard. I have never learned my mother's secret, and I never will. I doubt that I will ever see my mother again."

"Do you miss her?" Lae remembered her own loneliness for her mother after marrying Red.

"I wish I could care, but there has been no love between mother and daughter or father and daughter."

"Then you do not miss either parent." Lae thought about her relationship with Wyn. Would the child never love her?

"I do miss my mother. It was not that she was loving or even nice to me, but I miss the shuffling sound of her feet as she moved around the hut preparing meals, and the tuneless humming as she did the spinning."

"What did your mother do for you that you miss her?"

Egwinna shrugged. "What did my mother do for me? She taught me to tend to sick lambs, to spin, to card the wool, and to embroider." Egwinna looked at her feet. "She never held me. I do not think she liked me. I was something she had to feed, to clothe, nothing more." Tears slid down Egwinna's cheeks. "I promised myself I would never do that to my child."

Lae looked at the delicate features and slender hands of the woman in front of her. She did not have the features that most peasants had. Her hair was silky, her complexion fine. It would be easier for Lae to accept Stan if her mother were royalty. "Your mother never told you of your ancestry?"

"No, my lady. My parents still had the straight brown hair of their youth and not the white hair of old age. I have often wondered which ancestor gave me this." She flipped her curly auburn hair. "When I asked my mother, her answer was a scowl."

It was common, Lae knew, not to have feelings for parents or for children, but Lae had been reared with love. Threads of love built a tapestry that held the family together for generations. She found it sad that Egwinna had no one but Stan. "You love your son."

"With all my heart. I would die for him." Egwinna's chin quivered.

Lae remembered the bloody Viking that had been dispatched to Valhalla by Egwinna. "I have seen your words in action. You are a fierce warrior."

"I am not. I quake in your presence."

"Do I frighten you?"

"Yes, my lady."

"Why?"

"You have the power to take Stan from me."

Lae started to protest, but she knew that Egwinna was right. As soon as her father had discovered Stan, he was no longer Egwinna's. "That is true, but it should never come to pass."

"Not even you, my lady, can promise that."

Lae smiled. "You are being brazen, again."

"A terrible fault that my father said will be the death of me. I often argued with him. He used to beat me for it, but I never quit."

Lae heard the wonder in Egwinna's voice as if she had just made a discovery. "That life is gone. It is best forgotten."

The squealing of hinges as the door opened announced the whirlwind that had captured King Aelfred's heart. Lae watched Stan burst through the door and charge across the room. He stopped in front of his mother and tugged on her tunic.

"My grandfather took me to see the horses that belong to Queen Lae. He says that she has fine horses. You should feel them. Their noses are softer than . . . than anything!" Stan hopped on one foot, then the other. "Their coats are so shiny. When I am bigger, my grandfather said that I may have one! I want the sorrel horse!"

"That is my horse, Stan. I am reluctant to give him up. Tanton is a good friend."

"Horses can be friends?" Stan cocked his head and blinked at Lae.

"Son, you are being rude." Egwinna took Stan's chin in her hand and tilted his head up so their eyes met. "You must not burst through the door into a lady's chamber. You ought to knock."

"Like a gentleman?"

"Yes, Stan."

Lae watched the lesson with amusement. The boy had the natural charm of his father with looks to match. "You learn quickly, Stan."

Before Stan could answer, Lae's thoughts were pierced by a scream from Wyn. Lae whirled around to face her daughter who was kicking the unfortunate chest in rhythm with her cries. "Whatever ails that child?"

"She hates Stan." Egwinna's chin quivered. A tear slid down her cheek.

By the Blessed Virgin, Egwinna cries a lot, thought Lae. She watched Stan scurry behind his mother. He peeked out to stare at Wyn. Lae shouted, "What do you do to stop her?"

"Leave her." Egwinna pulled Stan toward the door. "Follow me, my lady, if it please you."

Lae was intrigued by Egwinna's child-rearing, and she trailed after her, ignoring protocol in favor of relief. She did step aside to allow Egwinna to shut the door. The three of them scurried down the steps. "Let us go to my chambers. It will be quieter," Lae said.

When the women were seated, and Stan was occupied by hanging out the window watching the inner bailey, Lae looked at Egwinna and burst out laughing. "We are like naughty children."

"I think so. Poor Wyn."

"Poor us. Her screeches are legendary. She could scare the Vikings straight out of Mercia and Wessex." Lae liked Egwinna, and she pondered the relationship she should have with her. Lae did not like Edward's whining wife, but she did have a feeling of loyalty for her sister-in-law. Egwinna was difficult not to like, for she had proven her bravery, her intelligence, and her ability to understand Wyn. It was an awkward situation for which there were no rules. Her father had put both her and Egwinna in this position, so Lae decided to make her own code of conduct. She was used to being in a world of men. It would please her to have a woman to talk with during the peaceful times.

"My lady, do you think it wrong of me to leave Wyn when she screams?"

"Does she hurt herself?"

Egwinna clapped her hands together as if in prayer. "I have never observed Wyn injuring herself. However, if it please you, I will return to her."

"You said that Wyn has shown some improvement. I have never had much time to spend with her, so I am ignorant about children. You have had the pleasure of watching your child grow hour by hour."

Egwinna glanced toward Stan. "Yes, it was fortunate for me. We should see to Wyn. If she is quiet, we should go to her."

"Mother, I do not want to go to her. She kicks and bites."

"Be quiet. You should not talk about your cousin in such a manner. You may go to the great hall and play with the kittens and puppies, if it is all right with my lady."

"Certainly." Lae was anxious to see her daughter. She knew she should spend more time with Wyn to teach her the ways of royalty.

Lae and Egwinna stood inside the tower room. The silence rolled over Lae like a wave from the Narrow Sea. She continued to stand quietly, but she looked at Wyn from the corner of her eye. The girl was watching her, and Lae was not sure about the ritual that had been established by Egwinna. She glanced at the nurse for guidance. Lae did not want to look into Wyn's eyes for fear the child would scream again.

"I want a drink right now." Wyn sat up and rubbed her swollen eyes.

Egwinna walked across the room to the plank table where a pitcher and mugs were kept. She poured water and handed a cup to Wyn. "A real princess would say please and thank you. A real princess is kind to everyone."

"Who told you that?" Wyn reached for the cup.

"My fairy godmother." Egwinna held the cup just out of reach.

"What is her name?"

"I cannot tell you. It is a secret."

Lae grinned, for she recognized the tale from her own childhood. It was odd that she had never thought to tell the story to Wyn. Lae spoke. "You cannot tell your fairy godmother's name, for if you do, she will fly away."

Wyn scowled. "She is mean. A real fairy godmother would never leave."

"If you want Egwinna to give you that water, then you must say please."

"I do not want it anymore."

"You are thirsty. Take a drink." Lae felt like stamping her foot. The devil had that child.

Egwinna handed the water to Wyn. "My lady, Wyn needs to be gentle broke. She is like a horse that has been beaten."

"What do you know about breaking horses? You are nothing more than a shepherdess." What made Egwinna think she could control that child? Lae felt anger flush her cheeks as she remembered the cruelty of Wyn's first nurse. She swept from the room without a word. The door slammed behind her.

Lae had almost made it to the bottom of the stairs when she met Edward coming up. "Edward, I did not expect you back so soon. What did you discover about the Vikings?"

"It is as you predicted. They continue to bring in supplies from Denmark. I have not sought you out to talk of the Vikings. I have a worse problem at the moment."

"What, pray tell?"

"My wife is on her way here. A messenger has given me this." Edward held a tri-folded piece of vellum. "It would be simpler if Elflaed would stay in Wessex. She is with child, again, and is too ill for this foolishness."

"Why is she coming here?"

"Elflaed has the misguided notion that she will be safer here since Father and I are here." Edward slapped the vellum against his thigh. "If one of us had been in Wessex, she would never have been allowed to come here."

"Does she not realize that the Vikings she fears so much are closer to us here than to Wessex?" Lae reached for the vellum, unfolded it, and read quickly. "This is most distressing. Our father, with his notions of inheritance, has put me in a bad position. I cannot have Egwinna in one part of the fortress and your wife in the other. It is not proper. What would the priest think?"

"It is too late to worry about what the priest will think. My wife will arrive tomorrow." Edward took the vellum from Lae. "If Egwinna leaves, then what will happen to my son?"

"Oh, Edward, I do not know."

"It is a woman's problem. I shall leave it up to you to decide on the proper course of action."

"Edward!" Lae frowned at the departing figure of her brother. Men always used the excuse that it was a woman's problem. They were no help in domestic issues.

Lae's peevishness with her brother caused her to whirl around to return upstairs, and she came face to face with Egwinna and Wyn. "I did not hear you coming." Lae felt foolish, but she did not know what else to say in her surprise.

"I wanted to take Wyn to the kitchen. I think she is hungry." Egwinna blushed.

"She is a finicky eater."

"I am not!"

Lae glanced down at the child who glared back at her. "I hope you find something to eat that will help your disposition."

Egwinna stepped aside. "I will see that she eats well."

"I have no doubts." Lae swept past Egwinna and crossed the great hall to her own chambers. She did not want to be the cause of Wyn's discomfort, and she did not want to be reminded by Egwinna's presence that she had a prickly problem. Lae just wanted to go to her apartment and read. The writings of her father usually consoled her, but today since he was the source of her problems, she would read the ancients instead while there was still daylight.

As darkness crept into her chamber, Lae gave up trying to see the words and, putting the book aside, stared at the floor. She had found no answer for her dilemma. She jumped up and stomped across the room. If her father created the problem, then he would just have to solve it. She pulled open the door and marched down the hallway toward her father's room. He had better be there, for the longer she thought about the preposterous situation, the angrier she became.

Lae knocked on the door as loudly as she dared. She wanted to appear as bold as she felt. When the servant opened the door, Lae brushed past him without waiting to be acknowledged by her father. Not only was she rude, but Lae knew she was contemptuous. She did not care.

King Aelfred sat on a bench near the firepit, one boot in his hand. Red sat in a chair nearby. Both men were in an animated discussion about the Vikings. Lae watched her father throw the boot to the floor.

"I would crush them to death with my bare feet to rid us of this pestilence," King Aelfred said.

Red chuckled. "I think a sword would suit the task better."

King Aelfred turned to Lae. "What brings my lovely daughter to my chambers?"

"Please do not stand, Father. The sight of King Aelfred in one bootless foot trying to follow protocol would be too difficult for me to fathom," Lae said. "You, too, husband. Forego ceremony in the privacy of the chambers."

King Aelfred patted the bench. "Sit here, Daughter, and tell me the news. What brings you here?"

Lae did as her father bade, folding back the sleeves of her tunic. "I have come about a domestic problem, nothing more, but one that was caused by you." Lae waved the servant out of the room. There was no need for the entire fortress to know her business. She had enough trouble keeping the gossips at bay. "Have you talked with Edward?"

"Not since this morning." King Aelfred tugged at his other boot. "Where is that servant of mine?" He looked around the room.

"I have sent him away, Father. He is the worst gossip in both countries."

"If the servants cannot hear, then it is a serious matter." King Aelfred took Lae's hands in his. "Tell me."

"Edward has informed me that his wife will arrive here tomorrow. What am I to do with Egwinna?"

Red cleared his throat. "Egwinna?"

"The new nurse who takes care of Wyn and is the mother of Stan." Could men remember nothing? Lae pulled her hands from her father's grasp.

"This fortress is large. She can sleep with the children and Elflaed can share the apartment with Edward," Red said.

"I see no problem." King Aelfred pulled off his second boot and dropped it to the floor. The thud punctuated the end of the issue for him.

"It is not a matter of space! It is a matter of having Edward's wife, his mistress, and his legitimate and illegitimate children all mixed in together. It is indecent. The priest will excommunicate us." Lae glared at her father. "All of us."

Red laughed. "Is that what this fuss is about? I doubt the priest would dare excommunicate two kings, a queen, and a prince."

"Do you not see how difficult it will be for the women to exist in this situation? Am I to keep Egwinna hidden away in the tower room?"

"With my granddaughter who screams? A terrible punishment for the innocent," King Aelfred said. "You worry too much about the priest. Let him demand donations to the Church for our transgressions."

"I can see that you are no help. How can two kings operate two countries, but cannot help me?"

"We trust in your ability to solve the problem," Red said.

"Please do not flatter me, Red. I have a dilemma. I do not know whom to fear most, the women or the priest."

"I would rather displease the priest," King Aelfred said.

"Exactly," Red said.

"I will send Egwinna and the children to Wessex. Mother will find the children a comfort." Lae frowned. "I do not know what she will think of Egwinna, but Father, I will be certain to tell her that was a problem of your making."

"I do not think the children should go." King Aelfred tugged on his mustache.

"Why not?" Lae asked.

"If we are to see to the future, then Stan should know his sisters. Strong alliances are made in childhood. We will need strength in years to come."

"What will I do with Wyn?"

"Keep her here. She needs to get to know her cousins as well." King Aelfred clapped his hands together. "Now, is there food being readied? I am hungry. Making decisions has always made me as hungry as a bear."

"Keep Wyn here? I will have to force one of the servants to care for her. Mayhap I will get someone young, but strong." Lae sprang to her feet. "I will send a messenger to Mother immediately. I think I will ask her to teach Egwinna some of the finer points of embroidery. Egwinna has the talent. Sometimes I do chatter on, do I not?" Lae patted Red on the shoulder as she left the room.

Lae kissed her signature on the vellum and folded it carefully. She smiled at the childish gesture, the kiss, but her mother had taught her to do that whenever writing to a loved one. Lae remembered that as a child she had watched her mother holding messages from her father next to her heart. She understood the fear that a wife had for a warrior husband now that she had one of her own.

Lae dripped candle wax on the edge and twisted her signet ring deep into the accumulation. She would send the message right away. Egwinna would follow it by just a few hours, but that would not matter. Lae pursed her lips. She had no soldiers to spare, but Egwinna would need at least six guards and two female servants. It would never do for any of her household to risk a bad reputation by traveling alone with only men. Lae laughed at the incongruity of her thoughts. She was sending her brother's mistress to her delicate and religious mother.

Explaining that it was her father's idea would put her mother in a good frame of mind. Her mother believed that King Aelfred could do no wrong. It was wonderful to see how much her parents loved each other, even though it had been a political marriage. Her mother said that love can be learned, but it was better when, unbidden, it wrapped itself around the heart.

It was cool in the great room, but Lae was too busy to do anything about it. She had pulled her chair as close to the firepit as was possible without setting her tunic ablaze. The messenger, a youngster of fourteen or fifteen summers, stood before her. He had nodded at each of Lae's instructions.

"You have been to King Aelfred's fortress before. You are to take a message to Queen Eahlswith. It is for her eyes only."

The messenger bowed, his brown curls falling in front of his face, and he left as quickly as he had come. The youngster was ambitious, and Lae admired him for it. He would make a good soldier when he was a few years older. He had the reputation of riding like the wind, clinging to a horse like a burr to wool.

Lae's favorite lieutenant had entered the great hall just as the boy left. "My lady, you sent for me. I await your command."

"I need an escort of a half-dozen men for Egwinna and some of the servants who will accompany her. They travel to King Aelfred's fortress in Wessex. How think you the roads? Are they dangerous?"

"If we travel inland, we should meet no Vikings except a patrol or two. Might I suggest that we take a dozen men for greater safety?"

"Good. With King Aelfred's army here, there should be no problem. Make preparations to leave at dawn. Do this in haste."

"My lady?"

"Yes."

"What of the child? Does he accompany his mother?"

"No, Prince Aethelstan stays here."

"Forgive my impertinence, my lady, but how are we to treat the mother of Prince Edward's son? Is she to be considered royalty or is she of the servant class?"

"Alas, I cannot answer. We make new roads through the forest of manners." Lae twisted her ring around her finger. How, indeed, should Egwinna be treated? Her father should answer this question, but he would not. Lae looked at her officer. "Treat her better than a servant, but not as royalty. However, Aethelstan carries the royal name and is to be treated as such if ever he should go with you on a journey."

"I understand, my lady. By your leave, I go to prepare. Until tomorrow."

"Thank you. May God be with you." Lae watched the lieutenant leave, then rested against the back of the chair. Why did life have to be so complicated? Was it not enough that she had to ward off the Vikings without having to invent new protocol?

The sound of movement behind Lae made her start. She reached for the knife she had hidden in her sleeve as she leaped from the chair and turned to face her attacker.

"My lady, no! Do you not recognize your child's nurse? It is Egwinna, my lady."

It took a moment for Lae to realize that her instincts had served her badly. She sheathed the knife, her pride chafed because Egwinna had caught her in a moment of weakness. "What do you mean by creeping up on me?"

"I am sorry." Egwinna stared at the floor. "It is my misfortune to be where I am not supposed to be and to hear what I was not supposed to hear."

"Do not speak in riddles. It irritates me."

"Yes, my lady."

"Neither should you keep me in suspense. Is there a problem with Wyn?"

"No, my lady. I have taken her to the kitchen for a good meal. She is eating like a beggar's child, fistful after fistful."

Lae wrinkled her nose. "I suppose table manners can be taught later. Why are you here?"

Egwinna raised her chin and looked directly at Lae. "I was on the way back to the tower room to get a wrap for Wyn. She was cold. I heard my name, so naturally, I stopped. It may be brazen of me, but I want to protect my son."

"From whom? Think you that we would harm him? Do not act like such a sheep." Lae waved her hand. "Go about your duties and do not worry about Stan or yourself."

"I am to travel to Wessex? Without Stan? I have never been separated from my son." Egwinna's chin quivered.

Lae tried to imagine the hurt that Egwinna must feel at having Stan stay behind and put her hand on Egwinna's arm. "I am sorry, Egwinna, but you must become accustomed to our methods. It is for Stan's safety that he stay here where two armies guard him."

"Why must I go? Have I done something wrong?"

Lae felt her face flush. "There is nothing to discuss. You will be ready to leave tomorrow at dawn. When the time is right, you will be returned to Stan."

"How long must I be in exile?"

"You are not exiled." Lae took Egwinna's hands in hers. "You must trust me."

Egwinna nodded. "Yes, my lady."

"Thank you. Go before Wyn misses you." Egwinna curtsied and left the great hall.

chapter

U

GWINNA DROPPED TO THE TOP STEP, letting her hands fall to her lap. The worst had happened. It was possible that she would be sent away never to return. She had never allowed distance to separate her from Stan, but now he was to be taken from her. Already her son had charmed King Aelfred, but she had not charmed anyone.

She closed her eyes and placed her cheek against the cold stone wall to cool the flame that burned there. She had acted without thinking. She had done something to cause her lady to send her away.

Egwinna's heart pounded. She had behaved stupidly, putting herself and Stan in jeopardy. As always her actions were reckless; her mother had often told Egwinna that she caused her own problems.

Egwinna thought about her son. Her mother had told her it was an honor to bear the child of a prince, that it might ensure Egwinna's future. Her future was gone now. There was nothing to do but run away with Stan before Lady Lae sent her away without him.

They would have to go where they would never be found, where they would least be expected to go, and that meant heading away from her village. If they went southwest, they would travel straight into Viking territory.

Egwinna shuddered at the thought of accidentally stumbling into the Vikings. If she went southeast, she would be in safe territory. She would definitely travel to East Anglia. She was wrong to think that she would be safe with royalty. Being so close to them only meant that they could scrutinize her more carefully.

Closing her eyes to calm herself, Egwinna felt her heart pound. She would sit quietly and plan her actions carefully. The escape must be perfect. What would she tell the guards? Could she convince the head groom to give her a horse? No, certainly not. Once Egwinna had ridden a horse, but had been terrified. She would not be able to ride these spirited animals. It would be less conspicuous to walk away from the fortress. A tear trickled down her cheek. Just when she thought she had a better life, she had ruined it. Egwinna did not know how long it had been quiet, but the sound was eerie. She jumped up. She had preparations to make.

Egwinna pushed open the tower room door. Wyn was asleep on the floor, her black hair matted from having rolled on the rushes that kept the room smelling sweet and fresh. Her swollen eyes were closed and one chubby hand was closed around the piece of wool she always carried with her. Egwinna felt sorry for the little girl. However, the child was no doubt the cause of her new problems. She looked at Wyn — kirtle soiled, face streaked — then gently lifted her from the floor and placed her on the massive bed that Egwinna shared with both children. She covered the girl with a soft wool blanket lined with fur.

Egwinna tiptoed to the firepit and placed another log on the grate. She squatted down and blew on the coals until the log caught fire. The crackling and warmth reminded her of the choice she had made, and she shivered with trepidation. She would be worse off than she had been any other time in her life. Egwinna bit her lower lip to keep from crying. She would do whatever was necessary to keep her son with her.

Egwinna went straight to the chest that held the things she had brought here a few short days ago. Other than food and a blanket, she would take no more than what she had brought with her. Tears ran down her cheeks. She was not a thief, but she was about to become the kidnapper of her own son. Egwinna took woolen tunics from the chest and, turning, stared at the frost-covered window. They would have to dress warmly. Fortunately, there were some advantages to being a shepherd's daughter. They had good wool clothing and sheepskin boots.

The moon was hidden behind thick dark clouds, and Egwinna had trouble finding her way down the path to the gate. Stan never questioned her, for which she was glad. He held the corner of her cloak in his gloved hand as they slipped past the elderly, dozing guard. It amazed Egwinna that the Vikings had not already attacked the fortress and carried them all off.

She shifted the bundle of clothing and food from one hip to the other and, holding onto the palisade wall, slipped beyond the fortress walls. Egwinna wished the moon that darted behind clouds at all the wrong moments had been full instead of half.

The howling of wolves, not so far away, reminded Egwinna of the times she had had to sleep at the edge of the pasture with a fire burning to keep the wolves away from newborn lambs. A wolf howled again. Egwinna shivered. She hated wolves.

There were so many bridges. Egwinna's heart was thumping. She wished she had had more time to find out about the bridges. Lundenburh was large and confusing to a girl from a small village. Egwinna squared her shoulders, gripped Stan's hand tightly, and continued walking, keeping to the shadows made by the timbered shops. Her footsteps sounded loud to her, and once when Stan sneezed, Egwinna was certain the guards would swoop down on them. She was so fearful that when she came to a cluster of thatched homes pushed against the dirt road, she decided to skirt that part of Lundenburh. When she got to the other side of the huts, she was not certain which bridge to take. They both looked familiar. The bridge to her left looked closer and more familiar.

The walk to that bridge took too long. Every minute that they were still inside the old stone walls meant their newly found freedom could be whisked away with a word from the queen. Egwinna stumbled on a clod of frozen dirt, and she reached out to steady herself. Her fingers brushed against the ragstone of the antiquated wall, and Egwinna remembered stories of an ancient warrior race that had come from far away. The wall surrounded Lundenburh and was still kept in good repair to keep out the enemy.

Peering through the opening in the wall, Egwinna could see the bridge. It looked like the one she had crossed a few days ago when she had come from her village, but she could not be sure. She waited for the moon to slide out from its hiding place. She did not know when her little finger had gone into her mouth, but the nail was bitten off before she caught herself. Egwinna jerked the finger down. She had always hated that nervous habit.

At last the fickle moon showed herself, and Egwinna looked at the bridge again. It had to be the right one. God would not punish her by sending her into Viking territory. Egwinna and Stan kept to the side of the bridge so that their shadows would blend in with the bridge railings. It would not do to be discovered now, for then she would certainly be guarded for the rest of her life if not killed outright. This was her one chance, and she would have to make it work.

It seemed that every shadow was a guard and every footstep they took was like a bell tolling their escape. Once across the bridge, Egwinna's fear of discovery was replaced by her fear of the unknown. In spite of the cold, she felt perspiration trickle down her spine. Egwinna pushed back the hood of her cape and let her hair fall loose. She hated the feeling of being closed in when she was nervous. She needed to see around her.

"Mother, is there a place to sleep?"

"Are you tired, Stan?"

"I am very tired, Mother. I am also hungry. Why did we have to leave? I liked my father and my grandfather."

Stan's pace had slowed until he was barely moving. In the darkness, Egwinna could hardly see the outline of the low rolling hills that surrounded them. "We will look for a place to sleep, Son. It would not be long."

A breeze lifted strands of hair away from Egwinna's face; a familiar odor caused her to turn into the wind. She looked toward the sky and inhaled deeply. "We are indeed fortunate, Stan. I smell sheep, and where there are sheep, there is either a shelter or a warm haystack. Let us walk to the top of the hill."

Egwinna pulled at the hand of her son, but he stood as if made of iron. "Come, Stan. You are a strong boy and can walk up this one small hill."

"I cannot."

"You will do it. We are not safe here. I promise you that there is a place to stay." Egwinna bent down and looked into his face. "Stan, you look like the horses who sleep while standing."

Stan giggled, took a few steps, and stopped. "I cannot."

Egwinna bent down and picked him up, balancing him on her hip and letting his legs dangle in front and behind her. She balanced his weight with the bundle of food on her other hip. He was heavy, and Egwinna thought that she would never get to the top of the hill. The trip up was worth the struggle, for at the bottom of the hill was a small shed. The sheep were grazing beyond the shed.

The shepherd was nowhere around. Mayhap he was asleep in the haystack at the edge of the field. She knew the sheep had a shepherd, for wolves were the bane of every sheep farmer in all parts of the island. Ewes were not very intelligent and did nothing to protect their lambs except to bleat pitifully.

Egwinna walked down the hill keeping the shed between her and the haystacks in case the shepherd was curled up in the hay. The barking of a sheep dog caused her to freeze just as she got to the shelter, and Egwinna prayed that he would not come after her. The dog would not recognize her scent, and he would continue barking until his master came to see what caused the commotion. Mayhap the shepherd was across the field where the dog was.

Her arms felt as if they were going to break, but she stood quietly, hardly daring to breathe. At last, the dog was still, emitting a low bark, then one last woof before deciding the danger was past. Egwinna moved around to the side of the building and, locating the door, opened it slowly. She stepped inside and waited for her eyes to adjust to the semidarkness.

The moon slid from behind the clouds and shone through the cracks in the wooden shed, throwing a pattern against the hay. Egwinna could smell old, but clean hay. No sheep had been in here yet, but the shepherd had wisely planned for early lambs. Egwinna dropped her bundle on the hay and laid Stan next to it. She took off her cloak and after covering Stan with hay, lay next to him, squirming into the hay to get comfortable. She covered them both with her cloak. She spent a few minutes listening to the sounds of the night: the wind in the trees, the familiar bleating of sheep, and the shallow breathing of her son, which soon lulled her to sleep.

The next morning, a faded sun peeked through the walls, awakening Egwinna. It took her a moment to realize where she was and why. She looked at Stan and found him staring at her with solemn eyes.

"I am hungry, Mother."

"No doubt. I have some good cheese and bread for you as well as a slice of meat. Unfortunately, I have only a small flagon of water. We cannot go outside the shed until dark."

"Why not?"

Egwinna sat up, pulling pieces of hay from her hair. "I do not want anyone to find us. We are playing a game. Remember? I told you about our game." She untied the bundle and pulled out food wrapped in individual bundles of linen cloth. Egwinna watched Stan chew a piece of bread with cheese. She had no idea what village they would finally settle in, but she thought she could still smell the salt from the Narrow Sea, which was peculiar. Egwinna had never lived close to the sea, so mayhap it was not unusual to have it blow this far inland in this part of the world. The wind had shifted in the night.

Egwinna chewed on a piece of smoked meat. Even though she found the stringy stuff distasteful, she knew she needed sustenance. Glancing at Stan sitting beside her she felt her love for him flow over her, and she kissed the top of his head. He rewarded her with a smile, his mouth circled with crumbs.

"We are going to have many adventures, Stan. We will be free, and we will not be stuck in that dreary old fortress any longer. We will be as free as the travelers who came to the fortress with their stories."

"I am glad we did not bring Wyn with us. She is too noisy. I do not like her. She hit me. I want a drink."

Egwinna helped hold the flagon for Stan as he drank. "When did she hit you?"

"All the time. She pinched me, too. I told her we were supposed to be cousins and friends, but that is when she kicked me on the leg." Stan pulled up his tunic. "See the bruise she gave me?"

Egwinna was surprised to see the newest purple splotch on Stan's calf. She had no idea that Wyn had hit her son again. "When did she do this?"

"She hit me whenever you were not looking. One time she pinched me when we were supposed to be sleeping. That hurt, too. I told Grandfather."

"What did he say?"

"He said that he would tell Wyn's mother."

"You will not have to put up with her anymore. We will make a new life, a better life for ourselves." Egwinna wished that she had the faith in herself that Stan seemed to have. How could she promise him a better life when she was inching her way into an unknown future? It would have been better had she gone straight south of Lundenburh, avoided her own territory and settled far away from Wessex or Mercia. She had been stupid to come this way. Why had she let her emotions rule her thoughts?

"I have to make water, Mother."

"Do not go outside. Use the corner." Egwinna flopped back down against the hay and listened to the rustle as her son moved. She would have to undo the mistake she made. Tonight they would retrace their steps, skirt around the north side of Lundenburh and head west. She could hide just as effectively in the west as she could in the southeast.

The next thing Egwinna knew, Stan was shaking her awake. "What is it, Son?"

"Mother! Mother! Get up!" Stan whispered. "Riders are coming."

Egwinna threw back her cloak and stumbled to her feet. Stan ran back to the wall of the shed, and stood a few feet from her, peering out a crack. Egwinna joined him, aghast when she saw how close the three horsemen were. "Come over here and hide in the hay!" Egwinna pulled her son down and dragged him to the far part of the shed. She grabbed her cloak and the bundle of food and crawled to the corner. "Put your face to the wall and breathe through the cracks. Otherwise the hay dust will make you cough."

Egwinna moved quickly, covering herself and her son with a much hay as possible. She could hear the sound of the horses' hooves as well as the voices of the men. She could not make out what they were saying, for even though it was in her language, their foreign accent distorted the words. She thought it odd that her lady would send foreign guards to find her. How stupid she had been to think that she could leave and take the future king with her.

Egwinna whispered to Stan, "Can you breathe?"

"Yes."

"Then play the game of silence. No matter what happens to me, play the game of silence. If I am taken, then you must go back to Lundenburh."

"How? I do not know the way."

"In the morning, keep the sun by this hand." Egwinna touched Stan's left hand. "In the afternoon, keep the sun by this hand. Now we must be still." Egwinna's throat constricted with fear. She would not have been able to scream even if the guards found her and ran her through with a broad sword.

The men were outside the shed. Their voices were loud enough that Egwinna could tell one man from the other two. He seemed to be higher born and in command. She heard the squeak of the saddles as they dismounted. They were laughing at one man and telling him he was too fat to get back on his horse without help. Egwinna hoped they would go away without coming into the shed. She heard wood rub against wood as the door opened. She could barely breathe, not that she wanted to. She felt Stan's hand grip hers, and she squeezed it.

"There is no one here." The voice boomed out. "This shed is empty. The shepherd's son is a half-wit. He must have imagined a woman sleeping here."

"His dog is not a half-wit. He was sniffing around here earlier. That is how the shepherd knew someone was in here."

Egwinna stopped breathing. It seemed as if the men were next to her. As small as the shed was, that was not far from the truth. "Then she has gone. The sun is high, for it is nearly midday. She was probably a traveler," the first man said.

"We have already had one spy in our midst," the second man said. "None other than the Lady of the Mercians. I expect other spies to invade our country as they prepare for war against us. We must be especially careful."

"Let us go. I have better things to do," the first man said.

"Let us investigate the hay. It strikes me as interesting that there is fresh hay on top of the old hay."

Egwinna's heart had stopped. No wonder the men sounded foreign. They were Vikings! My God, she wished for Lae's own guards now. Any punishment doled out to her would be better than to be caught by Vikings. Poor Stan. She had had no right to put him in this danger.

Egwinna hesitated only a second before sitting up. She dared not look to see if she had uncovered Stan. "Do you have no manners? Cannot a person sleep after traveling a long way?"

Egwinna stretched her arms over her head and yawned. She was surprised that in her state of mind she could create a pretense with a yawn. "Why do you not go away and let me sleep? I have come a long way, and I am lost, but I do not want to worry about that until later."

A man stepped toward her, smiling, his left hand resting on his sword. He stood before her, feet slightly apart, obviously not fearing a mere woman. Egwinna pulled her tunic straight, shifting her hips to loosen the material.

"I wish you would take your men and leave so that I could have some privacy. I do not suppose I will ever get back to sleep now. I am quite awake." Egwinna pretended to be interested in arranging her hair while she surveyed the men. The man in front was the leader. His status was revealed by his fine clothing and a peculiar silver ring on his finger in the shape of a wolf's head. The workmanship looked fine, but Egwinna was not certain as she had only one piece of jewelry. Egwinna noted his dark eyes that belied his reddish blonde hair. The other two men were dressed in coarser garb and were probably his servants. "Do I have the pleasure of knowing your name?"

"I am Eiric, son of the chief of Beamfleot. Who might you be?"

"I am a mere traveler." Egwinna had not thought of a name for her new life. She was quick and chose her mother's. "I am called Cymbre."

"Are you Welsh? Your name is Welsh."

Egwinna was startled by this idea. She thought quickly. The Welsh tolerated the Vikings. She smiled at the man who conversed so easily with her. "You are clever to know about my name. Do you speak Welsh?" Egwinna congratulated herself on not answering the question with a lie.

"I am to believe that you are wandering around my country, and you are not at all worried that you are lost? Mayhap you have been sent by the lady who rules the Mercians?"

"Lady Lae? I hardly think so." Egwinna almost bit her tongue, but it was too late to hold back the nickname that flowed so easily from her lips. Egwinna waved her hand to dismiss the intruders.

She tried to control the quiver in her voice that threatened to give away her nervousness. "If you would leave, I could do the things necessary. You understand this, do you not?"

Eiric leaned towards Egwinna. "I understand better than you think." In one swift, flowing movement, he drew his sword and thrust it into the hay next to Egwinna. He laughed at her gasp. "A problem?"

Egwinna glanced down the sword from Eiric's hand to where the blade disappeared into the hay. She saw no blood, but wondered at how close the blade had come to Stan. She knew she had to act like the bird that pretended to have a broken wing whenever danger was near her chick.

Egwinna stood, brushed the hay from her tunic, and stepped around Eiric so that as he turned his head to watch her, his attention was pulled away from the place where Stan was hidden. The other men watched her as well. She put her hands on her hips. "Why do you not take your men and leave me in peace?"

The knuckles on Eiric's hand turned white as he grasped his sword harder. She started to chew on her bottom lip, then released it. She was having a difficult time remaining calm. In fact, she was far from calm. She hoped the red splotches would not show up on her neck and face as they always did when she was nervous. "Cannot you depart so that I can find some water for washing? There are other things I must do."

Eiric pulled his sword from the hay and started to stab it, again. This time Egwinna was positive the sword would go through Stan, and she screamed as she lunged forward, knocking Eiric's arm aside. "Do not!"

"Why not? Is there someone you are hiding?" Eiric cleaned away the layer of hay with his sword, revealing the child.

Egwinna tried to step around Eiric, but he put his hand out so she could not see past him. His attempt at control angered her. Egwinna pushed his hand down, digging her nails into his wrist as she did so. She hoped he would bleed.

"He is my son. Do not . . . do not hurt him."

Eiric blinked. "I had expected to find a lover, not a child."

"Your mind is filthy, which befits a Viking," Egwinna said.

Eiric chuckled. "You are not in a position to criticize me."

"I am not afraid of you." Egwinna prayed that God would forgive her lie. "I ask that you spare my son."

Eiric put his sword back into its sheath. "I do not kill children, although the Anglo-Saxons would have people believe that of us." Eiric looked from Stan to Egwinna and back again. "His hair is the color of sun-bleached wheat. Is he truly your son?"

"He is mine and born of my flesh." Egwinna put her hand on Eiric's arm. "Do not harm him. He is all I have."

"As I said, I do not kill children." Eiric looked back at Stan. "Have him sit up. Why is he so still?"

"I have taught him to be as quiet as the fawn when there is danger. It seemed to be a good idea, since I am a woman and I have little defense." Egwinna could feel her heart pounding. "I have to travel to make a living for the boy and me. I am a poor shepherdess who is lost and in a strange country. I fear I have wondered beyond the Danelaw border." Egwinna stepped in front of Eiric and smiled at her son. "The game of silence is over, Stan. You may sit up."

Eiric chuckled. "That you are lost is possible. That you are a shepherd's daughter is possible. I could have guessed as much. I am curious, however. The hair coloring of the child is identical to the Lady of the Mercians. It is unusual enough to arouse my curiosity. If you are his mother, then who is his father?"

Egwinna felt her face flush. "He is no one of consequence."

Eiric grabbed Egwinna's wrist. "You are in no position to play games with me, and I am in no mood to sort through your lies. I suggest that you tell me the truth."

"I want you to promise not to hurt Stan."

"For the sake of the gods, woman. I do not kill children!"

"You may want to harm this boy or at least keep me from returning to my home with him." Egwinna sobbed. "He is my life. It is for him that I find myself far away from home."

"What mean you by that? Why have you chosen to wander the countryside?"

"I do not have to tell you." Eiric's laughter startled Egwinna. She stepped away from him.

"I admire your mettle even though it is couched in ignorance." Eiric nodded toward Stan. "Does he not speak? Has he no tongue or mind?"

"He speaks!" Egwinna felt anger surge through her. How dare this lowlife think her son, her perfect son, was dumb. She no longer felt like crying. She pushed Eiric aside and spoke to her son. "Tell this barbarian your name. No! Tell this . . . this Viking what you think of him."

Stan stared at the Viking. "I like his sword. I saw his horse through the crack. It is big and very beautiful."

This time the laughter from Eiric made Egwinna wince. She should have known better than to depend on Stan to speak of hatred when he could speak of horses instead. "Do not think that my son is ignorant. He is older than his years."

"Why do you flee your country with this boy?" Eiric hooked his thumbs in his sword belt and looked from Stan to Egwinna. "Who are you? Who is this child with the unusual hair color? Are you spies for the Royal House of Mercia?"

Eiric grabbed the fingers of Egwinna's right hand and bent them back. "I could break every finger."

Egwinna gritted her teeth against the pain. She would not tell this barbarian anything even if he broke all her fingers.

"So you choose not to talk. I can take your son. He is a fine boy and could be reared as a Dane. He could be taught to fight the Anglo-Saxons. I would be willing to teach him myself." Eiric stared at Egwinna. "I would suggest you start talking. No more stories. I demand the truth from you."

Egwinna glanced at her son. If the pain had not been so intense, she would have smiled at Stan. He looked so angelic sitting in the hay. Eiric applied more pressure to her fingers. The pain made her angry. How dare he assume that she would tell him anything? How dare he assume that a little pain would make her afraid? The pain of childbirth was more than anything he could do to her.

He leaned closer to her, pulling her to him. The only time she had been this close to a man was when she had been with Edward. She did not want another man to touch her. She had loved Edward, and he had given her Stan. Egwinna spat in Eiric's face. "That is the only answer you will get from me."

Egwinna watched the spittle slide down Eiric's cheek. His expression never changed, but his eyes narrowed.

With his eyes never leaving her face, Eiric spoke. "Yvor, Hroald. Take the boy outside."

Egwinna glared at Eiric. "He will not go. He will obey only me."

"We will see." Eiric pushed Egwinna away and drew his sword. He put the point under Stan's chin and pushed against the skin until it looked ready to burst. "You are to go with my men."

Egwinna held her breath as she watched Stan. He glanced at the sword once, then searched her face for help. He sat motionless, and she wondered if he were brave or too young to understand the danger they were in. She swallowed hard, partly to erase the fear she felt for her son and partly to push away the feeling that the sword point should be at her throat. Egwinna closed her eyes, then opened them. The tableau still played before her. She could not let her son be injured. "Put your sword away," Egwinna whispered. "I will do whatever you ask."

Eiric lowered the weapon. "Tell him to go with Yvor and Hroald."

"Yes." Egwinna smiled at her son. "Stan, would you like to see the horses? The pretty one is right outside."

"If you will be all right." Stan jumped from his bed of hay when Egwinna nodded. "May I?"

"Of course. Go with these men, and they will show you the horses. Be a good boy, and do what they tell you. Mayhap they will let you sit on one." Egwinna looked at the man that Eiric called Yvor. She tried not to stare at his bulbous nose that looked all the bigger because of the flatness of his face. His nose was like a pile of dough smacked down in the middle of a bread board. He was the ugliest man she had ever seen, but then, he was a Viking and probably none of them were handsome except Eiric.

Immediately, Egwinna chastised herself for thinking of Eiric as handsome. He was the enemy of Prince Edward, King Aelfred, her lord and lady, and her son. She must hate him.

She watched her son leave with the two men. Aware of Eiric's hand still around her wrist, she tried to pull away, but he held her tighter. The sound of his breathing nearly blocked the sound of Stan's happy laughter as it floated in from outside. She heard Eiric's sword slide into its scabbard. She held her breath until the click of the hilt against the leather told her the weapon had been put away.

Eiric touched her hair, and she felt like the half-wild kitten that had lived in the sheep shed on her father's place. The kitten had come close to her to eat what Egwinna had put down, but it would never let Egwinna touch her. Once when she had tried to touch the soft fur, the kitten had jumped back and swatted her hand with its paw, but it had kept its claws in. Egwinna felt like that kitten now, but she was afraid to strike out at Eiric. He ran his fingers through her curls. Egwinna shivered. "What do you want?"

"Where did you get such beautiful hair? It is the color of copper. Was there a Norseman in your family? Mayhap a grandfather? Your skin is the color of cream. It reminds me of my mother's. You are not Welsh, but a Dane."

Egwinna jerked her head away from Eiric. She ignored the strands of hair that were pulled out and left threaded through Eiric's fingers like a spider's web. "Do not insult me. I am Anglo-Saxon through and through. There are no Vikings lurking in my blood."

"You have the hands of a noble woman." Eiric grasped Egwinna's hands.

Egwinna pulled her hands free and held them up for Eiric to see. "I have the hands of a shepherd's daughter. I have helped with the birthing of lambs, I have learned to spin, to weave, to care for a child. I have scrubbed, cooked, and gone to market. I am nothing more, nothing less."

"You are much more."

Egwinna's pride controlled the words that tumbled out. "Listen to me. I am not Welsh. You forget that I am the enemy. I want all Vikings dead or at the very least sent out of the country that belongs to my people." Egwinna turned away from Eiric. She hated being trapped, and she said a prayer to the Virgin Mary to protect her. Her heart pounded so loudly that she was afraid Eiric would hear it.

She felt her face flush. How could she have been so stupid? How could she have gone against the wishes of her lady? Was she no better than a traitor to her lady and her lord? "I want to go back to my own country. Will you give me safe passage?"

"You could stay here. I would see that your son had whatever he wanted." Eiric put his arms around Egwinna and let his chin rest on top of her head.

"It is not simple. If I stayed with you, my son would give away the secret of his parentage. It would not be long before the color of his hair and his name would become known in Danelaw, Mercia, and Wessex. His grandfather would come for him. I believe this as strongly as I believe in God."

Egwinna allowed herself the pleasure of basking in the warmth of Eiric. She leaned back. Feeling the heat of Eiric's body made shivers run down her spine. "Stan's father would come for him with an army." Egwinna sighed and stepped away. Turning, she faced Eiric. "Ask me who his grandfather is. Ask me who fathered the boy who loves your horse. Then tell me if you have the courage to keep me here."

"You are serious." Eiric's eyes searched her face. "Tell me about your son."

Egwinna walked to the door and peered through a crack between the planks. Stan was hanging off the neck of a fine horse. He was ecstatic. Her life was nothing without her son. He had a destiny that went beyond her desires and needs. From this moment on, his needs had to come first, and his life had to be the most important.

Egwinna stared at Eiric. "I hope you do not kill us for what I am about to reveal to you. I trust that you have some honor since you are the son of a chief." Egwinna looked down at her hands. "My son is Aethelstan. He carries the name of the House of Wessex because his father is Prince Edward, son of King Aelfred." Egwinna was not prepared for the gasp from Eiric, and her head jerked up.

He stared at her, his mouth open. "To think that I almost caused a war because of my lust. Had I touched the wife of Edward. . . ."

"I am not his wife." Egwinna felt the heat rush to her face, and she knew the ugly red splotches covered her neck and her cheeks. She lowered her head because she could not look at Eiric.

"Not his wife? Then the boy is . . ."

Egwinna's head snapped up. "He is not to be called that. Aethelstan is to be King of Wessex."

"A pretty story, but one I find hard to believe. Was that what Edward told you when he bedded you?" Eiric grinned at her.

Egwinna slapped Eiric's face with such force that her hand stung. "I should have known that I could not talk to a Viking. I am not stupid. I had dreams when Prince Edward was with me, but I have no dreams now. I am not a woman who dreams impossible fantasies."

Eiric grabbed both of Egwinna's hands and jerked her toward him. He held her against him. "No woman has ever dared to slap me before or spit on me. You must like to live in danger. You are nothing more than the mother of a bastard. In Danelaw, we call those women prostitutes. You could serve my needs well."

Egwinna jerked her hands free and pulled away from Eiric. She did not want to remain close to him, for she had to admit that she was bewitched by him. She did not want to desire him, and she resolved to use whatever it took to get back to Mercia. Egwinna stared into Eiric's eyes. "I do not need to explain anything to you, but I will. When I saw that Prince Edward was infatuated with me, I did everything I could to make him desire me. I wanted his child. The moment I found that I could attract a prince, I knew no ordinary man would ever suit me. I resolved that I would have no ordinary child. Only a child of royal blood would be good enough for me." Egwinna looked away. "I was young and foolish. I thought I could be more than a shepherd's daughter. My son may be a prince, but I will always be no more than a caretaker of sheep."

"I could make you more."

"How?"

"I could make you my wife. I am to be chief someday. You could be beside me."

"Why would you do that? What reason do you have for wanting me as your wife?"

"I would want you as my wife so no other man could have you. I would want you because it would make Edward extremely angry that his son and his mistress were now mine. I would want you because you are beautiful."

Egwinna tried to keep her voice steady. It was incredible, but this man, this enemy, was offering her a life of wealth. She had no such offer from Edward. Edward's wife was pregnant, and if Edward wanted to do so after King Aelfred died, he could displace Stan with a legitimate son. She decided to bargain. "Vikings do not prize their women."

"You have been listening to the Anglo-Saxon lies. We value our women. I would especially prize you." Eiric reached for a copper-colored curl and held it between his fingers. "This hair shows me that you have Norse blood in your veins. You are one of us. Come live the life that you were meant to. I will give you fine clothing and jewels. You and your son will want for nothing. He will be reared as a fine Danish warrior. He will learn the sea and go on raids."

"Raids?" Egwinna's voice seemed to abandon her. She could picture Stan, strong and blonde, raiding the village where he was born, killing her childhood friends and their children and mayhap even her parents. She was foolish for thinking that she could have a life with Eiric. He was the enemy, not a gentleman.

"He has the makings of a fine warrior. We will have many sons and mayhap a daughter for you. You will not have to run from me as you have the House of Wessex. You are a Dane." Eiric wrapped his arms around Egwinna, pulled her closer, and kissed her.

She could not deny that she enjoyed the kiss. Egwinna kissed him in return with passion, which for so many years she had denied herself, but still she pulled away. "No."

"You want me."

"It is a gamble like playing knuckles and bones or tables." Egwinna pushed Eiric away. "I am not a Viking, and you cannot make me one. You are not thinking clearly, but I am. Having our two countries at war is not worth a few moments of pleasure. I do not think I could be happy with you, knowing that your commands would kill my people."

"We are not at war. I am trying to keep us from war. It would be a disaster for my people to have war. Egwinna, you are not beholden to the father of your child."

"Edward came to my village for Aethelstan so that his oldest son would rule Wessex. I cannot stay with you."

"You have not told me the truth. Why were you running away?"

Egwinna tried to keep the surprise from showing on her face. "What makes you say that?"

Eiric waved his hand toward the bundle that still lay on the hay in the corner. "It is obvious. So now what have you to say? Why did you run away? Your son cannot be king if he is not in Wessex."

"I owe you no explanation."

"You owe yourself one."

Egwinna matched the stare that Eiric gave her for a full minute before her eyelids fluttered and she looked away. "I was wrong to leave. I should have tried to explain why I did not want to be separated from Stan. I should not have jeopardized my son's future by taking him away. I must go back." Egwinna felt hot tears behind her eyelids, but she blinked them back. It would not do for Eiric to think she was weak. "I made a terrible mistake."

"You want me to help you get back to Mercia, I suppose. I will help you as best I can, although I will regret the choice you have made. Mayhap it is best. After the passion waned, we would fight," Eiric said.

"Why do you want to help me?"

"To prevent a war between our countries. You see, we have lived here for many generations. This land is part of me. I want my children to grow up here as I did, as did my father. We have plowed the land for centuries, and the dirt under our fingernails has worked its way into our blood.

"We have as much right as the Anglo-Saxons to this land." Eiric ran his hand through his hair. He turned away from Egwinna. "My father and I are aware of Lady Aethelflaed's hatred of our people."

"With good reason. Your people have raided our villages, raped our women, and killed our men." Egwinna had allowed her temper to throw away caution.

"Not all Danes wage war. Some of us want peace," Eiric said.

Egwinna pushed a few pieces of hay away from the bundle of food and clothing and picked it up. "I am ready." The banging of the door against the walls of the shed startled her and she jumped. Eiric's two companions were in the doorway.

"There are riders coming this way. I believe it is the Anglo-Saxon known as Prince Edward. His horse is the big black. A lady rides with him. They lead the others."

"The Lady of the Mercians," Eiric said. "How many men are with them?"

"More than two dozen men follow him. They stop and look at the ground occasionally. Are we to sound the alarm?" Yvor asked.

"No. I know why Prince Edward and the lady have come. Take the boy. We will be out soon." Eiric turned to Egwinna. "Do you want to meet with Edward? Do you wish to return with him?"

"I would rather meet with my lord than with my lady. I have no choice but to see them. I will do so humbly and ask their forgiveness." Egwinna handed her bundle to Eiric, picked up her cloak, and shook off the hay. She could hear the horses coming closer as she fastened the pin at her neck. "I am ready. It would be best to be outside waiting."

"As you wish." Eiric opened the door of the shed for her and waited while Egwinna passed by him to the outside.

"Thank you."

"I will not forget our short time together, Egwinna. If we were to have met in a different time, a different life, we could have been man and wife."

Egwinna felt her face getting hot, and she knew she was blushing. Eiric's laughter confirmed it. "Do not make light of my trouble. I was a foolish woman, and I will pay for my mistake. It will be more difficult for me if you laugh." Egwinna looked at Eiric's handsome face to preserve it in her memory. "I could not have been happy with the enemy, no matter how handsome the chief's son."

Egwinna stepped away from the shed so that the horsemen could see her. She was watching Edward when his eyes fastened on her. He motioned for his men to stop, turned his horse off the road, and cut across the pasture. As he came closer, Egwinna could see a frown that slashed across his forehead like furrows in a plowed field. She held out her hand for Stan as he came around the corner of the shed. She leaned down and whispered, "When your father gets closer, run to him. Mayhap he will give you a ride."

"I hope so." Stan danced up and down. "My father's horse is big. It is better than the Viking horses, do you not think so?"

"I would not know." Egwinna waited for Edward to stop before her. Lady Lae had stayed back, her face like a stone statue. Egwinna noticed that the two dozen men in the entourage stopped discreetly a few yards back. Almost to a man, they had their hands on their swords, nonchalantly, but their posture told Egwinna they were ready for anything. She released Stan's hand and watched her son run to his father's horse. He stood beside the big animal's left front leg, apparently not afraid of the dancing hooves as the horse, trained for action, pawed the ground and pranced in place.

"Father, may I sit up there with you?"

Watching as Edward reached down with a powerful arm and scooped the boy off the ground, Egwinna felt proud.

Edward swung Stan into the saddle in front of him. "You can see better from here," Edward said. "It is like being on a hill."

Edward shifted in the saddle and looked down at Egwinna. "Have you an explanation for your behavior?"

"I . . ." Egwinna hated when words failed her. It made her feel like a child again, caught doing something naughty. She was surprised to feel a presence behind her, then realized that it was natural for Eiric to be there. It was his country, and he was a leader.

"Good morning. You are Prince Edward of Wessex?" Eiric's voice was strong and clear.

"I am. From your manner, I assume that you are Eiric of Beamfleot, son of Thorsten. May I ask what you are doing with the mother of my son?"

"I was told that a woman and child were sleeping in the shed. Having a curious nature, my men and I came to investigate. I had no idea that I would find such a royal treasure. We have never met before a few minutes ago."

Edward nodded. "From the tracks, I could see that no one had helped Egwinna leave. I have a few questions for her." Edward stared at her. "The first I have is whether or not you want to return to Mercia with me. Do you?"

"Is my son to return with you?"

"He is my heir to the throne of Wessex. I will not leave him in Danelaw." Edward's voice was tinged with anger.

Egwinna took a step toward Edward's horse. "I have no choice but to go with my son."

Edward pointed to the man closest to Egwinna. "Give your bundle to Rand."

Egwinna handed the mounted warrior her pack and returned to Edward. She was surprised when Edward bent down and held out his arm for her. Egwinna pulled up her tunic as Edward jerked her upwards. She swung her leg over the horse's broad back just in time. As she settled herself behind the saddle, she glanced at Eiric. His face was expressionless, and she had no idea what he was thinking.

Egwinna waved tentatively to Eiric. "Thank you for your help."

"It was my duty as a host to one from a neighboring country." Eiric bowed and nodded toward Lae. "Please tell your Lady Lae that Eiric sends his regards and hopes that she is well."

Egwinna saw Eiric's eyes crinkle in merriment at the shocked look on her face. She could not ask how he knew her lady, but if she were ever brave enough, she would ask Lady Lae herself. "I will give her the message."

Edward saluted Eiric. "Again, thank you for the care of our lost family."

As Edward turned the horse toward Mercia, Egwinna heard Stan's laughter. She was glad that he was content. Mayhap a mother's only goal in life was to make certain her child was happy and safe.

The movement of the horse forced her to hold onto Edward's waist. She tried not to hold him too tightly. She did not want to get used to the idea of wanting him again, especially so soon after her encounter with Eiric. The fates had been unkind to her. Even now, they were probably laughing at her punishment. If she had never run away, she would never have known Eiric. It was a wicked punishment indeed.

As they rode up next to Lady Lae, Egwinna tried to read her face for clues to her temperament. Egwinna bowed her head in response to Lady Lae's gaze. "My lady."

"Have you an explanation for your behavior?" Lae's voice was tight and hard.

"No, my lady."

"Allow me to ask the questions." Edward turned his head and spoke to Egwinna over his shoulder. "I am curious as to why you ran away. Were we unkind to you? Did someone threaten you?"

She took a deep breath. "Lady Lae planned to send me to Wessex without my son."

"I do not understand that at all. Why would Lady Lae do that?"

"I do not think Lady Lae wants me to care for Wyn. I have allowed her to cry, and I pulled her through the great hall kicking and screaming."

"Is that all? Everyone has dragged that screaming child through the great hall at one time or another." Edward laughed. "If she were not so strong, she would have died a long time ago. We were alerted to your disappearance because Wyn was crying for you."

Lady Lae cleared her throat. "My daughter was upset because you were gone. She likes you."

"She likes me?"

"You are the only one for whom she has ever asked. You have been perfect for her. I am most anxious to make amends. When we return, we will discuss your future."

"I find this confusing."

"Can you tell me what you want? I will make it so." Lady Lae smiled. "I have an idea that it involves Stan."

"Yes, my lady. I ask that I never be separated from him. You could offer me all the gold in your treasury for Stan, but it would not heal my heart."

"It seems that you women make too much fuss about children."

Egwinna caught Lady Lae's glance and they both rolled their eyes. "My lord, you have not the sense of a goat."

Lady Lae burst out laughing. "Well put, Egwinna. I promise you that you will stay in the fortress. There is a problem we need to discuss. We women will have to agree to a truce in spite of Edward."

Edward coughed. "Well, I will leave the matter to you."

"As usual," Lae said. "I cannot afford to have you run away again. No one else has been able to handle that child of mine. Not even my strong will can control my daughter. You are the best nurse we have ever had."

Edward patted Egwinna's hand. "You are a good mother. It shows in the way you have reared Aethelstan. You have made me proud of my son."

Egwinna's heart nearly burst from joy. "I was proud of Stan on this trip. He was not afraid. My son . . . our son will make a fine king. That is all I wish. All I want is for Aethelstan to follow in King Aelfred's steps, and yours, and be King of Wessex."

"So he shall."

Egwinna leaned against Edward and closed her eyes. In her imagination she could see the crown on her son's head. King Aethelstan of Wessex wore the crown well.

chapter

ví

HE CRACKLING OF THE FIRE and its warmth lulled Lae into a sleep crisscrossed with dreams of past battles and future battles. In her dreams, the enemy was always the same giant of a man swooping down on her swinging a giant sword. Always her sword was miniature and just out of her grasp. She would run toward it, but it danced away from her, first glittering like gold, then shining dark red as if it had been dipped in blood. The huge Viking could run faster than she, and Lae would wake up just as he reached for her, the metallic rustling of his chain-mail ringing in her ears.

Tonight the dream was no different, and Lae awoke with a start, listening to the sounds of the night. The time would come when Lae would have an army strong enough to attack the Vikings and push them off the island. Then there would be no more dreams of a Viking pursuing her. She would not have a miniature sword, but a long one of a goodly size. She would ride through the enemy lines, lopping off heads.

Lae heard the sounds of horses' hooves, dogs barking, and the gates being opened and closed. Red and Edward had returned from another jaunt to the edge of Danelaw, coming back after the normal hour for sleep. She always felt relieved when her menfolk returned. She hated it when they went without her, but she had stayed up late the night before being a good hostess to Edward's wife, and she needed sleep.

Lae stretched her arms above her head and thought about Egwinna. Why the woman had felt a need to run away with Edward's child was still a mystery to Lae, and she intended to find out exactly what caused Egwinna's stupidity. She had been stupid enough to cross the bridge over the Thames to Danelaw. There could be reasons for her actions other than being lost. Was the woman a spy for the Vikings? Lae frowned at the thought. If Egwinna were a spy, she would be sorry she had ever deceived the House of Mercia.

If there were other reasons, she would find out later. She wanted a clear mind when she questioned Egwinna, since she did not know her very well.

Lae stretched and pulled her arms back under the warm covers. She thought she should get up and put another log on the fire, but she rolled over instead. Before her husband climbed into bed, he would stoke the fire. She had never understood how he could stay up so late. She smiled as she remembered that she used to try to stay awake while Red studied military history or read philosophy.

Lae yawned and snuggled under the blankets. At least Wyn was content to have Egwinna returned to her. How the child had grown fond of her nurse so quickly was a mystery. The child did not even appear to have a natural affection for her own parents. At best, the tiny four-year-old observed them with calm gray eyes. Lae wondered what thoughts drifted behind those eyes. She had never been a cuddly baby. Mayhap it was the difficult birth that made the child so strange. They had almost given her up for dead. Lae hoped that if the girl could not love her parents, she would learn to love Egwinna. A twinge of jealousy tore through Lae's heart, but she pushed it away. The child had to have someone. Lae wished it could have been herself. She drifted back to sleep listening to the snapping of the last bits of wood in the fire.

The next morning was cold. The frost on the window was like a colorless fern that spread itself across the panes of glass. Lae shivered, but did not leave the cold alcove that framed the window. She pulled the woolen blanket tighter around her shoulders and, following the shape of the fern-like frost, scratched a clear spot. She looked at the sky that was almost white. Pewter-colored clouds rolled inland. Even the sky was leaden. There would be a snowstorm before long. Lae shivered again, but, not wanting to interrupt her musing to call a servant, she went to the hearth and put a small log on the embers from last night's fire.

Lae pulled the blanket around her and sat back cross-legged on the floor, waiting for the room to warm before she dressed. She looked at the huge stones that ringed the hearth. It was attractive in a way, and she wondered about the men who had built the pit for Red's father. Although there was no discernable pattern, someone — probably the master mason — had made certain the stones fit in an efficient manner. It was rough, but artistic; the spaces between the stones were even and the colors blended from grays to browns and back to grays.

The hearth gave her a feeling of security. The men who had worked on it and the fortress were long dead. They had left something of themselves behind that gave Lae an awareness of the past. She was a continuation of her family from the beginning of time, just as the stones were a part of the builders' legacy.

Loneliness wrapped itself around her. She smiled at her vulnerability when routines were broken. Her father had returned to Wessex, and Edward was to come here with Elflaed and his children. It would be a delicate situation. Men! They cared nothing for decorum.

Lae's husband had not returned to her bed, but he often slept with the other soldiers in the great hall so as not to disturb her when he had to come and go at odd hours, although she had told him many times that she would welcome the disturbance. Lae watched the fire blaze higher, added another log, sat back, and contemplated the meeting with her brother's mistress. Should Lae meet with her in the great hall to emphasize that she was the ruler and Egwinna's life rested in her hands? Was Egwinna taking the Danes information? It was a preposterous thought, and Lae shook her head to rid herself of this idea. However, she would ask.

Egwinna was an intelligent woman who had won the heart of her daughter. Again, Lae wished that Wyn did not prefer a stranger to her own mother. Mayhap it would be better to break fast with Egwinna in the privacy of this apartment. It would be less threatening, and sometimes intimacy gathered more information than threats. If Egwinna were guilty of anything, an intimate meeting would serve a purpose. If she were not, then they could become better acquainted and draw closer to one another.

Lae sprang up and grabbed the tunic and under-kirtle the servant had laid out the night before on the bench close to the firepit. They felt warm to the touch, and she held the tunic against her cheek. She had chosen the plain gray tunic with the silver and rose embroidery, for she had noticed that it made her look more powerful. The rose-colored under-kirtle matched the flowers in the trim so like the wild roses in the summer fields, and she longed for the summer as much for the flowers as for the battles that would come.

Lae glanced back to make certain the fire was contained as she left for the bathing room. She looked forward to the morning bathing routine. The fire had better be warm and so had the water. One servant did nothing but tend to the bathing room and prepare the baths for her family and guests. It was the one ritual of the day in which Lae took time for herself. The rest of the time she felt she had to keep busy. It was impossible for her to sit and do nothing. Even as a child she had always run from one assignment to another. Her father had made her study for three hours a day, and although she loved learning, it had been difficult to sit for those hours with the books of parchment pages in front of her.

Lae pushed aside the tapestry that helped keep the winter drafts away from the bathers and let it drop in place behind her. She loved to relax in the tub and plan her day. She dropped the blanket from her shoulders, removed her night kirtle, and slid down into the water. The strong smell of soap assaulted her nostrils, and Lae sneezed. She took the offending lump of soap and rubbed it up her arms and down her breasts. She missed Red. Lae smiled at the memory of the peaceful times when she and Red had bathed together. She was certain that Wyn had been conceived during one of their baths. Lae took a cloth and rinsed herself, feeling the warmth of the water as it sluiced down her chest. She closed her eyes and let the steam relax her. She would stay here until the water cooled.

Food had been placed on the plank table by the serving maids when Lae returned to her apartment from bathing. She glanced at the table, but it held only the usual fare: slices of bread, slabs of meat, and hot broth. Since it was winter, apples had started to wither, and Lae wrinkled her nose. She hated soft apples. Most of the time she ate little fruit in the winter, except for the rare times when some arrived from the Holy Lands.

Lae stopped before the hearth, leaned over, and fluffed her hair toward the fire to dry it. It was so fine and long that she could not brush it herself. A favorite childhood memory was of her mother brushing her hair, one of the few private times Lae had had with her. Lae missed her mother more than she realized and vowed to ask her father to bring her for a visit. Lae needed her mother, not only because she missed her, but because she was certain that in the spring there would be war. If she died in battle, she wanted to die having had a good visit.

Her reverie was interrupted by the servant, who stood before her awaiting further instructions. Lae straightened and tossed her hair back over her shoulders. "Would you ask Egwinna to come to break fast with me? She should come immediately."

Lae watched the woman nod and back away from her toward the door. The woman was so thin that, as she turned, Lae could see her spine through the worn tunic. Even her hair was thin.

"Wait." Lae studied her face. The woman was pretty unless one looked at her features separately. Her nose was too long, her eyes too far apart, her mouth too thick, but put together, they were in balance. She was from the kitchen, so she should have had plenty to eat. "Why are you so thin?"

The servant looked startled, opened and closed her mouth twice before she spoke. "I am this way because I have been sick. I am well now, praise be to God."

"Have you been eating enough?"

"My lady, during winter, sometimes there is not enough food at home." The woman shrugged. "We are used to that. I will be well enough."

"I shall make arrangements for you to have food sent to your family. There is enough for that, I am certain." The servant curtsied, then shifted from one foot to the other. "You may go if you promise to eat as soon as you return to the kitchen." Lae watched the woman leave and wondered how old she was. Lae closed her eyes, trying to remember the woman's name. It would not come to her. She would find out another time.

Screaming came from down the hall, and Lae sighed. Obviously, Wyn had risen. Already the child had discovered a reason to have a fit. Lae turned back to the fire and pulled her hair forward to finish drying it while she waited.

The knock on the door was loud. Egwinna must have been waiting for a summons, for she arrived quickly. "Please enter."

The door opened, and Egwinna stepped inside, curtsying immediately. "My lady, you called for me. I came as soon as I could."

"I invited you to break fast with me." Lae motioned toward the table. "We must talk. Come, let us sit." Lae sat down. When she looked back, Egwinna still stood by the door. "Is anything wrong?"

"I have never eaten with royalty before." Egwinna's face was flushed.

Laughter erupted from Lae before she could stop it. "You have a child by royalty. I hardly think you should worry about eating with the aunt of your son." Lae saw that her manner had embarrassed Egwinna further, and she was sorry that she had been so thoughtless. "Come and eat. I have a favor to ask of you."

"A favor?" Egwinna walked slowly toward the table. She hesitated, then seated herself across from Lae. "What kind of a favor could a poor shepherdess do for a lady?"

"Wyn cried for you when you were gone." Lae watched Egwinna's face closely. There was a look of wary surprise in her eyes. Lae did not wait for an answer, but let her thoughts flow from her unchecked. "You are the only person for whom Wyn has cried. She has never wanted her own mother or her father. She is the most difficult child I have ever seen. My younger brothers and sisters were never this unreasonable. I do not know why she is that way, and I have given up looking for answers." Lae sighed. "Would that she had a disease that could be cured by powders. Wyn is to rule Mercia after her father and I die. Unless she can be taught to behave in a proper manner, she cannot rule in a proper fashion. Her only hope is you."

"Me?" Egwinna's mouth dropped open. She closed it.

"Yes." Lae carefully picked up a cup of hot broth and sipped it. She stared at Egwinna over the rim of the cup. Egwinna was almost pretty enough to be called beautiful. Her hair was her best feature, for it cascaded down her back in curls, and ringlets framed her face. Clear emerald green eyes, large and round like a cat's, watched Lae.

Egwinna's eyebrows were darker than her hair and her lashes were black. Her limbs were straight and strong. She came from good stock like the horses in the stable. Lae almost smiled at the comparison, but she liked fine horses. It was good to know that little Stan had such a fine mother.

Lae was impressed that her perusal of Egwinna did not seem to intimidate her, and she waited for Egwinna to begin to eat. Egwinna dropped her gaze first and picked up her broth. Lae chastised herself for enjoying the small victory.

Lae put the cup down harder than she ordinarily did. If Egwinna were to be entrusted with Wyn's care and the care of Stan, Lae had to be certain of her loyalty. "Why did you sneak off in the night?"

Egwinna's eyelids fluttered, then she stabbed a piece of meat with her eating knife and put it in her mouth. Egwinna chewed slowly, not taking her eyes off Lae, her gaze steady. She swallowed, then took a drink of broth. "The meat is very tender."

"Thank you." Lae hoped the words were not too clipped as she tried to force back the irritation she felt at Egwinna's obvious attempt to control their meeting. "Have you a good explanation of your departure from here into enemy country? Did you discover some piece of information that you wished to share?"

Egwinna laid her knife down. "I was under the impression that I was not a prisoner here. I believed that I could come and go when I chose. I believed that I could go wherever I wanted." Egwinna shrugged. "There was nothing happening here that would be of any use or interest to the enemy." She toyed with the edge of the trencher made from stale bread used to hold meat. She tore loose a piece of bread and dipped it into the cup of broth, then popped it into her mouth.

"Why did you run to the Vikings? Did you know them from before?"

"No, only by reputation." Egwinna continued to eat.

"If you were not giving the Vikings information, then why did you not go back to your own people? Why take my nephew to the enemy? Was it for ransom?"

Egwinna gestured with her knife, waving it in circles in the air. "I would not ransom my son to them. I was lost. The bridges all look alike to me. I crossed the wrong one." Egwinna shuddered. "I hate the Vikings. There is not enough money in the world to make me want to do harm to Stan. On the contrary, I was protecting my son." Egwinna stabbed the knife into a piece of bread.

"Protecting Stan? From whom?"

"From you, my lady."

"From me?" Lae blinked.

"It was not fear that caused me to leave. I did not want to be exiled to Wessex without Stan." Egwinna's voice broke. "He is my reason for living."

"I should have guessed." Guilt stabbed Lae in the heart, but she brushed it aside as she did the minor cuts she invariably received during training with the sword. She realized that Egwinna was an interesting person, although not as brave as she pretended to be. Lae wanted to reach across the table and take hold of Egwinna's hand to reassure her, but thought better of it. She had to know for certain that Egwinna was telling the truth. "That does not explain where you were going."

"I was going to East Anglia. I knew that if I went to my people, I would be found the next day, so I thought if I ran in the opposite direction, no one would discover me." Egwinna looked down at her trencher.

"You were not running to the Vikings? You are not a spy?"

"I hate the Danes as much as any Anglo-Saxon could. My mother told me that she had been hurt badly by a Viking during a raid on our village. I always asked her to show me the scars, but she had said hers did not show. She told me once that I was her scar, then she cried and told me not to believe it." Egwinna seemed to be talking to herself. "Mother said I was her beautiful scar. She only told me once. She cried only once." Egwinna shook herself. "I hate the Vikings for making my mother cry. I had no reason to spy for the Danes."

"Do not fret any longer. I shall not send you anywhere, for you are needed here. After you left, I . . . Wyn desperately wanted you to return. I have never seen her this way." Lae pulled off a chunk of black bread and chewed it. "Whatever you have done to make Stan so mannerly, I want you to do with Wyn."

"I am not sure I can do anything to help your daughter," Egwinna said. "I do not want Stan around her. She pinches and kicks."

"You may discipline Wyn however you want. Within reason, of course. Can you not find it in your heart to help a willful child become a better child?"

"But Stan might suffer for my decision."

"Is not your son of Anglo-Saxon royalty? Is he not able to overcome adversity by virtue of his birth?" Lae saw the pride in Egwinna as her chin tilted upwards.

Egwinna leaned forward on her elbows. "Why is Wyn so unruly? I have never had such trouble with Stan."

"I was not careful in choosing her first nurse, and she was too hard on the child. Tell me how you were going to support yourself?"

Egwinna's face turned red. "I had not thought that far ahead."

"With such a pretty face and that auburn hair, I am sure you would have found someone to care for you. Do not be so embarrassed. Women do what they have to for survival."

"I could have tried to sell embroidery, but I would not have had the money to do it. When the Vikings found me, I was prepared to offer myself to the handsome one in order to save Stan. The Viking would have taken me with him, but I could not betray Edward. I know that Edward thinks nothing more of me than a part of an entertaining evening, but I feel some loyalty to the father of my son. Edward used me to relieve his lust as all men do with all women. Edward cares not whether I live or die." Egwinna's eyes widened. "It was strange, but the Viking named Eiric told me to bring you his greeting."

Lae felt her face getting hot. It seemed that it was her turn to be embarrassed. She could think of nothing to say to smooth the situation. Her curiosity caused her to blurt, "exactly what did he say?"

"Let me think." Egwinna stared at a place on the wall over Lae's right shoulder. "He said, 'Please tell your Lady Lae that Eiric sends his regards and hopes that she is well.' "

"What an impertinent man! When we go to war, he will no longer be so brazen."

"My lady, I would like to be brazen and ask how he knows you."

Lae glared at Egwinna. How much should she tell this woman? "Why do you ask?"

"Well . . . well . . ." Egwinna licked her lips and began again. "It seems that he knew you, that he had met you personally."

"That part is true. I was riding into Danelaw one day to see what was happening, and he and his two servants caught me. He claims he does not want war. I do not believe him, of course, for his father is chief of Beamfleot. The Vikings have been raiding our country for hundreds of years." Lae felt her jaw tighten as she clenched her teeth. "Their days are numbered. I will push them out of our land with a killing sword." Lae took her knife and stabbed a chunk of meat, impaling it on the trencher. "They will leave or die."

"My lady, may I ask what it is that you want me to do with Wyn?"

"You are to treat her as the child she is and make her into the child that Stan is." Lae pushed the remainder of her meal aside and leaned her elbows on the table. "As you know, Edward's wife is coming here. I will have her sequestered in the far corner of this fortress. Do not worry about her. She is pregnant and given to illness. She keeps to her room most of the time. Actually, she keeps to her room, even when she is not ill." Lae snorted. "The woman is weak and has weak children."

Egwinna started to rise, then sat down. "Shall I find Wyn and Stan to tend to them?"

"Yes. Stan may be with my father. King Aelfred likes to dress him up as a soldier. I am afraid that Wyn may be found by her screams." Egwinna excused herself and left.

Lae reached for a book from the table behind her. She had been studying Caesar's conquest of Britain. Mayhap on the pages of vellum, she would find a clue to the Viking problem.

The image of Eiric flashed before her, and she could not help but think of Eiric as handsome. She reminded herself that he was still the enemy, no matter how comely he was. Lae turned several pages in the book and struggled to concentrate on the words, but Eiric's face kept getting in the way. What curse had been placed on her that she would be plagued by thoughts of the enemy?

She loved her husband. Never had she thought of another man. Did not the Church teach her that thoughts could be considered adulterous? She had dreamed of being the wife of Red from the time she was a young girl. Lae slammed the book shut. Military history had no meaning for her when she was wrestling with religion. Lae did not like the restrictions of religious rules.

Commandments were orders, and she had difficulty following orders save those given by her husband or her father. She would never have thought of disobeying King Aelfred, so why did she have so much trouble with the Bible? Her father and mother were pious, but she was not.

The sound of wood against wood made Lae shiver as she pushed the bench away from the table. When she was in one of these moods, she had to ride. This time, she would ride away from Danelaw. Just because she was fascinated by Eiric did not mean that she would seek him out. She never wanted to see him again, except on the battlefield. A ride was exactly what she needed.

Lae rode out of the gates at a trot, the clattering of Tanton's hooves on the wooden threshold filling her with happiness. She held the reins easily as she turned Tanton north along the river. He tossed his head and snorted, obviously as pleased as she was to have escaped the fortress. Lae laughed at him and as if in response, Tanton shook his head from side to side and snorted louder than before, filling the air in front of them with a veil of white steam. The wind in her face was chilly, but not unbearable. Lae wiped away the wind-caused tears that gathered at the corners of her eyes and tucked her head lower.

The water of the Thames sparkled as it dashed between the banks on its way to the Narrow Sea. The music of the contained water as it rushed past her made Lae's heart pound. She pulled Tanton up short and dismounted. She stood at the edge of the bank and looked at the river. The rushing water from the unexpected two-day thaw swirled and tumbled as it fought to escape from the river banks.

Lae stepped closer to the bank, curling her toes downward against the soft leather soles of her boots in order to keep her balance. If she fell into the river now, her woolen cloak would become heavy with water, and she would be pulled under. Life was too interesting to think about death. Better to think of birth. Soon Christmas would be here. What better way to celebrate life than with the birth of the Christ child? Lae loved the celebration of Jesus's birth. The music sung in the choir at Wintanceaster during Christmas mass swirled through her mind. She could hear the two choirs exchanging verses; her favorite words floated in her thoughts, clear and sweet. "Lamb of God, who takest away the sins of the world, have mercy on us," Lae sang.

Easter had always reminded her that Christ had been dead far longer than he had ever lived — eight hundred and ninety-three years, actually. She had never told her mother, who would surely faint at her daughter's blasphemy, but she could not understand how Christ had allowed himself to be crucified without a fight. She would never let anyone kill her that easily. She tried to feel contrite about her peculiar beliefs in order to apologize to God, but she could not. She would probably end up in hell. Lae shuddered, but she could not change her beliefs. She had tried.

The water rushed beneath her until her mind was cleared of thoughts. It boiled and churned with animal-like life, growled, clambered at the edges of the world and, even though harnessed by the earthen banks, still seemed free. She needed freedom, too, like the hawks in the sky. Freedom was so important to her that she had to go to war.

Lae remembered how she had feared that her marriage would shackle her, but now knew that her husband would never presume to control her through force. Red was much too mature to try to make her into an image of his design. He would not have been successful, anyway. Lae laughed aloud at the thought of anyone being able to change her. Even her father, King Aelfred, had thrown up his hands at her stubbornness. He always called her stubborn, but her mother said she was merely a person of conviction. Lae preferred her mother's explanation.

Turning away from the Thames, Lae led Tanton along the path parallel to the river. If the Vikings attacked by ship, she and her family would be ready for them. If they attacked from the north by land, it would be difficult to keep them out. There would be a bloody battle. Lae looked back at the fortification that sat on a bend in the Thames. There should be forts like that one all along the border between Mercia and Danelaw.

Lae stopped so quickly that Tanton ran into her, nudging her in the back with his nose. He pushed her again, but Lae ignored him. Forts along the Danelaw border! Lae felt her heart turn over as the thought gave her life purpose. It would take years to raise the money for forts and to pay for the battles that were certain to take place, but she could do it. With help from Edward and her father, a series of forts could be built to house armies. The Danes were going to be driven from her father's land, her husband's land, her land. All of England would be free of the Vikings. That was her goal and her dream. It could — it would be done.

The snorting of Tanton brought Lae back to the present, and she rubbed her hand up his nose, then ruffled his forelock. She loved to see the glittering red-gold of his mane. It seemed like sunshine had been captured in his hair. The huge animal pawed the ground.

"All right, you demanding beast. We will be on our way. We both need the exercise." Lae looked around for a rock and spying a boulder, led the horse to it. He was more than sixteen hands high, well-trained for battle, yet gentle enough to ride every day. It was an unusual combination to be found in a horse, and Lae felt fortunate that Red had found Tanton for her. He had given her the horse two years ago at the beginning of summer. Lae's memory of that summer was mostly of the wind tangling her hair as she rode without a cowl across the pastures, down the old Roman roads, and along the rivers. She also remembered that her husband had teased her about being in the sun so much that she was as brown as her horse.

Putting her left foot in the stirrup, Lae swung her other leg over the back of the horse. She adjusted her tunic and under-kirtle, and pulled her cloak tighter. "Ready, Tanton? Fly like the falcon." Lae kicked Tanton and let the horse have his head.

The run was long and exhilarating. To her right, the Thames sparkled like a streak of silver on white. Lae did not know how long she had been riding Tanton full speed when she noticed a figure riding on the other side of the Thames, matching her stride for stride. No horse was better than Tanton. She urged him to run faster and lay along his neck, burying her face in his mane. Incredibly, Tanton increased his speed.

"Holding back on me? You lazy beast. Do not let that other horse get the best of you." She glanced to her right and blinked tears from her eyes. The rider and horse were still even with her; the only thing separating them was the Thames. It had to be a Dane, for here the Thames was the boundary to Danelaw. The rider was good, especially for a Dane, and the horse well-bred.

Lae was curious. Pulling back on the reins slowly so that Tanton's mouth would not be cut from the bit, Lae sat up. Her shadow on the other side of the river slowed as she did.

A good rider, a good horse. Who was her adversary? She had to find out, even if it meant speaking to the enemy.

One of the few bridges across the Thames lay ahead, a narrow footbridge from one country to another, just wide enough for two people to walk side by side. Neither she nor the Danes felt it justified a guard. Lae dismounted, and tied her horse to the railing. Her shadow did the same on his side of the river. Lae stepped onto the bridge and stopped. I must be mad, she thought. It could be an assassin. She tossed her hair away from her face in order to see better and to stall for time. She should turn around and ride home.

The figure walked toward her, but stopped at the half way point. If she did not do the same, she would be angry with herself for her lack of courage. Besides, it would be to her advantage to know the strength of the enemy.

Lae heard her footsteps as she walked toward the man, a high-born Viking from the looks of his clothing. Her heart thumped and her knees felt strange. Stupid. She was being very stupid, yet she had to see who rode so well.

"It is the Lady of the Mercians, is it not? I knew that no one else could ride like the wind with such a lovely silver-gold banner streaming out behind."

Lae stopped as if she had been felled in battle. "You!" She felt trapped by her own curiosity as she recognized Eiric. "What are you doing this far north?"

"What are you doing this far north? Spying on us?" Eiric leaned against the railing and smiled.

"It was obvious that I was riding." Lae looked past Eiric to his horse. "Where did you get such a fine animal?"

Eiric turned and studied the animal. "He is from a long line of well-bred battle horses. He also has a heart for running."

"The better for retreat during time of war, no doubt," Lae said. She moved to the opposite side of the bridge and mimicked Eiric's casual stance.

"Would you care to ride my fine horse?"

"I have one of my own, thank you." Lae twisted a strand of hair around her index finger, pulling it tight until her finger turned dark red as the blood was trapped in the end. When she released the hair, it left marks.

A war between Eiric's people and hers would shed much blood and leave many scars. Lae looked up and felt her face flush as she saw his grin. He seemed to enjoy her discomfort. "You have no manners or you would not stare."

"I stare because you are beautiful. I forget my manners when I am near beautiful women."

"Vikings have no manners. I should not have been surprised to find you staring." Lae crossed her arms. She prayed that he would not notice her apprehension. Again she had let curiosity get her into a difficult situation. She would have to rely on Eiric to let her return home. He had released her once, but would he twice?

Lae swallowed. If Eiric harmed her, her husband and father would kill him. It would almost be worth it, except that she would rather have the honor herself.

Eiric tilted his head and surveyed Lae. "It is proper that a queen be lovely."

Lae turned away from Eiric. "Your flattery does not impress me." She leaned over the railing and stared at her broken reflection in the water as it rushed under the bridge. If she were true to herself, Lae would admit that she was attracted to Eiric. She pushed the thought away.

Lae should ride away from Eiric and pretend she was never here. There was something about Eiric that interested her. Lae frowned. What was she thinking? He was the enemy. She was supposed to want him dead.

She was aware of him next to her, his body heat suffocating her resolve, before she saw his reflection next to hers, broken and dancing in the water below. She stared at the two of them. She could see the reflection of her hair flashing in the water like a fish that had been hooked and was struggling to free itself. Eiric's image was dominated by the reddish-gold crown of hair that marked him as the enemy.

As Lae stared into the river, Eiric moved closer until their reflections merged. Lae felt as if she had been scalded. She stepped away from Eiric. "You are impertinent. You Vikings have never known how to keep your place."

"Spoken like a queen." Eiric turned away from the river and leaned against the rails. "Why do we waste our breath with words?"

"I will no longer make the mistake of wasting breath by talking with you. We shall meet on the field of battle." Lae turned away from Eiric and walked back toward her side of the river. Tanton was impatiently pawing at the snow to get at the juicy river grass, his mane rippling and shiny in the pale sunlight.

"Wait!"

Lae stopped, then chastised herself for obeying the command so easily. She started forward again, not looking back, when Eiric grasped her by the upper arm. She felt a shock of excitement surge through her, and she hated the loss of control over her emotions. She looked down at his hand, the silver wolf's head ring shining in the sun, and she was repulsed by the control he had over her at the moment. Lae jerked her arm away.

"Who do you think you are? How dare you touch me!"

"I apologize. I wanted you to see something. I could not let you go without showing you. It may explain some things." Eiric took her hand and led her toward the center of the bridge.

Lae wished she had not let him guide her. The warmth and strength of his hand astonished her. She had trouble breathing, and she felt an excitement she did not want. "Where are we going?"

"Right here. Let us pretend we are on neutral territory and, for the moment, that we are not enemies." Eiric pulled Lae to the railing, still holding her hand. "See the Thames that divides our countries? It knows not that we are enemies. It feeds both banks equally." Eiric swept his free arm back to take in the land. "Do the hills know to whom they belong? Do they refuse to grow grass or flowers because they are trod upon by Anglo-Saxons or Danes? Does the sun refuse to shine because I am a Dane or you are a Mercian? Why cannot we forget, like the earth does, who tramps across her face?"

Lae tried to pull her hand from Eiric's grasp, but he would not let her go. "You sound like a bard."

"Are you surprised that a Dane can love the land as much as a Mercian?" Eiric took her other hand and held both to his chest. "I was born in this country. I know no other home. If we were to fight, I would fight for this land that is mine. As an infant, I learned to walk across the land. As a child I learned to till the soil, to care for it, and as a man, I have learned to love it for what it has given to me. I beg you not to fight us for land that we have lived on and loved for centuries. Is not the land that belongs to both of us more beautiful in peace than in war?"

Lae tried to sort through the thoughts that bounced inside her head. Was he trying to trick her? Seduce her? Prevent a war because the Danes were not ready? Or was he really in love with the land? She stared into his eyes, hoping to see his soul, only to become more confused by the intensity of his look. "Why should you care if there is a war? You Danes have raided my country countless times. You have killed my people. What is one more battle to you?"

"I have a confession. A few months ago I would have been the first to argue for a battle with King Aelfred and his daughter in order to kill them and take their lands. I wanted to expand our country and finish the job my ancestors began."

Lae was startled to hear the very words she had spoken to her father repeated to her. It was like a knife twisting in her heart to hear a Viking talk of the death of her father. She felt compelled to understand this man. "And now?"

"I have fallen in love with the enemy." Eiric raised her hands to his lips and kissed them.

"What!" Lae jerked her hands away from Eiric. "You play me for the fool." She turned and, gathering her skirts, ran as fast as she could toward Tanton. How ridiculous she was to have let herself get trapped by his honeyed words. She wiped the tops of both hands against her cloak to rid herself of the kiss.

The ride home held no memory for Lae. She spent the next two days pacing her room, praying in the chapel, and tormenting herself for her stupidity. It was on the third day when she was kneeling before the statue of the Virgin Mary that the idea of going home lunged into her thoughts. She looked at the statue, the delicate features of the Virgin revealing nothing to her, and yet Lae wondered if the idea had been put there by the mother of Christ. Lae noticed the tiny smile on the statue. It had always been there, but to Lae it now held a message.

"I will go home. I can talk to Mother and my sister, who has taken the vows." Lae felt immense relief at having a direction in which to go. Not only would she be able to see her family, but it would put distance between Eiric and herself.

She stopped at that thought. Why should she worry about how close she was to Eiric? The man made her miserable. It would have been better had he hit her; then she would have an easier time hating him.

Home. The word gave her feelings of warmth and love. No matter how old she was or how long she had had her own fortress, home would always be where her mother was, where her memories were, and where her dreams had been dreamed.

Lae shook the snow from her cloak as she entered the great hall at her father's favorite fortress in Windlesora. A gust of wind entered with her, scattering ashes from the fire across the stone hearth. The smell of meat cooking sent a shiver of anticipation through her. Her mother was famous for the kitchen she kept.

Lae handed her cloak to the servant who had followed her to the firepit. He was an old man, small and bent, but with clear brown eyes that seemed to read one's mind, for he always anticipated everyone's needs. Lae wondered if he had been in service so long that he knew the people he served better than they knew themselves. She thought that mayhap he would understand her dilemma if she confided in him, but of course, it was improper for her to think such a thing. Lae let out a sigh. She was having difficulty with her thoughts lately.

The heat from the firepit made her cheeks burn in contrast from the biting pellets that had blown against her for the last half-hour of the ride. Lae looked across the flames and smiled at her mother seated on the other side of the circular hearth. Even though the ride took just a day, she had not seen her mother for almost two months, and Lae chided herself for neglecting her mother who had guided her through childhood years. Lae had learned to fight from her father, but her strength had come from her mother.

Her mother rose from the highbacked chair that was close to the firepit and extended her hand. Lae knelt before her queen and kissed her mother's hand.

"Rise, my child. I prefer a daughter to a subject."

Lae stood and was quickly enveloped in her mother's arms. She was slender, but not frail. Her mother always smelled of roses and cloves, and Lae felt comforted by the familiar scents. Her problems seemed to disappear in the safety of the arms that had always been there to hold her when she had been hurt. "I have missed you, Mother."

"I have missed you, too. It is the way of royalty. We rear our children to serve other people. Come, sit." Lae's mother returned to her chair and patted the one next to her. "Sit down, dear. Your father has gone on a hunt. This time of year the larder is low. Edward is to leave Lundenburh and ride to Wintanceaster. You look surprised. He had to ride there to talk with some of the men about gathering the army together for spring. I think you have convinced your husband, your father and Edward that it is time to strike at the Vikings."

Lae wished her mother had not mentioned the Vikings so soon. She found the memory of her last meeting with Eiric too confusing. "Is my sister coming from the abbey? I sent word to her to come. I have not seen her since she took her vows." Lae sat on the embroidered seat, undoubtedly done by her mother.

"She will come. I, too, sent word. I sensed that you were troubled."

"How?"

"Mayhap because of your hurry to come home, the way you worded your letter. I am not certain. Mayhap because I am your mother, or the fact that you left before your sister-in-law's arrival. Your fortress does not have a proper hostess for her visit."

Hanging her head, Lae stared at the floor. "I have been taught better, Mother. I am sorry I am not there to greet Elflaed. Mayhap I will return to Lundenburh before she arrives."

"It matters not. She is difficult to entertain. I have sent for supper to be served in my chambers. Tonight we will talk until the candles sputter and die."

"When will Aethelgifu arrive? I am anxious to see my younger sister."

"Tomorrow afternoon. There was a special mass to attend this evening." Eahlswith took her daughter's hand and squeezed it. "I have missed all my children, but the firstborn always holds a special place in the heart of a mother."

"Mother!" Lae chuckled. "I am not certain my first born will hold a special place in my heart. Wyn is still a terror, but Egwinna has a wonderful way with her. I hope Wyn improves."

"Are there no more children to come?"

Lae felt herself blushing. "Mother, my husband is as virile now as he was when we married. I am afraid the trouble lies with me. Because of the difficulty of Wyn's birth, I am certain there will be no more children."

"Oh." Eahlswith leaned back in her chair. "I was hoping that you wanted to visit to tell me good news."

"Mother, let us retire to your chambers. I feel that the stones have ears."

"A good idea. Whenever there is talk of war, I imagine spies everywhere." Eahlswith adjusted her cowl. "I am foolish, for our servants have been with us for years."

Lae rose and held out her arm for her mother, more as a gesture of respect than for any real need. Lae looked into the face that resembled her own, smiled at her living reflection and saw the smile returned. It would be a good visit.

They could not stop giggling. Lae snuggled under the wool blankets and fur throws of the big bed, sniffing the familiar odors of covers, people, and feathers. "I love this place, Mother."

"You were born in this bed," Eahlswith said.

Lae wriggled deeper into the covers. During storms, whenever her father was gone, Lae and her brothers and sisters were allowed to sleep in the massive bed with the heavy drapes down to keep out the sound of cracking thunder. Lae lay quietly for a minute, catching her breath after the last laughing session. She hated to break the spell, but she had a need to do so. "Mother, may I speak to you of a problem?"

"A problem can be lessened when two people share it."

Lae looked at the flickering shadows on the walls through the cracks in the drapes that hung about the bed. The only light was from the firepit. The candles had been extinguished by the servants an hour ago, and the hour was late. Lae decided to proceed before her mother fell asleep. "A Viking has been pursuing me."

"I see. How serious are your feelings toward him?"

Lae felt shock run through her like an arrow. The words sounded so ghastly coming from her mother. "I have no feelings for him. How can you even think that I might?"

"If you had the customary problem of battling with a Viking that we Anglo-Saxons have, then you would talk to your husband. When women come home to talk with their mothers or their sisters, it usually has to do with love. I will listen to you with an open heart, for you are my daughter and a part of me."

"I have hated the Vikings since that horrible time when we had to run from them. I am fascinated by this man, but I find the thought abhorrent. It goes against all that I have been taught and all that I believe in." Lae intertwined her fingers beneath her head and squirmed to get in a more comfortable position. She had many things to consider. "His name is Eiric. His father is chief of the Vikings in Beamfleot."

"Yes, that would be Thorsten," Eahlswith said.

"Mother, how do you know his name?"

Eahlswith laughed. "Do not think that you have caught me in a compromising position. I have more of an interest in politics than you know. Your father has mentioned his name."

Lae thought back to her childhood. She remembered her mother doing embroidery by the firepit in this room, in the kitchen overseeing the servants, or sitting by her father in the great hall during special state occasions. Never had she seen her mother in the company of a man alone. Could there have been the same need in her mother that she was feeling now? She had to ask. "Did you ever want to love a man other than my father?"

"You did not ride all the way home to discuss me, Lae. Let us concentrate on your problem. Tell me, have you been with this Eiric very often?" Eahlswith's voice betrayed her anxiety.

"Mother, only twice have I seen Eiric. Both times we met briefly. The second time he kissed my hand." Lae felt her face getting hot, and she was glad that darkness hid her embarrassment. "Mostly, he has been in my thoughts like a ghost."

"The problem is not great. Do not worry about these thoughts of Eiric. It is a harmless thing that happens to women who have been married for awhile. You have been married for more than seven years. It is easy to imagine love when a man takes an interest in you. Remember, the only man worthy of your love is the man who has given you a home and a child and who supports you." Eahlswith spoke softly, almost in a whisper.

"I know all that, Mother, but I still find thoughts of Eiric disturbing. How can I rid myself of them? It is as if my heart refuses to listen to my mind."

"I have no answer. He is the enemy. He is not worthy of you, and he is no match for Red, who has been a good husband to you."

"I am strong. I will no longer think about the enemy in soft terms. It is the only way I know to rid myself of unwanted thoughts," Lae said.

"Your sister will arrive after morning mass. Get some sleep. You are an honorable person, and I know you will not shame your family." Eahlswith yawned. "Sleep comes. I can no longer keep it away."

Lae's sister sat across from her on a embroidered chair that contrasted with her plain tunic. Lae could not understand how the lord could be served by an undyed tunic, but Aethelgifu had given up worldly goods, as requested by her order. It was a new idea, and, at the moment, only the nuns did this, not the priests. Mayhap it was just as well that she had become a nun, for Aethelgifu had not inherited the pretty coloring of their mother or even the distinctive looks of their father.

Aethelgifu sat with hands folded as if waiting to begin a prayer. Her round eyes opened wider at the sound of a door slamming from the vicinity of the kitchen, and Lae felt that if her sister had been standing, she would have skittered sideways like a horse about to bolt. Aethelgifu's nostrils flared, as if she hoped to sniff out danger before it struck. Lae looked at her sister's long face framed by a wimple, and it struck her that the quiet, ordered life of a nun suited Aethelgifu perfectly.

Everyone responded to danger in different ways. Lae had decided to hate the Vikings and to fight them, but her younger sister, mayhap too young when they had been forced to run from the enemy, had not been able to forget the fear. Lae had never before understood how her sister could tolerate the rules and the incessant reading and praying.

Lae felt compassion for her sister she had never felt before. She smiled at Aethelgifu. "Dearest sister, it was good of you to come. I fear that it has been for nothing. My visit with Mother, as well as the light of day, has made my problem seem small."

Aethelgifu returned her smile, although it did not appear to have come from the heart. "I have come to talk with you about a problem and give you guidance. I have a duty to my sister, and I will perform it."

"I feel it strange to talk with my younger sister, who is a nun, about a problem of love. Mother has helped me resolve it." Lae reached across the small distance that separated them and clasped Aethelgifu's thin hand.

"If the love involves a man other than your husband, the scriptures forbid it." Aethelgifu withdrew her hand from Lae's. "I must ask that you confess to a priest immediately. You could burn in hell for all eternity."

Lae tried to keep her voice even. "Spare me your platitudes. I have done nothing wrong. I have been intrigued by a man, but nothing more."

"You have not read the scriptures as I have. You were always too busy studying the strategies of war to understand the strategies of life, Lae. God intended women to be faithful. Your thoughts make you as unfaithful as any action."

"That is preposterous. We cannot lock up our thoughts." Lae felt her teeth clamp together. How dare her sister spout advice about love when she had never been in love? How could she talk of sin when no sin had been committed? Aethelgifu had lived in a protected world throughout her youth and now, while still young and still protected, thought she knew life. "You astonish me with your naiveté."

Aethelgifu's narrow chin tilted upwards. "I am not naive. I have studied the scriptures for years. I have been educated by the best priests and holy men. I know the Bible, I know philosophers, I know what I believe."

Her sister's words buzzed around her like flies in a stable. Lae waved her hand to brush them away. "I will not accept guilt for thoughts, Aethelgifu. Loosen your mind and think about what you have read. Life is more than words on a page. Life is about thoughts and feelings and problems. Philosophers cannot tell me what to feel or not feel. Religion cannot dictate punishment for my thoughts. My thoughts be as free as any falcon." Lae stopped when she saw a look of horror on her sister's face. Obviously, Aethelgifu thought Lae was being blasphemous. "What is your concern, Sister?" Lae said.

"I have admired you my entire life, Lae. You were never afraid, whereas I cowered at every strange sound. You are beautiful and I am ugly. Father loved it when you learned military history and strategy, but I hated the thought of war. I had nothing but my faith."

Aethelgifu grasped a small, wooden cross that hung from her girdle. She rubbed it with her thumb as her lips moved in prayer. Lae held back a smile at the realization that her sister probably did not know she was saying a prayer. Aethelgifu was obviously doing this for Lae, who had sinned. Lae waited for the nun to speak.

Abruptly, the cross rubbing ceased. Aethelgifu's cheeks were pink, and she let the cross hang from her girdle in its customary place. "Father praised me for my reading. He wanted me to go to a nunnery. I visited a convent and loved the peacefulness, the feeling of security. Here was a world that nuns controlled."

Lae looked at her sister. Aethelgifu wanted to control her world as much as Lae wanted control over hers. King Aelfred's legacy to them both was a desire to lead; they simply did it in different ways. She had never understood her sister. It was peculiar to hear this stranger telling her things that Lae could not quite fathom. She wanted to learn about her sister's fears, but being afraid was foreign to her. "Are you happy?"

"Yes. I will spend my life in the convent." Aethelgifu looked down at her hands. A tiny smile made her pretty. "I want to be an abbess someday."

"I am sure you will be. I have faith in you."

Aethelgifu looked up. "Do you?"

"Yes. I promise that as soon as I get back to Lundenburh, I will confess to my priest." Lae shuddered at the thought, but she would do it for her sister. She and Aethelgifu would never see the world in the same manner. Lae wanted to please her sister, but did not care if she pleased God. She would worry about God later. She had too much to do on earth.

chapter

VII

HE FULL MOON made the room as bright as day. Eiric sat up and looked across the darkened area toward the firepit in the middle of the forty-foot dwelling. He pushed back a pile of fur blankets and slipped out of bed. He stared at the figure curled up under the cover, brown hair streaming across the fur like a muddy creek, and tried to remember why he had chosen Nissa as a wife. Eiric shrugged. It was a political marriage, and he had nothing to do with the choosing.

What would it be like to have Egwinna's hair unfolding in ripples like sheets of copper across the dark brown of the covers? Or to have the Lady of the Mercians and her silver-gold hair lying in waves down the covers? It would never be possible. They were the products of different circumstances, and the circumstances were not favorable. They were enemies, and Eiric could not forget that. If he could not remember that fact for himself, he had to remember it for his children.

Eiric looked at his three sons sleeping side by side on a long cot against the wall. The hut was quiet except for the sound of sleepy breathing and the snapping of logs in the fire.

Eiric grabbed his cloak and wrapped it around himself. With a last glance at the children, he walked to the center of the hut to sit on the fieldstone hearth.

He watched the embers glowing beneath the remains of several blackened logs. It must be close to dawn, the coldest time of day in the winter, and for the third night in a row, he could not sleep. He wished he had never seen the Lady of the Mercians. She had enchanted him and had taken away his reason for fighting. If that were not enough, he was further bewitched by Egwinna. Two women who happened to be the enemy had taken his heart, and both were claimed by men of royal birth.

Eiric poked at the embers with a metal rod. To make his situation worse, he would meet Lae on the field of battle. That she wanted to kill him was evident, but what would she do if he refused to fight? Eiric stabbed at the embers again. What kind of thoughts were these? He was a Dane. He was born to fight. What would his father do if his own son did not go into battle? If the Vikings did not fight, if they stopped the raids, then mayhap the Anglo-Saxons would agree to a peace treaty.

Eiric dressed quickly and slipped out the side door. The blast of winter air hit him in the face like cold water, but he was not cold. He walked to the next hut and knocked twice on the door before entering. His father's hut was larger, although only his widowed father and a sister who had not yet married resided there. His father's senses were unaffected by his age, and Eiric found him standing in the middle of the hut, his sword in hand.

"Father, it is I, Eiric." He pointed to the sword. "Do you expect the enemy?"

Thorsten laid the sword down. "I was dreaming about a battle. What are you doing here?"

"I have to speak with you." Eiric waited to be acknowledged by the gray-haired man who stood before him. He was amazed at his father's continuing strength. In the firelight, although Thorsten's skin was wrinkled and leathery from the weather, his muscles were still hard. His father continued to teach the younger men intricacies of hand-to-hand combat, and no one had beaten him yet. The old man lived for war.

"What brings you to my hut so early in the morning? Have the Anglo-Saxons come to slaughter us?" Thorsten chuckled.

"They will not come until spring, Father. Come, let us sit by the fire. I want to talk with you." Eiric took a deep breath, and sat beside his father on the hearth stone. He twisted his fingers together, then stopped. He hated the childhood habit. "Father, we have lived here for many generations. This land has become as important to us as it is to the Anglo-Saxons." To Eiric it was as if two men loved the same woman. Eiric pictured Lae standing on the bridge between their two countries.

Thorsten leaned closer to his son, turning his head to catch the words. "We both fight for the land, that is true, but I do not understand your words. Speak clearly for an old man."

Eiric looked away from the older man whose small infirmities saddened him. Putting his elbows on his knees, Eiric stared at the earthen floor and wondered how he could tell his father that he did not want to fight the Anglo-Saxons. The reason, that he loved two of their women, would be difficult to explain. Voiced in his mind, it sounded ridiculous. How did he fall in love so quickly? Buoyed by the faces of the two women before him, Eiric looked at his father. "I believe it is time to make peace with the Anglo-Saxons."

The snapping of the embers in the firepit sounded like the cracking of bones breaking in battle. Thorsten stood and paced back and forth in front of Eiric, his hands clasped behind his back. "If any of my warriors had come to me with this ludicrous suggestion, I would have them put to death. They would be useless to me. They would be cowards. Since you have been a most trusted advisor, I will give you a moment to explain yourself." Thorsten pointed his finger at Eiric. "Before I label my oldest son as a coward only worthy of a coward's death, tell me why we should make peace with the Anglo-Saxons."

Eiric regretted his impulsive suggestion. He had let his fascination for Lae push him into action without thought. The ways of love were as foreign to him as the sea of sand that his father had told him about. In battle, he had hardly time to think, for his actions came naturally. He had been hasty to rush in to stop the wars. Eiric knew he had no valid explanation that would satisfy the man who glowered at him, but he made the attempt. "It is time we settle down as a people. Our numbers grow. We need to farm to raise food. That will insure our survival as a nation more than fighting for more land."

"That is an argument weak from start to finish. Unless you wish to lose your place as the next chief of this tribe and as my son, you will stop these stupid thoughts. It is only that I know you as a warrior riding into battle without fear that makes me give you a chance. I would have a lesser man killed." Thorsten's face looked like the god of thunder; firelight highlighted his cheeks, leaving his eye sockets dark and empty looking.

Eiric returned his father's stare, but he felt uncomfortable doing so. It was not often that he and his father were at cross purposes and Eiric did not like it. "I was thinking of . . ."

"My brother was thinking of women, as usual."

Eiric stared at Olenka who had arisen, unbidden, from her cot at the back of the hut. He did not know how long she had been standing in the shadows, but she always managed to interfere. "You know nothing of what I think."

"I know of the talk that has traveled through Beamfleot like a lightning bolt," Olenka said. "Father, your son has been expanding his horizons. Instead of seducing every female in our country, he has tried to seduce the ladies of Anglo-Saxon royalty."

"Amongst your despicable traits is that of a gossip." Eiric felt anger rising to choke out what little reasoning ability he had salvaged. Eiric had never understood his sister's animosity toward him, but he could not let her turn their father against him at this crucial time. "Do you spend your time listening to the gossip of old crones?" Eiric snapped his fingers. "Of course, you have to spend time with your own kind."

"I heard about your attempts at lovemaking from those two idiots who ride with you. They stick to you like burrs to a sheep. They know everything." Olenka stepped into the light, pulling a woolen blanket about her. She lifted her foot and wiped the bottom against her shin that was covered by the finely woven cotton of her night kirtle. "Father, Eiric wants to fight his battles in the bed chamber rather than on the field of battle."

Eiric jumped up and grabbed Olenka's shoulder. Before he realized what he had done, he shook her until the blanket fell to the floor. "You are a demon in a woman's form. What possesses you to be so hateful?"

"Unhand your sister. It is unfitting for a warrior to argue about women with a woman," Thorsten said. "I have doubts that my son is a warrior. It seems you have been bewitched by the Anglo-Saxon witches."

Eiric pushed his sister away and turned to face his father. "I have had no more than brief conversations with them. I was trying to find out if they were spying on us."

Olenka laughed. "It is obvious to any fool that a pretty face is more important to you than your own people. Of course they were spying on us. The Lady of the Mercians wants every Dane dead, and she will stop at nothing. You were stupid enough to play into her hands."

Rage surged through Eiric's body like a flash of fire. He pulled his arm back as far as he could strike Olenka. Before he could assault her, a large hand gripped his arm and jerked him away from her. His first instinct was to fight, but he knew better than to challenge his father. It was one thing to hit a woman, but no one would dare hit a father. "Olenka is a bitch. She has been a bitch all her life. No wonder she is not married. No man would want her."

"Enough! I know she is a difficult woman, but she is, unfortunately, your sister." Thorsten kept a grip on his son's arm. "Olenka, what is the meaning of this gossip?"

Olenka's facial expression was a combination of a smile and a smirk. Her heavy eyebrows, never even, converged to the middle of her face, making her look like one of the dark gods. "My dearest brother is a traitor. He should be treated as a traitor."

"You behave like Odin, trying to cause a blood feud in the family." Eiric felt his nails dig into his palms. He wanted to shrug off his father's hand, but years of subjecting himself to his commander's wishes would not allow him to do so. "Olenka, I cannot believe that you would listen to such manure. It is unseemly for a daughter of the chief." Eiric grinned at the sullen look his sister gave him.

"Enough of this." Thorsten's thunderous voice matched his temper. He stared at Olenka. "I will not have fighting within the family, for any reason. I forbid it." Thorsten turned to Eiric. "We will fight the Anglo-Saxons in the spring. Will drawing a sword and running it through the enemy be difficult for you?"

"Of course not," Eiric said. He drove away the thought of having to meet Lae on the battlefield at Fearnhammor. He had no choice but to fight. Not only was his honor important, but so was the honor of his family. Eiric glanced at his sister and his father. "Olenka does much damage to our family with her barbed tongue. Do you think she can silence it?"

Thorsten glared at his daughter. "It shall be so."

Olenka, still frowning, nodded. She picked up her blanket and went to the far end of the hut, disappearing into the darkness.

Eiric wished she would disappear permanently. He turned to his father. "I trust that the Apuldre Danes will join us against the Anglo-Saxons and the Mercians?"

"They have agreed down to the last warrior." Thorsten threw his arm around Eiric's shoulder. "It will be a great battle. We will gain much needed land. You said that we need more land. What better way to get it for our people?"

Eiric nodded. "Yes, father." He wanted to leave the hut. It had become oppressive to him. "The sun comes up. I must return home. The boys will be up early, for I promised that I would take them fishing."

Thorsten laughed. "That is good." He patted Eiric on the shoulder.

Eiric closed the door behind him and took a deep breath, letting the sharp winter air bite into his lungs. He let his breath out slowly, knowing that frost would form on his cloak. It was one of the mysteries of nature that intrigued him. How could life's hot breath turn so cold so quickly?

He walked across the snow-encrusted yard toward his own hut just as the sun rose, casting its bright pink rays over all that it touched. Instead of seeing it as an omen of a good day to come, Eiric saw it as the blood of a battle. He put away thoughts of war and death and replaced them with fishing and life.

Eiric laughed at his three boys skipping in front of him. They turned and yelled at him to hurry up every six steps or so. Part of the joy of fishing for them was that he carried their poles. He had learned a long time ago that the unlimited capacity for his sons to leap about caused the lines to tangle.

Eiric started to call the boys back so they would not get to the bay before him. They were excellent swimmers, but the water was edged with December ice. Eiric saw three heads bent over something in the path, and he relaxed as he watched Rorik. The child was obviously telling his brothers something important. Eiric smiled at his middle child, brought screaming and kicking into the world too soon after conception. The sun highlighted the red in Rorik's otherwise brown hair. Rorik gestured and his two brothers listened intently, captured as usual by the liveliness of Rorik's words.

Eiric watched Rorik take off at a fast pace, the other two jostling each other to be as close as possible to him on the narrow path. Hoskuld's short, stocky legs had to move twice as fast to keep up with his two older brothers. The constant running after his companions only seemed to make his body stronger and his lungs to have limitless capacity. Eiric would have laughed at the little boy with his bobbing yellow curls, but the child had such an earnest face.

The oldest boy, unfortunately, had his mother's coloring. His hair was the same dull, dirt color, and Kerby tended to have his mother's temperament which was also colorless. The boy never showed emotion even when Eiric took them fishing. Mayhap if he had been a better husband to Kerby's mother, the child would not have been so somber. The marriage was a match made because Nissa was the daughter of the Apuldre chief. Eiric wondered what it would have been like to have a woman that he wanted to come home to, a woman that would have responded to his touch, to his voice, to his needs.

It would have been better had Nissa screamed at him occasionally, but she never did. Once when she would not respond to his shouting at her, he upended the table and sent pots, pans, and dishes flying. Even then she said nothing, did nothing. He had stalked out, angry with himself for losing control and angry with her for making him do so. He had come back after a two-day spree of drinking and making love to as many women who were willing and to some who were not so willing.

He had had a terrible headache. Nissa quietly placed willow bark tea in front of him as if nothing had happened. The dishes and pots had been placed as usual on the shelves. He had noticed there were not as many dishes as there had been, and one pot had a nicked handle. Nissa had not reacted to broken dishes or his return home. He never touched her, again, in anger or in any other way. She was nothing more than the keeper of the household, the woman who fed his sons and wove their clothing. There were plenty of women to fulfill his needs.

Eiric was astonished to find himself at the edge of the bay. The mile walk had gone quickly. The boys were pulling at him, asking for their poles. Eiric handed the poles to the boys, admonishing them for getting too close to the edge. This part of the bay was good for fishing, but the bank was a straight drop down for five feet. The drop was not dangerous, but the water was close to freezing. It was an excellent place for the boys to learn the finer points of fishing.

Eiric walked to the edge and stomped on the turf. It seemed solid enough in spite of the amount of rain and snow that had fallen the last two months. He gave one more thud with the heel of his boot, and, satisfied it was safe, called the boys over.

Eiric gave them dried meat for bait and worked with them for the next hour. Kerby was the first to catch a fish. His matter-of-fact way of acknowledging the first catch was irritating to Eiric, and he tried to get the boy to express some joy. Finally, he gave up.

The next fish, a good-sized one, Rorik caught. He danced up and down after he had pulled the fighting, silvery fish from the water, and Eiric chuckled at his son. Rorik listened to his father who instructed him on how to remove the hook. Eiric tried not to show favoritism, but he could not help slapping the boy on the back. Hoskuld leaned over the fish and asked very seriously whether it hurt the fish to be out of the water. Eiric told him it was the manner of fish to be caught. It was their function on earth to provide food for the Danes.

Eiric put the fish in a basket to keep it from being stolen by a cat. He heard a scream behind him. He turned in time to hear, rather than see, a chunk of the bank sliding down the cliff toward the bay. It took him a second to realize that the scream was from Kerby. Eiric glanced around, hoping to see his son, but he could see only two of the boys.

Eiric's body reacted quicker than his mind. His heart thumped so loudly that he hardly heard the screams of Rorik and Hoskuld. Eiric jumped over the edge. As he fell through the air, he had time to see his son go under the water. A chunk of earth splashed into the sea close to Kerby. The resulting wave made the water muddy. It was deep in this part of the bay, and Eiric was afraid that he would not be able to see his son.

Eiric gasped so hard from the frigid water that he could not get a deep breath. He felt for his son, then surfaced. He tried to keep himself afloat while he shrugged out of his woolen cloak. As soon as he was free, he dove again, looking through the hazy water for a shape. He surfaced again, fearing the cold would force him out of the water, but he saw Kerby pop up a few feet from him, gasping for air. All the boys had been taught to swim, but not in freezing water.

"I am here, I am here!" Eiric swam toward the boy, who did not seem to have the strength to move. As the boy sank out of sight, Eiric kicked harder, his tunic imprisoning his legs so that he could not close the gap. "By all the gods in the sky, I will save my son," he prayed to no god in particular.

Eiric dove again to try to grab his son. He did not know whether he was closer to him or not. He reached out and felt the coarse material of Kerby's tunic. Clutching at it, Eiric pulled the boy to the surface. Kerby's eyes were closed and his face was pale. Eiric swam, pulling his son along with him until he got to a part of the bay that had a beach.

Eiric felt he had the strength of ten men as he walked from the chilly water into the frigid air carrying his son. He looked down at the white face of the boy and vowed that he would never again think of him as a colorless copy of his mother. He loved his sons, all of them.

The child awakened once as his mother undressed him. He coughed up more bay water, then lay back listlessly against the fur pallet that Eiric placed next to the firepit.

Throughout the next three days, Eiric matched Kerby's restlessness, waking when his son woke, and sleeping fitfully through dreams about muddy water. When Kerby cried out in fear, Eiric was there to comfort him, hoping that the child's dreams were not as bad as the ones he was having.

The third day was worse, for that was when the coughing started. Eiric recognized the rattling in the boy's chest as one that could kill. Nissa was there, her emotionlessness in the caring of her son disconcerting to Eiric. Where was this woman's heart? Eiric would have hit her again, but he knew that it would not awaken anything in her. Once he asked her if she cared whether or not Kerby lived, and all he got was a stoic stare.

The afternoon his sister, Olenka, came with her poultice for Kerby, Eiric merely nodded at her greeting. He had always been impressed by her ability to make use of the plants she found in the woods. Olenka was the witch-woman to the people in Beamfleot, for she could set bones and cure almost any illness. Almost. Eiric wanted to ask her to do everything she could for Kerby, but he could not. When he looked at her, the long scab on her lip reminded him that he had hit her. He had been stupid. If he had never been bewitched by the Anglo-Saxon women, he would not have betrayed his kindred. His own gods had punished him by trying to take his son. Eiric laid aside the tools he had been repairing and stared at the floor. He called on Thor to forgive him. Eiric promised Thor that he would no longer allow his anger to be used against the women in his family.

Eiric prayed to other gods, offering them everything to let Kerby live. He promised to fight the Anglo-Saxons with renewed energy to show that he was worthy of his people.

A week passed before Kerby improved. It was a small improvement, but a welcome one. The boy was hungry. Eiric wanted to feed the boy himself, but that would have been unmanly, so he sat close by as Nissa fed him and Olenka watched.

"Here, you must drink this," Olenka said. She held a bowl to Kerby's lips. He sniffed the liquid, shaking his head and wrinkling his nose. "It stinks."

"The stink is what kept you alive. Swallow." Olenka waited patiently while Kerby held his nose and gulped the medicine.

Eiric chuckled. He knew his prayers had been answered, and he was prepared to keep his part of the bargain. Every day his son gained strength. By the time the month was over, whenever Kerby was not begging to go outside, he was pestering everyone in the household. Spring would not come soon enough.

Eiric tried to entertain the boy by showing him how to repair tools. Kerby had grown impatient, and furthermore had ruined a good shovel. Eiric almost yelled at him, but reminded himself that the boy was not used to being cooped up. Even the cattle in the winter got tired of the barns and bellowed to be allowed out. It was just as hard for Eiric to be patient. He had not been out as much as usual since Kerby's accident.

Eiric heard the door open and turned in time to see his father enter in a blast of whirling snow. The older man stamped his feet and shook the snow off his cloak. Eiric stood out of respect for the older man who was his chief first and his father second. "Welcome, Father."

Kerby dropped a tool to the floor and threw himself into his grandfather's arms. "Grandfather, have you come to take me outside? You promised that when I was well, we could go for a walk." Kerby tugged on his arm.

"It snows outside. Did you not see the small storm I brought into your father's hut? We will not see the ground until spring, for this snow brings cold with it." Thorsten ran his hand through the boy's hair. "What have you been doing?"

"I have been trying to repair tools, but it is boring."

Thorsten laughed. "Repairing tools has always been boring, but it must be done. I have come to see your father. Run along and get a cup of broth from your mother for me."

"Sit down, Father." Eiric waved toward a bench close to the firepit. He waited for Thorsten to sit before he joined him. "What news have you?"

"I want to call the war council together. It is time to finish the plans we have started. We should be ready to invade Wessex and Mercia in April. We will be strong with the help from your wife's people. Her father, Haesten, is ready to join us. The Apuldre Danes are powerful and have been gathering their forces for a major invasion." Thorsten rubbed his swollen knuckles. "I have only a few years left in this life. I want to end it with my people in control of this entire island."

Eiric had heard his father's dream often, but this time it surged through Eiric with a vigor he had never felt before. "It shall be done."

Thorsten nodded. "I knew you would see the wisdom of my plan. I will arrange a meeting while you check our military supplies."

"I will do so." Eiric was elated. He would show the gods he could keep his part of the bargain. He smiled at Kerby who walked toward them, balancing a mug of broth as if it were a basket of eggs. Where would this child be if the gods had taken him? Kerby would have been robbed of his chance to lead the Danes in battle, and thus would have been denied a hero's place in Valhalla.

Eiric shuddered. He was content with the task he had before him. It was not so difficult to give up his infatuation with the Lady of the Mercians and her kinswoman, Egwinna. He pictured Kerby astride a horse charging into battle. Eiric silently thanked the gods for him.

Eiric helped his father prepare for war against the Anglo-Saxons and Mercians over the following months, and time passed quickly. The meeting with his father-in-law, Haesten, had been productive. The plans were in place for an attack on the enemy. Eiric admired his wife's father, a man of action. Haesten was loud and raucous, letting everyone near him know what and who he liked and who he thought unworthy to be called a Dane. He enjoyed killing, and he hated the Anglo-Saxons, especially King Aelfred, who had kept Haesten's two sons as hostages for more than a year. Haesten had never believed that King Aelfred had kept the boys to insure peace, but had used them to torment the father. Haesten had signed a peace treaty to get them returned, but he had vowed to fight King Aelfred when the time was right. The time would be perfect this spring.

When he was younger, Eiric had wanted to be like Haesten but could never gain as large a following, no matter what he did. After a few years, Eiric gave up the imitation of Haesten and had married the chief's only daughter, the oldest of the three children.

Eiric moved slowly down the streets of Beamfleot. The sun was out, warming the ground, but the air was chilly. Heading toward the blacksmith shop, Eiric wanted to see how quickly the smiths were working. Eiric winced at the high-pitched clang of hammer against anvil. The sound reverberated and almost dissipated before the hammer came down again in a song that was a prelude to war. The rhythm of the hammer, a familiar sound to a Danish warrior, beat out the song of death as it made a killing sword. Eiric watched a blacksmith bring his arm down and up and down, the muscles bunching and relaxing in tandem with the noise of metal against metal. Drops of sweat were squeezed from the tight-skinned brow of the blacksmith and arched upwards with each blow. The sweat beads evaporated in the heated air.

Eiric perspired as he stood inside the lean-to, away from the cool spring air. He looked around at the tense activity, camouflaged by the methodical beating of metal. The apprentices squatted by the fires, pumping the bellows. They seemed to be in a trance. Only when a blacksmith shouted an order and the bellows were pumped furiously, did they seem aware of their surroundings.

The smell of hot metal burned Eiric's nose and throat; its acrid odor made him cough. He wondered how the blacksmiths could endure it. Mayhap their insides were as tough as their outer skin.

Eiric walked over to the rack that held the almost finished swords. They had been molded, fired, hammered, and sharpened, but not polished. Still they were beautiful, standing as straight as the soldiers who would carry them into battle against the Anglo-Saxons and the Mercians. He ran a finger across the hilt of a sword. Which warrior would carry it, and which enemy would die? Would it be Lae? Eiric pushed her face from his memory. If they came face to face on the field of battle, could he run a sword through her? He chuckled. She would undoubtedly run him through and smile while doing so.

Eiric turned away from the row of swords and walked swiftly outside. He passed more sheds where the sounds of activity had distinct rhythms and melodies of their own. Chain-mail being manufactured had a lighter sound. Small hammers tapped the circlets into place, linking them to keep arrows out and life in.

As Eiric continued his walk, he passed the tanner's shed. The smell of curing hide was so distasteful that he could barely tolerate the people who worked in that trade. Consequently, his boots were always well worn before he could bear to be fitted for new ones. Eiric always had the shoemaker come to his hut, but still there was an odor that permeated the man's clothing, his hair, his skin.

Eiric circled the entire section, checking on the preparations for war and was satisfied that everything was on schedule. A hard morning's work deserved a little diversion. Eiric needed to ride. He had been born with the sea in his veins but he also loved the land. Just as being on a ship at sea had excited his ancestors, riding a horse across the earth filled him with pleasure that he had trouble explaining. Not being a man of poetic thoughts, Eiric had never really tried to explain the pleasure of riding. Lae shared this passion. He could tell by the way she completely gave way to the joy of riding. It showed on her face, in the way she sat on a horse, and in the total abandonment of caution when she let her animal run flat out.

Eiric sniffed the air as he neared the stables, inhaling the odor of straw, the sweat of man and beast, well-worn leather, and manure. This was a fine smell, not like the tanner's shed.

It was a good day for riding, with a sky blue sky and a gentle breeze that promised warmer weather but kept a touch of ice in it to remind Eiric that spring was fickle. He shivered as he rode north along the Thames.

Eiric looked up at the sun above him. He had been riding for over an hour. He flexed his fingers and smoothed his gloves. He kicked Astra into a trot. He had always marveled at the smooth gait of this mare. He rode her for pleasure. She was soft and easy compared to his war horse, and as they trotted along, Eiric forgot the impending war as he left Beamfleot farther and farther behind.

It was the flash of color that attracted him at first, then he recognized the Lady of the Mercians. Lae's hair streamed behind her like a ribbon of molten silver-gold. She was on the other side of the Thames, riding away from him at a fast clip on her sorrel war horse. Eiric loosened the reins and kicked the mare harder than he should have. She lunged forward, pounding her hooves on the ground in response to his command. This mare had the heart of a racer. She had won every race in which Eiric had ridden. No one would race him anymore.

Eiric was rapidly catching up with Lae, who rode at a fast trot, but not yet a full gallop. When Eiric was parallel to her and still separated by the Thames, he slowed his horse to match her horse's stride.

The Thames was wide at this point, and Eiric had followed Lae for more than a mile before she saw him. He wished he were closer so that he could see the inevitable anger on her face. Eiric waved his arm and yelled. "How goes it with the Lady of the Mercians?" He expected no reply, partly because of the distance and partly because he knew Lae would not acknowledge his greeting. He laughed and let the reins go slack as he leaned forward. Astra took her cue and stretched her neck as she gathered speed. Eiric could see nothing but a blur as he raced along the bank of the river that divided their two countries. He glanced to his left and saw that Lae was even with him.

"Come on, Astra." Eiric did not expect to lose a race against a woman. He lay against Astra's neck and shouted in her ear. "Are you going to let another horse beat you?"

Eiric looked across the Thames again. He was flabbergasted to see Lae's horse thundering down the south bank, riderless. Eiric's first thought was that his eyes deceived him. His second thought was that Lae was too good a rider to have fallen. He stared at the still-running horse. The saddle was askew.

Eiric slowed Astra to a trot, then a walk. He looked at the water as he turned his horse and headed downstream. He had to cross the Thames as quickly as possible. Eiric rode next to the river, looking for the ford he had seen on the way up. With the spring thaw and the rains, even the ford would be dangerous. He saw the ford near an oak tree and urged Astra toward the bank. She balked once before plunging into the bubbling water, and Eiric smiled at how well trained she was. "There will be extra grain for you later," he said.

The water pulled at Astra, and Eiric felt her struggling beneath him. His feet were wet. The splashing water was frigid, but his blood boiled inside of him, keeping him warm and giving him strength.

Eiric leaned over and looked at the water to help guide his mare. He could see nothing. With the turbulence churning up the bottom, Astra could step in a hole and break a leg. Eiric swore to Odin. He must be a fool to take a chance on injuring his favorite horse for the daughter of King Aelfred. The king had never done anything for him, so why should he risk his life for the enemy? Eiric was about to turn back when he saw Lae lying motionless on the far bank. Keeping his eye on her inert form, Eiric ignored the swirling water and pushed Astra harder. She slipped once when they were climbing from the water, but caught herself before Eiric tumbled off. He jumped down, dropping the reins over Astra's head, knowing she would not wander far.

Kneeling next to Lae, Eiric was alarmed to see how pale her face was. He stroked her cheek. It was warm. She was alive though her breathing was shallow. He felt her right arm for broken bones and, finding none, ran his fingers lightly down her left arm. The bone was broken halfway between her elbow and wrist. Eiric frowned. Unless someone skilled could set the bone, Lae would have a de-formed arm. It would be a shame.

Eiric checked Lae's left leg, then the other. He was relieved to find her legs unbroken. Eiric took off his fur-lined cloak and cov-ered Lae, being careful to keep the river-dampened corners away from her. He brushed her hair away from her face, looking for another injury. He found a large lump forming above her left ear.

Although unconscious, Lae still winced as Eiric touched the tender spot. Eiric held her hand and called her name, softly at first, then louder. He was frustrated to find that he envied his sister's training in the healing arts. He had never envied any woman before. Eiric snorted in disgust. He was becoming weak.

He shook the woman. "Lae, wake up. You can open your eyes, Lae!"

Lae stirred. Her eyes opened. "Are we in battle? Did you wound me? If you did, I will kill you in revenge."

Eiric laughed. "We have not yet met in battle. You are too eager to have my head. I fear that a loosened girth has led to an accident. You have fallen from your horse while racing me."

Lae tried to sit up. "My head hurts."

"The injury is worse to your arm. It is broken."

"Did you say a broken arm? My sword arm?"

"It is your left arm."

Lae inspected her swollen arm. "I hope it heals straight." She put her hand on the lump above her ear and cringed. "I seem to have a bump as well. Mayhap that explains the aching that pounds in my head."

"Are you in pain? Do you think you can ride?"

"I do not know." Lae glanced toward the woods. "Do you see Tanton? I fear wolves."

"He is still running. The saddle slipped, and it must have frightened him."

"Tanton is never frightened. He is trained for battle." Lae pushed Eiric's hand away and sat up. "Oh! My head spins, and my arm pains me." She leaned against Eiric. "I am sorry. I would rather die than have you help me, but I have no choice."

"If I do not help you, you will die." Eiric reached down and pulled out his dagger.

"What are you going to do, put me out of my misery?"

Eiric laughed. "Do not be absurd." He took hold of Lae's under-kirtle at the bottom and cut out a large piece.

"Are you mad?"

"Probably."

"You ruined a good under-kirtle."

"I left your tunic untouched. You are properly covered." Eiric took the triangular section of wool and made a sling for Lae. "I learned this from my sister. She is gifted in healing. Let me help you rise."

Eiric had placed his arm around Lae to steady her, and now he was aware of the scent of flowers that came from her hair, the softness of her skin and his desire to kiss her. The frightened nickering of Astra interrupted Eiric's thoughts before he could sort them out. He glanced toward the sound, whistling as he did so. The horse came galloping toward him, reins dragging. "May Odin preserve us. Look!"

Lae's intake of breath preceded a shiver. "Wolves!"

Eiric was intrigued and repulsed by the animals that were partially hidden in the shadows of the woods. He watched the leader, dark gray with ragged fur and a bedraggled tail, pace back and forth, lifting his nose to sniff the air. His eyes glistened in the light. His tongue was draped over huge teeth and hung out the side of his mouth. Foamy saliva dripped down his chest.

"They are vicious-looking. How odd he still commands them. This is no place to stay. Can you ride?" Eiric asked.

"I can try." Lae pushed Eiric's cloak toward him. "Is this yours?"

"Yes." Eiric brushed Astra away as the mare nuzzled his neck. Eiric, still holding onto Lae, stood. He grabbed his horse's reins with one hand to keep her steady. "She is more nervous than usual. The wolves." Eiric glanced toward the edge of the woods. "They have moved out farther."

"I have heard that some wolves have attacked people," Lae said.

"We have the same stories. I never knew whether or not to believe them," Eiric said.

"I see at least twenty of them." Lae held on to Eiric's arm and leaned against the mare while he wrapped his cloak about him. "The leader is huge. He may be the one that has been killing the sheep in this area. He is called the Viking Wolf because of his raids."

"I will take that as a compliment from your people to mine," Eiric said. He almost laughed at the look of consternation on Lae's face.

"I am sorry. It is a petty thing."

"We have bigger problems than insults." Eiric lifted Lae onto the saddle. She was as light and easy to handle as a well-balanced sword. "I will lead us away from here. Wolves are not supposed to attack people, but if they have the sickness, they attack anything. How far to the nearest settlement?"

"If we continue north, my fortress is five miles. If we go inland, we will reach a small village three miles from here. It is hidden by the woods that separate it from the Thames." Lae took the reins that Eiric handed to her. "I would rather go north. I am worried about Tanton."

Eiric glanced toward the wolves that had moved out of the shadow of the trees. He took hold of Astra's bridle. "I do not wish to walk through the woods, so we will go north. Do not worry about your horse. You said that he is used to battle. He will survive." Placing himself between the wolves and his horse, Eiric took hold of Astra's reins and walked deliberately along the river bank toward the north.

Lae held on to the pommel with her good hand. She leaned forward and whispered, "Do you have a weapon other than your dagger? I saw no sword."

"I am armed with just a dagger. And you?" Eiric watched Lae touch her sleeve.

"A dagger."

"How do you feel?" Eiric asked.

"Not well, but I could kill a wolf if I had to."

Eiric glanced over his shoulder. The wolves were following behind and still to his left. They had not begun to circle yet. "If the wolves attack, I will stay behind and hold them back. Astra loves to run. She will carry you to safety."

"Leave you behind? I will not let a Viking die for me. I would live the rest of my days hating myself for being a coward. I will fight to the death if need be while standing next to you." Lae stared at Eiric. "Let a Viking watch an Anglo-Saxon leave a fight? Never!"

"If I were not so worried about the wolves, I would laugh at your sense of misplaced propriety."

Lae snorted. "I cannot imagine a Dane giving me lessons in manners." She touched Eiric on the shoulder. "If the wolves start to close in, would Astra be able to carry both of us? She is finer boned than our horses."

"For a short while, but we could not outrun the wolves." Eiric shuddered at the thought of his favorite mare being torn to shreds by the pack of wolves. He did not like the thought of being shredded. "Is there not someplace that we can go to escape the wolves? An abandoned hut, anything?"

"No. Our best chance is to stand up to the leader. They should have deserted a sick leader. How odd."

"I do not understand it either," Eiric said.

Lae looked back over her shoulder. "They have spread out. Next, they will circle. We have to make a stand together."

"What makes you think that will help us?" Eiric was irritated that he had not thought of anything other than running away.

"What makes you think that it will not? Have you a better suggestion?"

Eiric shook his head.

"Then let us face the leader before the wolves circle." Lae pulled back on the reins. Astra danced in place and whinnied.

Her nervousness disturbed Eiric. "If I am to avoid being blamed for the death of King Aethelred's wife and King Aelfred's daughter, then I suppose I must stand by you in this stupid scheme. It would be best that my torn body be found next to yours."

"Good. Help me dismount. I am still dizzy."

Eiric swung her down from the saddle easily. He felt as he did at the beginning of a battle — calm. Eiric pulled out his dagger. "Get your weapon out. We will walk together toward the wolves. Whatever the end, remember that Dane and Mercian stood together."

"I am not certain my husband or my father will ever forgive me if I am found next to a Viking." Lae winced as she pulled a knife from her left sleeve and held it up. "This was meant for man, not wolf. I wish you the kindness of your gods and the protection of my God."

"I wish the same for you." Eiric took her elbow and walked toward the wolves. He had to force himself to breath. "Steady, Lae. Look the leader in the eye. Make him think we are stronger."

"If he charges, I will go for his throat. You keep the others at bay," Lae whispered.

"If he charges, let me take out the leader. I am stronger and will have a better chance of killing him." Eiric felt Lae stiffen. She jerked her elbow from his hand.

"Now is not the time to argue," she said. "Let me have the leader. I would rather concentrate on one animal while you take on the multitude."

"It would be better . . ."

"For the sake of both our lives, listen to me. I know my own strengths and weaknesses. I am not certain I can fend off multiple wolves without fainting. Wolves terrify me, and I feel ill." Lae hesitated, then continued walking toward the pack.

"All right. Anything to have agreement." He did not want to admit that Lae's point was good. He admired her determination and bravery. What a formidable foe. He was glad they were fighting the same battle this time. Mayhap fate would determine that they should die together on the same side rather than as enemies.

Eiric watched the leader of the pack. The wolf would not move, but neither did he look as if he were about to attack. His shaggy gray coat looked like motheaten wool. This wolf had trouble catching food and was unpredictable.

"There!" Lae whispered. "Did you see? The leader stepped back. We have him. Keep moving toward him."

Eiric looked at the lead wolf. He had indeed stepped back. The wolf's tail drooped. No longer was he curious and in the mood to chase. His golden eyes darted from one side to the other.

"He is nervous, Lae. Do not move too fast."

The wolf turned, and with his pack in tow, stumbled off toward the woods as if he did not care to dine at this hour. He looked back once before blending in with the shadows. As silently as they had come, the wolves disappeared. The only sound Eiric heard was the wind in the trees and Lae's sigh of relief.

"I think we are safe," Eiric said.

"May I ride your horse? I am weak." Lae leaned against Eiric as he walked her back toward Astra who waited a few feet away from them.

"You are a brave lady. I wish we could remain on the same side, but our lives are at cross-purposes. Let us declare a truce for now." Eiric lifted Lae onto the horse and swung up behind her. "Do you have a good physician at your fortress?"

"No. He has returned to Wessex."

"I would have taken you to Lundenburh, but without your horse, it is not advisable. We go to my village."

"What! If you think that you can abduct me and get away with it, you do not have the sense of a goat. If I do not kill you, my husband will." Lae reached for her dagger.

Eiric placed his arms around Lae, being careful to hold her gently. "Do not be stupid. I am doing you a favor. My sister will set your arm so that it will not heal crooked."

"I do not need your sister."

"If you want to be a warrior, then you will need two good arms. You need my sister. You will be an honored guest."

"An honored guest? Does a Dane know the meaning of honor?"

"We do. Mayhap we have learned from the Anglo-Saxons."

"I doubt that you learn that quickly."

"Vikings are honorable people. Did not your father treat my wife's brothers with respect when they resided with you?"

"We did."

"It will be for a short while, then you will be escorted home with an honor guard and me. Is that agreeable?" He watched Lae as she studied her broken arm.

"You will send a message to my husband?"

"Yes."

"It is agreeable."

Her hair flew in his face, and Eiric savored the feeling. The gods had found a perfect way to punish him. "Lae, I wish . . ."

"Do not say it."

"All right." Eiric rode in silence, listening to the sound of Astra's hoof beats on the soft earth. He wondered at his father's reaction when he brought Lae home.

Lae's arm had swollen so much that Olenka had trouble setting the bone. Eiric sat next to his father and watched as Lae gritted her teeth, but did not cry out.

"Take some more of the medicine that kills the pain." Olenka handed Lae a mug.

"Thank you." Lae drained the mug and handed it back.

"Once more, mayhap twice. If I do not snap it back into place, we will have to wait until tomorrow."

"I am ready."

Olenka put her foot against Lae's chest and pulled. The snapping sound was audible and Eiric winced. This time Lae could not keep from crying out, but then she smiled. "Is it over?"

"I will wrap your arm in bark splints and cloth. It will have to heal for seven days, and you will not be able to ride until after that."

"Thank you."

"You will be my father's honored guest. Please, you need sleep. I will show you where."

"I feel honored to have met you, Olenka. You have a remarkable talent."

"The better to heal the wounds inflicted on us by your people."

Eiric frowned at his sister's effrontery. Thorsten's voice was sharp as he scolded Olenka in their language. Olenka apologized to their father, unable to look at him.

Lae put her hand on Olenka's and spoke to her in the same tongue. "Do not worry about insulting me. I would have said the same."

Thorsten was clearly surprised at Lae's command of his language. He struggled to hide his astonishment. Thorsten said, "You speak well."

"I was taught by the sons of Haesten when they were guests of my father in Wessex."

Thorsten chuckled. "Haesten did not consider his sons as your guests."

Lae shrugged. "A necessary arrangement in a time of strife."

"Enough talk." Thorsten rose. "My daughter says that you are to rest. She knows best."

"Eiric, you sent the messenger with my words?" Lae asked.

"I did. We are following all the rules of good hosts. If you will excuse me?" Eiric rose at the nod from his father. He clapped his hand on his father's shoulder and left the hut.

chapter
VIII

AE OPENED HER EYES and looked around the hut. She knew exactly where she was. She moved her hand under the fur covering that she used as a pillow. Her dagger was still there. The good hosts had not removed her weapon although Olenka would have had the opportunity. The medicine that she had given to Lae was strong and had put her into a deep sleep.

Lae looked at the fingers protruding from the birch bark splint. She wriggled them. The swelling had gone down. They were stiff, but they worked.

"You are awake," Olenka said.

Lae was startled at how silently Olenka moved. She spoke quickly to cover her surprise. "How long have I been sleeping?"

"Two days. It was good for you. Is your aching head better?"

Lae felt her head. "The lump is all but gone." She swung her feet to the mat that covered the hard packed earthen floor.

"Do not move too quickly. You may be weak." Olenka put her hand on Lae's shoulder, steadying her.

"I feel peculiar. I would like to exercise. Is the weather good?"

Olenka chuckled. "I think you had better exercise inside first. The medicine I gave to you is powerful. Come to the table, and I will give you some excellent soup that Nissa has made for you."

"Nissa?"

"She is Eiric's wife."

"I know her brothers."

"Yes, so I have been told." Olenka stared at Lae. "Come, you need to eat."

Lae accepted Olenka's help, standing easily. She allowed Olenka to escort her to the table and watched as Olenka prepared three bowls of soup. Before Lae could ask about the third bowl, the door opened. Amidst a swirl of snow, a hooded figure entered the hut. Shaking off the snow, the woman took off her cape and hung it on a peg by the door. She stared at Lae.

"Nissa, please sit here. Our guest is about to sample the soup you so kindly sent to us."

"Thank you." Nissa sat at the table and watched Lae. Feeling like a fish in an a vivarium, Lae returned the stare.

"This is Nissa, my brother's wife."

"It is a pleasure to meet you." Lae wondered if the banality sounded like a lie.

Nissa lowered her eyes to the soup. "I have waited for you to awaken."

"Why, might I ask?" Lae watched Nissa surreptitiously to see if she would eat the soup.

"When my brothers were held hostage in Wessex by King Aelfred . . ."

"Nissa!" Olenka's voice was sharp.

Nissa's face turned crimson, and she dropped her spoon. She was as still as a stone. "I am sorry," she whispered.

"A hostage is someone who is taken against his will. Your brothers were given to King Aelfred's care without coercion." Lae's words were short and sharply delivered.

"I am sorry." Nissa looked directly at Lae. "I meant to give you a compliment. My brothers have often spoken highly of you. If they were here, they would be pestering you every day."

"How are they?"

Nissa smiled. "Both have grown to strong men. You would not recognize them."

"Where are they, now?" Lae noticed the furtive glance that Nissa gave to Olenka. Immediately, Lae was on guard.

"They are on a journey to our homeland." Olenka spoke quickly. "We do not expect them back while you are here. The weather is not good."

"I see." Lae took a spoonful of soup. "This is delicious." She ate in silence for the rest of the meal. There was something strange about the women's attitudes. She was their guest, and by Viking rules, she was not to be harmed. However, neither her hosts nor she could forget that they were enemies.

The rest of the early spring day was spent indoors. Lae was fascinated by the embroidery that Nissa did, and she marveled at each new stitch. Shy at first, Nissa grew bolder as her admirer marveled at the intricate techniques. The daylight disappeared too soon for Lae, and the lesson was over.

"Come to my home tomorrow, Lae. I have a loom that you must see. It came over from Denmark on the last ship. Even with your broken arm, you can learn to weave."

"I would be honored. Thank you." Lae touched the embroidery that Nissa had done that afternoon. "I will have to work hard to do as well as you. I hope I can remember your methods."

Nissa flushed. "I am designing something special for the border of Eiric's new tunic. I will show you tomorrow." Nissa jumped up. "By your leave, my lady. It is time to prepare supper. I must go."

After Olenka showed Nissa to the door, she turned to Lae. "I have some medicine that you must take. Your arm is swelling, again. Does it hurt?"

"Somewhat." Lae lied. Her arm throbbed, and the pain was giving her a headache. She did not want to continue taking medicine, for it dulled her senses.

"You must take this. You need a good night's sleep. It will help you heal faster." Olenka held a mug toward her.

Lae hesitated, then took the drink, gulped it down, and shuddered at the bitterness of it. "Thank you."

The medicine brought peculiar dreams to Lae of men discussing battles, blood, smiling faces, and embroidered tapestries of death masks whirling together with the faces of her menfolk. Lae pushed the covers back. The cool air was soothing. She tried to open her eyes, but she could not. She struggled to make sense of the voices she heard from the distance, but sleep pushed consciousness away. The dreams returned.

Lae was awakened a second time by loud voices. She did not know the time, but it was still dark. However, she was more alert than she had been. She looked down the length of the hut toward the flickering firepit and was startled by the sight of Eiric talking with his father, Thorsten, and two young men sitting on benches close to the fire. She could not hear what they were saying.

Lae surveyed the room. Olenka emerged from the shadows and handed a cup to Thorsten, whispering to him and gesturing toward Lae. Lae closed her eyes, even though she knew Olenka could not see her. What were they plotting? Surely not her death. It must be something worse. An invasion of Wessex or Mercia. How dare they do this under her very nose? She had to know what they were saying. Lae slid one foot to the floor, then the other. Keeping an eye on Olenka, Lae stood and moved closer to the men. Her arm throbbed, but she ignored it as she slipped through the shadows.

Thorsten clapped one of the young men on the shoulder. "It is good to see you, Raynor. Do not worry about our guest. She will not see you. The Lady of the Mercians would surely recognize both of you."

"We were children when we were in her father's court," Raynor said.

"She would not be fooled by you or Araldo," Eiric said.

"We had no way of knowing that you had company. We can take the ship into another harbor until Lae is well," Araldo said.

Lae's heart was pounding so hard that she knew they would hear her. A ship? Another load of fine steel for weapons and armor? She needed to get home. She had to get a message to her husband to come and get her now. How she missed him. How she missed her own fortress, her own food, her own bed.

Lae had heard enough. She stepped backwards toward the bed. She was halfway back when she stepped on a cat. It screeched and shot out of the darkness down the length of the hut.

Olenka whirled around. "What was that?" She stared at the black cat as it streaked toward safety.

Lae saw that Eiric, Thorsten, Raynor, and Araldo were looking in her direction. "Olenka, where are you?" Lae stumbled out of the darkness. "Olenka, my arm throbs worse than before. Do you have more medicine?" Lae kept her eyes half closed. "Are you there?"

"I am here, my lady. Let me help you." Olenka put her arms around Lae and turned her back toward the bed. "I will give you something to help you sleep. Where does your arm hurt?"

"All over. I had terrible dreams, and I am so sleepy." Lae allowed Olenka to help her to bed. She pretended drowsiness as Olenka checked her arm.

"It is not as swollen as it was, but everyone has a different response to broken bones. I will return in a moment."

With half-closed eyes, Lae watched Olenka return to the firepit and briefly confer with Thorsten before going to her chest of medicines. It was not long before Olenka returned. Lae did not want to drink the medicine that was held out to her, but she had no choice. As she drifted off to sleep, she wondered how long it would take her to awaken.

When Lae next opened her eyes, the hut was bright with the afternoon sun. She looked around for Olenka, but saw no one. Rising from the bed, she walked to the door and listened. The only sound she heard was a dog barking in the distance. Carefully, Lae opened the door and peered outside. There was none of the normal village activity. There was no hammering from the blacksmith, no laughter from the children, and no feminine voices drifting up from the market place.

Lae whirled around. There was still a fire in the pit. They had not been gone long. When it was this quiet in Lundenburh, it meant that a ship had come in from a foreign port. Lae rolled that thought around in her mind. The conversation she had heard last night was no dream. She did get out of bed and see Raynor and Araldo. She pushed the door shut, and leaned against it. A very important ship had come in last night. That explained the late night meeting with Thorsten.

Lae grinned. It must have been the first time that Thorsten did not want a ship to come in. Imagine his frustration at having her in his home and a ship full of arms and armament in the harbor. Lae could not wait to tell Red of this new development.

The thought of Red caused a spasm of loneliness to invade Lae's heart. Home seemed so far away. Lae looked at her healing arm and wriggled her fingers. The swelling was down. It would not be long until she could go home. She felt invigorated. Lae opened the door and peered out. Still there was no activity. She closed the door quietly and pondered the situation. How should she appear when everyone returned? Asleep? Awake?

Lae looked down at the tunic she had been wearing for too many days. It would be difficult to appear regal in wrinkled wool with one sleeve cut off. She could borrow a tunic from Olenka, but it would not be proper to take one without permission.

Before Lae could decide what to do, she heard dogs barking. The door opened and two young men entered in front of Thorsten with Olenka trailing behind. Lae grimaced inwardly. She would have to meet these strangers in a less than appropriate garment.

"I am sorry that I could not get here before them," Olenka said. She shrugged her shoulders. "Men never listen to reason."

Thorsten threw his arms around the two men. "You may not recognize these gentlemen."

"But I do, sir." Lae smiled to cover foreboding. "Raynor is to your left and Araldo stands to your right. How have you fared these last few years?"

"Very well, thank you." Raynor grinned. "You look as beautiful as always."

"You are the flatterer as always," Lae said. "Even as a young boy, you could charm any female."

"Except you, my lady. You were never fooled by my flattery." Raynor bowed. "How I wish I could have been worthy of you."

Araldo coughed. "He spreads veneration as thick as a fat lady spreads honey on bread."

"You, Araldo, have not lost your sense of humor," Lae said. "Nor astute observations of your brother."

"Remember when we were children in King Aelfred's court? You allowed us to hug you as brothers would a sister," Raynor said. "Do we have those privileges still?"

Lae hesitated. What role to play? She laughed. "You are a scoundrel, sir, but one whom I cannot resist." She held out her one good arm and embraced Raynor.

Araldo was soon by her side. "I claim my right as a foster brother, my lady, to your embraces. Is it proper?"

"I care not for some conventions, Araldo. You are as brothers to me. My heart is filled with happiness at seeing you."

Thorsten gestured toward the plank table. "Please, let us sit at the table, and let Olenka get us some nourishment. I am certain you have much to discuss."

"Yes, thank you." Lae placed herself opposite the two men she had known as boys. "Tell me about your trip across the sea. Was not the weather dreadful this time of year? You arrived so late last night. Were there storms?" Lae pretended that she did not see the look of surprise on Thorsten's face. The small victory tasted sweet.

"We had no fear," Raynor said. "We are Vikings through and through. The seas are no more trouble than walking across the pastures in summer."

"How have you fared?" Araldo asked. "Eiric told us about the wolves and your broken arm."

"A well-tended break should heal quickly. Olenka has cared for me better than anyone else could have. I should be able to ride and hunt again." Lae smiled at Olenka as broth was put before her by her hostess. "Her medicine is magic."

Araldo reached for Olenka and pulled her down on the bench next to him. "If her temper were better, she would make a man a good wife."

"If men were more useful, I would have a better disposition," Olenka said.

Lae joined in the laughter around the table. Olenka looked pleased. Lae had new respect for Olenka. She had a sense of humor that reflected an independent woman. Although she was the daughter of the chief, she was still a Viking woman and was expected to take a subservient role.

Thorsten crossed his arms. "Daughter, your barbed tongue is like a fence that keeps your heart in and the men out."

"Father, I prefer to think of it as armor against an enemy." Olenka turned to Lae. "Come, let us leave the men to their manly discussions. We have been invited to Nissa's to do some weaving." Olenka leaned over and whispered to Lae. "We have arranged a hot steam bath for you, too."

Lae felt her cheeks flush unexpectedly. In her haste to leave the men, she almost knocked over the stool on which she sat.

Thorsten grabbed it. He smiled at her. "In a hurry to leave the company of these two ruffians?"

"I would like the opportunity to work with Nissa. Your manly discussions are of no interest to me." Lae knew that she answered in a haughty tone. She often did that to cover chagrin, for the truth was that she would like to hear what they discussed. She was deftly being whisked away.

Three young boys peered at Lae as she sat at the loom in Nissa's hut. Lae could feel her mouth twitch as she tried to suppress a smile. She wanted to concentrate on what Nissa tried to teach her, but she could not. When she and Nissa locked eyes, they burst out laughing.

"I am sorry, Nissa, but they look so pensive," Lae whispered.

"They have heard how great a warrior you are. They are curious because you are a woman. We do not have any women who are allowed to go into battle."

Lae shrugged. "It is nothing. I have been taught to fight the Vik . . . been taught to fight since I was just a knee-baby."

"It must be thrilling to be so independent." Nissa pulled a shuttle through the threads.

"You have independence, Nissa. Are you not the daughter of a chief and the wife of a future chief?"

"I am."

"Were you not taught to fight?"

Nissa ran the shuttle back and forth several times before answering. "We were taught to support our men in other ways."

"Such as weaving?"

"Cooking, rearing children. Providing a comfortable home."

"Those are important."

"But it is not as exciting."

Lae touched the fabric on the loom. "No? How did you get such a wonderful color? It is as if the sky has wrapped itself around the threads. Do you not feel like an artist when you make something as beautiful as this?"

"I only feel like a wife. What do you feel like?"

"I feel as if I am being watched by three mischievous boys."

Frowning, Nissa turned around and faced her sons. "You have been taught to be polite."

"Let them come over. I do not mind."

"They will worry you to death with their questions."

"Good."

Nissa motioned the boys to come closer. "You may talk with Lady Aethelflaed for a moment."

Two of the boys scampered forward; the oldest stayed in the shadows. Lae smiled as they bowed. "You are well taught, I see."

"Our uncles, who lived with you, said that we must or you would cut off our heads and feed them to the wolves," Hoskuld said.

"Hoskuld!" Nissa dropped the shuttle, ignoring the clattering sound it made. "Go to the corner immediately and do not come out until I say so!"

After recovering from the initial shock of being portrayed as an ogre, Lae put her hand to her mouth to keep from laughing. "Nissa," she said between fingers, "it is your brothers who should be made to stand in the corner."

Nissa looked from her youngest son to Lae. "You are right, of course. Hoskuld should not be punished. Son, you do not have to stand in the corner. You are not old enough to know what to believe and what is unbelievable."

Lae held her hand out to Hoskuld. "Please come closer. Your mother and father would not allow me into their home if I were so bad, would they?"

Hoskuld inched toward Lae's outstretched hand and stopped next to her stool. "Are you the scourge of our people?"

Nissa gasped. "May the gods have mercy on your soul, Hoskuld. You bring pain to your mother. I am sorry, but he has not learned the finer points of being a good host."

"I am not offended, Nissa." Lae felt her happy mood of a few moments ago dissipate. The boy had asked a difficult question. "I would like to be thought of as . . . as a person who is in a position that demands painful decisions. Our two peoples, our countries, have disagreements, but I have no disagreements with you, Hoskuld."

"May I go outside, Mother? I want to find my father."

"Yes, you may."

Lae was relieved to see her young tormentor skip toward the door. A blast of cold air lifted the hem of her tunic away from her ankles and reminded Lae of her own hearth. She longed for Red's laughter. Lae rubbed her mending arm. When would she learn to be less impetuous?

The middle boy, Rorik, smiled at her. "You will have to excuse my brother. He is not as worldly as am I."

"I could tell that you were much more sophisticated," Lae said.

"I have many questions for you, but Father said that I was only allowed to ask one."

Lae glanced at Nissa who seemed to be as apprehensive as she was. "What might that be?"

"Would you sell your horse to me?"

"My horse?"

"Father said that you have the most wonderful horse. He told me how smart he is. I like horses more than anything else in the world. I would pay a good price."

"You are very intelligent to want a good horse, but let me explain Tanton to you. He is more than a horse. He is my friend. He has saved my life more than once in battle. You could not sell a friend, could you?"

"No," Rorik said.

Lae leaned forward and spoke softly. "I appreciate your love of a fine horse, but you do understand, do you not, why I cannot sell my friend?"

"Yes."

"Son, why do you not run outside and see to your brother? I think I hear him calling," Nissa said. She turned toward Kerby. "What is it, Kerby?"

Kerby stepped forward and bowed. "If I may ask a question of my own?"

Nissa sighed. "Please, not a question like those of your brothers."

Kerby tugged at his tunic. "I merely want to know if Lady Aethelflaed approves of Aunt Olenka's medicine."

"I do. She has the gift of life at her fingertips."

"Her medicines saved my life," Kerby said.

"Your father told me."

"Were you ever afraid of dying?" Kerby asked.

Kerby's face was so solemn that Lae realized there was more to his question than curiosity. Taking his hand, Lae nodded. "I have been afraid that death is coming to take me before my time is up. I was afraid of the wolves. Everyone is afraid sometimes. It does not mean that you are a coward. I think that God gave us the good sense to be afraid so that we would be careful."

Kerby blinked. "I was afraid in the water. I never told my father."

"Your father was afraid, too. He was afraid you would die," Nissa said.

"He was?"

Nissa's face flushed. "Yes. Say nothing to him. He would not want to talk about it. Go to your grandfather's hut and see what your uncles are doing. We women have work to do."

"Yes, Mother." Kerby pulled his hand free from Lae and scampered from the hut.

"Your children are delightful," Lae said.

Nissa turned back to the loom. "I love them so much, but I am afraid to show it for fear the gods will take them from me."

"How can children who bring you so much joy be taken by God?" Lae leaned forward to look more closely at Nissa.

"I must have loved Kerby too much. The gods almost took him," Nissa whispered.

Lae started to tell Nissa how ridiculous she sounded, but stopped. Nissa's face revealed her pain. Lae took Nissa's hand in her own good one. "Are your gods so cruel that they would give you the capacity to love and then punish you for it?"

Nissa glanced over her shoulder as if the gods were behind her. "I do not like to think much about them. Most of our gods scare me."

"Sometimes my God scares me," Lae said. "But most of the time I feel he protects me. Enough of this gloomy talk. Teach me about your weaving."

"You like the color?"

"Very much. I do not think we have that color in Mercia."

Nissa smiled. "I like it, too."

Lae turned in the saddle and looked back at the village. With her good arm, she waved at the tiny figure on the hill. She was certain that Nissa waved in return. Olenka probably did not. Lae smiled to herself as she thought of all the mistakes she had made in trying to learn to weave. Nissa had been a patient teacher, but an unsuccessful one. Lae could do basic weaving, and she had never learned anything else.

Turning around in the saddle made her arm hurt, so Lae faced forward. She caught Eiric staring at her. "Have I grown two noses?"

Eiric laughed. "Not at all. I was watching the sun shine on your hair. Your cowl has slipped."

Lae wanted to shove Eiric from his horse for his insensitivity to his wife. "I had a good visit with Nissa. She is an artist."

"Really?"

Lae pulled back on the reins and dropped behind Eiric to ride with Raynor and Araldo. "My father is most anxious to see you both, again."

"We are eager to renew his acquaintance," Araldo said.

"He treated us like sons, and so he seems a father to us."

"Then why do you join in the plot against our countries?"

Raynor shook his head. "We do not. We want to preserve peace and try to convince Haesten and the Apuldre Danes that they have nothing to gain and everything to lose by fighting you."

"Haesten thinks we are weak," Lae said.

"Your country and Wessex grow stronger day by day," Araldo said. "Your reputation astonishes even us."

"Can Haesten be controlled?" Lae asked.

"Of course," Araldo said. "You must believe that we respect your father, nay, even love him, and so do not want war between us."

"You brought him joy during a time when laughter was rare," Lae said. She wanted to believe him. She hated only some of the Danes, it seemed. Despair tugged at her. Did she want war? She glanced at Raynor and Araldo.

She rode along silently, homesickness overtaking her and becoming acute. It was odd that she was more homesick now that she was on her way home. "How much farther to the bridge, Araldo?"

"An hour or more. You are not on your famous horse now. You will have to be patient with this old nag." Araldo laughed. "I remember that you were never tolerant of slow horses."

"You always rode at the speed of a deer. It is a wonder you have not broken your arm before this, or your neck," Raynor said.

"Both of you exaggerate." Lae tried to put anger in her voice, but she could not.

Time passed slowly for Lae in spite of the comforting tales from the past told by Araldo and Raynor. Eiric rode beside them, laughing too heartily at some of the stories. He irritated her with his flirtatious manner. The bridge between Danelaw and Mercia would appear none too soon.

She thought about whipping the poor beast she was riding, but refrained. This horse was not meant to race. She was a beautiful animal, but was used primarily for breeding. They clattered across the wooden bridge in single file.

As soon as Lae reached the other side, she inhaled deeply. It was the same air as that in Danelaw, but somehow it seemed much purer.

"Who rides toward us? There are more than a dozen riders. Has King Aelfred ridden so far from his own territory?" Raynor asked. "I hope it is he."

"It is King Aelfred." Eiric waited for Lae to catch up with him. "Your father has moved quickly since getting the message that you were well enough to ride."

The sound of horses coming toward Lae penetrated her mind slowly, and, feeling as if she were awakening from a dream, she looked ahead. "It is indeed my family. My husband rides in front with my brother, Prince Edward. My father is to the right of him. Behind them are friends and supporters. My father was never convinced that you had not abducted me. Let me do the talking. It may save your Viking hide." Lae held up her hand and waved. "I did that to let them know that you have not abducted me. They would shoot an arrow through you on sight."

"A pleasant thought for an Anglo-Saxon," Eiric said.

"Keep your Viking mouth quiet, and you may keep your head." Lae waved again. "My husband! It is good of you to meet me. Father! Edward! I have been helped by Eiric, son of Thorsten."

"Remind King Aelfred that I am the son-in-law to Haesten. That will mean more."

"He knows that part of your lineage. It is good that he is fond of Araldo and Raynor, and that they ride with us. Aethelred, my husband, has a storm cloud on his face. Pull up and let them come to us. It will give him time to assess the situation. In the meantime, I suggest that you wave and smile. Can Vikings smile?"

"In the face of danger, a Dane can do anything necessary." Eiric lifted an arm in greeting as he pulled Astra to a halt.

Three men separated themselves from the entourage with nothing more than a hand signal by Red. The men who stayed behind rested their hands fitfully on the hilts of their swords, their bodies positioned for a foray. They must have found it difficult to believe that she had been safe all this time in spite of the many messages sent back and forth.

"I feel foolish sitting behind you," Eiric said.

"It is safer. I do not want to worry that an impatient relative will let an arrow fly toward you." Lae watched Red as he rode closer. His face was a mixture of anger, relief, and curiosity. She hoped the curiosity would be the strongest emotion.

"So this is the man you married," Eiric said. "He is handsome for someone his age. His hair is not graced with much silver and his muscles are still strong beneath his tunic."

"Simpleton! Contain your Viking rudeness. I would hate to have to defend you from my own people." Lae frowned. She would be glad to be rid of Eiric. He had hovered around her until she had been embarrassed for Nissa, who had worn a sad expression whenever the three of them were in the same hut. She had grown fond of Nissa and had pity for her. Lae glanced over her shoulder at Eiric. "Have you no manners?"

King Aelfred seemed reserved. Lae sighed with relief. That was good. She hoped his brilliant and analytical mind would see that she was not harmed. She believed that the king would listen to her. Lae searched her father's face. There was no sign of what he thought. Lae looked at her father as if seeing him for the first time. King Aelfred was thin of face beneath a brown beard barely streaked with the gray of age. His eyebrows were heavy, which gave him a grave look. His straight nose was more aristocratic than interesting. Lae was filled with pride at King Aelfred's bearing. The Anglo-Saxon king was an enemy who should not be misjudged by the Vikings.

Lae's brother, Edward, was as strong and as intelligent looking as his father. He resembled his father and copied his father's mannerisms as well as his coloring. He was a man that women always found appealing. No wonder Stan was so handsome.

Watching Eiric as he waited for the men to stop before them, Lae saw that he bowed his head just enough to show homage without degrading himself or his people. He waited for the Anglo-Saxons to speak, since he was in their country and their code of manners dictated it.

"My wife. It is odd to see you in the company of a Dane. I believe he is one of the enemy you wish to slaughter."

Red spoke with no sense of humor. Lae took a deep breath. "Good day, Husband. It is with great pleasure that I am able to see you in this life rather than the next one. Had it not been for Eiric, son-in-law to Haesten, I would have been food for wolves."

While she waited quietly for Red's response, she was pleased to see that she had piqued his interest immediately, while giving Eiric credit for saving her life. She could read the curiosity in Red's face, and it was all she could do to keep from laughing with relief.

"Please explain," Red said.

"My curiosity is aroused," Lae said. "In your message to me, you said you knew that I was in trouble before my note reached you. How?"

"Tanton returned riderless and with his saddle askew. I have told you that that particular saddle was old." Red frowned.

Why did her husband have to chastise her in front of the Vikings? It made her feel like a child. Lae shrugged. "I have always used that saddle. It is my favorite. It should have been in better repair. After all, it came from the stable of the Lord of the Mercians." Red's face flamed. Lae rushed on, hoping to undo the damage that her petulance had done. "Do you want to hear how this Dane saved me from the wolves? I was unconscious after the fall from Tanton. I think the wolves wanted me."

"How many wolves?" King Aelfred asked. "Were those beasts prowling around again?"

"That they were. A pack of twenty or more encountered us up the river. The leader has the sickness. I was lucky that this Dane saw me fall from my horse while he rode on the other side of the Thames."

Edward stared at Eiric. "Explain this."

"It was a simple matter. I saw the riderless horse and crossed the ford to investigate. I thought mayhap the rider had broken her neck. Fortunately she landed on her head and was none the worse for wear except for her arm."

King Aelfred burst out laughing. "It is good that she landed on the hardest part of her body. Her head has always been hard and that has made her difficult to manage. I am surprised the wolves dared to approach." King Aelfred rode closer to Eiric. "Tell me, are those gentlemen the two sons of Haesten? I found them delightful children when they were guests of ours."

"That they are." Eiric motioned to Araldo and Raynor. "Come forth and give greeting to King Aelfred."

Raynor was the first to reach the king. Forgetting custom, he leaned over and embraced the King. "It is a fine day when one meets a friend from the past."

"You look fit, Raynor. The years have been kind to you. And here is Araldo! Greetings to you. I am delighted to see that you have fared as well as your brother."

"I prefer to think that I have grown more handsome," Araldo said.

Eiric joined in the laughter of the group. "You can see through their words that they grow bolder with each sunrise. These two are excellent at games and have a keen wit that keeps our village elders laughing."

King Aelfred smiled. "Such as they were when young."

Red urged his horse closer to Eiric and Lae. "If you please, would you accept an invitation to Lundenburh? We could dine there tonight, and you could return to your village tomorrow. I would send a messenger to your wife and father."

"Thank you for your kindness, but I must return to my sons. They hunger for my companionship. With your permission, I would like to return the lady to your care." Eiric waited for a nod from Red, then slid from the back of Astra. He stepped back and, at a proper distance and with his best manner, held his hand out for Lae. She took it and swung down from the mare. "My lady, your company has meant much to my wife and sons."

"Convey my thanks to them for their kindness." Lae let go of Eiric's hand and stepped toward her husband.

Red swung down from his horse and, without comment, lifted Lae into the saddle. He saluted Eiric and silently mounted the extra horse that had been brought. Lae wanted to turn and wave to Eiric, but it would not have been proper. Her father should do the honor.

"Thank you, Eiric, for taking care of the Lady of the Mercians. She is a very special woman to us." King Aelfred touched his forehead with an index finger and turning his horse, rode toward Lundenburh.

Lae wondered whether or not the two countries could ever have peace. It would be difficult to do battle with the Vikings now that she knew Nissa, her sons, and yes, even Olenka. Would she be able to take the life of their menfolk? Lae shivered. Wars were inevitable. It was the way of things. She stared ahead, searching for Lundenburh.

chapter

IX

USBAND, THIS CANNOT BE SO!" Lae's throat was tight as anger surged through her. "After weeks of peace, the Danes have attacked us? After I was in their care?" Lae's voice cracked. "After I became friends with Nissa and her boys?" She threw the vellum to the floor.

"It is true. Haesten, Thorsten, and Eiric have banded together against us."

"So, Araldo and Raynor wanted to stop Haesten. I wonder if they deceived me as well."

"I am sure they meant what they said, but they do not have the power to stop Haesten," Red said.

Lae touched the sleeve of her tunic. "Nissa sent this to me not more than three weeks ago. Was this embroidered tunic a gift or a deceit?"

"Viking women do not make war, Lae." Red picked up the vellum that Lae had thrown. He folded it and laid it on the bed.

"After Olenka cared for me?" Lae held up her left arm. "She made my broken arm whole again. Too bad for the Vikings, for if the other is injured I will use this arm to swing a mace, to slice flesh from their bones with a sword, to spear the devils through their hearts." Lae paced with restless energy.

"I will send word to the councilmen that we will be in a state of war," Red said.

"The Council? They convene only once a year, and I think that is to trade old war stories." Lae put her hands on her hips. "I wish we could disband those aged soldiers. I fear they are old fashioned."

"It is an honor for minor nobility to be on our council. They do no harm."

"They do no good."

She crossed the room and grabbed her cape from the peg where it hung. "I must ride. I have need to think."

"I understand; however, do not tarry. We must act fast. The enemy has attacked us in large numbers," Red said.

"Really? Does that mean that Beamfleot is without protection?"

"It appears so. King Aelfred has asked that I join him to battle the Danes."

"I should like to attack Beamfleot." Lae pinned her cape, pulling her hair from underneath. "I will return in an hour."

"With a plan, no doubt." Red smiled. "If we split our armies, then you will need Edward's help."

"Yes. I will keep that in mind while I think." Lae felt guilty for leaving Red while she went riding, but she could not help it. She had a thousand furies inside her whenever there was trouble, and the only way to get rid of them was to race across Mercia.

"A kiss from my lady," Red said.

Lae stopped in midstride, rushed to Red, and stood on tiptoe to kiss his cheek. "You are a wonderful man, Red. You understand me better than anyone."

"Even more so than Eiric?"

"Ahhh! Do not tease me! That pig does not even understand how much his wife loves him and his sons." Lae shuddered. "Please, I do not want to remember the time I spent under their care."

"Painful?"

Lae buried her head against Red's chest. She loved the odor of wool and perspiration that was part of his tunic. It gave her comfort. "If the Vikings do not stop attacking us, in the future I may kill the very boys that Nissa loves so much." Her voice was lost in the folds of Red's clothing.

"The ways of war, Lae."

Lae stepped away from Red. "We have been fighting the Vikings our whole lives. I should have known there would be no peace." As she walked toward the door, she shrugged. "There is not room for both peoples on this island."

Lae pulled Tanton up and stared east toward Beamfleot. Turning in the saddle, she looked southwest where Fearnhamm lay. Her father and her husband would attack soon, sending the Vikings into a retreat. But which way? If the Vikings knew Edward and she were attacking Beamfleot, they would not come east. The Viking devils would escape to the northwest away from King Aelfred and Red. She did not want them to escape! Something was tugging at Lae's thoughts, but she could not capture it. She turned Tanton toward her fortress and rode slowly. An idea hit her with such suddenness and force that Lae was impatient to return to Red. She needed to see what he would think of it. Urging Tanton to a gallop, she raced toward the fortress.

Lae barged through the door to her chambers so quickly that Red leaped toward his sword.

"Wife, you put a fright to me that has stopped my heart!"

"I am sorry, Red. Listen to this plan, and tell me what think you."

"I knew you would ride home with a thought or two." Red pulled Lae into the room and shut the door behind them. He took her into his arms and laid his cheek against her hair. "Tell me."

"You and Father will keep most of the Vikings busy at Fearnhamm. In the meantime, we can presume that Beamfleot will be nearly empty."

"We can assume no such thing. Mayhap it is a Viking trick, Lae."

"You said that if we split our forces, I would need help from Edward." Lae pushed away from Red and marched to the window. "The Vikings will think that, too."

"They might not."

"We let them know it. They cannot fight two battles at once and protect Beamfleot." Lae whirled around. "That is not the best part of the plan, dearest Red. While I am in Beamfleot without Edward . . ." Lae held up her hand before Red could interrupt her. "Hear me out, Husband. While I am in Beamfleot without Edward's army, he is to the northwest of Fearnhamm waiting to catch the Vikings as they retreat from you and Father."

Red frowned. "Go to Beamfleot alone?"

"Yes, yes, yes! The Vikings have no choice but to go northwest. They cannot go toward Wales, you and Father have them cornered like rats in the south, and I will be in the east. It is a three-way trap." Lae held her breath, hoping that Red would see the strength of her strategy.

"Your plan depends on several things. One, your father and I must win at Fearnhamm, and two, Beamfleot must be almost unguarded."

It was good that Red saw the weaknesses, but Lae hoped he would not stop her. "Every plan has bad possibilities. Are not your men and my father's men ready?"

"Yes."

"Am I not ready for a little skirmish?"

"I could send Archer with you. I can spare him. He is my best soldier and most trustworthy."

"Edward would be free to hide out in the northwest."

"That is true."

"Oh, Red! Thank you, thank you!" Lae rushed across the room and threw herself in his arms. "I love you for giving me my own battle!"

"Most women want jewels, but not you," Red said.

"Most women do not have a jewel for a husband. You are all I need."

Beamfleot lay ahead. Lae stood in the stirrups and surveyed the tranquil scene before her. To the south lay the Thames, glittering like a silver necklace as it meandered through the April-greened fields. The trees were ready to burst forth with leaves, making the woods look as if the Creator had touched the branches with ochre. "I see no signs of the Viking army. My husband and father must be keeping them busy in the field." Lae turned to Archer. "You have fought with my husband for years. Do you think the Vikings could be hiding in their huts?"

"My lady, it is possible. They have used such tricks before." Archer pulled at his dark beard with a hand that was missing two fingers as he studied the town below them. "The sun is high enough and will no longer hinder us. They do not expect us."

"I do not care whether they expect us or not. I have come to destroy this gate to Hades. Ever since Haesten made Beamfleot his base, our people have seen that monster every week and sometimes more. If I see him or Thorsten or Eiric, I will kill them."

Lae knew that her voice sounded bitter. Haesten, Thorsten, and Eiric had worked for the last six months amassing more than three hundred ships to use against her people and her father's people — a grave mistake.

A greater mistake had been made by Eiric who thought that he could use his charm to disarm her. His charm would save him no more. If she saw him in battle, she would run him through with a spear or hack him in two with a battle-ax.

Lae looked across the field to where the second half of her army was waiting. She had smiled at the excitement in Edward's voice when she had told him of the plan to trap the Vikings in the northwest while she destroyed Beamfleot. It would weaken the Vikings considerably to have this base destroyed.

Lae was unable to resist leading her army against an enemy that she so deeply hated. She would have the chance to show Eiric how little his attempted seduction of her meant. Her only regret was that Nissa and Olenka would be in danger. She could be angry with Eiric, Thorsten, and Haesten, but she had trouble maintaining anger at the women who had befriended her.

Lae pulled Tanton around and surveyed her split hundred-man army. The front line of mounted noblemen wearing chain-mail was well armed with spears and bows. Directly behind the front row were the lesser equipped followers of her cohorts, and behind them the ceorls, fresh from the fields, in their Phrygian hats of boiled leather.

Lae wrinkled her nose with the memory of boiling hats in Tanner's Alley. The smell had to be endured if the ceorls were to have protection in battle. Lae looked at the men, dressed in their simple woolen tunics, drab but functional. She had a sudden rush of thankfulness for these men, the backbone of her father's nation and of hers. They were free to farm as they wished, and because they valued their freedom, they, too, hated the Vikings.

Lae held her spear high above her head. The noise turned to quiet in a wave from the front to the back of the army as Lae was about to give her first speech as head of her own men. She waited until she had their attention and, standing in the stirrups, consciously dropped her voice half an octave so that it would carry.

"Men-at-arms! I welcome you to this historic occasion. Before us is the town where Haesten has been a guest. The Viking fiend has been striking out at our people. It is time to destroy the hell-hole where he lives. While King Aelfred and my Lord Aethelred fight the Vikings in Fearnhamm, we will give Haesten's hell a taste of the flames. If the Viking army is hiding here, kill them. If they are not here, capture the Viking women so they will not bear children to bear arms against us. Take the bearns and children so that they will not grow into Vikings to wreak havoc on our people. Burn their huts so this blight on our land is gone. Take any Viking weapon so there can be none of our people's blood on them.

"We do this to return payment to the Vikings for the hell they have put our people through. There is to be one difference, however. I command you to treat the women as you would treat your own wives and daughters. Let not our men behave as the Vikings have behaved. Let us not ravish the women or kill the children." Lae looked from one side of the army to the other. "We go in honor to avenge our people.

"Let us pray to God and to St. Cuthbert and St. Oswald, both of whom watch over my father and thus over his family and their people. Let us ask that both saints deliver us from the monsters who inhabit our lands." Lae nodded to the priest whom she had insisted accompany her. She bowed her head with the army and listened to the sonorous voice of the priest, crossing herself in unison with the men at the end of their prayer.

Lae glanced at the sun. The time was right, and she turned Tanton toward Beamfleot. Her heart thumped loudly, her mouth went dry, and every part of her body screamed for action. It was possible that she could die, but it would be a glorious death. She was not afraid of death, but she wanted to finish a job once started. Her life was in the hands of God.

The beginning of the attack filled Lae with a calmness that she had heard her father discuss. She had never felt it before. Everything seemed clearer than normal to her from the moment she saw the other half of her army surge forward until she felt the pounding of Tanton's hooves beneath her.

She did not remember giving him the signal to run. The sounds of the army behind her, and the realization that her arm was up, raised in the signal for attack, startled her. Was she truly in the hands of God?

Lae coughed at the dust raised by the horses as they galloped toward Beamfleot, and she wished that she had worn a heavier head covering beneath her helmet. The smell of trampled grass reminded her that it was spring. There would be an entire summer of war.

As they neared the outskirts of town, Lae shifted her weight in the saddle to be in position to use the short spear she held in her right hand. Her sword had been specially made, and she was anxious to use it. Her hatred wavered when she thought of Eiric's sons, but she brushed this memory away.

She passed the first few houses, leaving them to the foot soldiers, and bore down on the center of town where lean-to structures dominated. These would be the best places to start looting for Viking swords and armor of the highest quality. This would also be an excellent place to be ambushed. Archer rode toward her, his mount's hooves clattering against the stones.

"Hail, my lady. Where are the Vikings you promised that you would kill?"

"Lest you become too confident, shall we check these buildings?" Lae swung down from her horse without waiting for a reply. She jammed her spear into the ground and drew her sword. "Come, Archer. Let us enter as one."

Archer laughed at her as he slid off his horse. "My lady, your cheeks are on fire. You have the infection of a first time soldier."

"Do I have to enter the enemy's lair alone or will you come with me?" Lae waited for Archer to stand to the left of the door. He kicked it open. A scream split her eardrum as she followed Archer into the darkened room.

Her eyes adjusted rapidly to the dim interior. Instantly Lae saw the deadened coals in the firepit, the bucket where the live coals were kept, a hammer and anvil, and a woman with three children cowering behind a rack of swords. Lae held her sword in front and walked cautiously toward the screaming woman.

Archer moved toward the woman in tandem with Lae. "Close your mouth, you stupid woman," he said in Danish. "There is no one to save you." He thrust his sword toward her. "Come out from behind the swords. If I have to come after you, I will run this sword through the curly-haired bearn that you hold in your arms. Never more will you be able to suckle him." Archer stepped forward. "Are you coming out?"

The woman was terrified of Archer, and she shrank back against the wall, pushing two toddlers behind her until Lae thought the children would be crushed. As Lae reached for Archer's arm to temper his outburst, a movement to her left alerted her. She swung around, sword ready. The figure leaped at her before she had time to think, and she thrust the sword toward it. She was aware of a stinging in her hand before she realized that her sword had left her grip and had clattered to the floor. Lae sidestepped the enemy's sword thrust easily. Had he been more skilled, she would have been struck.

As the swordsman stumbled past Lae, drawn by his own momentum, she stuck out her foot and tripped him. He hit the floor in an eye's blink.

Lae, angered at her stupidity, turned it toward the enemy and stepped on his neck, holding the writhing creature on the floor. What surprised her was the sudden stillness of the prone figure. Any seasoned soldier would have grabbed her ankle and thrown her to the floor. Mayhap it was good that she, unseasoned as well, had met her equal. Lae bent down and grabbed the soldier's heavy sword. She felt the strain on the muscles in her forearm, and the sword quivered. She placed the point of the sword to the man's back, hard enough to demand his obedience, but not hard enough to draw blood.

"Get up, fool." Lae stepped back to let the man roll over. She almost laughed at herself for dropping her voice down as low as it could go. She supposed she thought it would make her sound fierce.

"Do not hurt him, my lady. He is just a boy, trying to protect me. He is the apprentice to my husband, the swordmaker. He does not mean it." The woman sobbed.

"Get up and stand by the woman who saved your life," Lae watched the boy move slowly toward the woman who was still under Archer's sword. The boy's eyes never left hers. "Archer, we have a group of hostages and a nice rack of good swords. Shall I get help?"

"Yes. From the sounds outside, I would guess that our men are close by."

Lae backed toward the door, picked up her sword, and looked out. A soldier who was in the street responded immediately to her motion. "We need men to take these prisoners and swords." Lae pulled her spear from the ground where it stood by the door.

"My lady, it shall be done." The soldier touched his finger to his helmet as he disappeared into the crowd of men.

Lae turned and watched as soldiers herded women and children toward the north end of town. Smoke from the burning huts was already filling the air, along with wailing from the women and children. Lae swallowed hard. War was more difficult than she had imagined. She had imagined fear, pain, and suffering, but not sorrow.

Lae sheathed her sword, pushing it into its sheath until she could push no more. The hilt was resting on the top of the sheath and for now, the blade nestled in the lamb's wool lining. For her, the skirmish was over. Thinking of Nissa and her boys, Lae found that she had no heart for this necessary part of pushing the Vikings from her country. She also knew that if she did not help to force them out, they would take the rest of Mercia and mayhap Wessex. And the charming sons of Eiric would grow to be enemies of Stan and Wyn.

Tanton nickered, frightened by the flames. Lae led him down the street, following the crowd that was part of the confusion. She wanted to leave the noise, the chaos, the smoke. Archer would wonder what had become of her, but he would catch up with her later on the way to Lundenburh.

As she passed the two familiar huts of Thorsten and Eiric, Lae wondered about Nissa and Olenka. One of her soldiers was about to torch Nissa's hut, and all Lae could think about was Nissa's beautiful work curling in flames.

"Wait!" Lae shouted.

The soldier stared at her. "My lady?"

"Spare this hut." Lae looked at the neighboring structure and thought about the rows of medicines on Olenka's shelves. "Do not torch that hut either."

"Save these two huts, my lady?"

"Yes."

"These are the houses of . . ."

"Do you presume to question me?" Lae glared at the soldier. She knew that the anger she bestowed on him was really anger with herself for being so weak.

"As you wish, my lady." The soldier bowed at Lae's retreating figure.

Lae walked awhile before pulling up her riding tunic and putting her foot in the stirrup. She swung into the saddle easily while holding the sword to keep it from swinging against Tanton. She would be allowed to name her sword since she had confronted the enemy, but she would wait until she had led a real battle. She would not call this a battle. It had been too easy to round up women and children. She felt angry that she had been denied a true fight.

Lae rode out of Beamfleot, barely acknowledging the shouts of praise from the men she had led. She passed wagons loaded with crying women and pale-faced children, swords, boxes of household goods, and woolen blankets. Herds of sheep and cattle were being driven through the confusion. Chickens squawked as they were trussed up.

Lae rode hard. She could not wait to get home. She wanted to bathe. Mayhap she could wash away the disappointment along with the dirt.

The sound of galloping horses caused Lae to rein Tanton to a stop and wait for Archer.

"My lady, you left suddenly." Archer stopped next to her. "Forgive my impertinence, but your face no longer has the blush of excitement. Do you find war not to your liking?"

"It was not war. We raided a village much like the Vikings raid our villages." Lae rode at a slow pace. She glanced at Archer, who rode on her right. "This was not war, Archer."

"No, my lady. War is death."

"War is death," Lae repeated.

Archer kept his horse abreast of hers. "It is not a joyful thing to attack people who have no defenses, but there have been many times when our people have been in the same situation. We must stop the bloody Vikings. I have heard you say that many times."

"In my mind I know everything that you say is true, but in my heart I feel saddened." Lae listened to the sounds of the crying children behind her. "I never thought of the Vikings as having wives and children, homes and crops until I spent time with them. I knew they did, of course. I never saw fear until today. They feared us. They hated us. Their eyes were filled with the same feelings for our army that we have for theirs." Lae rode in silence. "But, Archer, still I will continue to fight. I will bathe my sword in the blood of the Viking warrior. If I die by the hand of a Viking, I will take pleasure in the fact that I have killed."

Archer cleared his throat. "My lady, war is a part of life." He held up his right hand. "My fingers lie on a battlefield thanks to a Viking sword. My wife lost more than I. She was brutally taken. Although her body has healed, her mind has not."

Lae shook her head to clear the sounds of the wailing children. "I know the reasons. I remember the pain of seeing my father lead us in retreat. I remember the fear. I vowed then that I would fight the Vikings. I remember that vow." Lae looked back at the cluster of prisoners who were following them. "Archer, we cannot feed all these people. What is the purpose in taking them?"

"We will hold them for awhile, then release them back to Haesten, Thorsten, and Eiric. It is only to show the chiefs that we can take whatever we want, when we want. I hope this will drive them farther north. The push is on, my lady."

"Well said, Friend. I rejoice in the beginning of the end for the Vikings. No more will you hear my weak cry. I will avenge your wife, your poor fingers, and other transgressions against us."

"My lady, you will want to train further. I would be happy to instruct you." Archer's face was serious. Archer rubbed the stubs where his fingers used to be.

"I accept, kind Archer. I would like to learn the finer points of the sword. What better teacher than one who has spent years on the field of battle?"

Lae savored her bath. She slid farther down in the wooden tub, cringing at the slime at the bottom. She would have to have one of the servants scour it out. Lae closed her eyes. She had wondered if a real battle would leave her more fatigued or if she would feel like celebrating as the men did in victory. She knew one thing; she would not drink so much wine that she would fall asleep on the floor in the great hall.

She had to get out of the tub, but she did not want to. Her husband had sent word that he and her father had returned victorious and wanted a conference. Lae held up a hand and wriggled her fingers. Would she ever lose them as Archer had? Or worse, would she lose an arm or a leg? She would rather die than lose a limb or even a finger. It was bad enough to have had her arm broken. It would not be the pain; nothing could be more painful than childbirth. It would be the disfigurement; the constant reminder that the Vikings had taken a piece of her.

As Lae descended the staircase to the great hall, she heard the laughter first, then smelled smoke from the firepits. It was April, but nightfall brought dampness with it. She had put on her best tunic, as pale blue as the sky, her most flattering color. The trim was dark blue silk with red embroidered flowers and her under-kirtle was dark blue silk. The material had cost Red many gold coins when he had purchased it for her from a dark-skinned Arab.

Lae wanted to look beautiful but regal when she met with the Viking women. She could not endure wearing the tunic that Nissa had made for her. Lae had shed tears when she folded it and placed it in the bottom of her storage trunk.

Red was sitting at the head table, with King Aelfred to his right. King Aelfred's scribe was seated behind both kings, writing furiously, his bald head shiny with sweat. Edward was talking to his father, but he was not sitting. Lae knew that Edward would spend the entire evening pacing back and forth, talking to the men, and slapping them on the back. She had seen him in this state many times before when a battle had been won.

Her place was waiting at Red's left. She smiled at him when he saw her. His face always revealed his feelings, and when she saw the love shining in his eyes, she wondered at her good fortune. She walked quickly across the room to him.

"Wife, sit beside me. I hear from Archer that you did a commendable job with a would-be assassin."

"A mere child, Red. No threat at all. I learned nothing except to check all corners before going too deeply into a building. Edward! Tell me of your encounter with the Vikings!"

"Your plan was brilliant, Lae. You think just like the Vikings."

"Edward, you have insulted me. To think like the Vikings is to be an ox brain."

The men laughed, then Edward said, "Would it please you to know what happened?"

"If you think my poor addled brain can tolerate such tales," Lae said.

"When the Vikings retreated, they sailed up the River Coln toward Thorny Island to the northwest as you foretold. We allowed them to trap themselves on that island where at this very moment my army holds them under siege."

"Wonderful news, Brother. I would like to toast to our combined victories this day."

Lae reached for a goblet of wine, took a sip, and swirled the wine. She liked the contrast between the silver of the goblet and the red of the wine. Holding the goblet high she said, "To Wessex and Mercia. May they fight as one, live as one, and become as one."

"Hear! Hear!" King Aelfred, Red, and Edward shouted.

Lae drank, then seated herself. "Where is Egwinna? I asked that she join us."

"I know nothing of that. Mayhap she feels it improper to be at the table with us. Or mayhap she has a problem with our daughter." Red motioned to a servant to bring a trencher of meat for Lae.

Lae held her hands above a basin placed to her right as a servant poured warm water over them from a pewter pitcher. She dipped her hands in the water and swished her fingers around, shook the water off, and allowed the servant to dry them with a linen towel as the day-old bread was placed before her filled with meat and broth. She took her eating knife from its sheath and stabbed a piece of meat. She had not realized how hungry she was until she smelled the food. The meat was tough. Although the marinating had done some good, it was not completely successful. "Where are the prisoners? Have they been fed?"

"We have most of them under guard in the outer bailey. They have been fed. I think they are as tired of turnips as we are, for the cooks reported a lot of grumbling. They should be happy to be alive. The Viking noblewomen will join us soon."

"Except for Olenka and Nissa. I wonder where they were?" Lae asked.

"Who knows?" Red placed his hand on Lae's. "You look especially lovely tonight."

"Thank you, my lord." Lae felt herself wishing that they were alone in their chambers. Lae saw Egwinna coming toward the table and smiled at her. The young woman was beautiful, and she wished

Edward could marry the girl. It was unseemly of her to be disloyal to her brother's wife, but she admitted to herself that she liked Egwinna better, and insisted that she be given privileges that Lae knew caused tongues to wag.

Egwinna slid into place next to Lae on command. "I have had a difficult time with Stan and Wyn. I could not leave them with the other servants until I had settled their quarrel."

"Started, no doubt, by my daughter," Lae said.

"Actually, for a change, I believe Wyn to be innocent. She wanted to see the prisoners close up, but my son refused to let her go. He barred the way and she began screaming, kicking, and biting him. I told him he had no right to stop her. He did not listen. Stan is as stubborn as his father. When I pulled them apart, they were rolling on the floor. I am having them bathed before I allow them to come downstairs. They got filthy and they stank." Egwinna clapped her hand to her mouth. "I chatter on, as usual. How unseemly of me."

"I do not mind. It is refreshing to have someone who speaks her mind."

"I am trying to follow protocol, but it is most difficult." Egwinna looked at Lae's food. "Is that beef?"

"Do not hope for such a delicacy. I fear this is an old deer whose muscles have long ago become hardened to life in the wild. It will take most of the night to chew enough meat to get sustenance." Lae chuckled at the look of dismay on Egwinna's face. "Never fear. The rolls are fresh."

A commotion at the rear of the great hall caused Lae to glance up. "What goes here?"

"I have ordered the wives and children of the Viking leaders to be brought here. I thought they should be given dinner in accordance with their station," Red said.

"You are kind." Lae watched the women and children herded to the trestle tables below theirs. She looked the women over and wondered how she would feel if she had been captured.

The oldest woman there was probably the wife of Haesten. She looked as if she had not suckled a child for a hundred years. She was a homely thing with white hair that trailed down her back like strings of wool on a sheep. To be fair, Lae thought, the woman has been through a difficult time.

Lae leaned across her husband to speak to King Aelfred. "Father, I do not see the sons of Haesten. I thought you had captured them."

King Aelfred peered down his long, thin nose at the prisoners. "They were not anywhere to be found. I have been informed that they had gone back to Denmark. It is too bad that in the past I had to hold them as hostages so that no harm would come to our people. I kept my word and released them several years ago, but Haesten broke his part of the bargain. He was responsible for building the forts at Apuldre and Middletun."

"Was it Haesten who had the ships brought in?" Lae asked.

"Yes. There were more than two hundred fifty at Apuldre, plus another eighty built in Middletun. Haesten means to destroy us. I mean to destroy him." King Aelfred spoke to his scribe. "Have you those figures?

"Lae, it is war again for our people. My time will be taken up with plans for the destruction of the Vikings." King Aelfred seemed to shake himself from his thoughts and smiled at his daughter. "Forgive an old man who rambles."

"Father, who is the wife to Haesten? Is it not the old woman?" Lae glanced at the woman. She was not surprised to see the woman appraising her.

"Haesten's wife has born him several female children, one of whom lives. I believe you know her. However, the boys were of an illicit union, and not hers. I know nothing more, so do not let your curiosity waste my time with questions."

"Father, I am no different from you when you question travelers about people."

"That is not the same. I do that so I know what goes on in the minds of men. It is a way of . . . of protecting our country."

Lae threw up her hands and laughed. "You are filled with excuses." She nodded to the guards who stepped aside to make room for the servants bearing trays of food for the captured Danes. "Our larder will be gone by tomorrow at this rate."

"What say you, Daughter, to giving them back to the Vikings?"

"I say that we make them slaves." Lae bit her tongue to keep from saying more, for her father looked at her with eyes that were too perceptive.

"I was hoping that your Christian values would supersede those of the pagans who plunder and sell our people into slavery. I hoped that you would want them released."

"Father, of course we should return them. They would not make good slaves. They would be quarrelsome. They would eat too much."

King Aelfred laughed. "Now I see that you were jesting. You are a strange one, Lae. I was hoping that, if we show them Christian grace, they will acquire some of their own. It is a plan for the future."

"You are right, Father. When do we send them back? May I be in the envoy? I would like to see the faces of the Danes when they confront the people who captured their women."

"Red, can you spare your wife for a journey? I think she wants to be a soldier," King Aelfred said.

"I can never spare my wife, but I have had to learn to let her go her own way. I sometimes see fragments of Lae in our headstrong daughter, Wyn."

"Red! You are too candid." Lae looked at the women seated below her. "I would be an asset and could help with womanly things. I remember how comforting it was to have Olenka and Nissa with me."

A furor on the stairway caused her to forget about the women. She spied a servant chasing Wyn down the stairs. When the servant saw Lae, she stopped. Wyn ran down the rest of the steps and across the great hall toward the head table. She seemed oblivious to everyone. Laughter followed her like the wake of a ship. She seemed formidable even at her tender age. Lae chuckled when she saw that Wyn realized the table directly in front of her held people that were not Mercians. Wyn stopped abruptly in front of a boy her own age. She stared at him. He screwed up his face and stuck out his tongue. Lae laughed when Wyn jumped back.

"You stupid Viking," Wyn screamed. "You are ugly enough without making your face worse."

"I will eat your heart, Mercian pig." The boy jumped up from the table.

His mother, face pale, pulled him back, whispering furiously at him while glancing at King Aelfred. She pinched his arm to keep him in tow. Wyn stepped closer to him and kicked the boy in the shin. Lae heard the resounding thud, but the boy made no sign that Wyn had hurt him.

"Egwinna, you have a way with her. Take her away before she hurts our hostages."

Egwinna moved toward the little tyrant and, with a practiced handhold on her arm, moved the child back to the stairs and out of sight into the upper chambers.

"Father, we had better return the hostages as soon as possible before my daughter destroys them."

King Aelfred frowned. "She is not afraid of anyone. Why does she strike out? Where did she get such a hard heart?"

"I have often asked that question," Red said. "I think she behaves like a brother of mine who finally met his end on the field of battle. At least it was an honorable death for a troubled man."

Lae pushed bread crumbs into a neat pile, then stabbed at them with her knife being heedful not to ruin the linen. There were stitches where servants had had to repair the linen table coverings because of Lae's past carelessness.

"Father, when do we move the hostages back to their own people?"

"I have sent a message to Haesten to meet us near the ruins of Beamfleot. We leave tomorrow at sunrise. Be ready to ride with us. I suggest you leave Wyn at home so that she will not cause a war before we are ready."

The sun was rising when Lae rode out of the gates with her husband, her brother, and her father. The captives rode on horseback or in wagons, escorted by guards from Red's Mercian army, as well as men from King Aelfred's army and Edward's army. Dogs trotted along with the horses, nipped at their legs, then dropped back as the horses' tails switched from side to side, and shooed them away as they did irritating insects. The dust rose in a brown cloud marking the path where men had trod, dissipating as horses and wagons clattered across the wooden bridge that separated the two countries.

Lae's station allowed her to ride in front, but as soon as they had reached a part of the road that was not so rut filled, Lae dropped back to ride with the captured women. Lae's courtesy was motivated by curiosity. She refused to chastise herself for it. To her right was Haesten's wife, who, despite her age, demanded to ride. She was lithe and sat well in the saddle. It was to her that Lae first spoke, but she found that the woman could not, or would not, speak English. She spoke in a tongue that Lae could not understand. Lae tried Latin and Greek, but the woman only shook her head.

"She can speak only the language of our mother country, for she came here after she was grown." A young woman spoke English with a trace of an accent. Her voice was distinct in that it had no intonation.

"You speak well," Lae said.

"Thank you. It seemed necessary that I learn the language of this land. I had hoped that I would never have to use it in these circumstances." The woman stared straight ahead as they rode, then, glancing sideways at Lae, she burst out with a torrent of words that she seemed to have been holding back. "You are the Lady of the Mercians? Aethelflaed is your name, but you are called Lae?"

"That is true. What should I call you?"

"I am Unn, a cousin to Nissa. My mother died when I was young, so I was reared by Haesten's family."

"Nissa? I have spent time with her."

"I know."

"Nissa is very talented, and she is a good mother."

"My cousin finds you beautiful and kind. It is difficult to place the kindness you showed Nissa with the warrior of a few days ago."

"Enough talk," Lae snapped. She did not like the way the conversation was going, so she rode away from Unn and back to the front of the procession to be with Red. "How much longer? Wagons travel so slowly." Lae touched his arm.

Red pulled back on the reins to ride with Lae. He patted her hand. "You are tired?"

"No, not of being on a horse. I am tired of trying to talk with those women." Lae gazed at Red's handsome face. "I am glad that I am not a Viking woman."

"I am sure the Viking men have the same sentiment," Red whispered.

"Red! I was about to boast that I was wise at such a young age to want to marry you."

"I, too, thank God that you were so wise. I thank King Aelfred for asking me to wait for you."

"Whatever happens, remember that I have always loved you, and I will forever. There can never be another man for me."

"You sound like a soldier. We have those thoughts before every battle. The hours before dawn are the ones where we think about our wives and children at home. The hours before dawn are the loneliest. It matters not that there are a hundred, two hundred men sleeping on the same hillside." Red held the hand that was on his arm. "I will never love another as I have loved you."

Lae smiled at Red. "Thank you."

Tanton's ears pricked forward, and Lae looked around King Aelfred and Edward, both of whom rode in front of her between an honor guard. She saw Haesten, Thorsten, and Eiric side by side, waiting for them on a grassy plain. They had come with an honor guard, but no warriors. Lae looked about. Her menfolk had chosen well. There were no woods to hide an army, no knolls from which to be surprised, and no buildings except the two Beamfleot huts that Lae had spared. They rose in the distance, a startling contrast to the blackened timbers of the less fortunate buildings.

As they drew closer to the Vikings, Lae looked at Haesten, Thorsten, and Eiric. Their faces were as thunderous as the storm clouds, and she loved seeing them thus. Mayhap they had learned too late not to trifle with the Mercian and Wessex armies.

Red rode forward to join King Aelfred and Edward. The Danes showed no emotion other than anger as King Aelfred saluted them. When her party was close enough to converse, King Aelfred held up his hand and everyone came to a stop. Lae was proud of her father. He was an imposing figure.

"Good morrow to you, Thorsten and to you, Eiric," King Aelfred said.

King Aelfred's historian rode closer in a wagon with a special built-in table. He was busy keeping notes for the history that King Aelfred insisted had to be done on a daily basis. She was certain that he would get every word correct, for the man was a genius.

Silence settled over the enemies like a woolen cloak. Lae realized that this was the last time her people and the Vikings would meet with any semblance of civility. Lae was glad that Olenka, Nissa, and the boys were not here. Her heart pounded with the realization that the war had begun. Both dejection and euphoria stole over her soul.

"Hail to Haesten, father of the children I had the pleasure of hosting." King Aelfred spoke loudly so that everyone could hear.

Haesten sat as still as a stone. His face seemed redder than before. The wind whipped his cloak away from his body, revealing strong arms. His hands held the reins tightly, and his horse stood absolutely still. "We do not consider it 'hosting' when the guests are unwilling."

King Aelfred waved his hand as if the semantics were of no consequence. His voice boomed out again, over the crowd of Danes, Anglo-Saxons, and Mercians. "It was our pleasure to have the inhabitants of Beamfleot as our visitors." Then King Aelfred's voice dropped from its cheerful register to one of anger. "Haesten, your people are fortunate that you were not in Beamfleot at the time, for they would have been killed in battle. As it stands, you brought in ships to destroy my people. You broke your treaty with me. You invaded my country, yet you have the arrogance to complain of the words I choose to use. My army and the army of the Lord of the Mercians defeated yours a few days ago in Fearnhamm. My son, Prince Edward, besieged your army on Thorny Island when you retreated. My daughter, Lady Aethelflaed, leading her Mercian army, captured your people and burned Beamfleot. We return your people to you with the advice to take them back across the Narrow Sea to your own lands."

Haesten's face mirrored the fury of King Aelfred's. He stood in his stirrups and gestured toward his honor guard. "We have as much right to this land as you do. My people have tilled the soil here, they were born here, and they will die here, but they will never, never leave this island." Haesten glowered at King Aelfred. "I would like to take my family and my people home."

King Aelfred sat as still as a granite statue. Lae held her breath. She stared into the distance beyond Haesten, but she could see no hidden army. She looked at the men who rode with her father. They had too much honor to attack Haesten protected only by his honor guard.

Her attention switched to Thorsten. He hid his feelings well probably because he was the craftiest of the three leaders. Lae shivered when she saw his stony face. Behind that face would be the deaths of many of her people as well as her father's people.

Eiric, wearing Nissa's handiwork, was dressed finer than anyone else in his party with a cloak of deep red wool thrown back casually over one shoulder to reveal a blue tunic trimmed with embroidered silk swirls that matched the cloak. Twin brooches of enamel and gold were connected by a chain of gold that flashed in the sunlight. When Lae looked at his face, she could tell that he had been watching her for a long time. He smiled at her, a smile that was imperceptible to anyone else, and she saw the corners of his eyes crinkle.

Lae frowned at him and looked back to her father who sat immobile on a broad war horse that was as quiet as his master. King Aelfred turned to the guards who had surrounded the prisoners from Beamfleot and ordered them to be escorted to Haesten.

The women moved with their children toward the wagon that awaited them. Lae would not mind fighting Haesten, Thorsten, or Eiric, but it saddened her to think that war could injure the women and children. That was war. Thousands of Mercian and Anglo-Saxon children already lay under the sod.

The group walked away from the Anglo-Saxons and Mercians to their own people. Without speaking, Haesten, Thorsten, and Eiric turned their horses and rode away, the wagons following them with their honor guard surrounding the Danes. Lae watched as they became smaller and smaller. How long would it take to wipe these tenacious people from her island?

The fire in the firepit was small, for the weather had not been cold. Lae had been escorted inside her own domain by Red, King Aelfred, and Edward, and now they sat around the firepit in her private chambers. They had come in quietly, each wrapped in thoughts of war. Her father stared out the window, Edward sat with closed eyes, and Red gazed into the fire.

Lae stretched one foot toward the fire and wriggled her toes. Her boots were muddy from the spring thaw, but she did not have the energy to call the servant over to remove them. She felt as if she were floating in a pond with no way of knowing which was up and which was down. She had never felt like this before. "Red, you are not speaking."

"I am always this way before a war." He slouched in his chair, twisting a part of his tunic between two fingers.

"I have not ever seen you so," Lae said.

"You have seen me only before battles. I speak of war."

Lae's heart thumped. She had not thought of war as anything other than a series of battles, but obviously there was more to it than that. "What is different about war?"

"The endless nightmares, the people suffering, exhaustion that settles in a soldier's bones." Red took Lae's hand. "You will learn of this. It is unfortunate but necessary."

King Aelfred stirred, and he looked from the window to his daughter's face. "If we are to have peace from the Vikings, we must first have war. Come here. I want you to see this."

Lae moved to her father's side and looked toward the Thames. The warmth of his body as they stood side by side gave her comfort. She fought back the notion that her father, her king, could die in battle though kings had died in battle before. She wavered at the thought of fighting the Vikings.

"What am I to see, Father?"

"Tell me what is out there."

Lae peered hard into the distance. She could see no enemy. "I see no one."

"What is there?"

Lae nodded in understanding. It was clear to her now. This was like the games they used to play when she was a child. "I see the trees, the wattle and daub huts, the animals, fields that have been well tended. I see the Thames. I see people."

"You see the parts that make up your country. If you let one part be taken, the Vikings will come for more. It is your responsibility to protect your people, to ensure their future. They trust you."

Lae tugged at her father's sleeve. "I am ready to fight, Father." Her people would be free of the Viking tyranny if it took her a hundred years to make it so.

"I remember that when we were children Lae would make me pretend that I was a Viking," Edward said. "She would beat me with a wooden sword, and I always had to die with my eyes rolled back and my tongue hanging out in a most distorted manner. She made me practice dying over and over. I am certain that if I were to die on the field of battle I would automatically assume that position."

"Edward! Do not speak so, else the furies will hear you and mock your words!" Lae knocked on a wooden shutter as she spoke. "I pray that Saints Cuthbert and Oswald will protect my errant brother."

The chamber door opened, and Lae turned toward the sound of heavy hinges groaning under the weight of the planks. Egwinna entered, followed by a trio of servants bearing trays of food and drink. She gestured toward the trestle table and watched while the cloth was spread and the linen napkins were put in place. A servant placed a silver tureen and silver bowls on the table before stepping aside to await further instructions.

Edward had stood as soon as Egwinna entered the room. "Egwinna, how pleasant it is to find someone who thinks of satisfying our hunger."

Lae glanced from her brother to Egwinna. It surprised her to hear his honeyed words. She did not think he had ever noticed Egwinna. Mayhap he finally appreciated her. Egwinna blushed and that made her all the more attractive. Lae looked back at her brother. He was smiling at Egwinna as he crossed the room toward her. Everyone in the castle would know Edward's feelings. Could he not be more discreet?

"Egwinna, where may we sit?" Edward asked.

"Do you think that I, a mere shepherdess, should tell a prince where to sit? Sit where it pleases you." Egwinna stepped away from Edward as he came toward her.

"If I sit, then you must join me." Edward took her hand and pulled her back to the table. "Father, come take nourishment with us. Forgive me, Lae; in my haste I have forgotten that you and Red are the hosts of this fine fortress. It seems that Egwinna's charms have addled my brain."

"Your enthusiasm is not taken as an insult. We are all family," Red said. "Come, let us eat and plan our future. Egwinna, you are a part of the family. After trying to care for my daughter, you deserve a place with us. Please sit."

Lae was shocked at Red's pronouncement. She decided not to notice that anything was amiss. Lae took her father's arm and walked with him to the table. She was surprised at how strong he was. Fighting side by side with her family would be exciting, tiring, sad, but ultimately good.

Lae was hungry. She ate with enthusiasm, hardly noticing her brother as he wooed Egwinna. Pushing back her trencher after she finished eating, Lae caught Red's eye. "I think we should make some plans for the war with the Vikings," she said. "Are we to attack them, or let them attack us?"

King Aelfred put his knife down and leaned forward on his elbows. "We have little idea where they will go, since we have burned several of their main villages. I think we should prepare for their attack on us."

"Where do you think they will strike first?" Lae asked.

"Not Lundenburh. This fortress is too well built. They will attack our weakest point, where there are no forts to protect the people or house an army." King Aelfred pushed the bowls and the stale-bread trenchers aside. He made a wavy indentation on the tablecloth with the back side of his knife blade. "This is the Thames. We control the south fairly well, but the Danes hold this area in the north and to the east of Wessex. Their lands are as vast as ours. If we want to push them out, it will have to be a coordinated movement. We will have to string our armies out along the Thames, covering hundreds of miles of frontier land. As of now, we cannot do that."

Lae stared at the indentation. "We cannot do what you say because of the lack of fortified castles. We have no place to house an army, no place from which to strike out and return for supplies. How fast can we build fortified castles?"

Red shrugged. "Not fast enough. We have very little money except for the gold stash we captured from Beamfleot. We have been fighting for many years in small skirmishes, which devours one's treasury quickly. Your idea is good, Lae, but too rich for our coffers. Mayhap when money is raised we can build forts."

"Years from now." Lae put her chin in her hand and concentrated on the imaginary map. "If we could anticipate their moves, we would know where to send the strongest army. They know our weaknesses as well as we do. I predict that they will move north into the center of the land they control. But where will they strike? Will they come down the Thames and attack West Mercia, or come around by the Narrow Sea and attack our east coast? What think you, Edward?"

"I fear, Sister, that your country will be attacked from the west. The Danes see Mercia as weaker. Remember, they know your western frontier is not well manned."

"They would have to pass Lundenburh if they chose to use the Thames. Why do we not fortify that river?" Lae asked.

"I do not think even the Vikings are that brazen. They will not risk passing so close to us," Edward said.

King Aelfred tapped the table with his knife. "Here and here are our weak spots; western Mercia and the border northeast of Lundenburh near Tamoworthig."

"They cannot take Tamoworthig. It is my favorite place," Lae said.

Red put his arm around Lae. "We shall all fight together. The Vikings will not get Tamoworthig. Someday we will build a fortress there, fit for the Lady of the Mercians, daughter of King Aelfred of Wessex."

Lae reached for a silver goblet and held it high. "Let us all drink to our continued pact of solidarity, and to the demise of the Vikings."

King Aelfred raised his goblet along with Red, Edward, and Egwinna. "To the death of the Vikings and to the birth of a nation."

GWINNA STRETCHED HER ARMS above her head; the woolen blankets fell to one side. She pulled them back up to her chin. She felt glorious. She rolled over and kissed Edward on the forehead. His gentle snoring stopped, he breathed, and snored again. Egwinna giggled.

"Edward, wake up. You sleep too soundly." She took a strand of her hair and tickled him under the nose. When that did not awaken him, she dragged the curl down his chin and across his chest. Egwinna laughed as Edward pawed at the air to rid himself of the instrument of torture.

Edward opened one eye and glared at Egwinna. "Woman, you meddle with danger. I am like a bear in the morning."

"That you are. You are slow and grumpy." Egwinna pulled Edward's beard.

"You cannot awaken the bear too quickly or he will hunt you down and devour you." Edward leaped across the bed at Egwinna as she retreated from him. He caught her by her leg, pulled her down, and tickled her.

"Edward! No!" Egwinna laughed and pushed at him, but he was too strong. "Please stop. I will do anything. Stop!"

"Anything? How wonderful to have you in my control." Edward kissed her.

Egwinna put her arms around Edward's neck and pulled him close to her. "I have always loved you," she whispered, pushing away painful thoughts. "I have always wanted to do whatever you wanted, but the circumstances were not right. As it is, you have a wife who carries another child at this very moment."

"It is doubtful that she will have a healthy bearn. Alas, I chose unwisely for a wife. Had I the sense to wait, I would have had you for a wife. I was impetuous and married too soon."

"You would not have been allowed to marry a shepherdess. I am not royalty."

"My father is a practical man. Witness that he is grooming Stan to replace me." Edward nibbled on Egwinna's ear.

"It is too late to imagine what might have been. What is done cannot be undone except by God. I have decided that I love you too much to worry about your wife or about the punishment God will hand me when I die."

"You women worry too much about God. You must do what I ask."

"What do you ask?"

Edward patted her stomach. "I ask that you give me another son."

"Edward, I cannot promise that I will make a son for you. This bearn is barely planted in my womb. It is just a fortnight past my time, and many women lose their bearns within the first three moons. Do not make me promise something that I cannot give."

"I want another strong son."

"Then continue to lie with your wife and keep her pregnant, too. Mayhap between the two of us, you will get your wish. I have given you Stan. I resent it that you think he is not enough."

Egwinna rolled away from Edward and buried her face in the blankets. She felt like crying, but she refused to let the tears come. Edward was no worse than other men. Her mother had told her men were all selfish, wanting tiny images of themselves. Never mind that women wanted girls to befriend. Never mind that women needed daughters to love, too.

"I do not know what upsets you so. Women know that men need more than one son. I have three daughters by Elflaed. She is like the cow that only throws heifers. Stan needs a brother. He needs someone to stand beside him during wars, to stand beside him when he is King of Wessex. I need someone to carry on my name and my father's name if Stan is killed in battle before he has sons."

"Daughters can stand beside their brothers in battle. Does not
Lae do this? Is she not trained in fighting as you have been? Why
not the same for your daughters as for your sister?"

"Some women are natural students of warfare. Most, however,
prefer spinning and cooking to fighting. The Romans showed us
that men fight better. The Bible reveres the woman who keeps herself at home."

"Edward, you have not read the part that talks of women who
tend their own fields and have their own animals so that they may
have money for themselves and learn to be independent. I wish Lae
could hear you speak thusly. She would beat you as soundly as does
her daughter our son."

"Where do you get these ideas? You dare to contradict me?"

"I repeat what Lae has read to me. We have discussed such
things at length."

"It is my father's fault for making certain the girls were educated as well as the boys. Thinking too hard about such matters can
addle your brain. Can I help it that my father had such strange ideas
and has tried to teach them to us?" Edward sat on the edge of the
bed and reached for his under-kirtle. "I must go. I have to meet the
escorts who bring my mother, my daughters, and my wife for a visit.
I will be sleeping in her chambers some nights."

"I will be sleeping alone. It seems unfair." Egwinna wanted to
throw a pillow at Edward.

"I will come by to spend part of the night with you. I have
enough craving for two women." Edward leaned over and kissed
the back of Egwinna's head. "I cannot help the fact that I married a
princess instead of you. You are first in my heart."

"Is it because I was the first in your bed?"

"You were not first in my bed. Ouch! Do not hit so hard."
Edward kissed Egwinna's shoulder. "When my wife arrives, she
will not want to know about us."

"Am I to be kept hidden in these chambers like a leper?"

"There is no need. Elflaed does not like it that I have a mistress. She will pretend you do not exist."

Egwinna rolled over and watched Edward as he dressed. "A
happy time for me, Edward. What of your mother? Will she hate
me, too?"

Edward shrugged. "I do not know."

"Lae says that your wife is pretty."

"I do not find her ugly. I do not spend much time at my own fortress, so she is not often in my thoughts." Edward pulled a cloak around his shoulders. "I shall be gone most of the morning, then I will be meeting with Father, Lae, and Red to discuss plans for repelling the Viking invasion."

"They will invade? When?"

"Soon, we think, but we know not where."

Egwinna watched Edward as he wrapped his sword belt about his waist, buckled it, and adjusted the belt and sword for comfort. She wished she had been trained as Lae had in the ways of war so that she could ride beside Edward in battle. When the Vikings came, she would be left at home to worry. She would not know of Edward's wellbeing until she saw him come home, grimy and exhausted. It would be worse if he were badly injured, for then death teased the living with promises of recovery.

Edward opened the door just as a small hurricane in the form of his son came hurtling through. "Mother! Wyn has hit me again! She kicked me on the legs. Look at the bruises. I am going to thrash her." Stan jumped on the bed and pulled up his tunic. "See here and there?"

Egwinna glanced at Edward. He was smiling and shaking his head. "Edward, come say good-bye to your damaged child. He needs a man's farewell, for he grows tall."

Edward strode across the room and grasped Stan's hand in his. "Son, you are to choose your fights wisely. Do not waste your power on your own kin, but save it for the Danes."

Stan stared into his father's face. "Yes, Father." Stan squirmed around until he could see into his mother's face. "But it is so hard not to beat Wyn. I would like to cover her legs with bruises."

Egwinna tousled Stan's hair, then kissed him on the cheek. "It is difficult, but you are a prince of the House of Wessex. You can be strong. You were born to it."

"I see that you have everything in hand, Egwinna. Farewell, Stan."

Egwinna hugged her son. She heard the door shut behind Edward and tried to forget that Edward's wife would arrive soon. "Where is Wyn? I must speak to her."

"She hides outside the door behind a pillar." Stan jumped up. "I will go get her."

"No, dear one. You will use that as an excuse to drag her by the hair. You go off and find a servant to bring us all food. I will talk with Wyn alone." Egwinna sat on the edge of the bed and let her feet dangle. "Come, do Mother a favor and fetch a servant." Egwinna watched as Stan bounced up and down on the bed twice before he leaped to the floor and ran across the room. He tugged on the massive door until it gave way and charged through, leaving it open, as usual.

Egwinna started to call for Stan to close the door when she spied Wyn peeking around a wooden pillar. "Come in here, Wyn. It is all right. I will not scold you. I want to talk with you." The child ducked behind the pillar. "I know you are still there, Wyn, for I can see your tunic." Egwinna laughed aloud as the material disappeared. "Wyn, I want to give you a hug, but I cannot if you hide." Egwinna waited for the child. She knew that if she kept begging, Wyn would become stubborn. At last, Wyn came out from her hiding place and walked slowly toward Egwinna.

"Do you not want a kiss and a hug, Wyn?" Egwinna slid from the bed and walked to the door. She was relieved when Wyn ran to her, throwing herself into Egwinna's arms. Egwinna hugged the tiny girl and received a fierce embrace. "Come inside. Let us talk before we break the fast." Egwinna shut the door and took Wyn's hand. They sat by the firepit. "Did not anyone comb your hair? It is very messy."

"I would not let them. I only want you to comb it." Wyn leaned into Egwinna and sucked her thumb. Egwinna pulled the child's thumb from her mouth.

"If you suck your thumb, you will have the teeth of a rodent."

"That is ugly." Wyn snuggled up to Egwinna.

"Why do you kick Stan?"

"I know not."

"Do you not like him?"

"No."

"Why not?"

"I do not know." Wyn hid her face in Egwinna's chest.

"If it makes you unhappy, then I will not ask you why, but I do not want you to kick Stan anymore. Can you promise me that you will not kick him again?"

Wyn nodded her head vigorously. Egwinna hugged the child, but she knew it was futile. They had had the same conversation a dozen times before. She wondered what was wrong with the girl and hoped she would outgrow her meanness.

Egwinna had just come down to the great hall from her chambers to see if Lae wanted help with the spinning when a commotion at the main doors stopped her. Her first thought was that the Vikings had invaded, and she froze on the staircase. She was relieved when the double doors opened and Edward's men entered. A woman dressed in a saffron-colored cloak lined with silk followed the soldiers inside. Edward was behind her, carrying a small girl. Two other little girls followed him. Egwinna's heart contracted with jealousy at Edward's other family. Her hands went to her stomach. Her bearn would be the son of a king, like Stan. No matter that Edward was married to the woman in the silk-lined cloak. Their children who lived were only female children and weak ones at that.

What was her name? Was it Eldred? Elflaed. The woman's name was Elflaed. Egwinna had wanted her to be ugly, but she was not. Her long hair was woven with saffron ribbons that matched her cloak and contrasted with the blue-black of her curls. Her skin was the lovely olive shade that never blemished and never aged. When a servant took her cloak, Egwinna looked at the woman's belly. She was in the middle stages of pregnancy. Elflaed had the glow of motherhood, but she was so frail that Egwinna wondered if she would break in two when the bearn was born.

Watching Edward, Egwinna was pleased at how he helped with the children. Not many men would come near any child, even their own. Handing a spindly-legged girl to her nurse, Edward shooed his other girls toward another servant, and led his wife toward the firepit. She was probably one of those women who was always cold.

Egwinna wanted to turn and go back to her chamber, but she was too curious to leave. She watched Lae emerge from the kitchen area and cross the great hall to Elflaed.

Lae held her hands out toward Elflaed. "Welcome to Lundenburh. Was your trip pleasant?"

"It was ghastly. It rained the entire way. The wagons were hideous. The road was terribly rough. I am so exhausted that I must rest. Show me to my chamber. I will be there until the evening meal." Elflaed wrapped her arms about herself and shivered while she waited for Lae to lead her up the stairway.

Egwinna was trapped. She would not run like a frightened rabbit up the steps. She held herself straight. She wished she had spent more time with her hair, and why, oh why, had she worn her oldest tunic? The color was ghastly for her, too. It was all she could do not to feel to see if her hair were in place. She watched Lae and Elflaed come up the steps, and she hoped her expression was neutral. That would be preferable to one of entrapment.

When Lae drew near, she seemed startled to find Egwinna on the steps. "Oh. Morning. How is Wyn, today?"

"She is fine, my lady. Her usual self." Egwinna swallowed. Her mouth felt dry. She moved toward the wall to give Lae and Elflaed plenty of room to pass on the wide steps. She held her breath as Elflaed stared at her.

"Lae, is this the whore that my husband keeps?" Elflaed asked. "I am surprised that you allow this woman in your fortress. Of course, you have always believed that Edward could make his own rules."

Egwinna felt her temper take over her intellect, and she spat out her anger in words. "I give Edward love. I gave Edward a son. What do you give him but trouble?"

"You let the whore talk to your sister-in-law that way? I would think that you had better manners." Elflaed slapped Egwinna across her mouth.

Egwinna tasted blood. She put her fingers to her lips to stop the blood from running down her chin. Egwinna's hatred had turned to fear. How stupid she had been to burst forth with her thoughts! This woman could have her turned out for this, or worse, order her death. Her mother had often warned Egwinna that her haughtiness would lead to her death. Why was she never able to keep her tongue? Egwinna stared at Lae and was amazed to see her astonishment turn to anger.

"I do not run my household around your husband's transgressions. That is your problem, not mine." Lae followed Elflaed up the steps, but in passing Egwinna, touched her on the cheek. "My dearest Elflaed, Egwinna cares for Wyn. She is the best nurse I have ever had."

"Your Wyn needs a guard, not a nurse. By the way, I have left orders for my nurse not to let Wyn near my children. I will also request that the whore not be allowed to contaminate my children."

Egwinna glared at the retreating figure of Elflaed. "If my thoughts were daggers!" she whispered to herself.

Turning, Elflaed stared down at Egwinna from the top of the steps. "If the whore needs to address me, she must use my title. I am not as lax with my servants as you are."

Egwinna's anger kept her from laughing at Lae's look of quandary. She watched Elflaed disappear with Lae trotting along behind. Egwinna looked down the stairway. Edward was coming up, carrying a frail little girl. Two other equally thin children were dancing up and down the steps behind him. When he was close enough to hear her, Egwinna whispered, "Your wife hates me."

"She hates everybody."

"How did she find out about me?"

"I told her a long time ago."

"Edward! Why?"

"I wanted her to know that you had given birth to my first son."

"To punish her?"

Edward shifted the child from one arm to another. He nodded. "She did not care."

"Every woman cares, Edward."

"I do not wish to discuss what was in the past."

"Have you told her about the child in my womb?"

"I will not use that piece of information as a weapon this time. She does not have to be told. She will find out soon enough. I must take the girls to her." Edward moved up the stairway. He turned as he neared the top. "She became hateful after I was hateful. I have regretted it since. She is much better at it than I."

Egwinna watched Edward as he took his daughters to Elflaed's apartment. Fortunately, Egwinna was in the tower chambers with Wyn and Stan. She would not have to come out if she did not want to. Egwinna stamped her foot. She was angry with herself for being so cowardly. To be hit in the mouth was nothing. She would come and go whenever she chose, and if Elflaed saw her . . .

Egwinna climbed the steps. She was past the doorway to Elflaed's quarters when a scream cut through her heart like a sword.

She shivered, for it sounded like a woman in labor. She stopped. Elflaed? Her time was months away. The door burst open and Lae rushed out. Her eyes were wide. "Egwinna, send for the midwife. Elflaed is in labor! Hurry, then come back to help me. I remember little about birthing."

Egwinna raced down the steps. She knew a lot about birthing from having helped with lambing season since she could walk. She flew into the kitchen like a falcon and stopped in front of a cook. "Show me where your dried herbs are kept."

The cook, fat and red of face, wiped her hands on her dirty apron and turned to stare at Egwinna.

"Show me your herbs. Hurry, or I will have you flogged."

"They are hanging along the wall in the back. Follow me." The servant waddled between the firepit and a long trestle table that held freshly cut beef. "There, missus," she said, pointing to dozens of bags of herbs hanging on hooks. "Which ones do you want?"

Egwinna pulled the bags from the hooks and opened them one at a time. She sniffed some, tasted others, then took three of the leather pouches that contained Guelder Rose, Marigold, and moxa. "Get me some boiling water. I want to make an herbal drink."

The fat cook tilted her head, her cheeks quivering with each word, and looked at Egwinna. "Are you a medicine woman?"

"Not really. I have only worked with sheep, but mayhap if I use the same herbs in a stronger drink, it will help Lady Elflaed." Egwinna pushed back the thought that she could kill Edward's wife if she made the drink too strong, for the ingredients could be poisonous when used together. It would stop labor, however. Her mother had used it countless times in the village when women had called on her. Egwinna had always accompanied her to help, but she had never done anything like this alone. "Is there a mid-wife?"

"Yes, close by," the cook said.

"Send for her."

Egwinna stood outside the chamber door and knocked softly. One of the servants opened it wide, and she thrust the cup into her hands. "Take this to Lady Aethelflaed and tell her that the princess must drink it quickly."

Elflaed was already on the bed with her feet elevated. Lae was holding her hand and speaking softly to her. Several servants stood nearby, twisting their fingers and looking as if they would like to hold their hands to their ears to shut out the angry accusations from Elflaed. In between moans, Elflaed lashed out at everyone and everything except God.

"Egwinna, you must come and help me," Lae said. "I know nothing of women's problems!"

"I cannot!"

"I command you!"

Egwinna crossed the room with a prayer on her lips and stopped beside Lae. "Make her drink to stop the labor. Quickly!"

Lae held the cup up to Elflaed's lips. "Here, this is to save the bearn. Drink."

"I will not. She would like to kill me so that she can have Edward." Elflaed gasped between spasms of pain.

"She does not want to kill you. Egwinna is not royalty and could never marry Edward."

Egwinna's eyes met Lae's. "Should I leave?"

"No!" Lae pushed the drink toward Elflaed. "Drink this!"

"It is poison."

"Egwinna would not poison you. Watch." Lae took a drink, made a face and swallowed it. "See, it is all right. If you do not take this potion, then you will certainly lose the bearn. Mayhap this is the boy that you wanted. You are dropping blood, but it is not much. The pain is made worse by your . . . your screaming."

"Get that whore away from me," Elflaed hissed between clenched teeth.

"I am disappointed in you," Lae said. "I thought you wanted another bearn for Edward. You are going to lose the bearn if you do not drink the potion."

"She is trying to kill me."

"Elflaed, she is not. I have drunk the potion and still sit here. Do you not want this child? You were meant to be a mother. All your daughters are sweet and lovely children."

"Does it taste bitter?" Elflaed gasped between spasms.

"Of course. The best medicine tastes bitter." Lae held the cup to her sister-in law's lips. "Please do it for your daughters. They should not be without a mother."

Elflaed nodded and grasped the cup with both shaking hands. She drank the brew, screwing up her face at its bitter taste. When she lowered the cup from her lips, she glared at Egwinna, then threw the vessel as hard as she could at her.

Egwinna saw the motion of Elflaed's arm and knew what was coming. She easily stepped aside and, never taking her eyes off Elflaed, heard the metal cup hit the wall before it clattered to the floor.

"Elflaed! Do not do that," Lae said.

Egwinna clamped her teeth around her tongue so she would not say anything to either woman. She wanted to leave. She slipped farther away from the bed and slid along the wall toward the door.

"Egwinna, where are you going?" Lae asked.

"The lady is distressed when I am near. It would be best if I left."

Elflaed pointed her finger at Egwinna. "I do not want you near me."

Stifling her temper, Egwinna prayed to the Virgin Mary for guidance. "I am sorry that you hate me. I wanted to help you." To Egwinna's surprise, Elflaed burst into tears instead of shouting at her.

Lae sat down on the bed and put her arm around her sobbing sister-in-law. "Everything will be all right. The cramping has stopped, has it not?"

"I am a coward. I am afraid. I am afraid that I will die. I am afraid that I will never have another son who will live to rule. My poor bearn." Elflaed pointed to Egwinna. "I am afraid that she will have the only living son for Edward. I am afraid that she will out-live me."

Egwinna was about to retaliate when she stopped herself. Elflaed's eyes rolled back until only the white showed, and she fell backwards against Lae's arms. Egwinna nearly fainted.

Lae supported the sick woman and eased her down upon the pillows. Lae looked at Egwinna with a puzzled expression. "What is wrong with her?"

Egwinna knew that her rival had slipped into unconsciousness. She felt fear wrap itself around every part of her. She had made the brew too strong, and Edward's wife was going to die! Egwinna shuddered at the thought of being hanged for a murderess. She did not want to be executed for the death of this woman. What of Stan? Would he lose his right to the throne? May Mary, Mother of God, have mercy on my soul and that of my babe! Egwinna crossed herself as she had been taught by the priest, a ritual she allowed herself only on the worst of occasions so as to not annoy God.

"What has happened to Elflaed?" Lae leaned over the prone woman and lifted an eyelid, then dropped it. "Her eyes have rolled all the way back in her head. Will she die?"

Egwinna crossed herself again. "I do not know."

"It was the brew you made her, was it not?" Lae's eyes were open wide.

"I did not mean to. I was trying to stop the labor as I had seen my mother do." Egwinna buried her face in her hands and moaned.

"Your mother? Did you never do this yourself?"

Egwinna wailed her answer.

"You should have told me this! I thought you were skilled." Laying her head against Elflaed's chest, Lae signaled for quiet, an unnecessary gesture since no one uttered a sound. "Her heart beats strong, praise be to the Virgin Mary."

"I will be hanged for a murderess, my lady," Egwinna whispered.

Lae placed a hand on Elflaed's chest. "She still breathes."

"I do not want her to die. I will grieve if only for myself and Stan." Egwinna peeked through her fingers at the still figure on the bed.

"You had better pray that she will not die. No matter how short tempered she is, she is still my brother's wife." Lae chafed the unconscious woman's hands.

"Would I be hanged for murder? Would Stan be sent away?"

"Oh, Egwinna. Do you think that we would be so cruel? I have no reason to suspect that you were doing anything other than trying to help Elflaed. You, a murderess? You do not have the mettle to murder anyone other than a Viking. You have no blackness in your heart. I would be more inclined to murder this woman than you. She gives me grief every time we are in the same fortress." Lae sighed. "You can uncover your mouth. You will not say anything that can shock me. Is there anything we can do for this woman?"

"No." Egwinna stepped toward the bed. "We must watch her, for her breathing is shallow. I sent for a mid-wife."

"A mid-wife will not help any more than you can."

"Does she still breathe?"

"Here, you sit down and stay with her. She breathes. I will go see to the rest of the household guests and wait for the mid-wife. The servants will stay with you to help. If she dies, please send for me first." Lae was almost to the door when she turned. "I will tell Edward that she is resting after her trip and does not want to be disturbed."

Egwinna pulled a chair close to the bed and sat down, resting her hand on the woman's chest so that she could feel the faint breathing. Only by closing one eye and watching her own hand rise and fall could Egwinna see that Elflaed's breathing continued. The number of breaths in a short span of time was alarmingly low. Egwinna closed both eyes and envisioned this woman in a shroud. The picture was not pleasant.

For the hundredth time, Egwinna looked toward the window. The sun had not set. Time dragged by as slowly as Elflaed's breath. It seemed that Elflaed was breathing deeper, but Egwinna did not know whether that was because she wanted her to, or whether it was genuine. All day the servants who stayed with Egwinna had tried to get her to eat, but she had no appetite. As the afternoon wore on, Egwinna had the courage to lay her head on Elflaed's belly. The mound of tight flesh pressed into her cheek as she lay against Elflaed's stomach. She felt no cramping. She was certain labor had stopped. If the bearn were to die, Egwinna would feel sorry, but it would not carry the fear with it that Elflaed's death would. Bearns died in the womb every day. Almost all mothers lost a child or two.

Egwinna watched with interest as the servants lighted the candles, standing on tiptoe to reach the half-burned ones that were in a ring at the top of a tall metal tripod. The candlelight flickered making tall, skinny shadows against the walls. It was like watching a dance.

Egwinna looked at Elflaed, and deciding that, after all this time, it would not matter if she stayed by her bedside. Egwinna got up, stretched, and walked around the room. She had refused another meal, accepting a bowl of mead instead. She knew that it would make her giddy, but she did not care. She drank it down quickly and when her eyes began to droop, she lay on the bed next to Edward's wife.

Egwinna remembered nothing else until her eyes opened at a sound. She listened quietly. The only sounds in the night were normal for the fortress. She could hear the log in the firepit shift as part of it burned away. She heard the calves in the stable bawling for their mothers. She heard the wind rattling the shutters on the window, and she heard an owl in the woods.

It was the coughing that had awakened her. She heard it again. Egwinna immediately rolled over and looked at Elflaed. Elflaed's eyes were open. Egwinna slid off the bed and went around to the other side so that she could see Elflaed in a better light.

"What happened?" Elflaed asked. Her voice sounded weak.

"You have been unconscious for a time. Are the cramps gone?" Elflaed held her stomach. "The bearn is still there."

"Yes, it is."

"I was so afraid that I would lose this bearn. I want a son for Edward that is of me and not of some whore . . . some other woman."

"I understand that." Egwinna leaned closer. She was startled to see that Elflaed's eyes looked sunken. "Would you like something to drink?" Egwinna called to the servant who slept in front of the firepit. "Get your lady a drink of cool water. Be quick about it." She clapped her hands to make the servant move faster and was startled at the loudness of the sound. "You will be all right. I think that you should stay in bed and not travel until your time."

"Do you know what that means?" Elflaed sighed. "That means that I will have to remain in the same fortress with you until this bearn is born."

"When will that be?"

"I think it will come in late June."

"I will stay in my own chamber with Wyn and St . . . with the children." Egwinna took a cup of water from the servant.

"Help your lady to sit up. Support her. That is good." Egwinna held the cup to Elflaed's lips and watched her carefully as she drank. "I will not be around you after this night. It does not seem proper, anyway."

Elflaed pushed the cup away. "Your position goes against the teachings of the Church, and I hate you for stealing away my husband's affections."

"I know." Egwinna did not want to remind the woman that Elflaed had taken Edward from her.

"Your skills with medicine are good. Stay the night and see that I do not die." Elflaed allowed the servant to lay her against the pillows.

"I will stay the night, for it will not be long until daylight. Are you certain you want me to do so? If you want to know the truth, I mixed the drink too strong."

"I am not half-witted. I guessed that. As much as I hate you, I would prefer your care to Lae's." Elflaed closed her eyes half way and peered at Egwinna.

"Why? Are you not afraid of what I might do to you?"

"You will keep me alive because it is in your best interest. Lae would sooner have me dead."

"How can you say that about Edward's own sister?" Egwinna shook her head. Mayhap Elflaed was delirious.

"She never wanted me to marry Edward. She said that I was too disagreeable. I know she said these things because I heard her talking to King Aelfred. She said that I had no lands that were worth having. She said that my father had nothing to give except a few warriors and foot soldiers. She thought I was unworthy indeed."

"Obviously, King Aelfred did not listen."

"Oh, but you are wrong. King Aelfred did listen. He advised Edward against me. However, Edward was young and thought he should control his own destiny. He insisted that we marry." Elflaed turned her head away from Egwinna. "There was only one way that King Aelfred would allow Edward to marry me. I was in my third month when we married. The simpleton priest almost had apoplexy."

"You need not tell me this."

"I seem to want to talk. Was there something in the medicine you gave me?"

"I do not know. I have never used it on a person before, just sheep, and they do not talk much." Egwinna was startled by Elflaed's laughter.

"Egwinna, after tonight I will hate you once again, but for now I seem to need a confidante. I thought my wedding gown was designed nicely. It hid my condition. Of course, it was my first pregnancy and a woman never shows much for the first child." Elflaed was quiet. "I was foolish. I was too young to realize that an impetuous boy can never make a true husband. You would have made a better wife for Edward, had you a better station in life."

Egwinna did not want to digest these facts. She felt as if too much had been said. "We need not discuss this."

"It was a difference of class. My father had the means to cause King Aelfred some discomfort; yours did not."

"I see." Egwinna wanted to be angry, but she did not have the energy. It seemed that the last few hours had taken more than she had to give. Egwinna looked at the woman who had the title instead of her. She wanted to hate someone for the situation she was in, but if she were to be truthful to herself, she should have never let Edward seduce her.

"Do you love Edward?" Egwinna clamped her teeth together to keep from blurting out any more foolish questions.

"I thought I did, but I think that I was . . . am more in love with the idea of being the next queen of Wessex. I wanted to be more than the daughter of a minor nobleman. I wanted to be more than Lae." Elflaed waved her hand. "This fortress and the way she helps rule her country only makes my quest more fruitless. She is a ruler; I will only be the wife to one."

"What a waste of your time to worry about that."

"The only thing I thought I could do right turned out to be wrong. I can have children at the drop of a tunic, but they do not appear healthy, and they are all girls except for my one dead boy. I am praying that this child is a boy." Elflaed patted her abdomen. "I am grateful to you for saving him."

"Thank you," Egwinna said.

"He will never be king."

Egwinna was startled more at the quiver in Elflaed's voice than in the news itself. She chastised herself for being surprised at Elflaed's sadness. What woman would not want her son to be king? "Why will a boy child of yours never be king?"

"I made a pact with King Aelfred. It cost him a lot in gold." Elflaed's voice cracked as she held back tears. "He said that I did not have good stock. Any sons of mine will defer their title to your son."

"Were you angry?"

"Very. I deserve to be the mother of a king," Elflaed said. "King Aelfred explained that his lineage seemed strong until they were in the prime of life, then a slow malady took their strength. They die young. He wants strong heirs. Is it my fault that his line is not strong?"

Egwinna sighed. "Does it not make you feel a bit like a brood mare? I am to be the mother of a king because I throw stronger children. It is a fact of life, I suppose."

"I should hate you more than I do. I could compete with you by having children. If I have enough, mayhap there will be a strong male, and King Aelfred would change his mind."

Egwinna sat quietly and watched Elflaed as she closed her eyes. Elflaed slept, but this time she was not ill. Tomorrow this conversation would be forgotten by both of them. She remembered similar nights with her village friends when they talked until dawn about their dreams and their fears. Sometimes too much was said and too much revealed. The next day, both secret sharers would pretend that nothing had happened.

Egwinna lay down on the bed and closed her eyes. Tonight would be a lost night for both of them.

The days were turning warmer. June came fast on the skirts of May. Egwinna leaned out the window of the tower room and looked across the fields to the river in the distance. The Thames was stitched into the emerald fields, hiding and reappearing like a thread of embroidery in silk. The sun, woven to the sky, was no longer below the forest. God's tapestry was most appreciated in the spring.

A warm breeze teased Egwinna's hair and lifted the end of her sleeve. Egwinna looked toward the sun and let it warm her face. She loved summer, but this summer would be difficult. The Vikings were certain to invade. Haesten, Lea told Egwinna, would not take kindly to having been insulted by King Aelfred. He would not be happy to concede defeat from the Anglo-Saxons and Mercians, either. The worst, so Lae had been told and had revealed to Egwinna, was that she and Edward had burned Beamfleot to the ground. Egwinna remembered Lae's laughter when she told of how stricken Eiric had been to discover that she had led her own army into his territory.

Egwinna thought of Edward. Were all men alike no matter what their country? Edward was much like Eiric. She wished that she were more like Lae. Lae made things happen. She never wavered in her hatred of the Danes. Lae knew the enemy and she knew warfare. She was a maker of her own destiny.

Egwinna turned from the window and sat on the bench next to it. She leaned against the wall. She should finish her embroidery, but she was restless. Mayhap it was because she was alone in the fortress with the children and Elflaed while everyone else was out with the falcons. Falconry was something she had never been allowed to do. Peasants are not allowed to do many things. She thought it was a ridiculous pastime, but the nobility seemed to enjoy it.

Egwinna thought she heard a bearn's cry, and she listened intently. She did not want to go see how Elflaed and her week-old son were faring. Elflaed had a wet nurse and two servants who could tend to her needs. Egwinna had not seen it and had no intention of doing so. Edward said the bearn was as spindly as all his other children had been at birth. He had also said that King Aelfred was not pleased, and Stan was assured his place. The bearn, named Edwin, was no threat.

Egwinna had not seen Elflaed since the near disaster with the potion. She had not helped with the birthing, at Elflaed's demand, but she had stayed outside the door on Lae's insistence. During one particularly long spell, Egwinna had poked her head in the door. She was amazed at her rival. Elflaed gloried in her labor, calling on the Virgin Mary and all the saints between exuberant screams that escaped between a tight-lipped smile. No wonder the bearns were so weak; their mother used all the energy for herself.

The banging of fists on the door brought Egwinna to her feet. She rushed across the room and pulled open the door, expecting a small army. Stan and Wyn pushed past her, both talking at once.

"I did not!" Wyn threw a fist toward Stan and would have hit him had he not sidestepped her.

"You did, too. You meant to hurt me." Stan pushed his cousin away from him. He laughed as she fell to the floor with a thump, landing on her bottom. "May the Vikings take you."

"Stop this fighting, or I will not take either of you for a walk." Egwinna put one hand on Stan's shoulder and, with her other hand, pulled Wyn to her feet. "What is wrong with you two? Every day, every hour, you fight."

"I hate Stan."

"I hate Wyn. She is mean."

"I have told you both before that kinship comes before anything." Egwinna let go of Stan and Wyn and closed the door. Servants did not need to be privy to everything. She was aware that there was talk that Stan was the favorite grandchild of King Aelfred. She did not want to add to their gossip.

"Come here and tell me why you fight." Egwinna sat on the bench and waited for the two children to assume their normal positions side by side in front of her. It was becoming a daily ritual. She hoped that one day they would stop their squabbling. Stan was to marry Wyn to bind the two countries together. Looking at Wyn's lower lip, which stuck out defiantly, and Stan's scowl, Egwinna could only hope that they would not kill each other before their childhood ended.

"I was practicing fencing with grandfather, and she took my sword."

"My sword was smaller than yours. It was not fair. They would not let me fight."

"You do not listen to instructions." Stan held his leg up. "See the bruises? She hit me again and again."

Wyn's lower lip protruded further. "It was only a wooden sword."

"You do not play fair! You do not follow the rules."

"I want to be a warrior like my mother, and you will not let me."

"You are mean. Mean people are Vikings, not warriors!" Stan pushed Wyn.

"Stan!" Egwinna grabbed her son's arm. "Do you forget what I have told you?"

Stan bowed his head. "No, Mother. I am to be a gentleman always. But Mother, she is no lady."

Egwinna forced herself not to laugh. "You apologize for your behavior."

Stan wrinkled his nose. He scuffed his foot in the reeds on the floor. "I am sorry you bruised me."

Egwinna considered correcting Stan, but thought better of it. He would make as good a diplomat as a king. "What have you been doing this morning besides sword fighting?"

Wyn leaned against Egwinna's knees. "I wanted to play knuckles and bones, but he would only play warrior."

Egwinna stroked Wyn's hair. "You should learn to wield the sword, too. You may want to lead an army when you grow up."

"Grandfather does not show me how to wield the sword like he does Stan."

"You do not listen, and Grandfather gets angry," Stan said. "I am getting ready for a war with the Vikings. When they come, I will be ready."

"Considering the bruises you have, Stan, I think that Wyn is ready, too. She can kick the Vikings to death." Egwinna laughed at her own joke, although it was lost on the children.

"Go play. There is a set of knuckles and bones by your bed. I have embroidery to do." Egwinna shooed the children away and picked up her stitching. She had not progressed much since yesterday. For some reason, she had not been able to concentrate lately even though she liked stitching the tiny flowers. The blue thread of the flowers looked lovely on the saffron background, but today she was restless. She stared at her sewing, her fingers motionless.

"Mother! You have heard nothing I have said."

"I am sorry, Stan. What did you say?"

"There is to be a war soon. Grandfather said so. My lady Lae said she was getting an army ready. She said when I am older, I can ride with her."

"It is generous of Lae to want you to be her squire. She is a good warrior and can teach you much." Egwinna tousled her son's hair. It was silky like the hair of a kitten. Would Stan live to adulthood if the war with the Vikings took place as King Aelfred predicted?

"I want to kill all the Vikings." Stan held out a handful of spear butt caps. "These are my soldiers. We fight a battle every day. Do they not look like soldiers? See, the little round part is the helmet."

"That is very nice, dear, but the armorer will miss all the caps he has made."

"No, Mother. He gave these to me. He said they were flawed. See, this one has a crack. That is my wounded man."

"Come and play, Stan. It is your turn," Wyn shouted.

"War is not a pretty sight, Stan. It is necessary, but many men and women are killed in battle."

"I will not be killed. I promise."

"It is a mother's worst fear to have her child sent into battle. If I had been trained in warfare, I would ride beside you to protect you."

"Stan!" Wyn yelled, again. "Come play."

"Enough talk of war. Go play while there are still games to play and time to play them." Egwinna picked up her sewing. It was a mother's plight to give life and have man take it away with his grown up games.

She glanced heavenward. The saints would watch over her son. Why would they allow a strong boy, heir to King Aelfred, to die in battle? She looked across the room at Stan. He was frowning at Wyn.

Wyn slipped a knuckle under the skirt of her tunic so Stan would not be able to capture it. Egwinna counted the game pieces; three knuckles were missing. Poor Wyn could never play games without cheating. From the sighs and looks that Stan gave Wyn, Egwinna knew that her son allowed Wyn to cheat in the name of peace. Egwinna wondered if she should permit Wyn to do that. It probably did not matter. Wyn was just a child.

Frantic noises from the outer bailey startled Egwinna. She dropped her embroidery as she jumped up and leaned out the window. The shouts were accompanied by a chorus of metal against metal as the chain wound around the windlass to open the gates. The dull singing of wood against wood matched the desperate rhythm of men running and dogs barking.

Egwinna watched Red ride through the gates before they were all the way open. He was followed by Edward and Lae, who, in turn, were followed by the master of the hounds and the falconer. The courtyard dogs jumped and nipped at the hunting hounds, who ignored the snapping of teeth; they seemed to know they were elite and that the other dogs were not worth their time.

The stable hands rushed toward the returning hunters and took hold of the horses' bridles. Lae slid off her horse gracefully, not waiting for Red to help her, and flew toward the fortress doors like a bird that needs to protect its nest. Her tunic and cowl rippled out behind her like a rainbow.

Egwinna leaned out the window as far as she dared to try to hear what was going on, but she could not. Red talked to Edward and a group of men from both armies who had been hunting with them. Egwinna could tell that something had excited the men.

The door to the tower room burst open and banged against the wall. Egwinna jumped and turned toward the sound. Lae stood in the doorway, cowl in hand. She came in, not bothering to shut the door.

"Egwinna! It is war! It is truly war! The Vikings have made a huge mistake this time. They had the audacity to sail up the Thames right under our noses." Lae waved her arms as she talked, the cowl flapping in the air like a cloth in the wind.

"When did they do that?" Egwinna felt fear grip her as it had never done before, not even when she thought Elflaed was going to die. She could tell from Lae's voice that the time had come for the real wars to begin. "When did they sail past us?"

"It had to have been a night or two ago. They had to have sailed from Sceobyrig." Lae marched back and forth across the room. "We should have burned that village to the ground as well."

Egwinna could no longer stand Lae's nervous pacing. She felt her heart would burst from so much worry. She ran to Lae and grabbed her arm. "How many ships? How many Vikings? When are they coming for us?"

"They will not come for us. We will go to them. I can only guess that they wish to invade the outlying areas where we have little defense. With the Vikings to the east and north of us and invading from the west, they plan to trap us. They want to force us south." Lae slapped a hand on the table. The crack echoed off the walls. "I will never let that happen. Until my last breath, I will fight Haesten, Thorsten, and Eiric. There will be no Viking blood mixed with Anglo-Saxon, because our swords will drain their blood."

Lae turned to Egwinna, her eyes bright with fevered excitement. "Come, Egwinna. Let us see what the men have to say."

Egwinna glanced back at the children sitting wide-eyed on the floor, their game forgotten. "Stay in this room. I will send a servant up to care for you." She could not wait for an answer. Lae had Egwinna's hand captured tightly as she pulled her from the room.

The great hall was noisy. Servants ran in and out carrying trays of meat, bread, and mead. Red faced and angry, men waved their arms about and bellowed. Two men sat quietly near the firepit, staring into the small fire that always burned, even in summer. Egwinna wondered if they were thinking of peace or of war.

Lae dragged her up to Edward and Red, who were talking with their captains. "How long before we can go after them?" Lae asked, bursting into their conversation.

Red placed his hand on her shoulder. "We must spend some time preparing."

"Time! We have spent time preparing. We must leave immediately. Vikings will enter our country soon, desecrating land, raping our women, killing our children. They care nothing for our Mercian people. I want to ride out now to stop them." Lae's face was flushed. She seemed to have a fever.

Red spoke slowly, as if trying to calm his wife with words. "Lae, it is better to wait until we know exactly where the invasion will come from. They could be invading Wales or Wessex. If they invade Wessex, we will be ready to fight with King Aelfred. If they invade western Mercia, he will help us."

"What if they invade Wales?" Lae asked.

"We will help the Welsh kings. It is their wish as well as ours to rid this island of all the Vikings," Edward said.

Egwinna looked at Edward. "When will the war begin?"

"Within a week or two." Edward took her hand from Lae's and held it gently. "The war will be long and bloody. I will send you to my father's fortress where you, Stan, and Wyn will be safe."

"No! I do not want to go there. I would never know whether you were alive or not." Egwinna tried not to let her fear for Edward show in her voice, but her voice quivered.

"No harm will come to me. God watches my enemies for me and tells me when my life is in danger. I have a destiny. How could God allow me to be harmed?" Edward leaned over and whispered to her. "I must come home to you so I may watch your belly grow with my son."

"You have two sons, now. Your wife has given you one. Do not be greedy." Egwinna blushed at the turn of the whispered conversation.

"A man cannot have too many sons. King Aelfred's line has to continue."

Egwinna pulled away from Edward. "Will the war last long?"

"It could take years. We have to march our armies so far to fight."

"What did you say, Edward?" Lae turned toward him.

"We have to march our armies so far to fight. That is why wars take so long. The soldiers are always tired. Your father's idea of keeping half the men in the army at one time and sending the other half to farm the land, then switching them is good. Still, it is tiring to fight after marching for days."

"Why do we march for days? There must be another way," Lae said. She paced back and forth again.

"We have to do so. There is no place for them to stay otherwise. There are no fortresses anywhere, so to speak." Edward was frowning. "Whatever are you thinking? You always walk the reeds ragged whenever you are about to hatch an idea."

"If we could spend our resources building forts along the borders between us and the Vikings, then our soldiers would have a place to stay." Lae spun around and smiled first at Red, then at Edward. "Do you not see? We would not have to march our men far. Each section of our border, our country, would have its own protection, its own army. I have said this before. It is such a simple idea."

"The banks of the rivers would be an excellent place to have forts," Red said. "The Vikings use the rivers like roads. Our forts would act as gates to keep them contained." He put his arm around Lae. "You have a mind that goes beyond my own. You are right. The time has come to build forts."

Edward slapped Red on the back. "Lae's idea will work. I will help build forts along your frontier, for that will protect Wessex as well. We will have to raise money to pay for waging war and building forts, but in twenty years, the future of our children will be better for it."

"We have some Viking gold," Lae said.

"True." Edward saluted Lae. "Here is to our future. May we have peace in the end."

Egwinna was not certain why the men were so proud of Lae, for she never would understand war and its strategies. She looked at Lae, who, contrary to her usual demeanor, blushed and stared at the floor.

Egwinna, filled with excitement, impetuously tugged on Edward's sleeve. He understood her signal and leaned down to whisper promises of love. With a smile, he dismissed her and returned to talk of war.

Egwinna turned to go upstairs, but her feeling of happiness was tempered when she glanced at the top of the steps and saw Elflaed watching her. It was not the sight of Elflaed that bothered her so much as the sight of a mother holding a week-old bearn in her arms. Egwinna watched as Elflaed's smile froze in place, then faded. She had obviously come to greet Edward on his return from the hunt. Egwinna looked at Edward. He had not seen his wife or son. She felt like a whore. She might as well be on the streets selling herself, for she was no better than the other whores, fortress or not for a home. She closed her eyes. When she opened them again, Elflaed was gone.

chapter

XÍ

CHILL CASCADED DOWN LAE'S SPINE. Pushing aside the web of dreams that entangled her mind, she sat up and looked at the sky. The stars were out in numbers so great that they seemed to obliterate the blackness. The moon was half full, its light still bright.

An owl hooted in the distance. That must have been the sound she thought was a Viking war cry. She had dreamed again of the battle that was to come. No wonder she was tired; she had fought the whole night long.

Lae touched Red. He did not respond. She wondered how he could sleep so soundly on the hard ground. She had put down plenty of leaves under her bedding, but after a few minutes, she felt every pebble that had not been swept away. Lae lay back on her pile of furs. She was bone tired from marching fifteen days in pursuit of the Vikings. A battle would be preferable to the endless riding and marching.

Her hair was so dirty that she did not think it would ever come clean again. She had tried to keep it washed and had tried to wear her cowl, but riding from sunrise to sunset had given her little time to keep clean. Lae remembered with fondness her mother's endless speeches about cleanliness. An Arabian servant had been instrumental in teaching Eahlswith the bathing ritual that she had passed on to her children. Her mother would be horrified if she could see Lae now. Thank God, Edward's family was safe in Wessex with her mother, having left Lundenburh in a timely fashion.

Rolling over, Lae pulled the furs around her shoulders. All soldiers had the same problems except they probably did not care as much as she did about their hair. She scratched her gritty scalp. She hoped the next camp would be closer to a river so she could bathe and wash her clothing. She scratched her stomach. Every part of her itched. If she had lice, she could not itch any more than now. Tomorrow she would look for bugs again, though so far she had found none. Red had laughed at her and said unless she got lice, she could not consider herself a real soldier. She said that she did not want to be a real soldier in that case, just one who killed Vikings instead of lice.

There were no campfire lights, but Lae knew that Edward's army was to her left. Her father was somewhere in the south, fighting against the Vikings who had invaded the western territory of Wessex by way of the rivers. King Aelfred had been able to send his thegns, Aethelhelm and Aethelnoth, along with their armies, to help track down the Vikings who had run toward the northwest. Both of King Aelfred's lieutenants were experienced in war. Edward was fortunate to have them with him.

Lae felt comfortable having those gentlemen to her left, but they were not enough to keep the dream from haunting her. Every night while on the campaign she had dreamt about the giant warrior who had come after her. The dream was always the same, and she had awakened with her hand on her own sword that lay next to her. She was always relieved to find the sword was normal in size and not the miniature one in her dream. Although she did not believe in omens, the dream bothered her more than she wanted to admit. Lae forced her eyes closed and tried to sleep.

She awoke without remembering that she had slept. Red kissed her as he had every morning since they had started on their journey. "Good morning, Husband." Lae yawned. "I am ready for action. I think that I would rather fight than spend another night on the ground. Had we had more time to get ready, I might have been able to bring our bed."

"Time was important. The Vikings have raided our people's homes and our churches, and they are carrying half of Mercia's treasures with them." Red pulled Lae close to him and kissed her again.

"I agree with you." Lae squirmed until she fit into her favorite niche against Red. "Do you remember the small village we passed through a few days ago? When the old priest came to me, I could see tears running across the wrinkles of time on his cheeks. He held a Bible toward me. Its pages were tattered and the beautiful leather cover was destroyed. I will not forget the old man's misery. The Vikings had ripped the silver from the cover of his Bible."

"I remember the look of pity mixed with anger on your face," Red said. "I knew then you were going to enjoy riding after the Vikings more than you ever had before."

"That is true, but I do not like sleeping on the ground." Lae stared at the eastern sky that glowed with the familiar crimson that preceded the sun. It would be a good day to catch up with the Vikings. She wanted to kill them all, even Eiric. The image of his family invaded her mind, and she shoved away the memory of their smiling faces. She must not think of Nissa as the woman who had befriended her and who had tried to teach her to weave, but as wife to the enemy.

Lae tried to think of Eiric as the one who might have torn the silver off the Bible, but she knew in her heart that he would not do such a deed. She had no doubt that one of his foot soldiers had. The Vikings had made an old priest cry. She would kill them for that.

It felt good to be in the saddle again after having spent the night on the ground. Lae had expected to be sore after riding so much, but she was not. Part of the time, like the men, she had walked to give her horse a rest as well as to exercise her own legs. She had always thought of herself as strong, but this trip had strengthened her further. In the evenings when she practiced war games with Edward, her sword felt lighter. She was able to fell small saplings by using a two-handed swing, something she had never done before. She smiled at the memory of the first one she had dropped. She had named it Eiric, and it had become so real to her she had expected it to bleed. She had plucked a leaf from the tree and had put it in her pack. She would use it to remind herself that she could learn to fight as well as anyone. If she died, then she would die as a soldier; a person of action. She hoped it would not hurt too much. Since she was the only woman of rank in the party, she did not want to cry.

Her reverie was broken by the noise of a rider coming down the trail at a fast clip. The messenger's horse kicked up dirt as it was pulled up short in front of Red. Lae reined in Tanton next to her husband. "Is there news?"

"Yes, my lady." The messenger looked back and forth between Lae and Red. "The Vikings are encamped just a few miles ahead in a place called Buttington. They are armed, but not expecting us so soon, for they drink, play games, and fondle their whores." The messenger's face darkened. "Excuse me, my lady. I am not used to such fine company in a group of rough soldiers."

"Your lady will pretend not to hear you as she feigns not to hear all the rough language that passes to her ears," Red said. "Your message is important. Take it to Prince Edward and to your lords, Aethelhelm and Aethelnoth. Tell them to get the troops ready." Red pointed to a nearby knoll. "Have them meet me over there as soon as they hear these words."

After saluting Red and nodding to Lae, the messenger rode away, his tunic flying out behind him.

"Red, how soon will it be?"

"As soon as we can. The wagon with our armor is not far behind. We will don armor and attack today in order to have time on our side."

"I can wait no longer. I am going to get my chain-mail."

"A wise idea. Return quickly to confer with the others."

As much as she had practiced getting in and out of her chain-mail, Lae could not fasten the buckles: her hands were shaking too much. The raid on Beamfleot had not been a battle. She could tell the difference in the way her father, husband, and brother had prepared for this fight. She was no longer the guileless soldier, and it made her quake.

The young boy who was assigned to help her was patient, but she could see his amusement. Finally, she asked him the question that had been rattling around in her mind. "Do others tremble as I do?"

"Please do not ask me to reveal secrets." He held the chain-mail cowl in both hands, ready to slip it over his lady's head.

"I feel like a coward because I am trembling." Lae wrapped her hair with a long scarf and pinned it in place at the nape of her neck. "I shall be hot in this armor. I hope I have enough strength to fight."

"I have been told that once a battle begins, there are no thoughts of heat or cold or anything but killing and survival. I have been told this even by those who tremble." The young boy never made eye contact as he said this.

Lae looked at him sharply. Did he realize that he had just told her that others feared as she did? She spoke not to the boy, but more to herself. "I want to make my people proud. I would rather go to my death at the hands of a Viking sword than to stand in fear or to flee from battle." She bent her head so that the chain-mail could be placed about it. "What is your name?"

"I am called David, my lady."

"It is a good name." Lae was conscious of the metal cowl's weight as David adjusted it for her. A single strand of hair caught in the joints of the rings, and she pulled the hair out by the root. Fortunately, she had thought to bind her hair after nearly going bald while the armorer had fitted her.

"Hand me the sword." David picked up the weapon and held it reverently for a moment before helping her to fasten the sword in place.

"It is a fine sword, my lady. It is not as light in weight as I thought it would be, but it is balanced so well that it seems to be a feather rather than a sword." David blushed.

Lae was amused by his apparent embarrassment. "Do you always talk so much?"

"No, my lady. I am instructed to listen, but not speak. It is too easy for me to forget that when with you. I have not served a lady before. You are not as disagreeable as the men I have served."

"Mayhap after I have fought in a battle or two, I will be disagreeable."

"I hope not, my lady."

Lae laughed at the seriousness of the boy. "Help me to the mounting block. I am ready to ride, although my husband is not yet ready."

"The time will crawl slowly, then it will race by after the battle starts, I am told." David held Lae's arm while she stepped onto the block. Tanton was tied to the side of the wagon. He stood still on command, an elegant animal that seemed to sense the importance of the moment.

Lae took hold of the pommel and swung her leg over the saddle while David pushed her into place by shoving her from the rear.

She settled herself in place, then looked down at his face. He was red, again. "Are you hot from the heavy work of pushing me in place or embarrassed by the method?"

David wiped his face with the sleeve of his tunic. "Both, my lady."

"I appreciate your help. Your lord was wise in choosing you." Lae took the heavy chain-mail gloves he handed her and laid them in front of her before reaching for her helmet. She looked up the trail as Tanton nickered at a group of soldiers who rode toward the camp. Lae's heart beat faster, for it was Red, and he was riding at a canter. She waved to him.

Red nodded to her as he pulled up quickly and jumped off his horse, pulling at the belt that held his tunic. "David, hurry with my mail. We attack when the sun reaches its peak."

Lae sat on her horse, stunned. The time had come and now that it had, she wondered if she were ready. She could not move.

"Lae! How do you fare? Your face is pale." Red touched her arm.

She blinked rapidly to clear her mind. "I fare as well as I can. The reality is frightening."

"War is frightening for every soldier. Those of us who have been in many battles are just as frightened, but we hide it well. You have been trained as much as or more than the men who fight today. You have ridden against the enemy before."

"Beamfleot was nothing."

"You will do right by your people, your father, and me."

Lae took a deep breath. "Thank you."

The sun was straight up, and even in the north where it was usually cooler, Lae felt the sweat trickle down her back. Tanton matched her mood, and she had to hold the reins tighter than normal to keep him from sidestepping into Red's horse. She was glad that she had heeded Red's warning and had worn a padded kirtle under the chain-mail to keep the metal away from her skin.

Lae placed the helmet on her head. She tried to adjust the long nose piece that always rubbed a sore spot on the tip of her nose, even though the armorer had tried to correct it. She had not had time to have a new helmet made.

She pulled on her gloves, checked the position of her sword, and glanced to her right where Edward and his army were waiting for Red's signal. She reached for her shield and waited patiently while David made certain it was placed comfortably on her left arm. The straps were thick and tough-looking. Lae was happy to have the shield, but it was heavy. She hated being burdened by it, but Red had insisted that she learn to carry it. She was glad that she had spent hours and hours riding with the shield attached to her left arm. How ironic that her left arm was as good as ever, thanks to a Viking healer.

The aroma of smoke and the barking of dogs signaled Lae that the Viking camp was over the next rise. She looked to her left and felt gratified that Aethelhelm, Aethelnoth, and their armies were waiting for her husband's signal.

At Red's gesture, the armies moved up the hill. When Lae looked down at the Viking encampment, she saw them scurrying about trying to prepare for the attack that they knew would come. Lae almost laughed aloud at the hastily built fortification thrown up around part of the camp. Its wooden walls would not keep the Mercian army at bay for long. "Let us destroy those who have tried to destroy us, Red," Lae whispered.

Red handed her a throwing spear. "You are more than ready. Get prepared to ride." Red raised his arm and with a shout, lowered it.

Lae squeezed Tanton's ribs and leaned forward. She held the spear at an angle under her arm, tightly gripped in her hand as she rode toward the Vikings. Even though she was in the first line of cavalry, the dust from the horses blocked her vision and made her cough. Lae was amazed at the volume of noise that made its way through the helmet and the scarf that she had wrapped about her hair. The pounding of the horses' hooves sounded like a thunderstorm. Tanton was a well-trained war horse who followed the commands she gave him through leg and hand signals.

The Vikings, who had been running in many directions, now formed their lines of defense. Lae wanted to scatter them before they were completely organized. She gave Tanton a signal and the war horse lunged forward, hooves pounding the earth, his ears laid flat, mane flowing.

Lae held her spear in a trembling hand. The pace was rapid and yet slow at the same time, and she saw every detail in brilliant color. The first of the Mercian cavalry struck down a row of Viking archers. Lae raised her spear above her head and glanced sideways at it to check the angle. It appeared correct. She could not depend on the feel of it yet, having just mastered the technique of javelin throwing.

A Viking came toward her with a double-edged battle-ax in one powerful arm. "Mary, Mother of God, help your daughter!" Lae's heart beat in triple time, and her mouth went dry. A vision of Tanton being sliced in half flashed through her mind, and she let the spear fly.

"Too soon! Too soon!" Lae cried. She pulled Tanton to the side, and he responded magnificently, swerving in time to avoid the battle-ax. She glanced at her target and saw that the spear had missed him, but in the process of avoiding it, he had had to drop back and lower the ax before he had a chance to swing. She had no time to think, for the second row of Viking archers let loose a hail of arrows that showered down on her and the other Mercian soldiers. She held her shield above her head. She could hear the whistling of the arrows just before they struck the shield with a sound like heavy drops of rain on a turret.

Lae could not see the Mercian foot soldiers, but she knew that by this time they were behind her. They would come in as the second wave of the attack. Their job would be the most brutal, since they were forced to fight hand to hand. Her job was to stop as many of the Vikings carrying battle-axes as possible. She did not relish that part of the fighting, but she could not fail her husband or her people or herself. The image of the tearful priest holding the desecrated Bible made her rage against the enemy.

A Viking warrior stood to Lae's right, shield in hand, double-edged blade held out, watching her. When he ran toward her, she held her shield away from her body so that she could pull her sword out with one clean motion. She felt vulnerable, and it was all she could do to force herself to follow through and draw her sword.

Tanton must have felt her fear and swerved left so suddenly that she was pulled away from her target. She tumbled from his back. The sounds of clanking metal made her feel as if she were inside a bell. Her breath left her, and all she could think of was that she was going to die before even killing one Viking. She was face down on the ground, her hand still clutching her sword, her left arm still carrying the shield. She could not take a breath and, in the noise around her, she could hear Tanton screaming. She tried to breathe. It was a horrible moment, until finally air did fill her lungs. She rolled over, pushed herself to a sitting position, and saw Tanton prancing in front of her. Reaching out with her sword, she slapped it broadside against his flank with a backhanded movement, and he bolted. He was useless to her now. She wanted him out of the fighting to keep him from being stolen by the enemy, or worse, killed.

Fighting raged around her. The bodies of Mercian, Wessexian, and Viking alike were strewn about the place like Wyn's dolls. Their blood mixed with the dust.

A Viking came at her from nowhere. Lae had no time to think about her own death. She leaped to her feet, stumbled, and pulled the shield close to cover her vital organs. The sword felt wonderfully balanced, and she grinned at the raging ox who lunged toward her with his sword ready for the kill. She saw his eyes full of laughter and a stupid grin on his bearded face. His arms and legs were huge, and she knew he expected an easy kill.

He thundered toward her and thrust his sword at her too soon. She parried quickly, the clang of metal against metal ringing in her ears. Her training took over her mind and body, and she met sword with sword over and over. Red and her father had prepared her well. She fought for what seemed like hours until one of her thrusts cut the man's bare upper arm. He was so surprised that he hesitated an instant too long. Lae returned her sword with a backhanded movement that she had used in spite of Red's tutoring.

His sword clattered to the ground. The Viking warrior snarled an obscenity at Lae and reached for his weapon. He held his shield over his vitals with one hand while he tried to pick up his sword with the other. Lae kicked it away from him. He crawled toward it, and she kicked again, but missed. He picked up the sword in one motion and lunged at her. For an instant, his shield moved to one side, and Lae drove her sword through his midsection, neatly slicing through his chain-mail, tissue, muscle, and entrails. There was a smell of iron and Lae wondered if it were the blood, her sword, or both. She quickly pulled the sword out of the writhing Viking. She avoided looking into his eyes. His time for crossing to Valhalla could be measured in seconds. Lae looked at the Viking's life dripping from her sword in bright red rivulets. The colors reminded her of red wine in a silver goblet. She would never again be able to drink wine without remembering her first killing.

"Lae! To your left!"

Lae was jerked from her preoccupation by the commanding voice of Red. She whirled in time to ward off the blow of another Viking sword with her shield. Red charged toward her on his horse and, with a swing of his own sword, cut down the man who had tried to kill her. She saluted Red to show him that she was once more in control of her senses, and waded into the fray with renewed vigor.

Mercian foot soldiers surrounded her, and she wondered if Red had ordered it so. If he had, she would be at best grateful and at the worst angry with him.

Lae pushed through the soldiers and spied a likely candidate for Valhalla. After she worked her way toward him, she saw that he was young, too young to be fighting. She dispatched him quickly, and turned away in time to see a Viking sneaking up behind one of the Mercians who was busy dispatching another barbarian to his gods.

Lae was startled to hear a soul-wrenching sound come from her throat accompanied by a primeval feeling of blood-lust. She advanced toward the Viking so swiftly that the shock on his face filled her with glee. He raised his shield at the same time she raised her sword, causing it to glance harmlessly to the side. Lae stepped back, then advanced before the Viking could discern her plan of attack. He stopped her sword time and time again. She tried to maintain her attack, but he seemed to keep her on the defensive most of the time. She changed tactics. He followed suit. The clash of sword against sword set up a rhythm that pushed away all other sounds and sights for Lae.

She advanced, fell back, advanced once more, like a dancer. Her wooden shield took the blows, but pieces of it flew into the air with each direct hit. Lae was getting tired, and she wished she could yell for the Viking to stop and let her rest. It was during one of the moments when she let fatigue control her mind that the Viking's sword nicked the chain-mail on her upper sword arm. A warm trickle of blood preceded the flaming sensation that raced down her arm.

Angered beyond anything she had ever felt before, Lae fought with a freshness that Red had told her would come if it were needed. She advanced, swinging her sword from right to left in a two-handed arc that she had not used with this man before. The third pass sent his shield clattering to the ground, and the fourth pass caught the Viking in the ribs as he was bringing his sword up. She swung at the man's sword arm and, although Lae could tell he tried to hold his sword, it crashed to the ground and made a clanking sound as it hit a flat rock.

Lae plunged her blade into his chest and hardly thought of death as she pulled the sword out of the Viking and turned to see where else she could inflict damage. She felt exhilarated, and she never wanted the fighting to end.

"Lae!"

She turned toward the sound of her name. Eiric stood in front of her, sword held down to show that he would not strike her. As was custom, she did the same. "How did you recognize me?"

Eiric saluted. "How would I not know you?"

She gripped the handle of her sword tighter. If only chivalry did not dictate. . . . "You could not know me. Who told you that I was in this battle?"

Eiric laughed. "After your raid on Beamfleot, all Danes expected you to join your husband in fighting. We need not bring our women to battle, for we can fight our own war."

"I see no shame in having a woman fight. I have been trained as a warrior the same as you."

Eiric glanced around the field of battle. "I agree that you have been well-trained. I saw the damage you did to my men."

"They deserved to die. They were Vikings as you are."

"They were men with families."

Lae's retort died when she saw the sadness in Eiric's eyes. "I had to," Lae whispered.

"I know. It is the way of men."

"And women, so it appears."

"Yes, and women. No longer will I be able to think of you as a carefree girl riding your horse along the banks of the Thames or sneaking into my country to spy. That girl is gone, replaced by a woman who kills like a soldier."

"I am a soldier. Do not try to take it away from me with clever words. I am a soldier." Lae turned from Eiric and walked away. The feeling of exhilaration she had had a moment ago was gone. Eiric had managed to confuse her. She turned to see what he was doing, but he had disappeared into the battle.

Lae raised her shield and sword, but the sounds of fighting were fading as she turned to look for another warrior. At first she did not understand what had happened until cheering from Mercian soldiers filled her ears. She looked toward Edward's troops and the armies of Aethelhelm and Aethelnoth. They cheered as well, waving their weapons in the air, hugging each other, heedless of the dead and dying from both sides beneath their feet.

The Vikings were running! They clambered inside what little fortification they had built and shut the gate. Most of the Vikings who were left ran to the northwest, farther into Wales. They would be less welcome in that country than they were in hers. The long process of starving the Vikings out would begin immediately. The war had begun, and it was glorious.

Lae ran with the foot soldiers toward the Viking fort, yelling as she went, and dodging the bodies that were strewn on the ground. Her memory of her first important battle would be the color of blood, the sounds of the dying, and the smell of iron. But she would also remember the exhilaration of her first kill.

The moon was reflected in the River Severn. Lae stood on the bank and dropped her kirtle to the ground. It was a relief to be out of armor. At least it had been easier to remove the chain-mail than to put it on. She needed only to bend down to remove the neck cowl. It had always rolled with ease over her head, dropping to the floor. Lae felt like a snake shedding its skin each time the ritual was performed.

Lae shook her head to remove any thoughts of fighting and called to her husband. "Red, I shall dive for the moon. Mayhap it will purify my soul. I am certain my soul was damaged today, for I swore at the Vikings more than once."

Red's laughter echoed across the still water. "You are concerned about swearing? I should think a Christian such as yourself would be more concerned about killing."

"Why, Red, you kill Vikings all the time. My father has killed Vikings for most of his life. I do not think God harbors ill will for you, so why should he feel less for me?" Lae turned toward her husband. "The water will be cold, but I feel so hot that I do not think I will mind. I have a need of a bath. We have laid siege to the Vikings for three days. I must have lice, but I looked and could not find any." Lae shuddered. "I hate the creatures."

"I would think they would fear a warrior like you."

"Lice do not know warriors from poor sheep herders. Lice are just looking for a warm place to sleep and a meal. I wonder if the earth thinks of us as lice. Mayhap that is why we are deluged by storms." Lae stared at the water that looked cooler by moonlight. She raised her arms above her head and dove in, slicing the water neatly with her hands. The shock of its coldness did not catch up with her until she touched the coldest part at the bottom. She pushed herself to the surface and popped up like a seal. She swam with long, easy strokes to keep warm. The weight of her long hair pulled at her scalp. She loved the feeling of the water against her skin. She dove to the bottom and touched it, then resurfaced.

"Come in, Red. It is as warm as a bath."

"You do not fool me, Lae. It is cold enough to freeze a normal person." Red stood on the bank and looked down at her.

"You had better come in and cleanse yourself or you will not be sharing my bed tonight." Lae splashed water at Red.

"You have declared war, Wife." Red pulled his tunic over his head and jumped into the water with knees drawn up, creating a splash followed by a wave.

Lae waited until Red surfaced. Grabbing his hair, she pulled him to her and kissed him. "That should warm you."

"I have lice."

Lae screamed and pushed her husband away from her. "Get away from me."

Red grabbed her arms. "You have no fear of a huge Viking warrior, but a little bug on me sends you running."

"Get away from me, Red, or I will drown you."

"Lae, I have no lice. They have all frozen." Red pulled her to him. He kissed her temple, her cheek, the nape of her neck. "The water is too cold for love. Come with me."

Lae allowed Red to lead her to the river's edge. She needed love to celebrate life and push the death away that had permeated her soul. There was no one else that she loved as much as Red, and no one else that filled her heart with as much joy. She would place this moment with Red in the folds of her mind along with other memories of her first campaign.

They laid siege to the Viking fort for more than six weeks before the enemy tried to break through the Mercian lines. Lae was not surprised to learn that they had eaten their horses. While she listened to the story from one of the captured men, she stood with her arm wrapped around Tanton. As she stroked his mane, she knew that she would prefer starvation to eating her horse. Her contempt for the Vikings increased. They had no love in their hearts. Mayhap they had no hearts.

Lae was thrilled to be riding between Red and her brother, Edward. They were so handsome with straight, strong limbs and field-toughened bodies. They were tanned and even the slight paunch Red had acquired from lounging around their Lundenburh fortress was gone. He was as powerful as any of the younger men in the army.

Lae looked at her hands, tanned and more supple than usual. She, too, had seen changes in herself. She had always been strong, but now she could ride for hours, stay awake on guard duty for two days, and go without eating for long periods of time. When she was off duty, she practiced swordsmanship with vigor. She knew the importance of the nuances that great fighters had perfected.

It was a long trip home, made longer because of her craving for Wyn, Stan and Egwinna. She wondered how Elflaed's bearn had fared. It was Edward's second legitimate son, and he had been named Edwin after Elflaed's people. Another boy named Aelfred had died before his first year. It was just as well, since he had never been healthy, poor child. The name Aelfred could be used for Egwinna's child, if it were a boy. Lae counted on her fingers. Egwinna would deliver in a few months. Thank goodness Elflaed had run like a rabbit back to Wessex as soon as she was able to travel. The mention of the Vikings was enough to cause her to grow pale and stop breathing.

It was a relief when midafternoon on the fifteenth day Lae knew that there was one last hill to climb to reach their own fortress. She motioned to Red and, taking her leave, raced Tanton up the hill. She stopped at the crest and looked down at the wooden walls that encased the rambling fortress of wood and stone. The four towers, one on each corner, gave it strength. Inside the walls, the outer bailey was crowded with stables and sheds for the armorers, the tanners, the laundress, and an extra kitchen.

Against the great hall was a tiny chapel. Lae needed to thank God for the safety of her loved ones, and she wanted to light candles for those who died in battle, never to return to their families. That was the saddest part of the victory. She would have to see to the families of the men who died. The children would be put to work, and the wives could find work in the fortress, mayhap.

Lae waved to Red and ran Tanton down the hill toward the gate, unable to wait any longer to celebrate freedom from armor, war, and death. The guards saw her coming and the gates swung open just in time for her to race through. Lae jumped from Tanton, letting the reins dangle, for she knew the groomsmen would care for him. She stopped half way to the great hall and shouted back to the stable boy, "Give him the best grain you have. He has earned it!"

Lae did not stop running until she saw Wyn flying across the great hall like an apparition, arms outstretched and white tunic flapping. She grabbed the child, picked her off the floor, and swung her around. "My baby! My baby! How I have missed you."

"I have missed you, too, Mother. Did you bring me anything?"

"I have brought you ugly prisoners. I have brought you your father with nary a scratch. I have brought you a lovely silver brooch from a dead Viking. It is very beautiful." Lae laughed for no reason except the pure joy of having her daughter in her arms. "You are heavy, Wyn. Did you eat rocks for breakfast?" Lae put the little girl down and kissed the top of her head.

Wyn giggled. "No, Mother. I am just grown up, that is all."

"Lae!" Egwinna called to her across the great hall.

"Egwinna, you are starting to have a belly." Lae reached out and grasped Egwinna's hands in hers. "Let me see. You are carrying a boy; I can tell."

"I hope so. If it is a boy, he will be named Aelfred for your father. Edward promised me before we left." Egwinna threw her arms around Lae. "I have been so frightened for you and Edward and Red. I was afraid you would be killed."

"We are safe."

"The messengers told such wonderful tales about you, Lae. They say you fought victoriously, as did Boadicea against the Romans. I am so proud of you."

"I did no more than any Mercian soldier. Do not let the fact that I am a woman make my stand against the Vikings be more than it would be for a man." Lae returned Egwinna's hug. "Now to more important things. Do you have some refreshments for the men? We are all parched and desirous of good food and drink. They are fast on my heels."

"Do you want to rest before dinner?" Egwinna asked.

"I feel as if I could stay awake forever. I have no need of rest, but tonight I will be happy to be in my own bed." Lae looked down at Wyn, who was pulling a piece of ribbon across the floor in front of a kitten. The kitten, black with a touch of white at his throat, wiggled his behind as he concentrated on his prey. He pounced on the ribbon, killing it instantly. Wyn laughed. The sound was so much sweeter than the sounds of battle. "Wyn, what is your kitten's name?"

"He has eyes the color of the jade stone you gave me. I call him Jade." Wyn scooped the kitten into her arms and danced around the great hall. "He does anything I want him to."

"I do not think he has a choice," Egwinna said. "Excuse me, Lae, and I will tell the servants to prepare for the men."

"Where is Stan?"

Egwinna shrugged. "When the messenger said that the army was within a half-day's ride from here, he begged me to let him go to the stables. You know how he loves horses."

"That is true." Lae went to the doorway and stared across the inner bailey at the familiar surroundings with relief. She would enjoy it while she could, for she knew that there would be years of battles with the Vikings.

There had been much laughter and noise as the leaders of the army had come into the great hall not more than an hour ago. The trestle tables had been dragged away from the walls and placed in a u-shape, with the head table in its usual place on the dais. From her vantage point at the head table, Lae could see and hear most of what was being said. She watched the men who slapped each other on the back while telling tales of their exploits.

The food was better than she had ever had, mayhap in contrast to camp food, and the mead sweeter. She was content to be between Red and Edward. Egwinna appeared periodically at the edge of the great hall, ostensibly to oversee the servants, but, as Lae noticed, she cast sidelong glances at Edward. Egwinna, too, was caught up in the celebration and was flushed with excitement. Or mayhap, Lae thought, she was happy to have Edward home.

Aethelnoth and Aethelhelm were down the table to Lae's right. More than once she caught one or both of them staring at her. Finally, she leaned across Red and asked, "Have I grown two heads that make you stare at me?" She smiled as she spoke to hide her underlying annoyance.

"My lady, pardon me for being rude. It is admiration for you that makes me stare. I thought you ruled side by side with your husband in name only, but I see that I was wrong. You are a soldier." Aethelnoth raised his bowl of mead. "A toast to a most worthy warrior."

"Thank you. I shall treasure your praise. To be thought of as equal to my husband is worth more than a fine ruby to me."

"I, too, would like to toast King Aelfred's daughter who shines as much as he said she did." Aethelhelm raised his bowl of mead. "Who trained you so well in warfare?"

"My good father and my husband trained me to be a leader and a soldier. A good soldier, Archer, who yonder sits, has trained me, too. I must confess, kind sir, that they never told me about the hard ground or the bad food." Lae raised her bowl of mead and drank with them.

"Let us have some good wine," Red said. He waved to a servant who carried a large silver tray with silver goblets of wine. "Bring the wine here, my good man. We are in need." Red stood, goblet in hand waiting until silence replaced the exuberant talking. "Let us drink to those of you who have changed history today. May we continue to have success."

Lae had placed her fingers around the silver goblet while her husband spoke, tracing the delicate bumps that made a grape design. When everyone raised their goblets, Lae did the same. The red wine rippled against the silver-vessel. All Lae could see was her sword as she pulled it from the gut of her first Viking kill. She felt dizzy and nauseated, but she could not create a scene. She was the co-ruler of Mercia and would not show weakness in front of the army. She gripped the table with her free hand and willed herself to place the goblet to her lips. She could only allow the cool silver to touch her mouth. Never would red wine pass her lips again. She would order it so.

Lae closed her eyes to the sight before her and waited for Red to finish. When it was deemed proper, she set her goblet down with a thud. Red wine splashed from it and Red stared at her.

"Are you ill, Lae?"

In answer, Lae clapped her hand across her mouth, pushed her chair back, and ran from the great hall. She heard two sounds — that of her chair hitting the dais with a thud and Red's footsteps close behind her.

She used the exit to the kitchen because it was closer. She barely made it past the cooks and servants, who stopped to stare, and she thanked God that the outside door was open to let out the heat from the kitchen. As she raced outside, the night air felt comforting, but she could no longer keep her dinner down. She vomited in a corner where the kitchen wall met the outside wall.

Lae pushed herself away from the rough wood of the outside wall and stepped backward. She inhaled a deep gulp of air and wiped her mouth with the hem of her tunic. "I need my mouth brush."

"You need to go to bed," Red took Lae into his arms.

"I am no longer ill."

"What made you ill?"

Lae liked the warmth of his body, the roughness of his tunic, and the way his voice vibrated against her cheek. "The wine in the goblet. It made me see my first killing, again. I am not a warrior after all."

"It happens to all of us after our first battle. If it did not, we would be no better than animals." Red squeezed her tighter. "You are a warrior. You will ride in front of the army any time you wish. You will have your own unit to command. You will do more than a raid on a village. You will lead men into battle while your father and I play chess and grow old by the fire."

"Grow old, Red? Never! I feel your youth. It will never diminish." Lae said the words too loudly, but she had to drown out the thoughts of old age for the men she loved.

"Lae, can you imagine Haesten's surprise when he learns you killed one of his best men?"

"I did?"

"You did. Unfortunately, Thorsten and Eiric had escaped before we were able to lay siege. It seems Haesten no longer fights with them. He has not been in the field for months."

Lae felt her heart jump at the mention of Eiric. She hoped Red could not feel it. Had she betrayed her husband and her country by not fighting Eiric? What would have happened to Nissa had she been made a widow? "Where are Eiric and Thorsten?"

"They have returned to Sceobyrig."

"Let us attack them in their lair and send them scurrying about like ants whose nest has been dug up." Lae heard Red chuckle; the sound was like a river tumbling over rocks.

"It will take us years of fighting. We have just begun. We meet tomorrow to talk of future battles. You should be there as usual."

"I will understand warfare better having tasted a large battle. I will be at your meeting." Lae listened to Red's heart beating. It comforted her.

The next morning the late June sun beat down, trying to push July on the resting army. Lae pulled her braids off her neck with one hand and fanned her sweaty neck with the other. She had made the mistake of taking a long, hot bath and now she was sorry. Her kirtle stuck to her, especially the part that was against the chair. She leaned forward and placed her elbows on the table, letting her braids fall. She had forgotten her cowl again, although she had to admit to herself that she had forgotten the hated head covering on purpose.

Lae looked around the table at the men who had spread maps over two tables that had been shoved together. Next to her husband and brother stood Aethelnoth and Aethelhelm, and beside them, Edward's companion, Claiborne, who traced a river with gnarled fingers. Archer sat next to Lae.

"Their strength is here in the waterways. King Aelfred is clever in building warships to thwart them." Claiborne leaned closer to the map, studying it with eyes that were dimmed by time.

Lae looked at her country crisscrossed with rivers, including the magnificent Thames. "It is unfortunate that we do not have the ships now."

Edward pointed to the map. "Our first concern is to get rid of Sceobyrig."

Red nodded. "Lae said that to me in private, and I concur. It would force them to move their base of operations farther north. If they do not, we will keep burning them out."

"If we use King Aelfred's fyrd system, we can keep the offensive strong." Lae leaned forward to see the map better. "With the fyrd system, half of our men would be in the army while the other half planted and tended the fields. It would work well for us."

"Yes." Red looked at Edward. "Do you want to raid Sceobyrig from the south, west, or from the north?"

"The shortest route is from the south, but then we would have to watch our flank. If we drove in from the west, we would have the advantage of speed and possible surprise." Edward traced a route from Lundenburh to the Viking fortification. "We let the current army go back to their homes and call up fresh troops. Red, can this plan work? You know the land around here better than I."

"Lae knows the land best. She has ridden it enough." Red leaned back in his chair. "How fast can we get an army to the Viking's lair?"

"It is an easy day's march. It would be better to start at night and attack at sunrise. They would not expect us." Lae pursed her lips. "Should we strike now or wait until King Aelfred has his ships?" Red stared at the ceiling. It was a habit that Lae remembered from childhood, and it endeared him to her.

"We strike now while they are still reeling from the blow we just gave them." Red looked at each of the others in turn. "We go in two days."

Lae felt every part of her body react to the words that Red had just uttered. Could she go back into battle so soon? She wondered if the men felt the same as she did. Lae thought about the raids that the Vikings had made into Wessex and Mercia. She remembered the women crying after having been raped. She remembered the sadness in her father's eyes when he viewed the destruction of his country and his people. Yes, she could fight.

"Lae, you have not been listening," Red said.

"I am sorry. I was just thinking of my father."

"No matter." Red signaled and Egwinna came forward, carrying Lae's sword. "It is customary after a soldier's first successful battle that the sword he carried by his side be named. It is an honor for the soldier, as well as for the spirit of the sword who kept the soldier safe. It is my honor to ask you to think of a name for your sword. Egwinna, you may lay the sword on the table."

"Am I worthy of such an honor?" Lae stared at the sword that had seemed to have a life of its own during the most ferocious part of the fighting.

Edward laid his hand on hers. "We do no more, no less for you than for any soldier. It is your due."

Lae looked down at the sword that lay before her. Its leather scabbard had been freshly oiled and the gold on the end and around the lip of the scabbard had been polished. A row of sapphires and rubies graced the outside of the sheath, following the curvature of the sword and its holder. The handle of the sword was solid iron wrapped in leather. Gold filigree decorated the hilt and pommel.

Lae stood and pulled the sword from its scabbard. The silver blade sparkled in light that came through the windows.

"It is my honor to choose a name for the sword that was beside me in my first battle. I have thought of this moment since I was a child in training with my father. I wish to name my sword for the Iceni queen who wanted freedom for her people. She fought the Romans with nobility and ferocity. She died an honorable death for her lands. Henceforth my sword will be called by a name that has sung in my heart for many years. It will be called Boadicea."

chapter

XII

SMOKE AND FIRE billowed and danced skyward as if the gates of hell had been opened on the River Thames. Lae sat astride Tanton, held a wet handkerchief to her nose, and watched the Vikings leap from their burning ships into the water, only to be snatched up by the people of Lundenburh as prisoners. First one ship was set on fire, then another. The Mercian soldiers moved around the decks, setting torches to the wood, to the masts, the sails, anything that would burn. They jumped from the ships as the fires became more intense, following the Viking enemy into the safety of the water.

Almost two years had passed since Lae's first battle. Fighting the Vikings had given her an inner strength. She was calm as she sat astride Tanton and watched flames lick the masts, eat the sails, and devour the decks. The sky turned red from the flames and black from the smoke, blocking out the late afternoon sun, making it dark before it was time. The Viking ships slowly disappeared in the flames.

She flicked an ash off Tanton's mane, patted him on the neck to soothe him, and watched the remains of another ship sink into the Thames, its deck reddened by fire. The river was laden with burning ships, and as each one went under, steam arose, hissing and spitting, adding to the smoke. The ships were buried in the water as the Thames conquered the burned-out hulls. It was hell on earth for the Vikings.

Lae rejoiced at the burning, for it symbolized the coming defeat of the Danes. She looked to her left where Red rode up and down the lines giving orders to his soldiers and the people of Lundenburh. She waited for his signal to bring her troops down to relieve his own. She glanced over her shoulder at her men lined up neatly behind, awaiting her command. She had been awarded these troops after the battle at Sceobyrig and the subsequent fighting where she had sent three more Vikings to Valhalla. The blazing ships reminded her of the incineration of Sceobyrig more than a year ago. That battle had forced some of the Vikings back to their homeland, for now they had no headquarters. The Mercians had captured a number of excellent swords and chain-mail. It had been a most profitable skirmish.

The ships below her had dropped down from the north on the Narrow Sea and had invaded Mercia via the Thames. Her spy system had worked well, and she was able to call in King Aelfred and his newly formed navy to trap the Vikings between Lundenburh's docks and the mouth of the Thames. Lae looked down at the sleek ships her father commanded, a contrast to the burning hulks of the Viking ships. Her father had said that the Viking strength had been the Anglo-Saxon weakness, but he had worked to correct that. King Aelfred was a master in strategy.

Lae squinted. She could see her father in the lead ship standing as still as a statue as he watched the destruction before him. Edward was on the ship to his right, looking as tall and as wonderful as her father.

The sound of pounding hooves caught Lae's attention, and she turned in her saddle. A man, riding toward her pell-mell, pulled up short, causing dust to fly about him, adding to the already dirty air. "My lady, your lord wishes you to ride south along the Thames to see if any Vikings can be captured."

"Tell my lord that his command shall be followed." Lae shouted orders to her foot soldiers as she turned Tanton away from the burning ships. Heat from the flames had come slowly, and so she did not notice how warm it had made the September air until she rode away.

Ahead of her lay a small woods that could hide a Viking or two. She signaled the men to spread out, and she slid off Tanton.

She wished she had taken time to don her chain-mail, but had not wanted to miss the burning of the ships.

Red had told her to stay away from the front lines. Well, she had her own army to protect her this time. She had strapped her sword over her tunic and placed a dagger in its specially designed sheath hidden in her sleeve. She was safe enough.

The men had started through the trees a few feet from Lae when she heard Tanton nicker. She glanced back and saw that his ears were pricked forward. Lae drew her sword.

"Look sharp!" Lae shouted to the men. She stepped deeper into the wooded area, listening and watching for movement. The forest grew dense, and Lae cursed her foolishness in drawing her sword in a place she could scarcely use it. She dropped back beside two of her men, sheathed her sword, and drew her dagger. Leaves rustled overhead. The floor of the forest was buried in last year's decaying foliage. Sun spots on the leaves gave them a dual color. If she had not been searching for the enemy, it would have been a pleasant interlude.

Her soldiers, most of them old hands at war, made her feel comfortable. She had asked Red the wisdom of giving to these old veterans a leader like herself who had had so little experience. He had told her it was normal that nobility led soldiers who were more experienced. When she had accused him of over-protecting her, he had shrugged and said that, too, was normal. She had been angry with him for a short time, but after thinking about it she realized that her father had done the same with Edward a few years ago.

Now she was glad that Red wanted her protected; in spite of the sunshine filtering through the forest canopy, the dark woods gave her an ominous feeling.

The cracking of a branch underfoot warned Lae too late, and the two soldiers on either side of her were knocked down at the same time. Lae felt a hand clamp across her mouth before she had time to scream. She rammed her elbow into her attacker's gut and felt grim gratification as she heard him gasp for breath. She forced open her mouth and bit the hand that held her. The Viking curse that burst from his lips made her chuckle, and she jerked away.

As she whirled around, she brought her dagger into position, but too slowly. The tall Viking lunged for Lae, and both fell to the ground. The fall knocked Lae's dagger from her hand. The Viking reached across her for the blade. She kneed him in the crotch, but not before he had gripped the dagger in his hand. He yowled in pain and slashed at her. She rolled away. The Viking cut her shoulder instead of slicing her throat.

Lae should have been grateful that she was not dead, but the smell of her own blood and the stinging pain made her angry. She shouted an oath and pushed her hand against the Viking's unhelmeted head. She did not have time to wonder how she would manage to get the huge man off her; one of her men did it for her. Lae covered her face to keep the blood from splashing into her eyes as she saw the soldier's battle-ax find its mark. The Viking was dead before she could scramble from the ground.

Lae let out a long breath, but she had no time to think about the dead man at her feet. Three of her soldiers appeared with two Vikings under guard.

"We have been through the woods. This is all we found." The soldiers stared at the dead man. "We will take care of this later."

Lae nodded. She knew that they would take the valuables from the man before disposing of his body. Booty was a soldier's right.

Blood soaked through Lae's tunic, even though she had clamped her hand across the gaping wound. She hoped that Egwinna could sew it without leaving too much of a scar. One of the men helped her to mount Tanton from a nearby stump. It was too far to walk in her condition.

"Egwinna, you do not look well. Does it make you ill to stitch people like some old tunic that needs to be repaired?"

Egwinna cut the thread with a knife. She placed everything back in a basket before putting a poultice on Lae's wound. "I am not feeling well. Little Aelfred is ill." Egwinna blinked rapidly, but tears flowed freely. "Lae, I have tried every herb that I know. He is not much more than a year old, and he has had not one day without illness."

Lae did not want to say anything to hurt Egwinna further, but little Aelfred had been sickly from the day he was born. It was ironic that Stan was so robust and this bearn so weak. "You need to let someone else care for Aelfred so that you can get some rest. Your next bearn depends on how healthy you keep yourself."

Egwinna looked down at her stomach. "I do not seem to be very large for the sixth month."

"It is because you are not eating properly. You owe it to this bearn to eat. Do it for the bearn if not the mother." Lae patted Egwinna's stomach. She winced at the pain in her left shoulder. "Send for a servant to watch little Aelfred. Let him have a rested mother."

"I spend as much time with him as possible, for I know he will not be on this earth much longer." Egwinna wiped her eyes with the hem of her kirtle. "He is going to die, Lae, and I cannot keep it from happening."

"If it is God's wish to have a little prince in heaven, then we must let it be so." Lae blinked to hold back her own tears. How could she comfort Egwinna when it had always been Egwinna's position in life to aid others? Lae lay back on the pillows and closed her eyes. Sleep came quickly even though she tried to keep it at bay.

Egwinna pulled her hand from under the covers as Wyn slipped into her chambers. "Come, child. Sit next to me." She patted the bed.

Wyn stared at her, then clambered into the bed that they still shared. She settled next to her nurse. "Are you ill?"

"Yes. I am very weak."

"I can get you something to eat. I will go to the kitchen and get it myself." Wyn's chin quivered.

"I cannot eat." Egwinna took Wyn's hand. "I have to talk to you about your mother. There are things that you need to learn before I . . . before . . ."

"You will not die. I will not let you." Wyn sniffled.

"Listen to me. Your mother is a very important person. You think she does not love you, that she goes away so she does not have to be around you, but that is not true. As a queen, she must put her subjects before her own wishes. She is a very good queen because she is not selfish."

"She is never here."

Egwinna licked her dry lips. "Your mother is one of the most important people in the world." Egwinna stopped to consider this. The world was a large place, but Lae commanded the people who lived in this land for as far as she could see in all directions. "She is so important that we must help her in her duties."

"I do not want her to have duties."

"You will have duties when you are a queen and rule Mercia. You will understand then."

"I do not want to understand." Wyn twisted the linen sheet around her finger.

"You will have children. . . ."

"I do not want any."

"In a few years you will marry Stan. . . ."

"No! I hate Stan!"

Egwinna sighed. It was as useless to try and talk with Wyn as it had been all the other times. "If you remember nothing else, Wyn, remember that whatever your mother does, it is for you." She lay back and closed her eyes. She would sleep awhile, then hold little Aelfred again.

The funeral for little Aelfred was poignant because of Egwinna's emotional pain. She had held the bearn until Lae forced her to give him to the priest. Lae looked from the tiny coffin to Egwinna who sat next to Edward, holding his hand. Her eyes were dry, and that frightened Lae more than the flood of tears from the last two days. Lae cried for Egwinna before the funeral, and she cried for Stan when he tiptoed to the coffin and kissed the dead bearn. She had seen Stan kiss little Aelfred the same way every night before bedtime.

Wyn sat next to Lae. In a moment of thankfulness, Lae kissed Wyn on the cheek. Wyn usually hated to be kissed or hugged by anyone, except Egwinna, but at least this time she did not wipe the kiss away. Lae wondered what Edward thought of Stan. He should feel fortunate that Stan was strong. It would seem that God had only one hardy son planned for Edward.

A few weeks after the funeral Egwinna, pale and with sunken eyes, went into labor. Lae had paced back and forth while the midwives worked with Egwinna. When Egwinna called to her, she rushed over and held her hand. Lae soothed Edward who vacillated from concerned father to leaving it all to the women.

Lae finally found a few moments to doze on the bench outside Egwinna's room. "My lady, you must come. She calls for you." A servant shook her shoulder. Lae jumped up and pushed her way into the chamber. She was not fully awake and everything seemed unreal.

Lae sat on a chair next to Egwinna and took her hand. "I am here."

Egwinna whispered, "The bearn is backwards. I am going to die, Lae. I have seen it so many times with the lambs."

"You are not a sheep. I have the best midwives here. Theresa is young, but skilled. You will be all right." Lae's voice broke at the lie. "Promise me you will be all right."

"When I die, cut out the bearn. Tell the midwives to take the bearn and save it. I have chosen names." Egwinna quit speaking.

"Egwinna, do not speak of such things or the witches will hear you." Lae closed her eyes. She hoped that when she opened them again Egwinna would look healthy. How could she live without Egwinna? Poor Stan would be without a mother. What would Wyn do without Egwinna to guide her? Egwinna had always been there for them. She loved Edward, she loved them all.

"Lae, if the bearn is a girl, call her Edith. If a boy is born, call him Aelfred. I want another Aelfred." Egwinna licked her lips. "Tell Stan I love him. Care for him as you would a son of your own. Tell Edward he was the only man I have ever loved."

Lae took a wet cloth from a bowl and dabbed it across Egwinna's lips. "Egwinna, do you want a drink?" Lae waited for an answer. There was no sound. "Egwinna?" Lae laid her head on Egwinna's chest. There was no heartbeat. "Oh, my God." Lae turned to Theresa. "Quick! Cut the bearn out before it dies. You must save Edward's bearn."

"We have never done that with success before, my lady. It is difficult . . ." Theresa's blue eyes filled with tearful horror.

"I do not care! I order you to cut the bearn out of its dead mother's womb." She was aware of the women glancing from one to another and to Theresa with curious looks. "Do you know what would happen to you if you let King Aelfred's grandchild die? Cut the bearn out!"

"My lady, if we cut too deeply, we cut the bearn." Theresa stared at the floor, her straight brown hair obliterating her face.

"If you do not cut at all, the bearn dies. Cut!" Lae looked around at the birthing tools that were placed on a tray. She grabbed the knife that was to cut the umbilical cord and thrust it at Theresa. "Cut!"

The midwife took the knife. "If you leave, I will do a better job."

"Hurry." Lae left the chamber and stood outside the door, leaning against the wall. She had not wanted to stay. She could not stand the sight of Egwinna's blood pouring out of her. It did not matter that Egwinna could not feel the cut or that she would never use the blood again. Lae shivered. She was thinking such uncommon thoughts.

Another funeral. Why had her life been suddenly turned toward death? Was it an omen of what was to come? Who was next? The cry of a bearn filled her with shock. Was it possible that the bearn lived? Lae rushed to the bedside. Theresa, smiling with wonder in her face, cut the cord as Lae reached her side. Not looking at the gaping wound in Egwinna, Lae stared at the bearn.

"It is a girl," Theresa said. She wrapped the bearn in the swaddling cloth that Egwinna had embroidered with flowers. "A strong bearn. The mother gave her all the strength she had. Her mother was wonderful."

"Her mother was wonderful in many ways. Give the bearn to me." Theresa placed little Edith in Lae's arms. "Poor bearn. She is covered with her mother's blood."

"A sad way to enter the world, my lady."

Lae hugged the bearn to her, amazed at the warmth she emitted. The tiny child had a perfectly round head. She was not splotched or misshapen in any way. "She shall have the best of care. Do you have a good wet nurse?"

"The best we could find, my lady. A young shepherdess. Her own bearn never lived through his first night. She is young and strong."

Lae grimaced at the irony of life. "A shepherdess to care for the bearn of a shepherdess. Fetch her immediately. She is to stay in the fortress. Tell her she will rear the bearn of a king. Get a cloth to wash the child's face."

"Yes, my lady." Theresa took the bearn from Lae. "I will wash her. You need to get some rest. We will also prepare the mother's body. We have to do this task too often after childbirth."

Lae forced herself to look at Egwinna. Thank goodness some-one had thought to cover her up to her shoulders. Blood had soaked the sheets and woolen covers, but Lae ignored it.

"She looks peaceful now." Lae felt some measure of relief to see that Egwinna looked as pretty as she had in better days. "Tell the wet nurse that the bearn's name is Edith and make certain the nurse is gentle and loving." Lae let the tears flow. She did not care whether or not the midwives saw her crying.

Lae did not know how much time she spent at the bedside holding Egwinna's hand, but she finally laid the hand gently on the bed, crossed herself after a small prayer to the Virgin Mary, and left the chamber. The task ahead would be difficult. She had to find Edward. Poor Edward. He always fled at the birth of his children, and she found it ironic that a strong soldier, a leader of armies, could not stand a simple birthing.

Lae found Edward in the stables, grooming his horse. As soon as he saw her, he smiled, then his smile turned to concern as she shook her head. She did not want him to have even a second's worth of hope. Lae took the rag from Edward and laid it on the manger. She took his hands and, without a word, led him to the orchard. He followed her like a faithful hound, and when she sat on a bench, she did not have to pull him down; he dropped like a stone.

"Tell me quickly and tell me the worst." Edward leaned his elbows on his knees and stared at the tufts of grass between his feet.

"Egwinna is dead. The bearn was breech and could not come out." Lae felt hot tears welling up in her eyes. She could not stop the flow, nor did she want to. Edward became a wavering figure before her.

"The bearn died, too?"

"She is beautiful."

"We will bury the bearn with the mother."

"Oh, no, Edward! The bearn lives. She is a fine, healthy bearn with hair the color of Egwinna's."

"How did she . . . ?"

Lae took hold of Edward's arm. "As soon as I knew that Egwinna had died, I ordered the midwives to cut the bearn free. I had to save the bearn, for Egwinna begged me to. I hope that God will not be offended."

"Why should God be offended that you saved an innocent from certain death?" Edward picked a leaf from a branch that hung overhead. "Why did God take the woman I love from me? Have I not been a good man? Did I do something to deserve this torment?" Edward tore the leaf into tiny pieces, dropping them one by one to the ground.

"God does not punish us by killing the ones we love. It seems that way sometimes, but God is not petty." Lae placed her arm around Edward's shoulder. She was surprised when he turned toward her and buried his head in her shoulder. The sobs began seconds later. Lae held him, her cheek against his chestnut-colored hair just as she had when he was a little boy.

He cried far longer than Lae thought possible. When the tears were gone, he pushed away from her, stood, and paced back and forth under the apple trees.

Edward stopped before her. "I cannot tell Stan."

"I will tell Stan."

"I want to see her."

"I will take you. You should see the bearn, too."

Edward shook his head. "Not yet. She is the instrument of death."

Lae jumped from the bench and stepped in front of her brother. "Oh, Edward. An innocent bearn cannot be an instrument of death." Her heart ached for her brother. She spoke softly. "It was Egwinna's concern for little Aelfred's health that weakened her. She loved her children too much. She loved little Aelfred, and she wanted to be with him."

Edward slumped against an apple tree. "You are right. I should never blame the bearn. Take me to her."

"Come." Lae took Edward by the arm and guided him to the fortress. As they entered the great room, Lae noticed a hush throughout. Servants were dabbing their eyes with their sleeves or hems. The news of Egwinna's death had spread through the fortress like a Viking raid. The servants would miss Egwinna's cheerful disposition as much as she would. Egwinna would have been surprised to see that so many loved her. She had been totally unaware of the effect she had had on people. It was one of her graces.

The door to the chamber was ajar. Lae could see that the midwives had done their job with efficiency. Edward hesitated, but she pushed him through the door with a hand in the small of his back, and guided him to the bed. She heard a pained sob. She motioned for the midwives to leave, then, with a pat on Edward's shoulder, she left him alone with Egwinna, closing the door behind her.

The next task would be most difficult. She had to find Stan. With Egwinna having been in bed for the past week, it was hard to tell just who might have been caring for the children. It was something that Lae had not thought about. The best place to find Stan would be the armorer's hut. Stan liked sword-making. The armorer liked having the inquisitive child underfoot even though he had to move more slowly.

It was a half-mile across the inner and outer baileys to the shed backed up to the outer wall of the enclosure. Lae was glad for the excuse to leave the gloomy fortress. She would grieve for Egwinna every day in her own small way, but now life had to go on. Lae knew that her grief would express itself in manic activity. She would force herself to rise at dawn and work until exhaustion overcame her at night. Only then would she be able to sleep.

She hoped that the Vikings would soon require her attention again. The smell and sound of hot metal hitting cold water assaulted Lae's senses. Though not a disagreeable odor it seemed so caustic. Her nose always dried up whenever she was near the sword maker's dwelling.

Lae stepped through the double doorway, pushing aside the leather curtain that hung haphazardly across part of the door. The hide had been nailed to the top of the frame, but over the years had torn away from the nails until it was only left as a reminder that the armorer had been too busy to do the minor repair necessary. The light inside was just as haphazard as the leather curtain. There were candles and lanterns placed around the room so that the armorer could see, but some of the candles had burned down and out and some of the lanterns needed oil. The strongest source of light was the huge firepit that dominated the center of the room. High-pitched ringing caused by the hammering of metal sheets with an iron mallet added to Lae's discomfort. She stood before Rhys, the armorer, who, when he caught sight of her, stopped his arm in midair. The abrupt silence was almost as painful.

"My lady. It is a pleasure to serve you. Do you have need of new chain-mail? Not a new sword, I trust."

"Neither, my friend. Both have served me well in the past and will continue to do so in the future. A finer armorer cannot be found in all of Mercia." Lae smiled at the square, squat man who stood before her, blushing at her compliment. This man was as soft on the inside as he was hard on the outside. No wonder children flocked around him from dawn to dusk.

Lae glanced around the room. Three boys were playing on the floor by the firepit while another trio of boys played war games, drawing in the packed earth with a stick. Apprentices were busy in the corners, cleaning chain-mail with sand and vinegar, repairing knives, or sharpening swords. She did not see Stan anywhere.

"I have come for my nephew. I thought Stan might be here." Lae glanced around the room again.

"He is in the back. I have asked him to read to my wife. She loves the scriptures but I am poor and cannot buy her a book. Stan brings his Bible and reads to her. He is a fine boy, a good boy. He is thoughtful of all people." The armorer laid down his hammer. "Wait here. I will get him for you."

"Thank you, Rhys."

Stan came bursting through the heavy curtains at the back of the shop and raced across the room. He held a huge Bible in his arms. "Lady Lae, I have just read about a great king. He was wise beyond all men and he ruled long ago in a far away land. When I am king, I want to be like Solomon."

"Where did you get that Bible?"

"I found it."

"You found it? Where?"

"I find it every week on the altar in the chapel. I put it right back. I do not keep it very long because Rhys' wife goes to sleep in a short while."

"You borrow the Bible to read to the armorer's wife?"

"She is ill and the stories make her feel better. Was I wrong to find it?" Stan's eyes were wide, and he shifted from foot to foot.

"You were not wrong, Stan, but the priest should be asked before you borrow the only Bible that we have for miles and miles. It is a precious book," Lae said. "Come, let us take the Bible back to the chapel. I have need to talk with you." Lae glanced at Rhys. "We will make some arrangement so that Stan can still read to your wife. It is good for Stan."

The chapel was cool, quiet, and smelled sweet compared to the hot and noisy armorer's shop. Stan pulled a stool up to the altar and replaced the Bible, turning it just so. It looked as if it had never been moved. No wonder the priest had never complained that the Bible had been stolen.

Lae helped Stan replace the stool and, taking his hand, led him to the altar. "Stan, I have something to tell you that is very difficult for me."

Stan stared at her pensively. "Are you going to tell me that I can no longer borrow the Bible?"

"It is much more serious than that. Your mother has been very ill the last few months. Today she gave birth to a little girl, your little sister. Your mother asked that you and I together care for our little girl." Lae inhaled, then let her breath out slowly. "Your mother was not strong enough. She died a while ago."

Stan blinked. "She died?"

"Yes. Her last words were of you. She loved you very much." Lae took the child in her arms and let him sob. She stroked his hair, as she had done for his father. When the deluge was over, she wiped Stan's eyes with the sleeve of her kirtle. "Come, let us go say good-bye to your mother. She looks beautiful."

"You are sure the bearn lives?" Stan took Lae's hand.

"Yes, a pretty little girl named Edith. She looks as if she is wearing a copper-colored hat."

"May I hold her?"

"Hold her? You will have to protect her all her life, for she has no mother and your father will be fighting the Vikings. It will be your responsibility to see that no harm comes to her." Lae looked at Stan from the corner of her eye. He stared at the floor. "Do you think you will be able to do the task?"

"Do I have to fix the hippens when she wets?"

Lae laughed. "No, we have a nurse to do that. You will have to do important things like make certain she is educated and married properly."

"Oh, that is easy. I can do that."

Lae wrapped her arm around Stan's shoulders as they stepped into the sunshine and left the chapel behind them. She bent down and kissed him on the cheek. "I have faith in you, Nephew. You will do well by little Edith."

Tanton's mane rippled in time with the soft canter that Lae preferred when riding for pleasure. She had to get away from the fortress and all its sadness. Never had death seemed to permeate every corner of the place as it had today. Lae was glad that although her father had grown thin, he was still much the warrior. His health was good, although he ate less. Her mother had assured her that this was normal. If anything happened to her father . . . Lae refused to finish the thought.

Egwinna's funeral had been heart-rending as it always was when someone was buried while still young. Egwinna had been placed in a grave beside her son, little Aelfred, as Edward had ordered. Stan had cried throughout the funeral, a quiet sniffling that had caused as many tears as the sight of Egwinna in a coffin on linen sheets. Egwinna had not had time to say what she had wanted done with her gold cross with the emerald stone that Edward had given her, but Lae could not bury it with her. Although it was against custom, Lae removed the cross from Egwinna before the funeral. Little Edith should have something from her mother.

Egwinna had looked incomplete without the Celtic cross she had worn every day for years. Lae had wondered at the wisdom of such a deed, but when she had placed the cross near the bearn's fingers, little Edith had grabbed it. Lae had taken it as a sign.

The sky was gray with wisps of clouds intermingled with fog rising from the River Thames. The air had a sting to it that made Lae's eyes water. Winter would be here soon. Mayhap the Vikings would not be sending out so many raiding parties now that winter was coming. They tended to pull back into their camps and fortresses and hole up like hibernating animals.

Lae sighed. What was she going to do with Wyn? The child had never cried for Egwinna, and yet Lae knew her pain was deeper than anyone else's. Wyn had loved Egwinna more than she loved her own mother. Lae winced. It hurt to admit that her own child loved another woman more, but it was the truth. How could she cope with Wyn as Egwinna had? She could not. Lae had expected a huge temper tantrum from Wyn. If the child had thrown her toys, broken her mirrors, or kicked Stan until he was black and blue, Lae could have dealt with that, but for Wyn to do nothing was uncanny.

The only thing Lae could do was to spend time with her daughter, though she did not think that an abundance of love could make up for the child's loss or her pain. Wyn would be like the tree that was injured. Instead of weeping, a tree enfolds its wound in hardened growth, hidden from view. As the tree ages, the injury often finishes it.

The wind became stronger and a soft rain fell, so Lae turned Tanton toward the fortress. She was surprised to see Red and Edward riding toward her. Mayhap there was another Viking raid that they could stop. She nudged Tanton with her heels and urged him forward at a run. As she rode up to the men, she was appalled at the looks on their faces. Something far more serious than a Viking raid brought them out to meet her.

"What is wrong?" Lae pulled Tanton to a stop. "Has anything happened to Wyn? To Stan? To Edith?"

Edward shook his head. "Far worse than losing a bearn, Lae. We are about to lose a father."

"You jest! Why do you say such horrors?"

"It is true, Lae." Red reached for her hand and clasped it. "Word has been sent to us. You and Edward are needed in Wintanceaster immediately. I will stay here with Aethelhelm and Aethelnoth to protect our borders from the Vikings. King Aelfred also asks that Stan, Wyn, and Edith be taken to see him."

"He has asked for Edward's other children, has he not?"

"Yes," Red said.

Lae reined Tanton away from the two men and rode alone. It could not be true, but she knew it was. Her father had become much frailer the last few years, though she had refused to acknowledge it. Each Viking raid took away a piece of his health. She put her hands over her ears, bent her head down, and closed her eyes so that she could think of nothing for a minute.

When Lae took her hands from her ears, she was ready for more grief. She turned Tanton back toward the fortress. Red and Edward had waited. "I will ride to Wintanceaster the day after tomorrow at sunrise. I will need at least four wagons, a pair of two-horse litters, several servants, and chests for clothing. I will take part of my army for an escort, and the rest can stay here to protect Lundenburh." Lae looked at the gray sky. "I am trying to contain my anger at God. I do not know why this has to be the year of death for us."

It was the longest span of five days Lae had ever spent, but at last she was inside her father's fortress. She fell into her mother's arms, marveling at the strength still there, and finally wept. She cried for her father, for her mother, but mostly for herself. Lae did not want to be the oldest generation.

"How selfish of me, Mother. I should not have burdened you with my tears. How is he?"

"Nonsense. I have had time to get used to your father's illness. You have not. I wish I could say that he was better, but the truth is, he worsens each day." Eahlswith's smile quivered as she tried to hold back her own tears. "I have prepared a meal for all of you. As soon as Edward comes in from the stables, we will eat. It is merely a small meal for the family. I am anxious to see the children. Where are they?"

"Your servants have taken them to the south tower. I wanted them kept away from Father until he was ready to see them." Lae untied her cloak and gave it to a servant. "Is Edward's wife coming?"

"Elflaed is here. She arrived a few days ago. My, I have never seen anyone breed like she does. She was with Edward for one night and now she blooms like the yowling cats in the stables."

"Mother! You are supposed to be a Christian woman. What a tongue you have."

"It is difficult to like someone who has lied about you, me, and even Aethelgifu, who is now in her grave. Thank god she became an abbess before she died."

"She attained her dream," Lae said.

"That she did." Eahlswith brushed a tear away. "It is always devastating to watch your children die. That is why I hate Elflaed. I cannot help it. She still makes up lies about Aethelgifu. How can one tell tales of the dead?"

"I have tried to ignore her lying, but I cannot," Lae said.

"Her tongue has never stopped clattering out with lies." Eahlswith shrugged. "When you age, you say what you want. I do not care what other people think, with the exception of your father."

"I am prepared to stay until he is better."

"Or until his funeral. Make no mistake about his condition, Lae. He is a dying man. King Aelfred has spent his life loving God, and now he is about to meet him."

"I will not be able to eat dinner. I will be anxious to visit with Father."

"You will have to wait until I say he may see you. I am ruler of this fortress, and I rule it as you do Mercia. I have sent for your younger brother and sister, but I do not expect them for a few days. You will have to comfort your sister, Aefthryth. She has always listened to you better than to me."

"Yes, Mother, I will. She seems a child to me in spite of her marriage." Lae impulsively kissed her mother. "My brother will grieve, but quietly."

The evening meal had been over for more than an hour before Lae and Edward were permitted into their father's room. Lae tried to prepare herself for the shock of seeing her emaciated father in bed instead of in battle, but she was not successful.

She sat near him on the huge bed at his right hand, while Edward sat in a chair next to the bed on his left. She reached for her father's hand and held it in both of hers. It felt as hot and dry as parchment, the result of a long, feverish illness. Lae wanted him to tell her that he was going to get well, but he only spoke to Edward about how he should rule Wessex.

"You will have trouble from your cousin, Aethelwold. He will claim the throne as the oldest son of my oldest brother," King Aelfred said.

"Some will follow him," Edward said.

"Most likely the Danes. They will do anything to cause a split in the nobility of Wessex," Lae said.

"And Mercia," Edward said.

"He has some claim to the throne," King Aelfred said.

"Our grandfather made provisions so that Wessex would not be divided," Edward said. "But he failed to consider the next generation — my generation."

"You told us, Father, that your father, King Aethelwulf, wanted the line of succession to go from one brother to the other in order of birth. Has that been satisfactory?" Lae asked.

"He sought to preserve Wessex and prevent brother from fighting brother. My oldest brother became king when I had seen only nine summers." Aelfred closed his eyes.

Lae looked at her father's face. His skin was jaundiced, his eyes were sunken, and even his beard, once shiny and full, had grown thinner, as if to mock the thinness of the man under it. In thirteen short years, Wessex had seen three kings crowned and three kings buried. Her father was king before he expected to be. The dead brother had a son too young to rule, and the line succession was as King Aelfred's father had wished.

"None of the other sons have contested Edward's right to rule. Aethelwold has always wanted power." Lae shook her head. "He would not be a fit ruler."

"Father, I know that Aethelwold will fight me for the throne," Edward said.

"And what will he use for money? Where will he get an army? Most of our nobility supports Edward," Lae said.

"He will go to the Danes," Edward said.

"Ah! The traitor. Of course!" Lae said.

"Lae, you have done well by Wessex. Will you promise me that you will help Edward as you have helped me? There is strength with our two countries acting as one." With his free hand, King Aelfred touched the pages of his latest manuscript that shared his bed. "I want the words written that our countries became strong together."

"Father, you need not have asked. I want both our peoples to live in peace. I love Edward and his children. That is a better reason than any other that I can relate."

"Well said. I feel I can rest for eternity knowing that my two oldest children will continue in my stead." King Aelfred lay against the pillows, his eyes closed.

"Father, you do not have to leave us." Lae swallowed the catch in her throat.

"I go to join your sister, Aethelgifu. An abbess is not a lowly escort into heaven. I dreamed last night that she waited for me. I would stay if I could. I had wanted to see the new century, but I fear that I will miss it by a month or two," King Aelfred said.

"How can you make light of your . . ."

"Lae, do not fret. I go to the greatest king of all. I will walk with God. Do not deny me that."

"I would that I could deny that to you, Father. It is not fair that I should lose a father from whom I have yet so much to learn."

King Aelfred withdrew his hand from hers. "You have a good teacher in Red." He opened his eyes. "I have need of sleep. Come see me tomorrow and bring my grandchildren to me. I am most anxious to see the youngest child. What is she named?"

Edward cleared his throat. "Egwinna named her Edith."

King Aelfred nodded. "A plain name, but solid. Is she a healthy princess?"

"She is a healthy bearn," Edward said.

King Aelfred waved his hand. "Forgive me. I must rest."

Lae plucked at the woolen cover that lay across her father's shrunken body. "There will be nine grandchildren. Elflaed is here, too."

"Good. It makes an old man's death easier if he see his lineage spread out before him like the tail of a peacock."

"Oh, Father!" Lae kissed her father's hot, dry forehead, slipped off the bed, and backed toward the door, not wanting to give up a second of seeing him. "Good night, Father."

Edward followed her out. "He will not live much past tomorrow. I knew someday I would be King of Wessex, but now that the time has come, I would gladly give up that honor. Were it possible for King Aelfred to rule forever, I would be happy."

October 26, 899, the day of King Aelfred's death was sunny. Lae hated the sky for being so cheerful when tears should fall continuously from the clouds for a great king and a wonderful man. Lae cried until she had no tears left. Her mother did well, crying at first, then busying herself with preparations for housing the extra guests who would arrive, comforting her children and grandchildren, and seeing to the servants. She won over Wyn, who took to her grandmother easily. Much to Lae's surprise, Wyn glowed when she was praised by Eahlswith.

It struck Lae that Egwinna had handled Wyn the same way. It was true that the child needed gentling as some horses did when they were saddle broken. Lae wished the nurse had not been so harsh with the child when she was a knee-baby. She should have known something was wrong with the nurse. The effects were long lasting. There were times, even now, when she was trying to soothe Wyn that her daughter eyed her warily, like a beaten dog. Could it have been that all the anger was a cover for vulnerability? Lae cried anew at that revelation. Was it too late to undo the damage? She had lost a father and driven away her daughter. Who could lose so much and survive?

Lae turned from the window. How stupid she was for her self-pity. She had many reasons to go on. She loved Wyn, and the child knew it. Lae had to get ready for the funeral. She wanted to visit with her brothers and sister before the long, public ceremony. There would be people from all the British and European countries here for the funeral. She wondered if Haesten would dare show his face. He had not fought them since they had burned Sceobyrig six summers ago. In fact, she remembered that her father had said that, although Haesten refused to sign a binding peace treaty, he had pledged to keep the peace for the Vikings he controlled. That, of course, did not include Thorsten and his son, Eiric.

She wondered what Eiric was doing. It seemed so long since she had spoken to him on the battlefield. She mentally berated herself for thinking of Eiric at a time like this.

The funeral was elaborate because of the nature of the man and his admirers. Lae glanced around the church at the leaders from all over Britain. King Aelfred had convinced them to unite, and then had led them to victory after victory. She felt a surge of pride for her father as she saw the stricken faces of his colleagues. They had loved him dearly. She wished Red had been able to leave the fortress, but times were unsettled with her father's death and Edward's coronation. For the first time, the Vikings would have three armies to fight instead of four. Red had to stay at the Lundenburh fortress to signal the Danes that everything was as it had been.

Lae had allowed the children to leave after the mass said in King Aelfred's honor. Stan and Wyn were like two young colts forced to stay in a stall, kicking and hitting each other until they had to be separated. Part of the time, Stan held little Edith, and they kept each other entertained. Lae noticed for the first time that Wyn ignored the baby.

Elflaed was there with her children, taking her rightful place next to Edward. It startled Lae to think that Elflaed was Queen of Wessex instead of her mother, and for a moment she felt the pain of what no longer was well up inside her.

Lae hastily said four Hail Marys for penance and vowed that she would confess her sin to the priest before she left the church.

She would have to be extra kind to Elflaed to make up for her resentful thoughts.

The day after King Aelfred's funeral, everyone assembled in the church for the crowning of the new King of Wessex. It was a bittersweet ceremony, as all such ceremonies were. Her father had been buried in the church yard, and Edward waited to be crowned where the coffin had stood. The sun had shone for her father's funeral and now, for Edward's coronation, it had hidden behind thunder clouds.

Was it an omen? No, it was merely normal fall weather. Lae sat quietly in the chairs provided for the family and watched Stan watch his father. Stan's mouth was open, and he leaned forward, gripping the back of the chair in front of him. His eyes never wavered throughout the entire ceremony.

Lae leaned forward and whispered, "See how handsome your father looks?" Stan did not notice that she had spoken to him.

The trip home was melancholy. Lae had stayed an extra three weeks to help her mother, but she had soon grown restless. She had used the weather as an excuse to return to Lundenburh. She had been shocked to notice the large amount of gray mixed with her mother's silver-blonde hair. It was difficult to see, but it was another reminder that her mother was growing older, making parting all the more difficult.

Their cousin, Aethelwold, had raced off to East Anglia as soon as Aelfred had died. Edward's spies had sent a message back that he left for Northumbria as soon as he had forged a treaty with the East Anglian Danes. Lae sent her own spies north to watch what Wold did there. She was not surprised when she and Edward learned that another alliance had been formed with the hated Vikings. Wold would be a problem, but he was not as good at war as she and Edward were. Lae sighed. Another complication.

Her heart soared when she saw the towers of her fortress. It would be good to get home. She had the driver stop the wagon, and she mounted Tanton without a saddle, her extra-full traveling tunic allowing her the freedom to do so. She liked riding bareback, but had not done so for years. She let Tanton go. The cold wind whistled through her hair and made her ears ache. She had not bothered with a cowl, as usual.

The gates opened and Tanton's hooves clattered across the wooden bridge as she rode into the outer bailey. She continued past the huts of the tanner, the armorer, and the others until she was at the gates of the inner bailey. They opened just in time for her to sweep through. She rode up to the doors of the great hall, slid off Tanton, and threw the reins to a groom who had run after her all the way from the stables.

She jerked open the doors and spied her husband running toward her. Lae loved him so much that at times like this, she could not get close enough to him. She thought her heart would burst at the sight of him.

"Red!"

"What with all the noise you created, I thought the Vikings had invaded." Red grabbed Lae and whirled her around.

Lae grasped him by the shoulders. "Take me to our chambers and shut the doors to everyone. I want a real homecoming. I have to celebrate life!"

BOOK II

907 a.d. — 911 a.d.

chapter

XIII

he pitiful crowd that stood before Lae was ragged and skinny. Some of the young men were Stan's age, nineteen summers, but they had no youthful glow, no hope for the future in their faces as he had.

Lae leaned back against the hard wooden throne and stared at their leader, Ingimund, who, by contrast, was dressed in a fine tunic of blue. With effort, Lae kept the contempt she had for this man from her voice. "I have a document from the Irish king that says you were forced from their country. They no longer want to tolerate a Viking who lies and steals from them." She gestured to a folded parchment that was held by Stan.

"Forgive me, my lady, but King Niall has misunderstood me. I am an innocent man. There was a plot against me, and I have been falsely accused by my enemies."

Ingimund's voice was as cold as the winter sky. Lae wanted to ask him why he was so finely dressed when the people he led were so ragged, but she knew that Ingimund would have another false answer. She wished Red had been able to leave his bed for this meeting. He was so good at burrowing the truth from people.

Lae glanced at Ingimund's entourage. She was concerned about one frail-looking woman who stood beside Ingimund; her worn, gray tunic contrasted with his fine tunic. The young woman's hair was the color of wheat, but it was lifeless and dull. The only sparkle about her was in her eyes, and Lae wondered if she were feverish from being half starved. She could not have been more than eighteen. Wyn's age probably.

Wyn, sitting on the dais with her mother but on a smaller throne, leaned over and whispered, "Mother, they smell. Send them away."

Would Lae never be able to teach Wyn how to govern? She glared at her impudent daughter. The child . . . no, young woman, was interested in her own comfort and no one else's. Lae placed her hand on Wyn's arm. "Do not be so hasty to judge. Hear Ingimund's arguments first. Think about what he has to say." She had been trying for the past year, without success, to teach Wyn the finer points of diplomacy.

Stan cleared his throat and frowned at Wyn. He sat to the left of his aunt in a similar throne made different only in that it had the crest of the House of Wessex instead of the crest of the House of Mercia.

Lae glanced at Stan and remembered that she had had to listen to these two argue and bicker since they had been children. It seemed now that they were almost grown, the bickering would continue from habit, if nothing else.

Lae turned her attention back to the Norseman who stood in front of her. Ingimund was not one of the Vikings who had attacked her country and her brother's, but she did not trust him. Given a chance, he would be as quick to invade Mercia and Wessex as they had been.

Igimund stood before her with hands clasped behind his back. If there had not been so many children who were obviously tired, ill-fed, diseased, and poor, she would have made him stand there longer before she allowed him to speak.

A bearn, whom a mother held in her arms, made Lae angry with the man who had dragged these people all over Wales and Ireland trying to find them a home. The bearn lay in a ragged blanket, listless and thin, his belly protruding above rags wrapped around his hips.

"What do you want from me, Ingimund? You have requested that I listen to you. Here you are in the great hall of my fortress, and here I am ready to lend an ear to your pleas. What have you to say?"

Ingimund stared at her from heavy eyelids and heavy folds of skin under his eyes. Thick brows made his eyes seem so deeply set so as to be almost nonexistent. "I would like to settle Wirral far to the northwest of Lundenburh. There is an abandoned town that has no name. We want to live there and give it life, as it could give us life."

"Close by, however, is Legaceaster. Many Roman roads lead from there in all directions. It would be a convenient point from which to attack the Welsh, the Irish, and the Mercians." Lae watched him blink as do lizards when hit by the sun unexpectedly. She looked for signs of sweat on his bald head that looked like a rock smoothed by a river. There was no sweat. This man was adept at deceit.

"Do I look like a man who has an army ready to attack?" He swept his arm around to include the pathetic women and children who stood with him. "This is my army. We fight hunger and cold, not men. Besides, Ireland holds no particular interest for me."

"Especially since King Niall used his army to escort you and your people from his country. From what I understand, you are lucky he did not require you to leave your head behind." Lae was pleased to see his startled eyes, but he was quick to drop his placid mask back into place. "It seems you tried to raise an army. Unsuccessfully, I hear."

Ingimund stood before her, waiting like a spider in a web for an unwary insect. His hands were angular and delicately veined, like a network of old Roman roads. Ingimund knew how to use those hands effectively. He did not look hungry, for his muscles were strong. Ingimund was broad-shouldered, with narrow waist and strong legs. He was not a handsome man; his lips were thin and his chin was cleft too deeply and veered off at an angle, but he commanded the space around him.

Lae made her decision. "The town you want has been deserted since we ran the Danes out. It will take much effort to repair it."

Ingimund nodded. "We know that. We have time."

"It is far from here. Your people do not look healthy enough to travel any more. Where are the men and the supplies?" Lae leaned forward and stared into Ingimund's reptilian eyes.

"The men are hunting. We have very few wagons and almost no supplies. We have not one goat to our name." Ingimund returned Lae's stare.

"It seems that a journey of such distance would be difficult for the women and children without wagons. Without animals, there is no milk. Your people starve. Why have you led them hither and yon with no home for them to tend, no pasture to grow animals, and no place to lay their heads?"

"We have been running from the Irish and the Welsh. They hate us as much as the Vikings hate the Anglo-Saxons and the Mercians. We were routed out of Ireland where we had lived for longer than I can remember. We tried to live in peace in Wales, but after they fought us long and hard, we had to leave there, too. I have very few men left. Many of the women you see here are widowed. We want to settle and live the rest of our days in peace." Ingimund reached behind him and pulled forward the young woman whom Lae had first noticed.

"See this widow? She will have a bearn before the year is out. The Welsh killed her husband. Before the snow flies, I must find a home for her and the others here." Ingimund whispered to the woman, who smiled shyly at Lae.

Lae frowned at Ingimund to show her displeasure at his obvious attempt to influence her. She waited before speaking. She wanted him to be nervous. "It is in my best interest to have the old town made livable again. You may as well try." Lae turned to Stan. "See that they have two wagons made up for them? One should hold food and the other building supplies."

Stan raised an eyebrow. "I will do as you ask."

"Thank you. Wyn, you will see that some tunics can be found for these women. They will need something warmer."

Wyn leaned toward her mother and whispered, "I cannot believe you want me to act like a servant and get these . . . these beggars clothing."

"Wyn, I am ruler of Mercia. Do not forget that." She turned back toward Ingimund. "We will have supplies for you assembled by tomorrow morning. Until then, you may camp in the outer bailey. We will provide you with a meal this evening." Lae nodded toward a trio of soldiers standing guard. "These men will help see to your immediate needs."

Ingimund bowed. "My people thank you. You have saved their lives." He bowed again and left the great hall, his followers close behind.

Lae would have some of her soldiers check to see that Ingimund did not have an army hidden somewhere, although the missive from

King Niall had said that most of Ingimund's men had deserted him. Lae turned to Wyn. "I have asked you to sit with me so that you could learn when to be stern and when to be charitable. You seem to have trouble learning to give to your fellow man."

"I fail to do anything to please you." Wyn jumped up and stomped across the room. At the door she turned. Her face was contorted, making her usually pretty features grotesque. She screeched, "If you want them to have clothing, then you tell the servants. I shall not help them."

"Wyn!" Lae stood and shouted at her headstrong daughter, but Wyn would not come back. Lae sat down and waited for her anger to subside. Her hands finally quit shaking, and she felt the heat leave her face. She looked at Stan, who had waited calmly for her as he had many times before. "I swore that I would not let her control me through my own anger. Once more I have failed to uphold my vow."

"She will not change, Lae. Wyn always thinks of herself." Stan laid his hand on Lae's arm. "I have some questions."

"Questions?"

"You have told me that Ingimund is not to be trusted. You said that to me last night when we discovered he wanted to meet with you. Why did you let him have land near Legaceaster?"

"It is better to know where a snake lives so that you do not get bitten unawares. And it never hurts to be kind to those who have no control over their own destiny. Someday I may need something from one of Ingimund's people."

"Kindness does not hurt, but I am certain it is more important to watch his movements," Stan said. "Father always said you were clever."

"Not always." Lae shook her head. "I was not clever enough to handle Wyn." Lae looked at Stan, who was more a mirror of her than he was his mother or father. Stan's silver-blonde hair matched hers as did his blue eyes. They both had the coloring of her mother, his grandmother. Lae missed her mother more than she had thought possible. It had been five years since her mother joined her father in heaven. The funeral had been attended by many people who had loved the quiet woman. Eahlswith could have been in the shadow of King Aelfred, but she was not. Strong and elegant, Eahlswith had been buried in Wintanceaster next to King Aelfred.

Lae squeezed her nephew's hand. King Edward of Wessex was proud of his son, and Stan had learned the ways of Mercia and Wessex well. It would help him when he ruled Wessex and Wyn ruled Mercia. Elflaed had continued to have children, but those who did not die were destined for the Church as King Aelfred had planned. The troublesome cousin, Aethelwold, had been killed five years ago by Edward in a battle for Wessex.

"Stan, you had best see to the supplies for Ingimund and his people. After that, wander among them for me, and see what you can hear."

"I will wear a worn cloak and keep my hair covered. It shines like a lantern in the moonlight." Stan stood, kissed Lae on the cheek, and strolled from the great hall.

It would have been wonderful to have had a son like Stan to carry on her name. Poor Wyn. She was not even a favorite in Lae's thoughts. She wished that Wyn would spend more time with her father, but she had refused, saying that Red's room smelled like death. Lae needed to talk with Red about what had transpired with Ingimund. Even though Red had been ill for almost a year and his body was weak, his mind was good.

Crossing the great hall, Lae climbed the steps to the chambers that housed Red. His illness was painful for her to watch. On some days he was better than others, but Red had told her that he always had a burning in his stomach.

The chamberlain was smoothing the covers across Red, who lay in a huge bed with pillows scattered everywhere. Lae dismissed the servant. She had more servants than she had ever had, but it was not that she wanted them. It was necessary for Red's care while she handled matters of the court and country and the council of old soldiers who tried to interfere at least once a year.

Lae sat on the bed next to Red at his insistence. She had been afraid at first, but he did not seem to mind. If she did not climb into bed with him, he would joke with her about being an old man. She would never think of him this way, and it distressed her that beneath the joking was his underlying fear that he was too old for her.

"Red, how fare you this morning?"

"Bored. Little Edith could not visit with me today. She is confined to her chambers by the priest until she learns her Greek letters."

"She reminds me of her mother with her stubborn ways. Some-times, when she tilts her head or smiles a certain way, I see Egwinna." Lae poured water into a cup for Red, but set it down when he refused a drink.

"What did Ingimund want?" Red pushed himself carefully into a sitting position.

"What you said he wanted. Land for his people." Lae looked at her husband closely. His coloring was better today, and he seemed to be in less pain than the day before. Maybe he would want to walk about later around the inner bailey.

"Did you give him land near Legaceaster?"

"I did."

Red nodded. "Good. He is wily and not trusted by the Irish or the Welsh."

"Nor by the Mercians." Lae shuddered. "He is like the snake from the Garden of Eden."

"Then let you not play Eve to his cunning ways," Red said. "You rule the country well, Lae. I rest easier knowing you can take care of our people."

"I learned from you. How could I do anything less?" Lae leaned forward and kissed Red's cheek. It saddened her to see how he had aged in the last year. His strong muscles were gone, replaced by a softness that belied the warrior, although his red hair was untouched by time. "I have been wondering about the wisdom of having Ingimund so close. I liked him better when he resided across the Irish Sea."

"You have something you would like to discuss with me?"

Lae's laughter echoed off the stone and timber walls. "How do you know?"

"I have been married to you long enough that I recognize the slight furrow of your brow when you want to talk about something important." Red folded his hands across his stomach. "Tell me about your idea."

"The Irish do not like Ingimund, and neither do the Welsh. It seems to me that now would be a good time for accolades to be sent to the kings of those countries. We could use them as allies should Ingimund or the other Vikings try to work a mischief."

"How do you plan to make those peoples our friends? They have not been so friendly before." Red watched Lae closely.

"We should send messengers with invitations to visit us. I doubt that the kings will make the trip, but they will be invited. We could also send Stan as an ambassador to those countries to seek a treaty. If they need our armies to help them, we will send them. They would do the same for us."

"I like the plan, Lae, except for one thing. I do not think we should send Stan on such a journey."

"He is a young man, not a child anymore. He should learn diplomacy."

"He could go to Wales, but Ireland is too far away." Red lay back against the pillows. His face showed the exhaustion of his body.

Lae would have stopped their conversation, but she knew that he would not want her to leave him with nothing to think about except his pain. "If I sent Stan to Wales and not to Ireland, that would not be diplomatic."

"Lae, Stan is not yet adept at diplomacy." Red picked at the woolen blanket. "I do not wish to say this, but I fear Wyn will not be a good ruler. She could never go on such a journey."

"How can you say that about your only daughter? She is to be queen after we are gone. She has been trained by both of us. She is to work with Stan to keep Mercia and Wessex as allies."

"Wyn hates Stan. How long before she attacks Wessex?"

"Red! She would not. She cannot. Wessex has been ruled by my family for generations." Lae pushed doubts about her daughter to the back of her mind. "Wyn is strong. Is that undesirable for someone who will inherit the throne? Is it wrong for her to be ready to rule a country that will have to fight its enemies for years?"

Red reached for Lae's hand. She wrapped her fingers around his. "It is like you to have no recollections of Wyn's behavior. You have been too kind when it comes to our daughter." Red turned away from Lae's stare. "It is difficult for me to tell you this, for in all other things we have always agreed. Our daughter is unsuitable for the throne." Red ignored Lae's gasp and continued. "She uses her power as a princess to extract favors from people. She abuses the peasants. I have often had to send money to some poor farmer who has lost a valuable crop because she ran a hunting party through it. She is demanding and mean-spirited."

Lae jerked her hand from Red's. "I will not listen to your accusations. Do you hate her because she was not the son you desired?" Lae sprang from the bed and stormed across the room, pacing back and forth in front of the firepit. She had always felt the sting of not having given a son to Red.

God had chosen to give her but one child. Lae glared at the man who lay against the pillows. How dare he blame her for not having more children? The sight of his wasted body twisted her heart, and her anger at him fled. She was left with the shame of not having had another child. She wondered again, as she often had over the years, why God had chosen to punish her.

Lae rushed back to the bed and almost threw herself across Red, but pulled away from him in time to prevent him from wincing. "I am sorry. I did not mean to startle you." Lae chewed on her lower lip. "It is not your fault that I had no more children."

"I have never blamed you for that. It was God's will that we had but one heir. Mayhap the reason will be clear to us in the future." Red closed his eyes. He seemed to sink deeper into the pillows. "I wish to speak of politics, not our daughter." He opened his eyes.

"I listen to you as always, Red. Your advice is as sound as was my father's." Lae sat in a chair and folded her hands in her lap. She was glad that he did not want to discuss Wyn anymore. It was the only argument they had had consistently over the years.

Red pulled the covers to his chin. "If you want the help of the Irish and the Welsh against Ingimund, then you should plan to take the trip yourself."

"Me? I cannot leave you."

"You will have to. Your brother can watch both Wessex and Mercia while you are gone. It is imperative that you make the appeals to the kings yourself. A messenger will not do, not even the son of Edward of Wessex." Red's breathing was labored, but he spoke in spite of his problem. "We ask for help from the Welsh who are more foe than friend. I expect that once they talk with you, your natural charm will convince them to help us against Ingimund or any other Dane. The Irish would accept Stan because they hate Ingimund as much as we do, but they would be insulted if you visited the Welsh and not them."

"I will take Wyn with me. She should learn a lot from a trip such as this."

"If you do take Wyn, then you must take Stan. The Welsh and Irish will not care for our daughter's haughty ways. We must show them that Stan is of a better temperament."

"I do not like to hear you speak so of Wyn."

"Someday you will know her for what she is. I hope it will not be too late." Red closed his eyes. "Be cautious with our daughter."

"To please you, Husband, I will go to Wales and Ireland. Stan and Wyn will accompany me along with an honor guard and a small army, but I do not want to leave you."

"Our country and our people have always come before our own needs. It will take you a month or more. You should see the King of the Ui Neill. Niall Glundub is a fierce warrior when it comes to the Vikings. King Cadell of Wales is the same." Red opened his eyes. "Do not worry. Little Edith will keep me entertained with her stories about the priest who attempts to teach her. I promise that I will not die while you are gone. My body may be full of sickness, but my heart will not stop beating. It is full of love for you, and that keeps it strong."

Lae rose and kissed Red's cheek. "My love for you grows stronger each day, dearest. I have been blessed." Lae smoothed the covers over his legs. "I must make preparations. The sooner I leave for Ireland, the sooner I will be able to return."

Lae kissed Red again and left the room before he could see the tears that flowed down her face. She felt certain that he would be there when she returned, but Red's time was limited. She wanted to spend as much of it with him as possible before the sickness took him from her.

They left before dawn on a day in May that promised to be bright and warm. Wyn refused to ride a horse and insisted on a litter. Lae argued with her, but finally yielded to Wyn's demands to save precious time. When they finally set out toward Ireland, Lae was restless. Red had risen from his bed and stood in the inner bailey. Lae knew he watched her as she mounted Tanton. He looked more rested than usual, and she felt some relief at the sight. Lae waved at him as the party moved out, then looked down at Wyn reclining in the litter. "Are you not going to wave to your father? He waves to us."

"I suppose so." Wyn flipped her hand upward, but did not look in his direction.

Stan called out, "Good-bye, Uncle. Good health to you." He rode up next to Wyn. "Why do you hate your father so?"

Wyn frowned at Stan as she brushed the skirt of her tunic. "Can you never ride a horse without throwing dust everywhere?" She glared at Stan. "My father never liked me. I have been nothing more than an embarrassment to him from the time I was a small child. You have never had to see the looks of pain on his face as I have. He spends more time with your sister, Edith, than ever he spent with me."

"You have never had to see the looks of your own countenance during one of your fits." Stan pulled at his blonde beard. "You look ugly at those times."

Lae frowned at Stan. "It is unseemly for you to quarrel with Wyn. We have barely begun our journey and are not outside the walls yet."

Stan bowed his head. "I apologize. It was thoughtless of me."

Lae sighed. "Forgive me also for being so curt with you. I do not want to leave Red alone for so long."

"He is stronger today," Stan said.

"He is not. His strength comes from necessity. He did not want me to worry about him." Lae nudged Tanton in the ribs and pulled away from Stan and Wyn. She did not want to listen to their arguments, for it angered her. She could listen to the cook and his wife argue day in and day out about every little thing that went on in the kitchen, but she could not tolerate the same behavior from Stan and Wyn. If Stan and Wyn could not agree on minor things, how would they be able to work together for the good of their countries?

A cool breeze unexpectedly lifted the edge of Lae's cowl from her face. She shuddered involuntarily, then crossed herself to ward off the evil eye that had caressed her soul. She hoped her mood would improve. It had not helped her anxiety to have to scold Stan already. He was right. Wyn had been disrespectful to her own father and king. Lae did not know which was worse — Wyn's arrogance toward the man who begat her or the king who ruled her.

Lae let the thoughts flow over their well-worn path once more. Would Wyn have been different had Egwinna lived? Lae shook her head, the cowl's rippling reminding her of its heaviness. She longed to remove the circlet crown that held it in place so that the wind would blow the thing away. She thought about going against tradition and riding bareheaded as she often did when alone, but knew that she would not.

She was going to Ireland, and she would meet with the ruler as her father and mother had taught her. She would follow all the rules of etiquette. Lae hoped that Wyn would not embarrass her. She had been surprised when Stan had expressed his reluctance to go, citing a need to stay with Red.

Stan was usually anxious to travel. He liked to study everything from the lay of the land to the way people built shelters to the mannerisms of the rulers. Lae had been just as surprised when Wyn decided it would not be too much trouble to go to Ireland and Wales. Lae remembered her own excitement as she explained the reasoning behind the trip. Looking back, she realized that Wyn had been bored by the hours of instruction about the manners of the foreign courts. Lae wished she had stopped her diatribe. She had known Wyn was disinterested, but she had continued to instruct, hoping that a spark would be ignited. It had not.

Lae did not have to look behind her at Wyn. She could envision the young woman's sulky face. Wyn's interest in the trip had waned when she discovered they would be on a horse, in a wagon, or a ship for twelve days. The promise of gifts to be given and received were of no consequence to Wyn. Did she not have everything she wanted already? Lae allowed that thought to grow. Was it possible that Wyn had never had to work for anything? That was preposterous. Lae had had everything that she had wanted, and so had Stan.

She pushed away the thought that had broken through her defenses. It articulated itself again in Red's voice, and she heard him as plainly as if he had been riding next to her. The voice said, "Wyn does not have the temperament to be a good ruler. She will destroy the work of generations for Wessex and Mercia."

Lae shook her head to dispel the voice. She used the defense she always had: Wyn would grow into her position when the time was right.

The trip to Ireland was uneventful, and most of the time Lae rode Tanton, taking to the litter only once when Wyn chose to ride for awhile. Lae did not avoid her, but whenever the two of them sat side by side for longer than five minutes with nothing to do, the sparks flew between them like lightning. First Wyn's face would gather darkness like a storm cloud, then she would fly into a rage, her words thundering and hurtful. Lae did not want to be tormented. Thus the trip progressed with mother and daughter parrying positions and words.

Lae looked out the third floor window of the fortress. She was glad to be on solid ground again after having crossed the water in the ships provided by her host. She liked to sail, but this time tension had prevented her from enjoying the salt water, the warm air, and the sun.

It was most important that she convince King Niall to join her against Ingimund. It would not hurt to work together against the other Vikings either. King Niall had thrown Ingimund out of Ireland for his transgressions, and she was anxious to learn what these were. Ingimund was hated by everyone it seemed. Even the Vikings would not tolerate having him near them.

Ireland, spread before her like a velvet coverlet, lay beyond the window. The rolling hills changed shade, but never color. It was the greenest place she had ever seen, and she understood why the traveling singers sang lonely songs of beautiful Ireland with its beautiful women.

The women were beautiful. Lae turned from the window and watched her women trying to speak Erse with the lady-in-waiting, King Niall's sister, who had been assigned to her. The Irish princess moved with the grace of a deer and deer-colored silky tresses revealed auburn highlights in the sun.

"My name is Heather, like the flowers that grow in my mother's homeland." The princess' voice had the sing-song lilt of Ireland.

"An interesting name and beautiful," Lae said. She hoped her Erse was adequate.

"My mother was from Scotland. She longed to return, but alas, could not." Heather smiled. "She said I was her window to the past."

"A fine window for a mother," Lae said.

Even though Heather was slender with a tiny waist, the princess looked heavier than she was because of large breasts. She must have many suitors who had asked for her hand, and Lae pondered the reason that she was not married. Mayhap the girl did not want to be wed and had convinced her brother to let her remain single a while longer.

Lae wondered how old the king was to have a sister so young. Lae picked up some of the language that Heather spoke. She had not heard Erse spoken since she had been a child with an Irish priest as her tutor. Her father had insisted that all his children be instructed in every language for which he could find a teacher. She thought back to the years she had listened to the priest and was startled to realize that he had talked often of the beauty of the country. He had been sick for his home, but because of her father's insistence, the priest had taught them for more than five years. It had been ironic that he was never to return to his land. The good priest had died during one of the Viking raids when he was in the village praying at a funeral. The last rites for a peasant had been for himself as well. Lae sighed. Always the Vikings.

Lae was escorted into the great hall by Melvyn, brother of the king. They led the procession; the king's cousin, Gearoid, escorted Stan and Wyn who followed directly behind Lae. Melvyn tried to speak to her in her own tongue, but he stumbled so badly over the pronunciations that she took pity on him answering his question — at least what she thought he had asked — in his own language. She spoke haltingly at first. His astonishment made her laugh, and he laughed with her.

Thank goodness Melvyn was not as serious as she had believed him to be. The smile was more natural than the solemn face he had presented to her. His freckles danced when he smiled, and Lae liked that. She guessed he was about Wyn's age. If Wyn had not been betrothed to Stan, this young man would have made an interesting match.

Melvyn helped Lae up the platform steps and to the head table. King Niall stood. She bowed to him, then heard his deep voice as he greeted her in his language. Lae looked up and her breath caught in her throat at his handsome face. She was staring into the deepest gray-blue eyes that she had ever seen. His hair was black and thick and glossy. He had not been ravaged by age, but tempered by it. Hardly any lines creased his face and it was with a start that Lae realized he was not as old as she had expected. He was probably younger than she by five or six years. He was as handsome as her own husband so far away, and Lae felt her heart constrict as she thought of Red. She wished that her husband were beside her now. She missed him, and the pain that had been hidden surged forward.

Lae realized that King Niall had asked her a question about the trip. "It was an easy trip. I especially want to thank you for the ships that you sent for us to cross the sea. They were beautiful and well designed." Lae noted with some pride that he seemed startled to find she could converse with him so easily. The language was returning to her quickly. When he took her hand to lead her to the chair to his right, he stared into her eyes until she felt her eyelids flutter like a simpleton. She looked down at the floor. Saints preserve her! She was acting like a peasant girl with her first lover. The manners of this court could not be so different from her own, but she thought that King Niall was flirting with her.

Lae forced herself to ignore the warmth of his hand wrapped gently around hers and concentrated on seating herself without tripping. She pulled her hand from his with a jerk when he kissed her palm. She settled into place hoping that her face was not as red as it felt. Lae bowed her head and let the cowl divide her from King Niall so that he would not see her blush. If only Red were here.

Lae reached up and touched the circlet crown that adorned her cowl. It gave her comfort, for it matched the one that Red wore on state occasions.

Stan was her protector in Red's absence, but he was too young to notice King Niall's flirtatious ways. Having never been in such a situation before in a supporter's court without an older man as an escort, Lae found that she was ill equipped to fight this duel.

Lae was unaware of anyone else in the room except the Irish king. Lae forced herself to look away from him and survey the crowd of people before her. The feast was not much different than those in the great hall of her own fortress. A sea of people sat at trestle tables below. Dogs lurked about, waiting to snatch pieces of meat that dropped from the knives of the guests. Lae spied a mother cat with two tabby kittens in the corner close to the firepit. The mother cat sat with eyes half closed, but Lae was not fooled by her apparent inattention. The striped cat's tail switched from side to side, scattering reeds. The kittens crouched down, their little twitching behinds in the air. They were ready to attack the enemy tail.

"Do you like our kittens?"

Lae turned toward King Niall, relieved to have a safe topic to discuss. "I love to watch kittens. I have been entertained all my life by kittens. I have not had one of my own since childhood, however."

King Niall leaned closer to Lae. "You have missed one of life's pleasures. In my own apartment is an old mother cat that I have had for a decade. She sleeps on my favorite chair, and I do not dare disturb her or she will growl."

Lae chuckled. "I find it amusing to think that a cat controls a king."

"It is a mother cat. They are used to boxing their kittens around. When she thinks that I do not comb my hair properly, she perches on the back of the chair and bites the imaginary tangles free. She is more formidable than was my old nurse."

"A cat of strength then. Nothing seemed as strong to me as my nurse. When I was a child, she struck terror in my heart more times than I care to remember. My father even bowed to her wishes. I suppose he had memories of his own nurse." Lae laughed. "Do you suppose nurses are bred somewhere just for the purpose of terrorizing children?"

"Yes, in hell."

Lae could not help the giggling fit that his pained expression caused, and after she struggled to control herself, she gave up. Tears streamed down her face, and she was vaguely aware of the other guests peering at her with more curiosity than they had before. Lae laid her hand on King Niall's arm. "I am sorry to make such a fool of myself." She took a folded cloth handed her by King Niall and wiped tears from her eyes.

King Niall laid his hand over hers and leaned too close. "It was good to laugh. I have not laughed like that for a long time. The Viking problem has made my life somewhat unbearable. Ingimund, especially. Your message said that Ingimund was living near Legaceaster with your permission."

"Yes. I thought that he should be where I could find him when I wanted to check on his activities. He is more than a day's ride away. It is close enough to watch him, but far enough away to keep him from breaching our defenses."

"A wise move. Did he talk to you of his poor band of ragged urchins who needed a place to live? Did he tell you of the cruel Irish king who banished him from Ireland?"

"No, I told him."

"You have good spies."

"I pride myself on having a good army with leaders who know things. It is important to me in these times. My goal is to rid the entire island of the scourge of Vikings. I am furious at the killing of our innocent people, the raids, the burning of our churches, and the raping of our women. I hate the Vikings. I will watch Ingimund with particular vigilance." Lae was surprised at her own vehemence, and she stole a glance at King Niall to see his reaction. To her surprise, his face matched her mood.

"It has been my misfortune to witness some of their atrocities." He leaned closer and whispered, "My own wife was murdered by Vikings not more than a year ago. She was heavy with child, our first." King Niall's voice caught on the memory. He made no attempt to hide his distress.

"My lord, I am sorrier than words can express. I did not know this."

"I should have remarried by now as is the custom, but I have not found a suitable woman." King Niall shook himself from the past. "I will support you in your quest to rid your country and mine from the pestilence that poisons us. A treaty between us will show the Vikings and the rest of the world that we have met face to face. We will stand as one against the Danes." King Niall reached for his chalice. "Let us drink to a newly formed alliance. May it continue forever."

Lae raised her chalice in response to King Niall. She pretended to drink, for it was red wine that shimmered in the silver chalice. Lae fought nausea and replaced the chalice carefully in the circular indentation in the tablecloth. She never remembered having been so concerned about the placement of a chalice before. Her hands shook. She placed them in her lap, fingers intertwined tightly.

She was sorry that Red was so far away, for she needed him. Not only would he understand her aversion to red wine, he could share in this moment of triumph. Having the Irish king as a supporter meant that her dream of routing the Vikings was closer to becoming a reality.

When Lae's eyes met King Niall's, he reached out and took her hand. Lae gently pulled her hand away. She hoped she had not offended him, for their coalition would be most important politically.

Lae glanced down the table and was startled to see Wyn watching her through half-closed eyes, a crooked smile on her youthful face. No doubt Wyn enjoyed watching her mother's consternation in her bout with nausea and the flirtatious manner of the king. Unfortunately, Wyn would read Lae's excitement at the proposed treaty as love sickness.

Lae glanced at Stan, but he was busy talking with King Niall's brother, hands gesturing wildly. Lae would have laughed in any other situation to see her nephew struggle with the unfamiliar language. He had studied it for only a few months last year. Lae decided that she must try again to find an Irish priest to tutor Stan, Wyn, and Edith as she had been. It would be most important now.

Lae looked around the great hall. No one seemed to notice that she was ecstatic except Wyn. She forced herself to look at Wyn again. Thank goodness she was busy arguing with Stan. It was probably the only time Lae was relieved to find them fighting. From the look on Stan's face, he was in great pain, although he tried to hide it.

King Niall leaned close to Lae and whispered, "I cannot play the proper host any longer. I am a man of great control, usually, but tonight you have me in your spell. Would you consent to a game of chess in my chambers?"

Lae gasped at the impropriety of the request. "I think not. It is not proper." She looked down the table at Wyn. Thank God her daughter was still irritating Stan. "I . . . I am surprised at your . . ."

"I am sorry. Forgive me."

Lae took a deep breath to steady her voice. "Although I am a ruler in my own right, I am first a woman with Christian upbringing. I cannot act the part of a man and play chess in your apartment."

"I have seldom had such interesting company, and I fear that I do not want the night to end. Would you consent to a game of chess if we set up the game board here, in the great hall?" King Niall asked. "Forgive my manners. My nurse would have been horrified at my offer, as would have been my mother."

"Consider your request granted. I see nothing wrong with a good game of chess here, except that it is not a womanly pastime. Do you believe that you can beat me?"

"I will be easy with you, but I cannot let you win. It would pain me no end to lose a game of war in front of my people."

"Prepare to be embarrassed, my good King Niall. I do not take kindly to opponents who think they can be easy with me. I see it as an insult. As in battle, I fight hard, and I fight to win. Are you man enough to be beaten by a lady?"

Cocking his head, King Niall regarded his guest. "Mayhap I have been too generous. I accept your challenge. There will be no grace given because you are a lady. I would not want to offend a guest, so I will play as if you were a man."

Dinner had been over for a short while when King Niall had sent for the chessboard. Now, with the hour late, Lae concentrated on her next move. She had to admit that this man played better than anyone she had encountered before, save her father.

She was aware that a crowd had gathered around them whispering among themselves. They thought that she was trapped. Lae agonized over the next move. She could not lose. She hated to lose. It appeared that she was trapped the same way that she had once tried to trap her father, only he . . . Lae smiled to herself as she moved her queen. "Stalemate." It was not a victory, but it was no loss, either. Lae enjoyed the murmuring of the people as they approved of her move, but most of all, she loved the look on King Niall's face.

"We are well suited."

"Mayhap. I challenge you to another game. The night is young, and I feel victory is close."

"The night is not young. Morning slips in like a thief to steal the stars. However, another game. When I win this one, I will allow you a challenge game." King Niall's words were softened by his smile.

"Agreed. You may make the first move."

King Niall laughed. "I will not fall for any tricks of yours. You are the guest in my fortress, you move first. I want to study your methods."

"My methods are simple. I play to win."

"As in love."

"You are too bold. As in war, nothing more." Lae reached out and moved a pawn.

"An odd beginning."

"Not so when you see the end."

The candles in her room had burned down to stubs in the hours that she and King Niall had played chess. Her lady-in-waiting, Princess Heather, slept quietly in the corner bed. Lae pulled off her clothing and slid her night tunic over her head. She was ready to climb into bed when a quiet knock on the door shocked her. Who would be so bold as to come to her chamber this time of morning? She hoped it would not be a messenger with bad news.

The knock came again and Lae crossed the room hurriedly, pulling her gown down over her hips. She opened the door a crack and peered out. "Wyn! Whatever are you doing awake at this hour?"

Lae opened the door to allow Wyn to enter. "Are you ill? Do you need anything?"

Wyn made no attempt to enter. "I was restless. I cannot sleep when my mother is not in her room." Wyn's eyes crackled with contempt. "My own mother plays the prostitute. Do you make all your treaties that way?"

Lae's hand whipped across Wyn's face with a cracking sound that startled both of them. Lae saw the look of shock on her daughter's face, followed by hatred. It was Lae's turn to be shocked. What had she ever done to make her daughter hate her so much? The difficult child had grown into a difficult woman. She had to find out why. Lae grabbed Wyn's arm and dragged her into the inner chamber away from the sleeping Heather. Wyn tried to jerk away, but Lae was stronger, and she tightened her grip. Lae kicked the door shut behind them and shoved Wyn into a chair.

"You have some peculiar ideas, but this one is unfathomable! Whatever are you talking about?"

"You cannot do this to me!" Wyn started to get up, but was pushed back into the chair.

"I just did." Lae pointed her finger at Wyn. "You will sit there and talk to me. You will not treat me the way you just did. I am more than your mother; I am your queen. I have power of life or death over you. I gave you life as your mother, and I can take it away as your queen."

Lae paused to take a deep breath. Her own anger surprised her. She had not felt this way since the last time she led a raid on the Vikings. Could it be that she hated her daughter as much as Wyn hated her? She continued to stare at Wyn, who sat straight in the chair. She had recovered from the surprise of being slapped by her mother. Lae felt some pride in Wyn's quick revival.

Wyn's face was like a stone statue. Only her eyes, made darker by the low candlelight, seemed alive. "You may kill me if you wish so I cannot tell about your affair, but you will have to explain it to Father."

"Do not be stupid. Your father would understand that a chess game in the great hall is not a love affair. He trusts me, and I him. Whatever are you thinking? You know nothing of love or people. You do not know the difference between a few games of chess to while away the hours and a love affair. What manner of person have you become?" Lae folded her arms across her chest. She thought back through the years. Wyn had never been able to relate to anyone. Without meaning to, Lae voiced her musings. "You have no heart."

"I have no heart because you never gave me one."

"I never gave you one? What kind of accusation is that?"

Wyn shook her head. "You gave everything to Stan. You gave him your approval, your attention, your love. I had nothing."

"Stan did not come to us until you were four years old. You were the only child in the castle and had both your father and me."

"You were never there."

"I was there for you more than you remember." Lae looked at the woman in front of her. How could she make her understand? How could she help Wyn heal?

"I always saw you from afar. You never wanted to be with me."

Lae thought back to the child who threw the best tantrums in Mercia. She should have made herself sit with Wyn, tantrums or not.

"Everyone always hated me."

"Not true. Did you try to love anyone? Did you try to put your arms around anyone or kiss anyone or be kind to anyone?"

"No. I did not want anyone to touch me. Except Egwinna." Wyn said the name softly. "I loved Egwinna."

"Yes, Egwinna loved you." Lae watched as Wyn glared at her. There were no tears. Wyn's white-hot loathing for her dried any tears she might have had. There was to be no reconciliation.

"Egwinna was the only person who spent time with me. She knew what I needed. She knew me. Me," Wyn said. "She cared about me. I could behave any way with her, and she still loved me." Wyn held out her hand. "See this ring? She gave it to me. I have worn it every day since." Wyn turned away from her mother and stared at the floor. "Of all the people who could have died, why did Egwinna have to be the one?"

"No one knows the ways of God, Wyn. We must learn to bear the painful. . . ."

Wyn burst from her chair. She stood in front of Lae, shaking and her eyes rolling like those of a wild horse. "Do not try to explain Egwinna's death with religious platitudes. She deserves better memories than that. She died giving birth to Edith. A love child. Mayhap you and King Niall could do the same. I will tell Father of the lust that shows on your face."

"Stop that." Lae stepped toward Wyn and grabbed her by both shoulders. She dug her fingers into Wyn's soft flesh. She whispered, "Do not try to intimidate me. Do not try to control me with threats of made-up stories. Remember, I hold your future in my hands."

Lae pushed Wyn away from her. Wyn whirled around and left the inner chamber, ran across the sleeping room, and pulled the huge door shut with a bang. Lae shook as she collapsed in a chair. She hated herself for having let Wyn make her angry.

Lae rubbed her forehead to rid herself of a headache that had just begun. She could not afford for her daughter to distort the truth of tonight. Why had she been unable to rear her only child to be a good person? Was it not a mother's duty? She loved Stan as much as any mother could love a son, and she loved Edith. The little girl had filled the void in her heart caused by Wyn's hatred. It was harder to love Wyn, but whose fault was it that her daughter was difficult?

It was not yet time to get up. Mayhap she could get some rest. She left the suffocating confines of the inner chamber and collapsed on the bed. Today would be difficult for several reasons. The most important was that she had to meet with King Niall's council to convince them that Ingimund and the other Vikings could be eliminated if Ireland and Mercia worked together. For the most part, the men were old and conservative, but they had shown her respect yesterday at the banquet. They had been impressed with her chess playing as well. She felt confident that an alliance would be forged between her country and King Niall's.

She had been surprised to discover that they seemed to know about her battles against the Vikings. It had surprised her further to learn that the men had wanted all the details of her exploits. They had nodded their approval at descriptions of her tactics and had encouraged her when she told them she had started with one fort at Legaceaster near Ingamund's location at the border between Mercia and the Viking infestation. She had explained that when more forts were built and housed armies, she could protect more people. She would also be able to attack the attackers much quicker than by sending troops out from a central point. That had brought about much nodding of heads amongst the old soldiers. Ireland would benefit from the forts as well, especially if a treaty were signed. Compared to the ordeal she had just gone through with Wyn, working with the Irish Council would not be difficult.

The moment for saying good-bye had come. Lae wondered why the past three weeks had flown by so fast. Mayhap it was the endless meetings and the evening games of chess. The king had won one more game than she had, but it had been late, and she had not kept up her guard. She learned something about herself from that chess game.

She smelled the salt of the sea air and heard the waves as they lapped against the side of the boats and the dock where she stood. She was aware that King Niall stood closer to her than protocol would permit. She had grown fond of him and hoped that he would find a suitable wife soon. She thought of him the same way she thought about her brother. Lae touched his hand. "I wish you luck in finding a wife. You deserve someone who is beautiful and kind."

"I will teach her to play chess, but not too well. I like to be challenged, but I do not like to lose. When we meet again, the games begin."

"We will probably never see each other again."

"That is true." King Niall looked toward the ships that would carry Lae's party to Wales. "We had an interesting time and a good alliance has been formed. I shall always remember our games of chess. It is much better to have played the game with a beautiful woman than some old man."

"Your impertinent manners need to be refined, sir."

"Without my impertinent manners, I would have had no memories worth thinking about. This way, we have memories — wonderful memories to carry us into old age." King Niall touched Lae's hand.

"Memories, sir? Of what? A few games of war on a board? You lack for entertainment, I can tell." Lae pulled her hand away.

The king laughed. "Your barbed words wound me. Those few games may not have meant much to you, but to my poor court, it was wonderful entertainment."

Lae curtsied. "I am glad to have been of such importance to you."

King Niall bowed in return. "It was my pleasure. If ever the need arises when we must gather our armies together, I hope that you are on my right hand to help me win the battle."

"I on your right hand? To help you? I think not. I think that I prefer to lead the armies myself with mayhap some help from you."

"You are a soldier for certain, my lady. I pity the Vikings," King Niall said.

"I am the leader of my country, now that my husband is ill. I must fight the Vikings. I have lived my entire life with hatred for them. Mayhap it is fate that we will one day fight together."

"The fates have nothing to do with your life. You make your own destiny."

"Mayhap." Lae looked toward the ships. Everyone was on board. She could see Tanton tied at the rail, along with other horses they had brought. They waited for her. "It does us no good to prolong the agony." Lae turned to King Niall and curtsied. "I take my leave of you. Send me word when you find a wife. I care for you as I do my brother, and I care what happens to you."

"You will live in my heart, also." King Niall kissed her hand.

Lae turned away from King Niall and boarded the ship. King Niall waited on the shore and waved to her as the ship slid across the sea. She waved in return until she could no longer see him.

She stood in the bow of the ship most of the day, watching the waves break, throwing froth upwards, admitting to herself that she was avoiding Wyn. Wyn would spread rumors about her. No matter. No one would believe Wyn, but for a few unfortunates that liked to live with filthy gossip. Lae hoped that Wyn would not be able to subvert her plans to gather allies about her.

The trip to Wales had been uneventful and now Lae was seated with the council of warriors. The great hall was hushed, and many of the warriors stared at her. She should have been used to such stares, but she was not.

King Cadell sat at the head of the table, Lae to his right. He sat as straight as if someone had planted a rod down his spine. Because of this he seemed taller.

Lae had expected the Welsh to be unruly, since their reputation was almost the same as the Scottish Picts who were known to paint themselves blue and ride naked into battle. King Cadell was as stoic as the hawks in the woods. His hair was steel gray, thick and shiny. Heavy eyebrows, gray like his hair, were drawn together. Lae wondered if he ever relaxed or laughed. He had not stopped frowning since she had arrived three days ago. A thin upper lip was topped by a hawk-like nose and gray eyes. King Cadell was handsome and dignified and appeared as cold as a winter day, and she had come to think of him as Gray Hawk.

During the meetings he had been fast to pounce on those who were stupid or whose thoughts were different from his. Like the hawk, King Cadell needed no one. He could perch above the rest of the world and look down on the unfortunate ones below him.

Lae knew that she would never be able to think of Gray Hawk as having a life outside his position. He was always formal, never bending, even during the banquet that had welcomed her. She had been astonished to watch him drink bowl after bowl of mead and never droop. Lae had to be careful not to become inebriated from the mead, for she did not want to incur the wrath of Gray Hawk. At one point she had almost called him that. She had tried to wipe the name from her thoughts, but it did no good. He would be etched in her memory forever as Gray Hawk.

The treaty to fight against the Danes together had been signed without difficulty and before Lae realized it, preparations were being made to travel to Wessex to see her brother before returning home. She had to show Edward the treaties and explain all that had happened. She knew that Stan needed to see his father and form some alliances with his half-siblings.

Home seemed far away, and Red seemed like a dream. Lae could not wait to make the circle. Home was heaven to her and, like a wearied pilgrim, Lae wondered if she would ever arrive.

chapter

XIV

AE'S HAND TREMBLED as she broke the parchment
seal. It was King Niall's seal and for a moment she
held it to her heart, not wanting to read what was
inside. Lae wanted to prolong the peace that had
been hers for the last fortnight since returning home.

She looked across the apartment toward Red.
He was asleep, his breathing shallow. He had seemed the same
when she had returned home, but during the last few weeks she had
noticed that he slept more. She did not know whether the illness
was taking its toll, or that he had relaxed since her return.

He had confessed to her that he had been concerned about her
continuously while she had been on the journey. Red had also told
her that he had worried more about her while she was on this trip
than when they had ridden together into battle.

She walked to the window where the light was better, still
holding the letter against her breast. Lae stared at the sky.

"You are beautiful with the light on your hair, Lae."

"Thank you." Lae dropped the hand that held the parchment to
her side, letting the folds of her tunic cover King Niall's letter.

Red pushed himself up on his elbows. "What have you in your
hand?"

"Nothing that need worry you. How are you feeling? May I
send for your supper?"

"I am not hungry. What have you in your hand?"

"I told you it was nothing."

"I saw King Niall's seal. Read it to me."

"May I get your supper first?"

"Do not bribe me as if I were a child. I want you to read that letter to me. I order you to read it to me. I am still king." Red threw back the covers and slid from the bed. "See, I stand like a man, not a mewling infant, so treat me like a man."

Lae took a step toward Red, her hand out to steady him. "Red, I did not mean . . ."

"Stop! Stay where you are. You do not have to hold me up. I will come to you." Red walked unsteadily toward Lae, holding onto the furniture and the wall for support. "I still have the legs for walking though I have not had the strength to bed you as a husband for too many months to count."

Lae willed herself not to cry as she watched Red struggle. "It matters not to me whether you bed me. I love you more each day."

"You always pleasured me, and I you." Red held his back straight and looked Lae in the eye. "You need a healthy man who can love you. You are too young to live with memories. Did King Niall bed you?" he whispered.

"Red! I swear to you that no man appeals to me as do you. I did not allow impropriety to occur. I would not do anything to cause you shame."

"Wyn has told me . . ."

Lae threw the parchment to the floor. "Wyn has told you? What has that scheming wench told you?"

Red flushed, but did not look away from Lae. "She said that you spent many nights with King Niall."

"May God forgive me if I strangle our daughter. I was in the great hall playing chess with King Niall many nights through. I did not tell you, for I had forgotten the incident. A few chess games were not important enough to remember. Not only was Stan with me, but most of the knights and ladies stayed up to see which of us would win."

"Did you win?"

"You accuse me of adultery, then dismiss the insult with a question about a game? I know not whether to be relieved or angry with you. How could you doubt my fidelity? My belief in the commandments? Most of all, how could you doubt my love for you?"

Lae looked away from her husband, aghast at her own insensitivity. "I am sorry to have spoken with anger toward you when, in truth, it is Wyn who angers me."

"It is my fault, Lae. The weakness of my body causes a weakness in my head. I should never have believed anything that Wyn said." Red clung to the back of a chair, his knuckles white. "Help me back to bed."

Lae rushed to Red's side and slid her arm around his waist, holding her frail warrior gently. As she helped him into bed, she noticed that his fingernails were tinted blue. She knew that she would never see the healthy pink in Red's nails or lips again. She vowed to increase the amount of medicine that he was getting.

"I want to send for Olenka."

"No. She can do nothing more than you have."

"She is better than I."

"I have the illness that my father had. My heart is dying and nothing can prevent that."

"Olenka may know of something . . ."

"No." Red's voice rasped from exertion. "Read King Niall's missive to me."

"It may not be pleasant news."

"There is no news that is pleasant these days. The Vikings strike at us all the time."

Picking up the parchment, Lae took several deep breaths and opened it. The name Ingimund leaped from the first line of the letter. She read slowly, partly to translate the Latin in an unfamiliar hand and partly to absorb the news. "Ingimund!" Lae said. "That snake has not waited long before playing the traitor to us."

Red pulled himself into a sitting position. "What troubles you?"

"King Niall of Ireland says that Ingimund has called a secret council of Danes and Norsemen to meet with him in Ireland. Ingimund wants to pull all the Vikings together into one unit to lead a massive army against Mercia and Wessex." Lae slammed the parchment against a writing table, scattering vellum and pens. "I will see that unfortunate piece of filth dead before he places one foot inside Lundenburh. What an absurdity to assume that he can be a leader of men against us."

Red threw back the covers and swung his legs to the floor. "Let us send for some dinner. I want to work out some plans with you."

Lae turned and stared at her husband. She had not seen him this animated since the day she arrived home several weeks ago. He was a different person from the one he had been just a few minutes past. His eyes were bright. It was not the brightness of a fever, but the excitement of a good fight that made them so.

"If an invasion by Ingimund makes you feel better, then I am happy to have him become a thorn in our sides." Lae held out her arm for Red. His hand grasped her arm with some of the strength he had from days gone by, and Lae led him to a chair by the firepit. He had complained of the cold, even in the summer, so Lae had ordered a low fire to be kept burning. She sat next to him, but pushed her chair back from the heat.

"Lae, is there more information in that letter?"

Lae reread the letter. "Yes. King Niall says that Ingimund has built a fort. He started it as soon as his men could bring in supplies." Lae looked at Red. "He must have started it last year. It cannot be more than a wooden wall around an outer bailey. If the town is inside, so much the better for us."

Red tapped the arm of his chair. "If he has had a year to build the fort, then it could be formidable. Send someone to spy."

"I wish we could have sent some of our men to spy on Ingimund. As it was, they are needed along the border where we are building forts. I did not think Ingimund was a threat."

"Anyone that cunning is a threat. I should have guessed his intentions," Red said.

"I want to attack immediately before he has a chance to build up more of an army." Lae felt her heart beat faster, and her cheeks burned. She could hardly wait to encounter the arrogant Ingimund.

"Haste could cost you the battle. You need to pull in an army."

"We have our standing army."

"Yes, but they are about to rotate back to their fields and families. I ordered it so three days past."

Lae twisted her braid around her finger. "Do you not think they would want to fight before going home? It would take a hard three days' march to reach Legaceaster. I do not want to wait, but I want to be fair to the men."

"I have no feeling for that. If you want men with some experience, take the army that stands now. If you want men who are fresh, take the new army." Red leaned back in his chair and stared at the ceiling. "If I were ready to fight with Ingimund, I would surprise him as quickly as possible. Take the standing army. I believe that after three months of little activity they would welcome a fight."

"It shall be done." Lae jumped from her chair, grabbed both of Red's hands, and pulled him to his feet. "Dress yourself, Red. Let us talk to our lieutenants. We shall ride in two days, and in less than two weeks, Ingimund will cease to exist."

"What about Edward?"

"I have no time to send for him. Besides, we can deal with Ingimund ourselves. I shall take Stan. He needs experience in killing the enemy."

"I am sorry I cannot ride with you." Red kissed Lae's cheek.

"You cannot go? Even in a litter? Could you not direct the battle from a safe distance?"

"I would not degrade the Kingdom of Mercia by leading a battle from a litter. I have no need to defile the people of Mercia that way. I have the utmost faith in you, Lae. You have proven yourself a warrior many times over. You will lead the army against Ingimund."

Lae felt her heart thump inside her chest. She could not speak. It was the first time that Red had admitted he was too ill to fight. She knew that he loved a good battle. "I cannot lead an army without you."

"You can, and you will."

Lae wrapped her arms around Red. "I shall send for Edward to help me."

Red pushed her away. "For God's sake, Lae. Think about what you have just said. Do not underestimate yourself! You have traveled to Ireland and Wales and have come home with treaties worth triple your weight in gold. You have successfully fought the Vikings before and beaten them. You have a gift for strategy. Your father and I trained you for battle. Do not think yourself or us unworthy. Fight!"

"It is easy to say, but have you forgotten the disastrous Battle of Corebricg three years ago? I fought alongside King Constantine and his Scottish soldiers, to no avail. We were beaten soundly by those damnable Vikings in Northumbria. I was lucky to escape with my life." Lae's eyes clouded over as the memory pushed itself forward from a foggy hiding place in the back of her brain. "If one of my men had not died for me, I would not be here."

"The winter of 903 was our worst, but death is the price of war, Lae. Always someone dies." Red sat heavily in his chair. "You have to lead the army. You are the leader."

"On the contrary, Red, you are the leader of the Mercians."

"We ruled side by side until my health failed me. But now, you must keep our people free. It would have been a victorious battle for us at Corebricg if your troops had been rested. Constantine should never have forced you into battle so soon." Red pulled his beard, made pale by the white hair mixed with the red. "You must go after Ingimund before he gets stronger."

Lae paced back and forth across the floor, the reeds crackling as if to punctuate her agitated state. "I have always had you or Edward by my side or another king."

"There has to be a time for every warrior to lead a first battle. This is your time. Do we not all send our children forth in our stead when the hearth fire is kinder to us than the campfire?"

"Of course. Why do I feel so . . ."

"Frightened?"

"Yes."

"You had never lost a battle before Corebricg. I think it brought back memories of your father's lost battle when you had to run for your life."

"Mayhap."

"I was fearful for a month before leading my first battle. When I stood before my army to give them the battle plan, I realized that I was responsible for their lives. If I led them well, most would come home to their wives and children. If I failed in my duty, many would die. I was alarmed by the trusting looks in the youthful faces of those who had vowed to fight with me. I was even more concerned about the graybeards who had joined. Was it right to take them into a fight for which they might not have the strength? Was it right to make widows of grandmothers who were too old to find other husbands? I wanted to abandon the campaign."

Lae gasped. "You, Red? You, one of the bravest men I know, wanted to quit?"

"Yes, I did. However, a truly brave person goes on in spite of fear. Fear is God's way of giving us a bit of caution." Red held his hand toward Lae.

She knelt before him, grasped his hand, and held it to her cheek. "I will make you proud of me, Red. I will lead the army against Ingimund."

"I will be beside you in spirit." Red kissed her hand. "Send for Stan. I want him to learn the plan for attack from you. You teach it well."

A loud knock on the door startled Lae and she sighed. It seemed that she had too little time for her husband. Even a quiet moment such as this one could not last as long as she wanted it to. She rose and opened the door. A gust of damp air pushed its way past her servant, and a messenger dressed in foreign garments stood before her. "What is it?" She tried to keep the sound of irritation from her voice.

"My lady, this messenger has ridden without stopping."

"Make certain he has a good meal, a place to sleep, and provisions for his return trip." Lae reached for the vellum that the messenger held out to her. She noted the seals were from Legaceaster, and her curiosity almost overcame her manners. "Thank you. I will have a message for you by afternoon. Eat and rest well, for you will have a difficult return trip." Lae waited until both men bowed and closed the door.

"What is it?" Red asked.

"A most interesting message, I am sure." Lae walked across the room to her writing table, and, picking up a knife, ran the silver blade under the seal. The parchment popped open, and she read the letter inside. "It is from several freemen in Legaceaster just across our border. They have asked that we ride to their town to rescue them from Ingimund. They say that he is amassing an army to fight them before the fort we just built on the river is manned. We only needed a fortnight before the army moved in." Lae grinned. "This gives our war against Ingimund that much more credence."

There was no sound in the apartment except the tapping of the vellum scroll against the palm of Lae's hand while she was deep in thought. After a few minutes, she turned to Red. "I have a plan. As soon as Stan arrives, I will lay it out for both of you. It is unusual, but it has been tried before in another place, an ancient time." Lae felt mischievous and she laughed aloud. "I am looking forward to a fight with Ingimund. It should be invigorating."

"I am not certain but what the Furies have taken hold of you, Lae, when I hear laughter such as that."

"Red! Be careful when you mention them. They may hear you!" Lae knocked three times on the wooden arm of the chair.

Red laughed. "You are not afraid of anything, even the Furies, so do not pretend to be shocked."

"What if a priest heard you? Or a servant girl? The rumors would fly."

"It would be good for your image. Armies would run from you."

"I do not want armies to run from me. I want them to die by my sword. I want their spirits sent to their otherworld so that this world may have peace." Lae stared across the room at the plank wall. The wall before her disappeared as her imagination laid out the plans for the forthcoming battle.

Time flew so fast that Lae had hardly any moments to herself. She was busy instructing Stan and the other lieutenants in her strategy, stressing that, because it was unusual, no words should be spoken about it to the general army. She had all the meetings in her chambers so that Red would be a part of the proceedings. She needed his experience and advice. Stan and the other men admired him, asking him questions about the battles he had been in with King Aelfred during his youth. At times like these, Lae watched the sparkle return to Red's eyes. Even his spirit seemed to revive. At other times, when his fingernails turned blue and the color drained from his face, she made him drink the foxglove tea she had prepared for him. He would excuse himself and lie down. The plans for the protection of Legaceaster continued, but Lae found that a part of her mind listened to Red's breathing.

The day came when Lae rode out at the head of her army, looking back at Red who watched her from the apartment window. He saluted her. Lae returned the salute as one soldier to another and as wife to husband. When she had told him she did not want to leave him, he had said that each time they parted, he feared that he would never see her again.

"Are you that ill, Red?" Lae had said, hoping to hear that he was not and that her imagination had run wild.

"I do not worry that I am going to die, but that you will be killed in battle," Red had said.

Lae remembered the momentary confusion as she realized each of them had worried about the other's death. She had such a look of surprise on her face, so Red had said, that he laughed until tears rolled down his face. She had laughed with him, a needed release for them both.

Remembering the laughter with Red seemed so long ago that it was like another life. In the three days that it had taken the army to march from Lundenburh to within striking distance of Legaceaster, Lae left thoughts of her husband behind and concentrated on the battle before her.

Before sunrise Lae had led the army from its encampment toward the walled town of Legaceaster. Now she watched nighttime shadows dissipate as the sun peeked over small hills behind her. Her scouts had told her that Ingimund, with an army of fewer than a hundred, would come from the west and ride into the sun. She sat astride Tanton, holding him under tight rein. He always sensed when it was time for battle and pranced and snorted.

Lae glanced at Stan, who sat calmly on his warhorse next to her. Lae was proud of him. She wished that Egwinna could have lived to see what a good soldier her son had become.

Lae touched his arm. "Stan, are you ready?" She noticed that his countenance was serious. "Send part of your men inside the walls. Hide them well. Tell the townspeople to get ready for an attack. Put someone on the gates who will open them to Ingimund at the right time. Be careful of him. He is a snake."

Stan shifted in the saddle and looked at Lae. "It would be safer for you if you went inside the walls and let me hide in the woods."

"I have had more battle experience than you, Stan. It is better that my army remain outside." Lae grasped his arm. "It is harder for me to have you involved in this war than I can ever explain. You sit before me as a grown man, but I still see the child who played at my feet. Forgive me, but I feel a need to protect you. Allow me that. And who will rule Wessex?"

"Ah," Stan said. "I am no longer the child that you remember, but will do as you say. I am eager to meet with the leader of the Legaceaster freemen. He will undoubtedly be pleased with your plan." Stan looked around at the peaceful countryside. "And Ingimund will be surprised that we are here. He expected an easy conquest. How soon do you expect his army to appear?"

"Within an hour or two. It is time to hide in the woods. Remember the signal." Lae held her arm high above her head and listened for orders that told her the army was being readied by her lieutenants. "God bless you, Stan. May the angels guide your spears."

"The same to you, my lady." Stan saluted her.

Stan rode back to where his army awaited him, then Lae dropped her arm as she pressed her heels against Tanton's ribs. He tossed his head as if to say he was glad to be moving. They rode toward the woods and within a quarter-hour, more than two hundred men were hidden amongst the giant oak trees. Lae and her commanders sat silently on horseback while the infantry sat on the ground behind her. Not one man whispered, not one man snapped a twig. Only the normal sounds of buzzing flies, the ripple of leaves, and the occasional snorting of a horse interrupted the summer morning.

It seemed as if they had been hiding forever, but Lae noted that the sun had barely moved each time she looked at it. Finally, she heard Ingimund's army before she saw it, and she glanced across the meadow at Stan. Had he heard the army coming toward him? She watched Stan closely. He was talking with one of his men. She saw him sit up and look in the direction of the marching. Good.

Lae stood in the stirrups to get a better look at Ingimund's army. They seemed well enough equipped, but then the Vikings were noted for their swords. She said a prayer to the Virgin Mary and crossed herself. If she died today, she wanted it to be with valor. She licked her lips that were always too dry just before she went into battle. She could take time for one last drink, but she did not want any movement to be seen. She was only twenty-five feet into the woods. She watched as Stan signaled his army, and she said another prayer for him.

Lae could envision Ingimund's surprise as he and his army drew close enough to see Stan waiting for them. Ingimund's army surged forward, swords drawn, shields held in place, and spears in throwing position. Lae could hardly bear to stand by and watch a battle going on without her. She caught herself rubbing the hilt of her sword, a habit that had left a permanent shiny mark on the handle. She continued to rub the sword as she watched a shower of spears fall on Stan's army. Most of Stan's men stopped the spears with their shields, but in so doing, rendered the shields useless. These were thrown aside, and Lae could hear the ringing of sword against sword as hand-to-hand combat began.

Stan drew his sword and struck with lightning speed. More than one enemy left a widow and children behind because of Stan's ability.

Stan's army was smaller than Ingimund's, which Lae had intended. Stan was quick to give the signal to retreat behind the walls of Legaceaster. The gates opened, and the army pushed its way into the town with Ingimund right behind. The few Vikings who squeezed inside the town no doubt regretted their haste as the gates shut in the face of the rest of the enemy. Ingimund gave the order to send the battering rams against the gate and the walls.

Lae heard the creaking of wheels as the battering rams were pulled into place. The townspeople had no way of knowing that Lae was waiting to attack Ingimund, and she worried about what they would do. They would think the end was near. She watched the battle, trying to decide when Ingimund and his army would be so engrossed in their task that they would not notice her approach. Movement at the top of the wall interrupted her thoughts.

Lae grabbed her lieutenant's arm. "Look!" She laughed. The townspeople were not going to give up without a struggle. They poured steaming water, and from the smell, Lae detected boiling oil, too. She could not decide what the women were pouring over the timbered wall. The slow-moving liquid from pots, pans, and cauldrons from the top of the wall flowed onto the army below. Lae watched the sun sparkle off the gold liquid that clung to the enemy. Ingimund's men were writhing from the sting of the burning liquid that must have made their chain-mail unbearable.

Lae shaded her eyes and leaned forward. "What is that dark swarm those women are dropping over the walls?" Lae watched in wonder as the dark liquid refused to follow nature's laws. Instead of gushing down, it swooped down, then up, then whirled around and dove toward the hapless army.

"Bees! Bees! First honey and now thousands of bees! Let us ride!"

Lae raised her arm and let it fall as she spurred Tanton forward and rode like lightning toward Ingimund. The wind whistled through tiny holes in the mesh. Lae hated the weight of the mail against her face, but she had no plans to have her face cut to pieces by a sword.

The enemy apparently had no idea an army was behind them until Lae, riding hard with sword drawn, lopped off the head of an unfortunate Dane. Lae laughed aloud at the confusion that followed. She barely held the reins, allowing Tanton to avoid danger as she became dangerous to the enemy. Her sword swung down again and again, mixing the blood of many soldiers. Next to her, her commanders fought magnificantly. The gates to the city opened, and Ingimund led his army inside. He had fallen into the trap even easier than Lae had imagined. Stan and his "defeated" army were inside, waiting to be the right side of the vise to her left.

Pushing her army forward, never letting Ingimund and the Vikings rest, slaughtering them from all sides, Lae pressed onward. If Ingimund did not surrender soon, his entire army would die. She did not care. She was exhilarated by the battle. It was almost like the wooden horse that the Greeks had given to their Trojan enemies. If Ingimund had been better educated, he might not have fallen into the trap she had set for him.

Lae looked for Ingimund. She had lost him in the middle of the battle. She glanced to her left and was startled to see Ingimund within striking distance. He was riding toward her, his lower face unshielded. His jaw was set in a hard, tight line and his lips were compressed. His visage was one of fury.

Lae felt her own anger rising. How dare he be angry with her! He was the ingrate who attacked. She turned Tanton toward him, expecting to meet him on horseback, sword to sword. She was shocked when she saw a spiked mace in his hand and his sword sheathed. Lae barely had time to pull Tanton aside. She was not fast enough, and the mace hit a glancing blow to her left shoulder. She gasped at the pain and prayed that her shoulder was not broken. The blow unseated her and she tumbled head over heels.

Ingimund circled around and rode toward her at top speed, holding his sword down like a spear. She had held onto her own sword, but without Tanton beneath her, she was at a terrible disadvantage. Lae knelt on the ground, watching Ingimund ride closer. Just as his sword came down to drive through her midsection, she leaped in front of his horse, slashing her sword across the horse's chest as she sprinted to the other side. Blood streamed out of the animal's wound as he screamed in pain. The mount went down, rolling over Ingimund. Lae turned and stared at the horse. She could see the skin pulled back, exposing muscle and tissue beneath the spurting blood. The horse's eyes rolled back, and he screamed again. Lae trembled at the horse's agony.

She raised her sword and, even though she knew she should not take the time, she sliced through the shaking horse's jugular. Blood splattered across her chain-mail as the horse convulsed and died at her feet.

Ingimund leaped across the body of his mount and grinned at Lae. She swore to herself for the act of mercy that would probably cost her her life. She did not even have time for a small prayer.

Lae swung her sword up to ward off the blow from Ingimund. The clanging of metal against metal caused her ears to ring. Sweat trickled into her eyes. She blinked so as not to loose sight of the experienced warrior. Lae stepped back as she felt her way around the dead horse. She almost slipped when her foot caught in the downed animal's mane. Lae watched Ingimund's sword flash to her left, then right, then left again. She was able to parry each of his blows, but her arms felt heavy and slow. Lae saw the sword swing above her once more, and as soon as she held her own sword up to block the blow, she knew she had made a mistake in the way she held it. Her sword shattered near the hilt, the blade catching the sun as it fell to the ground.

Lae whirled away from Ingimund, leaping sideways. Glancing down, she saw no dead man's weapon to help her. She stood and faced Ingimund with a calm that she had no idea she possessed. She would die as a soldier.

Lae heard the whistle of an arrow, followed by a thud as it hit the ground next to Ingimund. During the moment that Ingimund glanced at the arrow, Lae lunged forward, head down, and dove into his midsection. She knocked him to the ground and sent his sword flying from his grasp. She did not know what she would do next, but a surge of energy rushed through her as she realized she had a second chance at life.

Ingimund tried to shove her away, but she held on to him, and they rolled down a gentle slope. He held her to the ground. Lae hated the pressure of his weight on her, and she tried to push him off, but he was too heavy. The weight of his body plus his armor made her feel as if she were being pressed to death. She could hardly breathe.

With one frantic shove, Lae managed to force Ingimund onto her left side, then took advantage of his momentary lack of balance to push him farther away. It was at this moment she saw the flash of metal as Ingimund drew his dagger. Lae squirmed away as the dagger came down, glancing off her chain-mail, just missing the flesh encased beneath. She reached across with her left hand and grabbed Ingimund's wrist. He jerked away from her, but with a sudden strength born of desperation, she pulled back her leg and kicked Ingimund away from her.

Lae could not understand why he grunted and moaned until she saw the blood flowing from his abdomen, making a dark river across his pewter-colored chain-mail. She watched, fascinated, as Ingimund's blood wound its way like a creek across the links of his mail and dripped onto the ground, where it soaked into the dust.

Ingimund moaned again. "Lady of the Mercians, you have caused my death."

Lae sat up and studied Ingimund's wound. "I have caused your death? It seems you give me too much credit, Ingimund. I merely pushed you away. Your own carelessness caused you to fall on your dagger."

"A woman . . . the cause of my injury! The gods may not let me enter Valhalla." Ingimund's anger was apparent even through the pain in his eyes.

"I have no doubt that you will enter your soldier's heaven, for your gods are not very particular. I have fought you as a warrior, though I myself would have preferred giving you a more honorable death. I am robbed of the chance to tell an exciting story of how I avenged my people by cutting you down with my own sword."

Lae tugged her helmet off. With Ingimund down, the fighting would cease as soon as the word was passed from man to man. Lae held the helmet in her lap. "Ingimund, I place you under arrest for the attempted overthrow of Legaceaster, a village that is under my protection. For that crime, you will be imprisoned there until the end of your life."

Ingimund tried to laugh, but the sound was rasping, like the grating of stone against stone. "I will not live long enough for you to send me to a dungeon. It is my wish that I lie here until I cross to the other side."

"You are not trying to trick me, are you? You are a cunning Viking." Lae leaned forward and watched the blood flow from Ingimund's injury.

"My lady, I am hardly in a position to trick you. My life's blood flows on this land that I coveted, but can no longer take from you. I die within the hour." Ingimund closed his eyes. "Even as I speak, light leaves me, and this world seems far away."

Lae glanced up as a shadow fell across the helmet she held on her lap. She was relieved to see Stan before her. "Ingimund has been wounded."

"I see that." Stan pulled Lae to her feet. "He will be cared for. The battle is over. Legaceaster has been saved by you, my lady."

"With abundant help from you, Stan." Lae tilted her head toward Ingimund. "See that his wounds are tended to. I do not want God to think that we are as barbaric as the Vikings." Lae looked down at Ingimund. "I will see that you have a good place to rest if you die. I have my doubts that the wound is that serious. Your dagger was not long."

"You wound me with words." Ingimund closed his eyes and turned his head away.

Ordinarily, Lae would have been insulted by Ingimund's action, but sorrow for a downed warrior prevented her anger from rising. Ingimund was pathetic. She dismissed him from her mind as soon as she saw her own soldiers carry him away on a litter.

Stan draped his arm around his aunt's shoulder. "You have proven yourself an apt teacher once more. I have been sent by the town's people. They want you to ride through the city in celebration."

"I will do so as long as you are by my side. Egwinna would have been proud of you, Stan." Lae leaned against Stan, ignoring the metallic grating of their chain-mail.

"She was always near to me, whereas my father was always so far away."

"War made it so." Lae sighed. "It seems we have had wars all my life and all of yours. If our countries are to enjoy peace, we must build forts. Many forts. Legaceaster is almost a proper fort. If it had had an army, Ingimund would not have attacked."

Lae waved her arm to encompass the entire area. "I see a line of forts built across our frontier to keep the Vikings out. I will build a series of fortified cities that will house a permanent army so the people will be protected."

"A series of forts?" Stan's gaze followed her outstretched arm. "Do you mean to continue what you have already started? Down the border between Mercia and the land that the Vikings inhabit?"

"That is exactly what I mean. The people will have an army close by in case of a Viking attack. It will also give us a base of operations from which to attack them."

"It will take a long time to build these forts."

"If it takes the rest of my life, I will not care. I want to protect my children, my grandchildren, and the children for generations to come," Lae said. "Our countries can survive only if they are united. That is the future for this land; one country. We cannot survive with those barbaric Norsemen attacking. Eventually, they will wear us down. My plan will end the constant fighting." Lae looked toward the battlefield where the bodies of men from both armies were being readied for burial. She raised her fist toward the north where the remnants of the Viking army had retreated. "I will push every last one of them out of this land. By the saints in heaven, I will do it."

The victorious return ride to Lundenburh was joyous. Lae could not wait to tell Red about the celebration in Legaceaster. Her head still ached from too much mead, but she did not care. When the fortress came into sight, she could no longer restrain herself, and she allowed Tanton his head. He sailed across the field toward Lundenburh, and they galloped through the streets.

The gates to the outer bailey opened for her, and she raced through, not stopping for the inner gates to open fully before Tanton bolted through. She pulled him up short near the doors to the great hall, slid off the horse, dropped the reins and burst through the door.

"Where is your lord?" Lae shouted at a startled servant girl.

"In his chambers, my lady."

Lae hiked her riding tunic up and took the steps two at a time. She pushed open the heavy plank door and forced herself to stop inside the darkened room. As soon as her eyes became accustomed to the dimness, she could see her husband on the bed, covers pulled to his chin. She closed the door as quietly as she could. "Red?"

He opened his eyes, blinked, and grinned. "Have you returned so soon? You must have been victorious."

Lae tiptoed across the room. When she reached his side, she took his hand and held it. She did not like the coldness of it and rubbed slowly, trying to get life back into the hand that had comforted her, held her, taught her to fight. "It was a victory, Red. I wish you could have been there."

"I wish the same."

Lae winced at the sadness in his voice and was sorry she had brought up such a sensitive point. "Ingimund is sorely wounded. He tried to kill me. I expect festering to finish him off. Tonight we will tell you stories at the banquet. How is life here? Have there been any problems, anything that you had to take care of?"

Red took Lae's hand and pulled her to the bed. "Sit and let me talk to you without having to look up. It tires my neck."

"I am sorry to have been so thoughtless." Lae climbed onto the bed, pulling her tunic above her ankles and folding her legs under her. She kissed Red on the cheek. "I have missed you. Now, tell me about the trouble. Have the Vikings bothered Lundenburh?"

"It is worse than that. It is our daughter."

Lae sighed. "What has the girl done now?"

"She accused her servant of stealing her necklace. I had no choice but to question the servant girl." Red pulled his hand from Lae's. "I had the girl searched, and I had her hut searched."

"Wyn has told me this same story in the past. Whenever she loses something, she says the servants have stolen it."

"Lae, I had to search. We have had things stolen before. I have to believe our daughter for the sake of appearances."

"I understand the politics, but I wish you had waited until I had returned. I know how to handle Wyn."

"No, you do not — any more than I can. I cannot ride into battle with you, and now you are telling me that I cannot even settle domestic chores properly." Red turned his head away from Lae.

"Oh, Red. I meant nothing of the sort. I am sorry."

"You are always saying you are sorry. I loath that word, especially coming from you."

Lae cupped Red's chin in her hand and forced him to look at her. "My dearest, let us not quarrel about Wyn or the servants or anything. Mayhap the servant did steal Wyn's necklace."

"She did not. Wyn came to see me later. She was wearing the necklace. When I asked her about it, she just said she had found it. I got another servant for Wyn — an older woman," Red said.

"I know how difficult that had to be. No one wants to be with Wyn. They fear her." Lae patted Red's hand. "I will find a place for the servant that was sent away. Mayhap she will be happier in the kitchen."

"That will not be possible," Red said.

"Why not?"

"The girl was so distraught that she ran away. Her body was found in the Thames yesterday." Red took a deep breath and continued. "She had been badly beaten, probably raped." Red stared at the firepit. "I gave her father money to pay for the funeral plus some to replace what she would no longer bring home."

"You gave them a pension?"

"I had to. Our daughter gave me no choice."

"No, she did not," Lae said. "Poor servant girl. I should talk to Wyn. Why does she hate me so much?"

"She does not hate you."

"You are too kind. She hates me." Lae kissed Red on the cheek. "You do not have to protect me from Wyn. I have known about her feelings since she was a child." Lae slid from the bed and crossed the room, hesitating at the door. She took a deep breath and opened it. A short walk down the hall took her to Wyn's chambers. Even before she got there, she could hear Wyn's tirade against the woman who served her. Wyn could not even manage one servant.

Lae pushed open the door to Wyn's chambers without knocking. The sight before her was even worse than normal. Clothing was scattered across the bed and dripped to the floor where it made puddles of color.

"Not that tunic, you dolt! It makes me look like a hog." Wyn whirled around and threw the tunic on the floor along with several others. "Why are you staring? Get me a tunic that fits."

"Yes, my lady."

"Wyn, you are too harsh with people who try to help you."

Wyn's head snapped around. She glared at Lae. "Well, if it is not my mother with advice. 'Wyn, you must treat the servants better if you are to rule effectively. Dear Wyn, you must think about how people perceive you. Wyn, dearest, you must not have temper tantrums in public. It will cause people to wonder what kind of ruler you will be.' All my life you never once thought of me. It was always them." Wyn put her hands on her hips. "When did you ever think about me?"

"I always think about you." Lae looked at her daughter closely. Wyn stood next to the bed in her silk kirtle. It clung to her like a second skin. Wyn had always been slender and pretty, but Lae was startled to see that her daughter had grown beautiful.

Lae turned to the servant. "Tend to something else now." The woman scurried from the room unable to hide the relief she felt.

Wyn dug through a pile of tunics on the bed. It looked like a rainbow had crashed into the bedroom and had died on the linen bed covers. Wyn stopped digging and turned toward her mother. "Why do you stare? Have you not something better to do?"

Lae felt her temper flare, and she tried to keep her voice steady. "I have nothing more important than you."

"Oh, Mother. No wars to fight? No Vikings to kill? No sick people to make well? Then I guess you may spend a minute or two with me." Wyn stamped her foot. "How very like you to ruin my solitude."

"You want me to leave before you have found out why your father sent me?"

"I see. You would not come on your own. Father probably told you to check to see what I have been doing. What sin have I committed against the House of Mercia?"

"You caused the death of a servant."

Wyn held up a saffron tunic. "What of this? Does it do justice to my coloring?"

"Did you not hear?"

"I heard."

"It was the girl you accused of stealing your necklace."

"I know all about it. I caused nothing. If she is such a rabbit, then she does not deserve to live."

"How can you be that soulless?"

"You bore me, Mother. Always the same speech. Always telling me how horrible I am." Wyn tossed the tunic back on the bed. "You never had time for me when I was a child, so do not waste my time now."

"I gave you enough time."

"You gave me nothing!" Wyn shouted. She reached back and grabbed a handful of colorful tunics. "This is what you gave me instead of time. You gave me clothes. You gave me servants. The only thing you gave me that was worthwhile was Egwinna. And God took her." Wyn choked on her last words. "When Egwinna died, then God died for me, too."

"Wyn! Do not say such things! You will incur the wrath of God." Lae reached toward Wyn, but Wyn backed away from her mother's touch.

"It is too late now. I shall make my own life. Cannot you tell what I am doing? I am packing. I will leave here."

"Leave? You are an unmarried woman. You cannot leave without an escort. You have no place to go."

"I do not need someone to escort me. I can take care of myself."

Lae sighed. "Remember your servant? Could she protect herself? Do you want to end up in the Thames?"

"Why should you care. I was always a problem to you. You will not have to worry any longer, Mother."

Lae felt the old distrust of Wyn returning. "What do you mean?"

Wyn laughed. "I should not tell you, but I will. I intend to go to the Vikings. Eiric, to be exact."

"You have lost your senses. Why go there? You will become a slave to them, or worse. I will not allow it."

"Do not be absurd, Mother. I always get what I want. I want to go to the Vikings." Wyn laughed. "Can you imagine what the Mercians will think when your own daughter sides with the enemy? What will they think when I seek out the man that you have always loved? Oh, you pretended to hate the Vikings, but you were at their camp for many days. Did you let a Viking make love to you? I know you did. You let a Viking make love to you while pretending to fight the so-called enemy. What a hypocrite you turned out to be."

Lae felt the blood drain from her face. Every nerve in her body was on fire. "You would not." The memory of the physical attraction for Eiric caused her cheeks to flame. She put her hands up to hide the obvious red spots that she knew blazed forth with shame. "Wyn, it was not what you think. I was injured. I stayed in his father's hut, and I was always with another woman. I never let him bed me."

"You wanted to."

"I . . . I did not. He is a Dane."

"He is a handsome man. Did you not want Eiric to hold you, to undress you, to love you? How could the Lady of the Mercians allow the enemy to touch her? You charlatan!"

The sound of a slap startled Lae. She did not even know she had hit Wyn until, with a cry, her daughter fell to the floor. Lae stood over her and looked down. "Get up and stop acting like a beaten servant. To your feet!" When Wyn did not move, Lae reached down, grabbed her by the hair, and jerked her to a standing position. She let go of Wyn and wiped her hands on her tunic to remove the strands of black hair that had been pulled free. Lae no longer felt shame. It had been replaced by the anger that had always helped her to survive. She felt as if she had stepped from her body and someone else had taken her place.

"You are a Mercian princess, and you shall act like one. I am ruler in Mercia. I am the queen and you the subject. You will do exactly as I say. If you do not, then I shall have you imprisoned or executed. Whatever suits my needs at the moment will be done." Lae grabbed Wyn as she tried to turn away from her mother's wrath. Lae deliberately squeezed her daughter's arm. "Make no mistake. I will tolerate your disgusting behavior no longer."

"Let go of me!"

Lae jerked Wyn's arm. "You will do what I say. You will answer each of my questions. Is that clear?" Lae waited a moment, letting the silence between them hang like a heavy tapestry. "Are the terms clear?" Lae spoke between clenched teeth. For good measure, she jerked Wyn's arm again.

"It is clear that I am getting your complete attention for the first time in my life, Mother."

"Fine. Play the down-trodden soul if you wish. Mayhap it will make you feel better. Your words are no longer full of surprise, so the sting is gone. I pity you. You will never be blessed with real love, for you live only to hurt."

"I will run away."

"You could not wound me as much as you wound yourself. I will have you sent somewhere and guarded."

"No!"

"Yes!"

Wyn turned away from her mother and threw herself on the bed. She sobbed and kicked, thrashed and screamed. Lae waited for her to calm down before she spoke.

"You cannot stay here. I no longer trust you. You would become a spy and give secrets to the enemy. I will make some excuse for you to leave. I will take you myself if I have the time."

"Where will you take me? To a convent? Where?"

"I do not know yet, but one thing is certain. I will not take you to Wessex. I would not bring shame on the House of Wessex." Lae paced the room. "I cannot allow you to marry Stan." Lae whirled about and pointed her finger at Wyn. "You have thrown away the chance to be ruler of Mercia. Mercia and Wessex will be ruled by Stan. If I die before Edward, then, as my brother, he will rule Wessex and Mercia jointly. Even you must see that neither can exist alone. If you rule, then your hatred of Stan would divide the two countries and both would perish."

Wyn pushed her mother's finger away. "Is that all you can think of — Mercia and Wessex and who shall rule? I do not care to rule. Does that shock you? Have you never stopped thinking about politics and war?"

"Where would you be if I had?"

"Mayhap I would have had a mother like other little girls." Wyn glared at Lae.

Lae felt disgusted by Wyn's baiting of her. "Do not try to make me feel guilty for doing my duty to my people. If you had learned the lessons I tried to teach you, you would have known that leaders cannot have a life without their subjects. For whatever reason, we are born to this position."

"Then you should never have allowed me to be born. I do not aspire to lead. All I want is wealth. I admit that. At least I do not pretend to be something I am not." Wyn turned toward the window. "All that land means nothing to me except money."

"There is nothing more for us to discuss while I decide your future. Until then, you are confined to your chamber. I will have guards outside your door. Do not try to bribe them. They will be my most trusted men."

Lae left the room, shut the door behind her, and leaned against it. She had to protect Wyn from her foolish ideas. She wondered how she could have reared her daughter any differently. The sounds of sobs from the other side wrenched her heart, but the damage had been done. She had no idea how to undo the hurt. If she were such a bad mother, why had she been able to love Stan and Edith? Edith was more of a daughter to her than Wyn. Lae shuddered. It was a good thing that she had not been able to have more children. Mayhap God had been kind to her after all.

chapter

XV

YN THREW HERSELF ON THE BED and sobbed. She did not want to be shut up in her chambers like a prisoner. It was degrading for a Mercian princess.

"I will not let her do that to me." Wyn sat up and dried her eyes on the hem of her kirtle. Wyn quit crying and listened. She heard nothing. She could run away before her mother had a chance to gather the guards. Even if they were in place now, the guards were like any other men. They could be bribed. For that matter, the gatekeepers could be bribed. Everyone had a price. Her father had a price. Even her mother had a price. Wyn had learned as a child that all she had to do to get her own way was to smile sweetly at her mother. Her mother was so eager to see a smile. What a fool.

Wyn slid off the bed, slipped a dark blue tunic over her head and tied the girdle loosely around her waist. She grabbed a leather sack off the peg where it hung and threw in a few clothes, her brush, an ivory comb and a mirror. A sack of coins followed. Even though it was summer, Wyn took a woolen cloak from the trunk at the end of her bed. It would keep her warm in the cool evenings as well as disguise her.

She opened the door carefully and peered out. The guards were not there yet. She had no doubt that her mother would indeed place them, but it was obvious the queen needed time to find the most trustworthy. Good. Her mother's prudence gave Wyn the advantage.

Wyn slid out the door quietly and walked nonchalantly down the steps. She crossed the great hall without anyone noticing her. She had always been able to come and go at will. Usually the servants scurried out of her way, pretending not to see her. Most of the time it infuriated Wyn, but today she found it laughable that no one paid attention to her.

It was not difficult to make her way to the stable among the noise and confusion of her mother's victorious army. A customary frown at the groom made him move quickly, and he got her the gentle mare that she loved. The simpleton was afraid of her and seemed relieved when she rode across the inner bailey.

Things were hectic, but household chores went on as usual. Amid laughter and flirting with the soldiers, the laundress and her helpers beat the linens in a trough with wooden paddles. The smell of strong soap wafted across the grounds, and Wyn was surprised at the pang of homesickness that attacked her. She set her teeth in determination and rode through the gates, refusing to look at anything else. A frown at the guards on the outer gate assured them that they would incur her wrath if they tried to stop her. As soon as she was through the high wooden wall, she kicked the mare to a trot and they headed across the northeastern bridge that would lead her to Viking territory. It would not take her long to find their new settlement since the Danes only controlled a small section by the Narrow Sea.

Wyn felt a tear run down her face, but she wiped it away, furious that her emotions were playing havoc with her plans. She deserved better than what her mother had planned for her. Her mother had never been a mother. She was too busy fighting the enemy instead of trying to make peace with them. And her father. He never had enough backbone to stand up to his wife. Wyn remembered that, as a child, she had always been angry at the two of them. She remembered her entire childhood as one long scream. The only person she had allowed herself to love died a long time ago. Wyn cursed, daring God to punish her further.

The clattering of the mare's hooves on the bridge brought her back to the present, and Wyn glanced over her shoulder. Her mother's guards were nowhere to be seen. That stupid Viking, Eiric, would probably take her in. After all, she could help him embarrass her mother.

Would not Stan be dumbfounded to find that she had the gall to hide out amongst the Danes? Wyn wrinkled her nose in distaste. Imagine her mother thinking that she would ever let Stan near her. He was much too serious. He was as serious about wars and territory as her mother was. Well, he would not marry her now. She would be ruined as soon as it was discovered she had gone out without a chaperone. Wyn giggled. Without a chaperone and in the middle of a Viking village. She would be treated the same as a prostitute. Let her mother try to get her out of this mess.

Wyn stopped riding a half-mile from the Viking village, dismounted, and let her horse drink from a tiny spring. When the mare had her fill, Wyn led her past a hedge into a grove of trees. She would wait here until dusk so that she could search for Eiric without being seen.

In the distance a horse neighed, and Wyn quickly grabbed some grass and shoved it under her mare's nose to keep her from answering. She heard no more neighing and, in surveying the area, saw nothing.

Wyn waited until she thought she was safe, then plopped down on a grassy knoll and ran her hand through the silky grass. The sun shone through the trees, and Wyn lay back. She was sleepy. The sun felt warm on her closed eyelids, and, for the first time in hours, Wyn relaxed.

A twig cracked, and her mare snorted. Wyn's eyes flew open, and she found herself at the sharp end of a broad sword. She looked at the Viking who held her life in his hands. Wyn could not move nor could she speak. Her heart thudded against her chest, and she felt like she had a mouth full of wool. How could her mother ride into battle knowing the enemy held such swords?

"Who have we here? A Mercian noblewoman, it seems."

Wyn stared at the man who seemed near her own age. His brown hair was straight and unruly. He did not seem so dangerous, after all.

"I am hardly in a position to attack you, not that I would care to dirty my hands, so you can sheath that sword."

"You are the enemy. I could kill you and not even care." The man did not move the sword.

"You are shaking."

"Danes do not shake."

"The sword is shaking, and it is not from its weight." Wyn gently grasped the blade with her fingers and pushed it aside. Sitting up, she brushed debris from her tunic. "Have not you ever been in a battle?"

"I have. I have ridden with our warriors many times."

"Have you ridden against the Lady of the Mercians?"

"Not yet, but someday I will."

"I hear that she is a good warrior. Is she?"

The man shrugged. "She could be a Dane the way she fights, but it is unnatural for a woman to ride into battle. My father would never allow my mother to be trained in warfare. Women were born to keep a good home."

Wyn laughed. "The Lady of the Mercians would kill you in an instant for that remark if she were here."

"I do not think so. I know her."

"You know her? How?"

"Once she and my father had to fight off some wolves, and she was injured. She stayed with my aunt who nursed her back to health."

Wyn shrieked with laughter. "This is too easy. You are the son of Eiric, are you not?"

"I am Kerby, son of Eiric. Who are you?"

"I am your new house guest. I have escaped Mercia. I seek sanctuary with your father." Wyn jumped up. "Take me there this instant."

Kerby studied Wyn. "Tell me who you are."

"You do not need to know."

"You are the daughter of the Lady of the Mercians, are you not? They call you Aelfwyn." Kerby's face paled.

"It does not matter who I am. I have come for refuge. I want to be a Viking, not a Mercian."

"The Lady of the Mercians has a formidable temper. If I took you back to my village, I would not only bring down the wrath of Lady Aethelflaed on my head, but that of my father, too." Kerby turned away from Wyn and ran his fingers through his hair. "I do not want either one of them angry with me."

"Angry with you? What about me? I am the one who has given up so much. I have left my family, albeit not much of one; I have given up the throne of Mercia. What have you done? Some warrior you are. You cannot even escort one lone woman into your village."

Wyn spat out the last words, the venom in her voice propelling Kerby around to look at her. She noticed for the first time that, even in the sun, his hair was the color of mud.

"I did not ask you to come here. It is not my fault that you have run away." Kerby's voice had an edge to it. He was almost whining. He kicked at a clump of weeds. "You are not worth starting a war over. I think you are a spoiled child. Go home where you belong. I am not going to take you to the village."

"You will, too!" Wyn lunged forward and beat his chest with both hands. "You will take me there!"

Kerby backed away from her. "My father would kill me for starting another war."

"So what is another war?" Wyn reached for her mare's reins and began walking toward the village. "Are you coming?" she shouted over her shoulder. "If you do not, I may get shot by an arrow, and then my death will be your fault. My mother would wipe out your entire village in revenge. Did she not do that once?"

"If you go with me to my village, you must follow behind."

"You do not want me to go as your prisoner?"

"It would be no great honor to have a Mercian woman as a prisoner. Hold your horse back as our women have been taught to do."

"It will be a unique experience, so I will try it. How many paces behind, Kerby?" She giggled as Kerby rolled his eyes.

The Vikings watched Wyn as she followed Kerby through the village, her horse almost keeping pace with Kerby's. She did not especially like the Vikings' nosy manner. She glared at them, holding her head high. She refused to think that they might rise up and attack her. She was angrier with her mother than she was with the Vikings. Besides, Kerby was her protector, such as he was.

The sounds of the village quieted hut by hut as she and Kerby rode past. Wyn noticed a woman had turned away from a loom that leaned against the side of a wooden hut to stare at her. The loom dwarfed the woman, who held a shuttle motionless halfway through the warp. She turned as Wyn came closer, her ankles brushing the warp weights made of soap stone. The material she wove was in bright blues, reds, and saffron in contrast to her simple tunic of dark brown held in place by a pair of large circular brooches of gold and silver.

Wyn tossed her head. If the woman were wealthy enough to own such jewelry, she should have a servant do the weaving. The jewelry could not be valuable. Wyn glanced down at her gold ring. A green stone glistened in the sunlight. Wyn wore gold jewelry with gemstones.

The children who peered from behind their mothers and older sisters irritated Wyn. She glared at one until he buried his face in his mother's cape. Wyn had to suppress a grin. Children should be kept out of sight at all times until they were civilized.

When she and Kerby stopped before the largest hut, a man stood outside, arms folded, making him look bigger than he was. He scowled and, momentarily, Wyn was taken aback. Wyn rode as close to him as she dared and stared into his surprisingly dark eyes which did not seem to match his reddish-blonde hair. "I have come to seek asylum."

Eiric stared at her. "You are one guest that I do not wish to protect. I will not be a party to anything that would bring duress to your mother."

"You know who I am?"

"Yes." Eiric turned to his son. "Escort her back to her own country."

"You cannot send me back like a piece of baggage." Wyn's voice was calm, but her tone was like ice: harsh, hard, and colorless. "I am Princess Aelfwyn, daughter of King Aethelred and Queen Aethelflaed. I am certain that you know her well. I have asked for asylum. You must protect me from her wrath."

"I said I know who you are." Eiric, arms still folded across his chest, tapped a finger against his forearm. "It will never do for you to stay here. I do not wish to see your mother wage war against us as she has Ingimund."

Wyn laughed. "You are afraid of my mother?"

"Only the ignorant have no fear of the Lady of the Mercians. She is a fine warrior and has caused many a fine Danish soldier to speed his way to Valhalla."

"You surprise me with your words of fear, for you are Eiric. You are afraid of a woman?"

"Your mother has the heart of a wolf. A she-wolf who protects her cub is dangerous. I do not wish my people to be attacked, so Kerby will have to return you to Mercia."

"I will not go." Wyn slid from her horse before Eiric could stop her. "It is your duty to protect me."

"My duty is to my people. As far as I can see, returning you to Mercia is the best thing I can do for my people." He spoke brusquely to Kerby. "I doubt you can handle this woman. Get down off that horse and take her into the hut until I can arrange her return."

Wyn wanted to stamp her foot and scream, but she knew it would not matter to Eiric. He would do what he wanted. Her only chance was to convince him that she should stay. She watched Kerby dismount, unhappy that he did nothing. He would not argue with his father, and he would not talk to her. Kerby had no strength of his own. She frowned at Kerby, then marched in front of him, pushed open the door herself, and stepped into the hut where he lived, followed by the two men.

When her eyes adjusted to the dimness, she was surprised at the spaciousness of the hut. A large pit in the center of the room contained a bank of coals, even though it was summer.

Wyn smelled a stew and her stomach rumbled. "Kerby, get me something to eat." Wyn swept across the room, brushed imaginary dirt off a stool with her cape, then seated herself. "Hurry up, Kerby. You are so slow." She frowned at Eiric when he chuckled. "What do you find so amusing?"

"I find your attempt at acting royal comical. You shall have your dinner, but my son will not serve you. It is our custom to have the women wait on the men and guests." Eiric snapped his fingers. "Wife, bring a bowl of stew for our visitor." Eiric sat across from Wyn and leaned toward her.

"Notice that I call you a guest. You are that and nothing more. I do not care that you are the spoiled brat of a great lady. I do not care that you want to hurt your mother. I do care that you have put my people in grave danger."

"What do you mean?" Wyn arranged her tunic. She did not like this man's tone of voice. Just because he was to be the chief of this putrid little village did not mean he could talk to her that way. She raised an eyebrow and stared down her nose at the uncouth man before her. "Who are you to talk to me this way?"

"I am the one who will lead my army against that of your mother's. I am the one who has vowed to kill her. Does that not make your heart hurt a little? Fear me a little?"

Wyn's laughter was light. The picture of this man in mortal combat with her mother was amusing. "I have no feelings for her. You may run her through for all I care."

Taking a bowl of stew without comment from Nissa, Wyn began eating vigorously. She knew that her manners were worse than usual, but she was starved. She ignored Eiric's contemplation of her and, when the bowl was empty, handed it to Nissa. "More." She watched Nissa dip more stew into the bowl from the cook fire. Reaching for it, Wyn started eating as if her hunger would never be satisfied. When she finished the second bowl, she smiled at Nissa. "Thank you. It is good."

Nissa spoke for the first time since Wyn had arrived. "I feed you because my son brought you here, and because you are the daughter of a fine lady. You are not welcome. Your presence will bring death and destruction to our village. I am old and can no longer stand the pain that goes with the death of my people. You will leave."

"Are you going to allow your wife to talk to me that way?"

Eiric's smile was wry. "It is too late to take back the words that have already been spoken."

"I am not leaving."

"Then I have no choice," Eiric stood and crossed to the firepit.

"Finally, you understand what I demand," Wyn said.

"I have no choice but to make you a slave. My sister, Olenka, could use a good slave. Or mayhap prostitution would suit you better. Many a soldier would love to bed a Mercian lady. You are fair to look upon even though your temperament is ugly."

"What? You cannot do that! My mother would have your head on a pike. How dare you speak to me like that!" Wyn glanced around the hut for the first time. The man, Kerby, looked as surprised as she felt. Nissa looked as serious as her husband.

"Do you think your mother would come here to rescue you? Unfortunately, she has no need for an excuse to wage war against us." Eiric picked up a small log and poked at the fire in the pit. "What have you done for her? Your actions tell me that you are spoiled and impetuous. You have none of the attributes of your parents."

"Who are you to tell me what my parents are like? I am the one who has lived with them my entire life, not you." Wyn stood up and marched to the door. "I am going home."

Eiric threw the log in the fire with such force that sparks mixed with ashes flew about the hut. He jumped up and grabbed Wyn's arm. "You are not going anywhere. You need to learn a lesson or two. We do not allow women to do as they please."

"Let go of me! I am Aelfwyn, Princess of Mercia, daughter of King Aethelred and Queen Aethelflaed. How dare you touch me with your barbaric hands." Wyn tried to pull away, but Eiric's hand closed tighter around her arm. "Do as I say, you pig."

Eiric laughed and took his hand away. "I hope you never rule Mercia. Your disposition would create havoc for your people and mine. I prefer a good battle with competent soldiers like your parents to the likes of you."

"You know nothing of my mother."

"I know a great deal. She is to be admired. Her name will live in history long after history has forgotten mine." Eiric brushed ashes from his sleeve. "I will help you return home. You are too much trouble."

"I defied my mother. I cannot go back without consequences." Wyn hoped her voice sounded helpless. She had no intention of ever seeing her mother again. She could not return, for to do so would mean defeat.

"You do not belong here." Eiric's gaze never left Wyn's face.

"I had nowhere to go. I will be imprisoned if I go home. Can you allow that to happen?"

"I do not care what happens to you. You made your own problems."

"She has already ordered the guards. That is why I came here. She hates Danes."

"The Lady of the Mercians does hate us. That much is well known, even by our children." Eiric laughed. "They play games of war and die honorable deaths at the hands of a child chosen to play Queen Aethelflaed."

"It is no game for me. Did you mean it when you said that I would become a prostitute?"

"What do you think? You and I are no longer going to try to outwit one another. Tomorrow morning, you will be escorted back to Mercia."

Wyn sat at the table and folded her arms across her chest. "Like a prize goat. I will not go back."

"Why is it that we are always plagued with runaway Mercian women?" Eiric asked.

"You have had other women from Mercia? Here?" Wyn asked.

"My husband exaggerates. It was many years ago when your mother was our guest," Nissa said.

"My wife should know better than to countermand my words. She knows not that I speak of Egwinna, who, with Lord Aethelstan, was here as a visitor." Eiric laughed aloud. "I see by the look on your face that you did not know about that secret."

"Egwinna was here?"

"She ran away," Nissa said.

"Ran away?" Wyn knew her mouth was open, but she could not gather her wits about her enough to close it.

"Egwinna was not like you," Eiric said. His voice was soft, and his eyes had a far away look. "She came here by accident. She had meant to run to East Anglia."

"Egwinna ran away? Why?"

"I know not." Eiric slapped his hands against his knees. "So I will tell our people to prepare for war."

"War?" Wyn asked. She felt her heart beating faster. "Is there to be a war?"

Nissa threw down a pot. "Of course there will be a war over you. I am certain by now Lae has discovered that you have gone. She will arrive with an army."

"She cannot know that I have come here. I was careful to leave no trail."

Eiric laughed. "I should think that you told your mother the truth because you wanted to make her angry."

"Why do you say that?" Wyn asked.

"It fits your temperament. You probably said it in a voice filled with rage. I pity us if we have to fight for you and win. This battle with your mother is one that I wish we did not have to fight. The thought of the prize to be gained is terrifying."

Wyn pounded her fist against the table, causing the platters to jump. These people were no better than her own kind. No one seemed to want to help her. "I will just have to go elsewhere. I would not want you to win the battle and hate the prize." Her words dripped with acid, and as she marched across the earthen floor to the outside door, she flicked her skirts at an old cat sleeping near a bench. The old tabby hissed, but refused to move. "I hate cats."

She had no idea where she would go, but she had a good horse and some jewelry she could trade for food and a place to sleep. She would not go to Wessex. Uncle Edward would take her back to Mercia, probably under guard. She hated Uncle Edward almost as much as she hated Stan. Never were two men more alike and both were just like her mother. They talked of wars, of battles, of pushing the Vikings out of their island. The three of them thought always of the future, but they neglected to live now.

Just as she reached for the door handle, the door burst open. Wyn jumped back, then scowled at the two young Vikings in the doorway. They had obviously been running a great distance, for their faces were red and perspiration soaked their tunics.

"Watch where you are going, oafs!"

"Father! The Lady of the Mercians rides in front of a great army. They are armed, but not in chain-mail."

"How far away, Hoskuld?" Eiric leaped to his feet. "Rorik, did you count them?"

Wyn turned toward Eiric and saw that he had his hand on his knife. "You are going to fight them for me?" She glanced down at his fingers resting on the intricate gold filigree handle. A picture of blood flowing from a mortal wound in her mother's breast forced its way into her mind. She felt a pang of regret at having placed her mother in such jeopardy. How could she have been so stupid, so rotten to her own flesh and blood? Wyn shivered at the use of the term. Mayhap flesh without blood would be a better phrase in a few hours. If her mother died, it would be her fault. Her father would never speak to her again.

Wyn shut her eyes to block out the knife. "Do not fight her." She was startled into opening her eyes at Eiric's growl.

"You have never learned the lessons your mother tried to teach you. They ride without chain-mail for two reasons; they had no time to don armor, or they do not expect a fight. I am certain your mother knows your temperament. It is a sad day when a child disowns her parent." Eiric shook his head. "They carry arms in case we attack. We will not."

Wyn gritted her teeth. "Thank you." The words came out pinched.

"Do not thank me. I do a favor for a great lady and for my people." Eiric draped his arm across the shoulders of Hoskuld and Rorik. "Ride with me to greet the Lady of the Mercians. You shall have that honor since you were such good observers. The lady will remember you, and she has a fondness for you."

Wyn's eyebrows shot up at Eiric's words. She opened and closed her mouth like a dying fish, but she could not ask the questions that clattered around in her mind.

Eiric called back over his shoulder. "Kerby, you ride on my right as usual. We have much to discuss with the enemy."

Wyn glanced from Eiric to Kerby, then back to Eiric. "What of me?"

"Yes, what of you?" Eiric opened the door and stepped through, nearly knocking Wyn off her feet as he brushed past her.

Wyn watched as Kerby, Rorik, and Hoskuld followed their father outside. "You will not leave me behind like a piece of offal. I will decide my own fate." She stepped through the door and slammed it. The rafters vibrated in protest.

"If you ride with me, you will obey me. I am not your kindhearted mother, but the enemy. I could slice you in half with little provocation," Eiric said.

Jerking the reins of her horse from Kerby, Wyn mounted the animal with no help. She arranged her tunic to avoid looking at Eiric and his sons. She kicked her horse with more force than she should have, and the mare leaped forward. Cursing quietly, she decided against following demurely behind Eiric and his sons. She pulled up next to Kerby. It did not matter to her that the Viking women were not allowed such liberties. She was a Mercian.

Wyn caught herself. She was trying to run from Mercia. "How far away is the Mercian army?" She asked no one in particular.

Rorik answered. "They are less than two miles by now. She must have discovered your absence quickly. You were not difficult to follow."

"I thought I would have more time," Wyn said.

Hoskuld pointed. "Look, there are some of your tracks. Your horse's feet are small. There is a nail missing from the back left foot. Why did you not just leave a missive as to where you were going?"

"You are impertinent." Wyn felt her cheeks blaze. She had always been hasty in making decisions and often, such as now, she had to admit that she created her own trouble.

"Look ahead, Father. I see movement on the horizon. They come across the mud flats." Hoskuld pointed. "They must be in a hurry to cut across there. It is difficult for the horses."

"They do not follow my trail. I came around the flats," Wyn said.

"You underestimated your mother's determination." Eiric pulled back on the reins and turned in the saddle to face Wyn. "You would do well to learn from her. If you were not so stubborn, you would be like your cousin, Prince Aethelstan, an d study her methods."

Wyn wrinkled her nose. "Stan is pathetic. He was always running around asking for her opinion. I swear he could not sleep without her permission."

"He will be a greater threat to my sons than you." Eiric shaded his eyes with his hand. "They come at a fast pace. I see flowing silver." Eiric spoke softly. "Lae has forgotten her cowl again."

Wyn noticed a catch in his voice, and she searched his face. His eyes were shining, and there was a slight smile on his lips. "She is your mortal enemy."

"Yes."

"You act as if you are in love with her."

"I am in love with a dream, that is all." Eiric moved his small entourage forward. "Let us hope that the lady believes me when I tell her there are no hidden Danish soldiers in our woods."

Wyn was not happy with the blazing pace at which they rode. The distance between the Mercians and the Vikings disappeared too quickly. She cringed when she was close enough to see her mother's face. Wyn knew by the set of her mother's jaw and the tight line of her mouth that the negotiations would be swift and to the point. She stole a glance at Kerby. He, too, was grim. His face was pale and his eyes wide.

Wyn tried not to feel pride, but it stole up on her. "Have you not had a chance to fight the Mercian army yet?"

"I have fought in several skirmishes, but never have I faced an army of this size. There must be more than two hundred soldiers." Kerby sat quietly, the muscles in his jaw bulged as he seemed to fight to hold his courage. "Allow me to ride forth and greet the Lady of the Mercians."

"Granted," Eiric said.

Wyn licked her lips. They were dry. She felt her stomach churning. Fool, she said to herself. Your flight has made a mockery of you, for your mother comes to retrieve you like a lost cow. She kicked her horse to a gallop and chased after Kerby. "Wait!" She rode along side of him, ignoring his silence. "I have need to come out of this as gracefully as possible. Do not worry. I will not create trouble for your people."

"That is the first time you have thought of someone instead of yourself since you came to our village."

"I still think of myself first. Vikings are no better than leavings, like soap from a butchered hog."

"I would rather be the soap than the hog," Kerby said.

"I could not think of any other example," Wyn growled.

"Since you do not have a way with words, why not keep them inside? I will do the talking."

"You? You hardly speak. It is not your nature."

"Unfortunately, it was my request."

Wyn rode toward the Mercians silently. Her mother rode Tanton as effortlessly as any warrior who had fought and won battles. Wyn tried to push away the pride for her sovereign that threatened to overshadow her anger at her mother. She would honor Kerby's wish to keep silent, for she had no idea what she could say.

Her mother held up her arm, the wide sleeve of her tunic sliding toward her shoulder, revealing the sleeves of her deep blue kirtle. The tunic's night sky color accented her skin that was as milky as the moon. She still had the beauty and strength of a woman half her age.

The small gesture halted more than two hundred soldiers. The Lady of the Mercians rode toward Wyn and Kerby. When the distance between them dwindled to a few feet, the queen pulled back on the reins and stopped. Wyn shivered at the look on her mother's face. She had never seen such coldness.

"I have come for my daughter."

Kerby cleared his throat. "My lady, I believe there has been a misunderstanding between us. I have come to rectify a mistake."

Lae held Kerby's eyes locked with hers for a moment before speaking. "Mistake is a slight word for a grave error. You should never have given sanction to this woman. Your mistake could cost your people their village, their lives, and their tenuous future on this island."

"I wish to prevent an altercation between us." Kerby's Adam's apple bobbed up and down several times. "I have no desire to take up arms against a Mercian army at this time."

"Are raids more to your taste? Mayhap the burning of homes, the murder of the men and the rape of women is all that suits you."

"No, my lady. I do not care to fight that way. I do not care to fight with you at all. I have come in good faith to change a wrong to a right." Kerby took a deep breath. Perspiration dotted his forehead.

Lae looked at Wyn for the first time. She motioned for her daughter to ride to her. "I originally came here to drag you away from these disgusting people and take you home, but on the ride here, I thought that mayhap it would be a fitting punishment to leave you here," she whispered. "The Vikings have no regard for their women. It would be a bitter sentence for someone so haughty to have no power and no privileges. Do you want me to send your belongings? Actually, I shall send only those belongings that will serve you as a Viking wife. Your name shall be forever stricken from the history of Mercia, and it will never again be spoken. You shall cease to exist in the past or the future."

"No! Oh, no, Mother! My queen! Please. I have been so wrong." Hot tears ran down Wyn's face. She was shocked by them as much as she was by her outburst. Her words were not what she had expected to say. She did not care that she had no pride. She wanted to go home. She would go home on her mother's terms. It was no longer fanciful to live with the Vikings or to have crossed over to the enemy. It was no longer a charming dream of revenge. "I will do whatever you say if you will let me come home. I want to see my father."

"Not so loud. They will hear you."

"Please! I beg you!" Wyn watched as her mother struggled with ideas of punishment. Anything. She would take any punishment, even forty guards and bread and water if she were allowed to go home.

Lae motioned for Kerby to come closer. "Would you be agreeable to housing my daughter?"

Kerby cleared his throat. "We find that a Mercian princess is hardly a fit companion for our Danish women. My father wishes you to take back your daughter."

"It might be the best thing for her to stay with you. Mayhap she would learn humility."

"I would rather that she learn humility from her people than from mine," Kerby said.

Wyn was relieved to see her mother try to suppress a smile. "I will do everything you say, Mother."

"Doubtful." Lae motioned for Wyn to follow her. "Let us have a conference. Excuse us, please."

Wyn rode along side, hopeful and reluctant. "As you wish." She hated the subservient phrase, but she could think of nothing else. They stopped a second time out of earshot.

"My daughter, you have disgraced yourself twice in one day. That is difficult even for you. Do you have an explanation for your actions?"

Wyn shook her head.

"I will not accept that for an answer."

Wyn hung her head. "I wanted to wound you."

"I was not wounded."

"I know that." She looked her mother straight in the eyes. "If you had loved me even a tiny bit, I could have hurt you."

"How little you know." Lae turned her head away from the sun and stared across the mud flats into space. "Oh, Wyn."

"I was going to live with the Danes. I wanted to help them fight you. I thought I wanted to see you dead, but when I heard that you were coming and saw Eiric as a warrior, as your enemy, I . . ." Wyn choked back a cry. "I could not bear to see you dead."

"It would take more than Eiric's sword to cut me down. I have become a capable warrior. Alas, I was not a good mother."

"You were meant to be queen, not a mother."

"I should have made the time to be both. Enough. If you want to return to Mercia, then you will do as I say. I have put the mother in me, what little there is, aside. Your queen now talks to you. Are you ready to listen?"

"Yes."

"You will not be allowed out of the fortress without armed guards."

"Yes, Mother." Wyn hoped that her mother would forget that threat in a short time. She hated being escorted anywhere.

"You will no longer be betrothed to Stan. I will find a more suitable queen for him."

"Mother! You shame me!"

"I shame you? Look in the mirror for the truth."

"Let me marry Stan. How will it look if he will not have me? We have been betrothed since we were children. I can make Stan a good wife and a good mother to his children."

"Do not be absurd." Lae sat still. A light breeze rippled her tunic. When she spoke, it was in a tone so soft it seemed as if the wind had said the words. "The real reason you cannot marry Stan and have his children is that you would make an improper mother. It is the only legacy that I have given you."

Wyn was stunned. She had always pretended that her mother hated her, but she had never known that her mother blamed herself. To hear her mother's confession was like a sword through her heart. She wished she could cry, but the tears would not come. They had died along with her soul.

"Do you agree to that? Those are my terms," Lae said. "It is for your protection."

Wyn flinched, for she knew her mother was right. "I agree."

"Then let us return to Mercia."

Wyn felt like the pillar of salt that had once been Lot's wife. She waited while her mother rode over to Kerby. She did not want to know what was said. She did not want to look at them.

Wyn was startled when Lae rode over to Eiric. She leaned forward to catch the words as they floated on the wind, but she could hear nothing.

Eiric smiled. Her mother smiled in return, and then they clasped hands. Wyn was shocked. These enemies who wanted to kill each other acted like good friends. They even saluted each other as they parted! Wyn waited for her mother to join her. When Lae did,

Wyn noticed that her face was flushed. Wyn leaned over and whispered, "Is he not charming?"

Lae's head jerked around. "Let us not discuss the charm of the Vikings. They are like the fox who smiles before attacking the lamb. Remember that." Lae urged Tanton into a fast trot.

Wyn chuckled at the sight of her mother riding away from the Vikings. It was a rare sight, indeed.

Wyn's bedroom looked like a sanctuary to her instead of the prison she had believed it to be. She let her servant remove her clothing and slip her night kirtle over her head. Wyn fell into bed without dinner in spite of her mother's protests.

The night had come before they had returned home, and it was moonless and starless. Sometime in the night, Wyn awakened briefly to thunder and lightning. The rhythm of raindrops against the window lulled her to sleep.

It was late when Wyn awakened the next morning. The sky was gray, and the rain tapped against the window panes. The furniture and woolen blankets smelled damp. Wyn shivered and slid down further in bed. Mayhap she would not get up today. Mayhap she would sleep until nightfall.

She was trying to drift back to sleep when the scraping of wood and the rasping of heavy, metal hinges announced that she had company. She opened her eyes, ready to yell at her servant, when, to her surprise, her mother came into the room, carrying a tray. Wyn sat up in bed. "Do my eyes deceive me?"

"Not at all. I wanted to . . . to . . ."

"Do not explain." Wyn waved her hand. "You are feeling uneasy. It is all right to placate me. Mayhap I will be easier to handle."

"You have always been fussy when it comes to food." Lae kicked the door shut with her foot.

Wyn winced at the loud thud. Her mother had to have powerful legs to send the heavy door into the frame so forcefully. "Do not try to mother me. You never have before, and I am not sure but what, at this late date, neither of us would be comfortable."

"I have brought your favorite."

Wyn slid from the bed and walked to the table. "What is that?"

"Lamb stew with beans, barley, and carrots and thickened with amulum."

Wyn started to protest that the stew was not her favorite. She felt the old anger return. It was Stan's favorite, not hers. She looked at her mother, but seeing her placid face, decided not to destroy her dream. Let her try to play the mother game for awhile. She would tire of it soon.

"Thank you." It was all that Wyn could say. She watched her mother put the tray on the table by the window. Wyn wished she were not hungry, but she was. One thing about being a Mercian princess was that one was guaranteed good food. For as long as she could remember, her mother had always been adamant that the food be excellent. Even during the cold, winter months, the food was still edible although their stores were depleted.

Wyn waited for her mother to seat herself, then sat opposite her. Someday, others would have to wait for her to sit first. Someday when she was queen. She winced. She had agreed never to be queen. Mayhap she could behave and change her mother's mind. "What is there to drink?"

"Milk."

Wyn wrinkled her nose. She had never liked milk. It was difficult to keep fresh, and it soured quickly. She leaned over and sniffed the cup. It seemed all right. Wyn searched for something to say to the woman who sat across from her. The silence was awful. "How is Father today?"

"He . . ." Lae cleared her throat. "He is not well. I have ordered more medicine for him. I want the dosage increased."

"May I see him?" Wyn was surprised to find that tears were forming. She had always seen her father as an extension of her mother, and therefore someone with whom to fight.

"I am sorry, dear. I fear that he is too weak. Mayhap with more medication, he will be stronger." Lae laid aside her spoon and stared out the window. "I wish I could do more. It saddens me greatly to see him suffer."

"Saddens you?"

"Of course."

Wyn propped her chin in her hands, food forgotten for the moment. "I do not understand."

"What do not you understand?"

"How can you love one man and be married to another?"

Lae gasped. "You are incorrigible. Do you want to make me miserable? Is that your intent?"

"I just wanted to know. I want to know how you can have feelings for Eiric when you are married and appear to love Father." Wyn watched her mother's shoulders drop and a smile appear as she visibly relaxed.

"Oh, that. It is merely a natural attraction to a handsome man. All women tend to be flattered when someone seeks them out. I think it is a wonderful way to keep young." Lae laughed. "As long as you remember not to be serious, it can do no harm."

"I have never found any man who flatters me." Wyn picked up her spoon and resumed eating.

"Given your beauty, I can hardly believe that."

Wyn dropped her spoon. Stew splashed from the wooden bowl and spotted the plank table. "Do you think I am beautiful?"

"Very beautiful."

"Did I cause you a lot of trouble when I was growing up?"

"At times, like yesterday, you handed me a load that made me wonder whether or not I could carry it. I expected a Viking army to pull me down, but not my own daughter."

With nothing to say since she did not want to apologize, Wyn sat silently, waiting for her mother to continue talking. She liked her mother's voice. It was soft and musical.

"When I was pregnant with you, I thought you would never come. My stomach got fatter and fatter. I was afraid that I would split open and you would come tumbling out." Lae took her daughter's hand. "I am sorry I could not have been with you when you were growing up. I often wished that I could have been merely a princess so that I could have been with you."

"You were always talking of battles," Wyn said.

"Always. Even when I was not at war, I was thinking of how to prepare for war. It is a rare ruler who can relax."

"Grandfather took time to play with me."

"Your grandfather was exceptional. He knew how to put war from his mind." Lae stirred her bowl of stew, pushing aside a turnip with her spoon. "King Aelfred was admired by all his people. Even before he died, he was called Aelfred the Great. His name will live beyond this world." She finished her stew in silence.

Wyn watched as her mother closed inward, like a flower that folded in retreat from the evening shade. The intimate interlude was over. She could only salvage a little bit of respect from her mother now. "I want to be Queen of Mercia. I will do as you ask."

Lae pushed her chair away from the table and stood. "I will send a servant for these dishes. Keep to your chambers. I will think about your request. I want you to be queen, too."

"Keep to my chambers? What shall I do for exercise? Walk circles around these rooms like a caged wolf?" Wyn stood as her mother crossed the room. She watched the Lady of the Mercians regard her.

"If you must exercise, then you will exercise with guards in tow." The queen pushed the door open and swept through, disappearing as it shut behind her.

The week passed slowly for Wyn. Now, as she leaned out the window, she could smell rain in the air. The wind from the north seemed to promise snow, though it was too early. By the time the snow came, it would be too late for war. Mayhap her mother's meeting with Eiric had something to do with the peace that had settled across their countries this past week.

Wyn looked across the inner bailey. A wooden lattice enclosure held a dozen partridges, a pair of pheasants, and more chickens than she cared to count. A little girl was busy scattering feed around the pen, causing a small riot among the fowl. The sun shone on the feathered birds, wrapping them in miniature rainbows.

Beyond the window, the trees were touched with the gold and reds that signified the beginning of fall. Wyn was tired of viewing the world from her window every day. She turned from the window and stared at the spinning wheel. She was so bored. She had nothing else to do except embroider. Wyn walked over to the chair where she had been working and picked up the distaff. She laid it back in the chair and wandered around the room, touching each piece of furniture. She wished she had not sent her servant off to do errands. The woman was taking a long time to return, but Wyn understood why. She did not like being confined to the small chamber either.

The dizziness struck her so suddenly that she had no time to prepare herself for the fall. The floor rose up to meet her face.

"She awakens, my lady. The fever is high."

The voices came from far away. Her mother's voice was faded, but calling her over and over. Wyn opened her eyes. "Water." The voices evaporated with her will, and Wyn let darkness take over.

chapter

XVI

AE LEANED AGAINST THE PILLAR outside Wyn's chamber. She was exhausted, so she knew Wyn was beyond that. Lae closed her eyes, beyond caring about anything at the moment. She allowed herself to slide down the pillar until she was sitting on the floor, knees bent. Lae draped her arms across her knees and waited for the nurse to come out.

"My lady?"

Lae opened her eyes and looked up. She did not know how long she had dozed. She rubbed her neck. "How is she?"

"I cannot lie to you. She will die in two, mayhap three days."

"You confirm my fears. Send for Aethelstan."

"I am here, Lae." Stan knelt next to his aunt.

"There is no time to lose. Mount up with two of your best men and ride to the Viking village."

"Ride to the . . ."

"Wyn is dying. Ask, beg, or pay Olenka to come. We have no one who is as good as Olenka. Over the years, she has saved many a Viking warrior. She may refuse. If she does, ask for medicine. Tell her that Wyn has the fever and wastes away. I have no pride when it comes to saving Wyn's life. Go."

"You will be indebted to them."

"I know, and it galls me. I will worry about that later."

"Farewell, Aunt. I shall return by morning. You have my word."

"Wait! It would be more proper if I sent a missive." Lae jumped to her feet and ran to her room. Flinging aside the charters she had been working on, she pulled a small piece of vellum from the pile. Quickly, she scratched a note to Olenka. She knew that it was not considered proper by the Vikings to have a woman receive a note, but she hoped that Olenka would appreciate the tribute. Lae wrote in Latin, not knowing whether Olenka could read it, but Lae could only speak their tongue. She knew that Eiric could read Latin, however, so she penned her thoughts carefully.

"Here, Stan." Lae barely let the seal dry before thrusting the note at him.

"Farewell, Lae. We leave before first light. Pray to God for Wyn and for me." Stan walked briskly from the room without closing the door behind him.

Lae wasted no time in returning to Wyn's room. "How fares my daughter, Hope?"

The nurse shook her head. "I have sent for more cool water as you instructed, but her fever rages. She is delirious and calls for Egwinna."

Lae groaned. "She may see Egwinna sooner than any of us would like."

Hope nodded, her gray curls bouncing. Her cowl had long ago been draped around her shoulders. It was smudged with sweat and dirt where she had wiped her face and hands.

"Please sit and rest, Hope. You look exhausted."

"Oh, no, my lady. It would be improper."

"As your queen, I order you to sit. Would you disobey your queen?"

"No, my lady." Hope lowered herself slowly to the chair, arranged her dark gray kirtle and folded her hands.

Lae wrung a cloth out in a bowl of water. She was shocked at how hot Wyn felt. "Did you give her the medicine?"

"Continuously while you slept."

Lae pulled up the cloth that had been folded across Wyn's chest. It was hot and smelled so strongly of herbs that her eyes watered. Lae had no idea what to do. Finally, gathering her courage, she asked, "Do you think I do the right thing in preparing a poultice even though she does not cough?"

Hope clasped and unclasped her hands. "My lady, I do not presume to question you."

"I wanted truth from you, not fear."

"I meant no disrespect, my lady." Hope's eyes were wide and she continued to knead her hands together. "I meant no disrespect."

Lae patted her hands. "I know you did not, and I meant none to you. I value your opinion highly. I am asking you as one mother to another. Did I do the right thing?"

Hope pursed her lips, stared at the floor, and twisted her gnarled fingers together. "I would do the same. To do nothing and then lose a child is worse than doing the wrong thing. Besides, how could a poultice be wrong? It cannot harm the dying."

On hearing the truth, Lae felt faint. "You are a wise counselor. You do not merely tell me what I want to hear, do you?" Lae looked into Hope's pale blue eyes made milky with age.

"I am too old to hide my beliefs. It will take a miracle for your daughter to live. Allow me to get more hot water." Hope scrambled to her feet, agile for a woman of her age.

"Be certain to get something for yourself to eat. You have been here all night."

"My lady, may I bring you something?"

"No."

"My lady, you are light in weight. Do you not eat properly?"

Lae brushed the back of her kirtle to rid it of dust from the floor. "I often forget to eat. Thank you for your help from one mother to another."

"From one mother to another, I wish that God be with you." Hope nodded at her own words. "We live for their living, and die a bit when they die before us."

"I know."

"The Viking woman — I have heard that she is supernatural when it comes to healing."

"I pray you are right." Lae was silent, letting the silence build a wall between subject and queen again. With daylight came the old barriers. "I must allow you to your duty, and I must attend to mine."

Lae acknowledged the bow from Hope, then turned to attend to Wyn. Lae stood by the bed and looked down at the woman whose black hair lay limp against the pillow as a testament to the hours of fever. Regret tugged at Lae's heart at the torments her daughter suffered. If only Olenka had the power to rid Wyn of whatever demons had invaded her soul. Poor child, poor woman.

Lae could not see breath in Wyn, and she shook her immediately. "Wyn, speak to me." Finally Wyn opened her eyes and focused on her mother's face. "Listen to me. Are you awake?"

"Egwinna calls to me. I want to sleep." Wyn's eyes closed.

"You cannot sleep! Egwinna does not want you to come with her now. She is telling you to stay here. Your time is not up." Lae shook Wyn once more, but this time Wyn refused to open her eyes. Lae slumped against the bed and folded her hands in front of her to keep them steady.

Lae kissed Wyn's cheek, and her daughter stirred. Lae hoped it was a sign from God. Wyn looked vulnerable for the first time in her life.

Lae closed the door softly behind her. She had to get some rest and make certain Red was kept informed of Wyn's progress, or lack of it. The servant would call her if there were a change, and Hope would return soon.

Someone shook her. Lae pushed him away before she recognized Red. "What is it?" Lae sat up in bed.

"Stan has returned. He calls for you."

Lae threw back the covers and said a prayer as she ran down the hallway toward Wyn's chambers. When she pushed her way through the door, she saw a figure leaning over Wyn. A kettle of boiling water had been placed near the bed and a servant was fanning steam toward the patient whose head and chest had been placed in a tent-like affair.

"Olenka. How kind of you to come."

Olenka slammed down a jar of medicine. "I came because Nissa insisted that I must. She reminded me of the time years ago when you saved our huts. The woman is soft in the heart. Eiric was not certain I should help this daughter of yours. He said she is a tyrant."

"I thank you anyway."

"I also came because your nephew promised me gold. I cannot refuse gold. With gold comes independence."

"How true — in both our countries." Lae stared through a crack in the tent. "How do you find her?"

"Your instincts about healing are almost as good as mine. The poultice on her chest did no harm and may have prevented her death."

"Thank God."

"I will try to save her. What is one more Mercian to taunt us? At least this one does not fight."

"I wish . . ."

Olenka held up her hand. "Do not say it. We cannot change what has to be." She turned to Lae. "You look as if you could become ill very easily. Do me the favor of returning to your rooms. I cannot save more than one Mercian at a time. It goes against my Danish heart."

Lae did not know whether to laugh or cry at Olenka's words. She whispered, "You do us a great kindness," and left the room.

When Lae awoke the sun was high in the sky. She leapt from her bed and ran down the hall, slowing when she heard Stan's voice coming from Wyn's room. When she entered the room, Wyn was pushing Olenka's hand away.

"I do not want any of your foul-tasting potion. Are you trying to poison me?"

For the first time in her life, Lae welcomed Wyn's bad temper. Her daughter defied everyone, even Death.

"Take that medicine," Stan said.

Stan held Wyn's hands while Olenka pried open her mouth and poured warm liquid down her throat. Along with Olenka's determination in curing her patient, she seemed to get pleasure from causing Wyn's discomfort. Lae could not blame her. Wyn had probably caused Olenka more than enough trouble.

"Stan, she is much better."

"Yes." Stan wiped perspiration from his forehead with his arm. "I do not think heaven is ready for Wyn." Stan glanced at Olenka. "The angels do not have that much fortitude."

Olenka's mouth twitched, and she clapped her hand over it to try and smother her laughter. "My lord, you speak the truth."

"Wyn, how do you feel?" Lae reached into the tent-like affair and brushed dampened hair away from Wyn's face.

"How do I look, Mother?"

"Terrible."

"That is how I feel." Wyn coughed, her whole body shaking. "Water."

Olenka held a bowl to her lips. "Here."

"You look tired, Olenka. Can Hope care for her while I send for sustenance for you?"

Olenka scrutinized Lae from her face to her feet. "I will only eat if you join me. I have told you before that I cannot save two Mercians. If you become ill, it would be difficult for me to save an enemy who wields a sword against my people."

"Why do you care about me?"

"I wish I knew. I berate myself daily for my weakness," Olenka said.

"Come with me. It is quiet in my rooms." Lae whirled around and left the room, assuming that Olenka would set aside her pride and follow.

Olenka ate as someone would who had been tilling the fields all day, and Lae had trouble believing that the food had dwindled from the dishes so fast. "May I have something else brought?"

"No." Olenka wiped her mouth with a cloth. "It was good." She leaned back in her chair and looked around the room. "This is very pretty. I like it better than our long huts."

"It is not much better. We have built towers, that is all." Lae reached over and took Olenka's hand. "Why did you really come here? I know you well enough to know that you have ample gold, and you demand independence."

"I wish I knew. Eiric was surprised. He thought he would have to order me. I think it was something that Nissa said. She reminded me that I loved my nephews more than life itself. It was she who said that to lose a child was the worst thing that could happen to a woman." Olenka squeezed Lae's hand before withdrawing her own. She tore off a corner of the bread trencher and put it in her mouth. Olenka chewed slowly. "You have only one child."

Lae felt a lump in her throat. "You are so kind, Olenka. I owe you much."

"In another time, my lady, we could have been good friends. I can see why my brother finds you fascinating."

Lae blushed. "Please, I have always been true to my husband."

Olenka laughed. "In thoughts, too?"

"Always. You are too bold for me." Lae fanned herself with her hand, but she could still feel the heat in her face.

"So Eiric tells me."

"Will you stay the next few days with Wyn?"

"Of course."

"I would like to ride with you to your village when it is time for you to return."

"So we can visit as if we were childhood friends?" Olenka asked.

"Yes."

"Will it not make it more difficult for you to strike against my people?"

All thoughts left Lae's mind at the brazen question from Olenka. When at last she could think, she answered with a simple, "Yes."

Less than a fortnight later, Lae rode away from the Viking village and toward Mercia accompanied by a small army. Wyn was in a weakened state, but had improved day by day in a most dramatic fashion. She was now well enough that Lae could escort Olenka home. Lae had to leave the fortress so as to be relieved of Wyn's angry accusations toward everyone who tried to help her.

She and Olenka had indeed talked like childhood friends all the way to the Viking village, but they had avoided their obvious differences. The closer the two of them had drawn to Olenka's home, the quieter they had become. However, visiting with Nissa had been like seeing a sister. The three women had stayed up most of the night like naughty children, laughing and gossiping. Before Lae had left for home, she accepted gifts of medicine and embroidery, which made wars with their menfolk more poignant.

Lae had only seen Eiric once from a distance, and for that she had been relieved.

"My lady! My lady!"

Lae awoke quickly from her reverie. The voice sounded like the utterance of a nightmare; she recognized the sound of urgency. She turned toward the rider. "What is it?"

"A hundred soldiers ride toward us. I fear they are Vikings."

"How far from Lundenburh?"

"An hour's worth."

Lae instinctively reached for her sword. When she felt nothing, she shouted, "Where is my sword? Get it for me. Stop the supply wagon!" She leaped from Tanton before the wagon stopped and raced toward it. Although their mission had been one of peace, she had ordered a wagon with swords and armor to follow them. Lae realized that Olenka had noticed, but had said nothing.

"If I had not played the good hostess and proper guest instead of the soldier, I might have been armed. I should have thought about possible skirmishes with the enemy. They have spies everywhere." Lae muttered to herself as she stood next to the wagon that held the armor and armaments. She took her sword belt from a soldier and fastened the familiar leather girdle around her waist. Her sword, placed in her hands, was one that Red had had made for her to replace the one broken in battle.

Lae kissed the pommel and said a prayer to her favorite saint, Oswald. She did not forget St. Cuthbert and prayed to him as well.

"My lady, you should put on armor."

Lae glared at the young soldier. "Do you have time to put on armor?"

"No, but I am a man."

Lae stared at him until he blushed. "Do I not have the same capabilities in battle as a man?"

The young man stared at the ground. "I am sorry, my lady. I have little experience in your army. I had forgotten your skill."

"We have no time to argue. Arm yourself as best you can and prepare to kill a few Vikings. It is exhilarating work!"

Lae whistled for Tanton, waiting impatiently while he trotted to her side. She swung herself into position, pulling at her riding kirtle to get it out of the way, and rode to the front where her more seasoned soldiers had already formed a battle line. "I will lead the right flank charge with these men. You, Archer, take the left flank with the younger soldiers who ride behind the wagons. Hold up for awhile." Lae shielded her eyes with her hand. "It is not Eiric or our usual bunch of Vikings. These seem to be from the north. They cannot help but see that I am a woman. With their prejudices against women warriors, they will not know my strength. I will drop back as if unable to fight them. When they have followed me, you cover their left flank. I will turn back, and together, we will have them in a vise." Lae watched Archer run his fingers through his black beard. "What say you to the plan?"

"A fine one, if the Vikings do not know who you are. If they know you are the Lady of the Mercians, they will not be fooled. In that case, when you drop back, they will not follow you. If that happens, we will have to rush them together. Does that second plan suit you?"

"I will watch for your signal. If the second plan is to be in place, you will lead." Lae did not wait for an answer, but rushed along the lines shouting orders for her soldiers to prepare themselves. She stopped in front of the soldiers, so many of them younger than she ever remembered being, and searched their faces for a clue to their thoughts.

It was a young army because they had not expected this short journey to be dangerous. Lae could see no emotion in their faces nor did she expect to. It was the older, experienced soldier who was unafraid of passion and would recite his prayers aloud. She glanced over her shoulder, alarmed at the number of Vikings riding toward them. "We are outnumbered, but have no fear of that. God protects the true Christian."

The words froze in Lae's throat. She had grown fond of Olenka and Nissa, and they were not Christian.

Lae looked out at the Mercian army before her, then glanced over her shoulder at the advancing enemy. God, why did you send so many when we are so few? She turned back and looked at the men before her. Gathering her strength from somewhere deep inside her, she spoke. "Remember St. Oswald who was outnumbered by Cadwallon? On the eve of the great battle, he dreamt that St. Columba spread his cloak over his sleeping troops and promised them victory. I have always prayed to St. Oswald before every battle. He has protected me. I will vow on his grave that if he helps us slaughter the Vikings who come to attack us now, I will have his remains taken from behind the Viking territory and reburied at Gleawanceaster. He is a Mercian saint and should be buried in Mercian soil." Lae looked from man to man. "Raise your spears and ready yourselves. We fight!"

Lae held her sword in the air and waited for the Vikings to come closer. Her nerves were taut, and it was all she could do to resist leading the men out too early. The reins cut into the fingers of her left hand, forcing her to give Tanton some slack. Tanton, prancing about as usual, leaped forward. Lae pulled back on the reins, angry with herself for not having been more alert. "Tanton, hold yourself calm. Remember your training. You have been a war horse for a long time. You are experienced."

The Vikings poured over the crest of a small hill. They were partially armed, which meant that they had rushed off in a frenzy.

Lae wondered at their stupidity, but had no time to dwell on it. She dropped her sword and yelled, "Death to the Viking heathens!"

She spotted her first victim and bore down on him, holding her sword in front like a spear. The Viking sneered at her as she rode toward him. He did not try to pull his horse out of the way but held a battle-ax firmly in one hand. He grinned at her, and Lae wished she had not put Tanton in such danger. She loosened the reins so that her horse could maneuver as she rode toward the Viking.

It was easier than she thought possible to run him through, and his entrails spilled like fresh cheese. She pulled her sword out of the man, his blood running down the blade. Strangely, he sat still, staring at her, a look of surprise on his face. Finally he fell, trying to swipe at Tanton with his battle ax. Lae pulled Tanton to the left. The ax fell to the ground like its master, no longer a threat.

Lae jerked Tanton in a circle to put the horse between the next enemy that lunged toward her. She re-positioned her sword as a Dane leaped at her, swinging a battle-ax above his head with both hands. Lae's sword thrust was too short; his arms were long. She pulled Tanton back, back until he stumbled over a body. Lae looked around. The Vikings had closed in on three sides. She yelled the command to retreat and pulled Tanton sideways as she sliced the air with her sword to keep the enemy at bay.

Her men, on foot and on horseback, dropped back with her, slashing their way as they spread out. When their lines, thin but solid, had flowed around the Vikings on two sides, effectively sucking the enemy into a trap, Archer and his men closed in from the left. The Vikings were trapped in a circle with no room to draw their swords. Lae and her men surged forward with a renewed enthusiasm. Their trap had worked. In less than an hour, the Vikings had been slaughtered.

The few who had escaped would be valuable, for they would spread the word of the power of the Mercian army. Mayhap it would deter other Vikings from ambushes.

Lae smiled as a shout of joy went up from her young army. For many of her men, this had been their first battle.

Lae ripped a piece of material from her sleeve and wiped the blood from her sword. No one wanted to talk, for they had their own men to bury. "Archer, how many men did we lose?"

"No more than five, my lady. We were most fortunate."

"Still it is a high cost since we had a mere forty." Lae wrapped a piece of cloth over her fingernail and dug blood out of the engraving on her blade. She wiped the sweat from her forehead with her cowl. "Get a detail together. We will bury our soldiers in Lundenburh."

"Yes, my lady." Archer rode away from her, yelling orders in a voice that had ordered such things many times before.

Lae would not permit herself to mourn the dead in front of her men. After her first battle, she had told herself that the deaths of soldiers were to be expected for the good of Mercia. She had forced herself to become immune to seeing slaughter so that she could continue her fight against the Vikings. Her brother and her husband had both told her that was true for every leader. A soldier could cry for his friend or his family killed, but a ruler must never let emotion get in the way of the ultimate goal. Tears for a death in the family had to be in private.

Lae sheathed her sword. It was time to ride on, time to go home. She looked over her shoulder for a last look at the scene of battle. It would be one of many to come over the next few years. The Vikings were being pushed from her land. She looked toward the horizon. Her destiny lay with the Vikings. She turned and faced the southeast. Her husband waited for her. She would have good news to tell him, and he would be pleased for her.

When they neared Lundenburh, Lae could smell the salt air and the mud from the flats. Tanton's nostrils flared, and he strained against the reins until Lae gave him his head. He raced toward the timber huts that ringed the small town, the noise of his thundering hooves driving women and children from their homes. They waved and jumped up and down as Lae rode down the road into Lundenburh. The ever-present dogs yapped and jumped around Tanton's legs, but the proud horse never noticed them.

Lae rode through two sets of gates as they opened for her and her army. A huge dust cloud rose behind them and drifted toward the sky.

Lae was anxious to have Tanton rubbed down and threw the reins to her favorite groom. She slid off the horse without waiting for assistance and walked as quickly as she could toward the fortress, answering the questions thrown at her as succinctly as possible without being rude and without breaking her pace. She had been gone only two days, yet everything looked so different. Mayhap it was life, not death, that she viewed. Now she could think about home, and she wondered how Red and Wyn had fared.

The door opened for her and she nodded her thanks as she rushed through. She crossed the great hall and climbed the steps two at a time.

"Red, you are up." Lae saw him standing by the window as she entered the room. "Do you feel better?"

Red opened his arms and enveloped his wife. "The increase in medicine that you ordered has helped me more than I expected."

"It cheers me to hear you say that." Lae snuggled into the familiar curve of Red's arms. She raised her head and kissed him on the cheek. "It is good to be home."

"Is that blood I smell?" Red held her at arm's length. "You are tattered. Why do you come home with one sleeve?"

"A small conflict with some Vikings from the northeast. It was nothing."

"How many did you dispatch to Valhalla?"

"Only three or four or five. I do not remember. It was a small band. Well, not so small." Lae took Red's hand and led him to the chair by the firepit. His face was gray beneath the excited flush that dotted his cheeks. "You must sit."

"You command me like a dog." Red sat down and chuckled as Lae dropped to his feet.

"I do not. See, I am the dog who sits at her master's feet. I want to be here. It has been my favorite place since I was but a child."

Red laid his hand on her head. "You are much taller now than the youngster that begged me to tell her stories of all the battles I had been in. What a bloodthirsty child you were. Your eyes always lit up when I described a killing."

"I had no sense of life or death. I never knew death." Lae kissed Red's cheek. "I wanted to be exactly like you and my father."

"Most little girls want to grow up and become wives and mothers. You always wanted to rip the insides out of the Vikings." Red did a mock shiver.

"Oh, Red. You jest. I am surprised you had the courage to marry me."

Red kissed her on the forehead. "I would not have it any other way."

Lae sat quietly. Red's love had been steady and secure for most of her life. It was comforting, especially in battle. "I love you more than I can ever show you. I could never love another with the same depth."

"Dearest Lae, I have been blessed by God for having you. Look at me." Red placed his hand under her chin, raised it, and looked into her eyes. "My beard is white with age. My skin hangs loose over muscles that have grown soft. I am an old man about to die."

"I do not want to hear about your age. You will never be an old man to me." Lae closed her eyes to the whiteness of his beard and the lines that were etched across his face. She grasped his hand that still held her chin, and kissed it.

"I am sorry to have distressed my lady. I will not be so rude in the future. Please forgive me, Lae."

"Forgive you? Red, it is I who must beg you for pardon. I am strong enough to ward off the Vikings, but not strong enough to stop death."

"Let us not waste what time we have by talking about death. I have lived a long and wonderful life." Red leaned against the brocaded backrest. "Edward will be here soon."

"Edward?"

"You sent a messenger to him before you left asking him to come, did you not?"

"Yes, but I did not expect him immediately. He must have understood the urgency." Lae frowned. "The Vikings are too dangerous."

"Stan sent patrols to ride up and down the river while you were gone. He said the Vikings were amassing armaments. Many ships have been seen coming into their harbors."

"What else has our nephew said?"

"The blacksmiths have been working day and night in the Viking villages. He has set ours to work as well."

Red was agitated at the talk of Vikings. Lae waved her hand to dismiss the conversation. "Let us not talk of the Danes. I have had my fill of them today. Tell me of our daughter. Has she been well?"

"She is much better. The young recover quickly. She has been to see me several times today and yesterday while you were gone.

Wyn has suddenly become aware of my illness. Or she wants something from me."

Lae laughed. "Probably the latter." Lae settled her head on Red's lap once more. "Has she been sweet?"

"Most of the time. Sometimes her impatient nature took a hold of her, and she had to force herself to sit by my bed, but I feigned sleep so she would have an excuse to leave." Red lifted a strand of Lae's hair. "Have you been riding without your cowl? Your hair is as tangled as the wild roses."

"I must have lost it."

"I think you should make a law that says cowls are never to be worn. It would save a lot of fabric."

"It is church law, not mine." Lae rubbed her fingers together. Dried blood flaked off. "I shall have to go have a bath, Red. I am like a pig in a mud hole." Lae stood and kissed her husband on the cheek. "I love you."

Red held her hand for a moment before letting her go. "I will order supper for us here. We can let the soldiers celebrate alone tonight."

"Red! You may be excused, but I will not be. I will make a quick toast to our victory, then I will be up. Keep my supper for me."

The next day was gray with huge thunder clouds. Lae sat on the bed next to Red in his chambers while she awaited her brother's arrival. She stared at the frontispiece of a book that was opened on her lap. The intricate design of red, green, and gold of the first letter on the page did not hold her attention. She had been staring at that page for more than a quarter of an hour, and no words would stay in her mind.

"What are you reading?" Red asked.

"Nothing, actually. I thought a little of *Bede's Historia Ecclesiastica* would be an inspiration, but I cannot concentrate." Lae closed the book and laid it carefully at the foot of the bed. "My father left this book to me. His books are a wonderful legacy."

Lae stretched her arms above her head and tapped her fingers against the head board. "I expected Edward this morning. See? I even had a table brought in here so we may confer." Lae pointed to a long table covered with rolled maps of parchment and vellum. "I am just impatient. Mayhap Wyn gets that from me."

Red held his finger to his lips. "Listen. I hear someone on the stairs."

"You do?"

"I have developed an ear for company from spending so much time in this bed."

The door burst open and Edward strode in. "I did not bother to knock. I have such bad habits. Good morning, Red. Has my sister been kind to you?" He opened his arms as Lae ran across the room and threw herself at him. He whirled her around. "My sister gets heavy with age."

"You are terrible, Edward. It is not my weight but your weakness that makes it seem so." Lae tugged at his brown beard. "What is this? Do you cover your handsome countenance once more?"

"I cover my handsome face so that the women do not faint." Edward dropped Lae on the bed. "I have asked that food be sent up for me. I knew that you would want to start discussing war immediately, my vengeful sister. Stan is on his way to bring Wyn. They should be here soon. I see you have the maps."

Lae bounced off the bed and seized one of the maps. She tapped it against Edward's chest. "I am ready with a plan that cannot fail. I know we can rid our entire country of the Vikings. The plan is so simple that I do not know why it has never been attempted before."

"Do you have a secret pact with the Furies?" Red asked.

"No, but I do have this plan." Lae threw the map on the table. It struck another stack of maps and bounced.

"Has she told you anything about this plan, Red?" Edward asked.

"No. She would not give me a hint."

"Come, Red. Can you join us at the table?" Lae looked at him. His color was good. He seemed to be thriving on the excitement.

"I will."

The servants arrived with food just as Stan and Wyn appeared. Lae helped the servants unload the trays, ignoring their startled glances. "Sit everyone. Hurry and eat. I have much to discuss with all of you."

"We had better eat as much as possible," Edward said. "I am sure we will not be allowed out of this room for a long time."

"Edward! You picture me as a tyrant."

"You are a tyrant when it comes to the Vikings. I do not know how you are going to do it, but Stan tells me that you want the Vikings to give you the body of St. Oswald."

"I will find a way. I promised St. Oswald that since we beat the Vikings in the last little battle, I would move his remains to a Mercian burial ground. I shall keep that promise." Lae reached for the butter plate. She sniffed the butter. "Hand me that chunk of bread. The butter is not rancid yet."

"Keep eating butter and you will be as round as the cook's helper," Edward said.

"Do not be absurd." Lae buttered her bread and ate quickly. Before anyone else was finished, she had unrolled the largest map. "Look at this. Danelaw cuts across this island from southeast to northwest. We have always wanted the Vikings out, but we have not the offensive strength to do so. Although since you killed that damnable cousin of ours a few years ago, it is been easier."

"Aethelwold opened the gates for the Vikings, though. We still fight because of his traitorous treaties," Edward said.

"The Vikings are expert at the quick, jabbing raid." Stan traced a blue line on the vellum that represented a river. "They sail in, destroy a village and its people, and sail out. Our armies are never fast enough to stop them."

Wyn slammed her bowl down on the table, rattling the pewter plates. "Is that what this important meeting is all about? Vikings? Why am I here?"

"You need to know military tactics so that you can control your own army someday," Lae said.

"I do not want to control an army. I find that idea very boring." Wyn pushed her chair back and stood. "If you will excuse me, I have something else that needs my attention. I am tired. I think I will take a nap."

"You sit down here and . . ." Lae hesitated when she felt a hand on her arm. It was Red's.

"Mayhap she is still tired from her illness," her husband said.

"Mayhap." Lae fought to control her temper. Wyn looked healthy to her, but this discussion was serious. It might be better if Wyn did not know its contents. "Have a good nap."

"Thank you, dearest Mother." Wyn smiled at Lae as she left the room.

Lae watched her go. She could not tell whether Wyn's smile was genuine. If she were judging an enemy, she would not trust such a smile as that. She looked at Stan who watched her, then she glanced toward Edward. Both their faces said the same thing. They wondered how long Mercia and Wessex would remain allied if Wyn were at the helm. Lae did not feel like revealing her pact with Wyn. "She is just tired."

Stan cleared his throat. "Then she must be tired quite often."

"Stan!" Lae frowned at her nephew. "You should not be so harsh with Wyn. She has a delicate nature."

"Delicate! I still have scars from where she bit me when we were children, and I am sitting on those scars."

Red laughed and at last Lae joined him. Edward and Stan laughed as long and as hard as she did. Wiping tears from her eyes, Lae shook her head. "All of you are impossible. Quit your silliness and listen to me."

"I am listening." Edward held his hand over his mouth.

Stan took Lae's hand in his. "I promise that I will behave."

"All right." Lae tried to frown at Stan, but she smiled instead. She was proud of him, for he had learned well. "I am speaking of the forts, again."

"We have talked about this for many years," Edward said.

"I am still intrigued by this idea of forts, Lae. Tell us what you have planned for the Vikings," Red said.

Lae unrolled the map a second time. "Stan is right when he says that the Vikings are quick to raid. Their strength is their fast entrance by land or water, a bloody raid, and a quick retreat. What if we could get our army to a Viking raid as soon as it started?"

Edward leaned over the map. "That is easy. They would be slaughtered. The Vikings do not have the power or ability to wage a long-term war. The problem is that we never know where they will strike. They come up the rivers."

Red traced the Thames on the map. "This is our lifeline, and the Vikings strangle it."

"Not anymore, since we have this fortification. Since our father wrested Lundenburh away from the Vikings, we have been able to keep them out of here." Lae pointed to the top of the map. "Two years ago we built a fortification at Legaceaster in Wirral after the battle with Ingimund. We have controlled River Dee and that part of the country since."

"Are you suggesting that we build another fort?" Stan asked.

"I say that we build many forts. I have said it often, but we have always been too busy to follow through. From now on, we act. Together, Edward, you and I could start the drive against the Vikings. Too long we have looked for a way to push them out with one huge army. It is not effective."

Lae's excitement caused her to talk faster than normal. Barely stopping for breath, she continued. "Well-placed forts could protect our armies and provide a garrison for attack. We could station armies anywhere in Danelaw. We could respond quickly to their raids and eliminate the Vikings."

There was silence. Lae studied the faces of the men. They stared at the map. Lae could hear her own breathing. She knew it was a good plan. She prayed that they would see it.

Edward was the first to break the stillness. "We would need several forts in the middle of the country as well as on the rivers."

"Do not forget the Roman roads. The Vikings travel them almost as well as they travel the water." Red pointed to a brown line.

"We can do it, Lae." Edward grabbed his sister and gave her a hug. "Your idea will work. We will not only block the Vikings with small armies of our own, but we will attack the attackers."

"Yes," Stan said. "Each fort will house a garrison equipped to fight."

Red leaned over and grasped Lae's hand. "The only question is where shall we start?"

"I want to start at Scergeat and Bridgenorth." Lae folded back the sleeves of her kirtle and pointed to a spot on the map. "Scergeat would protect Lundenburh from western attack down the Thames. Bridgnorth would be on the River Severn and would protect our people in the northwest."

"I want to build at Witham," Edward said.

"Inside Viking territory? Edward!"

"You will keep them so busy on the western front that I will slip in and build a fort before they know I am there."

"It is so unknown that it will probably work." Red studied the map. "Would you also build a second fort here?"

"At Heorotford?" Edward pulled at his ear lobe, mimicking a habit of his father's. "It could lie across the river from the stronghold the Vikings have there already." He slapped his hand on the table. "What better way to know what the Vikings are doing than to sit and watch them? It is a fine idea, Red. I will do it. I will build two forts at the same time."

"Father, while they watch you build a fort at Heorotford in their own backyard, you will sneak in and build another fort way inside their lines. You are as devious as Lae," Stan said.

"Together we will build so many forts that the Vikings will be squeezed out." Lae rolled up the map and placed it next to the others on the table. "Do we have a plan? Do we start building as soon as we gather the men?"

Stan clasped his hands behind his head and leaned back. "I assume we will use trees in the forests near each fort for the walls and such."

"It will go quicker that way. We want to surprise the Danes," Lae said.

"What a surprise it will be for them to find us on the offensive all the time," Red said. "I am glad that I will be able to see that in my lifetime."

Lae winced at his words. She wondered how long his life would last. She pushed the morbid thought from her mind. "Red, do you think Mercia is strong enough to take the offensive?"

"I think so. Even if she is not, the offensive must be taken anyway. You have a good plan, but if we wait too long, the Vikings will weaken us with little jabs into the heart of the land."

Edward pushed back his chair and paced the floor. He stopped in front of the window and looked out. Turning abruptly, he pounded his fist against his other hand. "We can do it. Wessex has the manpower. We have the strength, but most of all we have the desire. Together, Lae, we shall conquer the Vikings. I will pledge my support to you this moment." Edward crossed to the table and picked up his bowl of mead. "A toast to the House of Mercia and its very fine lady. To our success."

Lae watched Stan and Red pick up their bowls. All three watched her as she sat stunned. She finally picked up her bowl and held it against the other three. "To victory. No matter how long it takes, the Vikings will die to the last man."

"Hail to a new beginning," Red said.

Lae drank the sweet liquid. It slid down her throat, and she was glad God had given the earth bees to make honey. She felt warm and comfortable. If she died tomorrow, it would not have been in vain. She looked from Red to Edward to Stan. Her husband, her brother, and she were of an older generation, but Stan would carry through if anything happened to them.

The mead made her sleepy and as soon as Edward and Stan took their leave, Lae helped Red back to bed. She lay down beside him and promptly fell asleep.

The pounding on the door made her groan. She rolled over, pulling a pillow over her head to quell the pounding of a blacksmith that must have taken up residence inside it. He was obviously making shoes for a thousand horses. Her mouth felt like someone had milked all the moisture from it and stuffed it with flax. Someone shook her. "Go away."

"Lae, you must awaken." It was Red.

Fearing that her husband was ill, Lae snapped out of her mead-induced sleep and sat up. "What is wrong?"

"Edward is here with a message."

"Edward?" Lae squinted into the darkness of the room. Edward was lighting the candles in the stands and on the tables. He ordered a servant to light the sconces on the walls and then leave. When the door shut behind the young man, Edward waited until footsteps had died.

"For God's sake, Edward, what is wrong?" Lae felt like screaming at him. He always had a peculiar need for light. She could have listened to him in the evening's first darkness, but he could not. "Speak quickly, Edward."

"Your spies have just come in from the northwest, and mine from the northeast. Both have similar messages. The Vikings are amassing for an attack."

"Where?"

"We are not certain yet. They are coming from many parts of Danelaw. There are three kings who ride from the east, the west, and the north."

"No, it cannot be! We have not had time to build our forts yet. They cannot attack us now." Lae jumped from the bed, her headache replaced by anger and fear. "We cannot fight the entire Viking country. We can fight them if they are in small groups."

Edward grabbed Lae by the shoulders and shook her. "We have to fight them. No matter how large their army is, we have to fight."

"Oh, God, Red! What are we to do?" Lae threw herself across her prone husband.

"Lae, I am surprised at your fears. Why do you act this way? You have killed Vikings before. They have come after you with numbers greater than yours."

His voice soothed her with vibrations that affirmed life. Lae pulled herself away from Red, looked from him to Edward. "I do not know why I behaved so badly. I wanted to surprise the Vikings with our forts. Instead, they surprised us."

"We will still surprise them, Lae." Red took her hand in his. "Only this time we will surprise them twice. We will fight them wherever they invade, and we will build forts."

"Yes, we will. What else have our spies said?" Lae's mind was whirling. She had much to do.

"There are thousands of Vikings. We must gather our armies as quickly as possible. I have taken the liberty of telling several of your men to prepare to ride tonight." Edward walked to the door. He turned. "Lae, you have met the Vikings before, and you have always been victorious. You will this time, too, I know it. I feel it here." Edward placed his hand on his heart.

Lae smiled. "I had a moment of weakness. Better in my own chambers than on the field of battle. I shall be strong when I need to be. I have but one regret."

"What is that?" Red asked.

"I am sorry that Eiric and Thorsten have chosen to attack. I have grown fond of Olenka and Nissa."

"As had our father grown fond of Nissa's brothers. They fight us as well," Edward said.

"For what? Land. So be it. It was our land long before they came, and it shall be ours again," Lae said.

chapter

XVII

HERE WERE THOUSANDS OF THEM. From her vantage point on Tanton, Lae stared at the hordes of Vikings who marched toward her, spears high, swords sheathed for the moment, and round shields held casually to their sides. There were three distinct groups of Vikings each separated from the other by a few hundred yards.

Lae took a deep breath. The field of battle was far to the northwest of Lundenburh, almost to Tamoworthig. She said a prayer for the safety of her men and for those she left behind — Red and Wyn.

"I wish that your father were here to see this sight," Lae told Stan. "It will be a battle recorded in the chronicles for certain."

"How so, Lae?"

"There are so many Vikings, that to defeat them, to slaughter them, will weaken Danelaw permanently." Lae turned in the saddle and looked at the army gathered behind her. She, too, had amassed thousands of men from Heorotford, Weogornaceaster, and Gleawanceaster, and from small villages as far away as the border of Wessex. It had taken more than a month to gather an army. The standing army would not have been enough, and Lae was glad she had listened to the advice of her husband. Even from his sickbed, he had had a premonition that this battle would be important. It would have been better had Edward been able to be here.

"Lae," Stan said, "Father will miss one of the best fights of all time."

"I wish Edward were here. The Vikings knew he was fighting them and too busy to come to our aid."

"They did not create a problem in the southeast to lure my father there without some reason." Stan looked up at the sky. "See, the birds gather already. How do you suppose they know they will soon be feasting on the dead?"

Lae shuddered. "Stan, promise me that if I am killed today, you will not let those disgusting birds peck out my eyes and eat my flesh."

"I would not think the birds would dare do that to you."

"The birds know no difference between a dead rat and a dead queen. They are the most democratic of all of us." Lae patted Tanton absently as she drifted into a world of her own. She started to pray to St. Oswald and smiled at the irony of his reburial in Gleawanceaster. She had no way to get his body from deep inside Danelaw without grave danger to herself or anyone she would have sent. She had decided to enlist the aid of Eiric although she had not really expected him to answer her letter or to agree to get St. Oswald from Lindcylene. She chuckled.

"Why do you laugh?"

"I was just thinking of St. Oswald. Thanks to a Viking chieftain, he now rests on Christian soil rather than heathen ground."

"You never did explain how you talked Eiric into giving up something that was valuable to us. I am surprised they did not destroy St. Oswald for revenge."

"I do not understand it myself. I promised Eiric gold and jewels, but he refused, saying that he had no need for my baubles. What Viking does not like gold? I think it is because it sparkles. People cannot resist the call of gold."

"Eiric had too much pride, mayhap," Stan said.

"Yes. I, too, have pride and do not like being beholden to him, but it was most important to me to get St. Oswald returned."

A horse galloped up behind Lae. "Who is that, Stan?"

"One of my men. He has been seeking information for us." Stan held up his hand in salute. "What news have you?"

The messenger stopped his horse quickly. The animal snorted in response to the dust that swirled around his legs. "I have come to tell you that three Viking kings have three armies coming to fight. The first king is Agmund."

"Agmund! He vowed never to set foot in our country. He has signed a peace treaty with Mercia." Lae slapped her hand against the pommel of her sword. "I have named this sword for a warrior queen of old. May this sword, Boadicea, slice off the head of that lying ingrate. Who else leads an army against us?"

"They are called Gunter and Egil." The messenger licked his lips. He could not look at Lae and turned his head. "I have it on good account that they want to capture you."

Lae drew her sword and held it across her breast. Her anger at their impudence made her words sharp. "See this sword? They will not capture me. I will kill myself before I let a Viking murderer touch me." She returned the sword to its scabbard. "Thank you for the information. You may return to your ranks. Stan, we have forced the enemy into one last major battle. They are gathered together as one unit instead of fighting us and each other. We have made the enemy cohesive. The end of the conflict is near. We will see if they can capture me."

Stan waited for the man to leave, then he spoke to Lae in a low voice. "I do not think you need worry about being captured."

"Never underestimate the enemy. Look, they are nearly in range of our arrows. It is time to make the last preparations."

"May we meet again at the end of the day to celebrate our victory." Stan saluted and rode to the left where his men were positioned.

Lae took her helmet from the apprentice blacksmith responsible for her gear and positioned it on her head. She lifted the veil of chain-mail that hung down from the banded eye holes and shouted to the blacksmith. "Go back to your wagon. You belong at the back. Hurry. We are about to ride out." She dropped the chain-mail down carefully over her lower face and neck and arranged it over the chain-mail shirt she wore over her tunic. Tunic and chain-mail were both gray, a somber color for a somber day. She looked at the sky. It was too cheerful. The beautiful August blue sky and fluffy clouds would be witness to a bloody day.

She looked across the field at the Vikings, then at Stan. He was in position, waiting for her sign. Lae stood in the stirrups, drew her sword, and held it high above her head. The stillness settled over her men like a blanket. The silence roared in her ears, the ultimate quiet that came before the noise of battle. It was a collective prayer to God from each man for his soul.

She swung her sword downward and at the same time dropped into her saddle. Tanton leaped forward. From the shouts of the men behind her, the thundering of the cavalry, and the running of the infantry, Lae knew there was no turning back. This battle would be fought to the death.

"St. Oswald, protect my men from the Vikings." Lae did not have time for another prayer. She rode straight into the Viking infantry.

The infantry was no threat to Lae as she held her shield in place and swung her sword down, slicing away arms and hands. She knew her men followed her, especially the six hand picked soldiers who were her best fighters. They would protect her flank as she tore through the Vikings. Lae saw a figure in front of her in a fine tunic under chain-mail. She wanted the man who wore the tunic decorated at the hem and sleeves with brocade: a king. He would die for making the remark that he would capture her. The man she rode toward was broad of shoulder with muscles that had known hard use. Flaxen hair escaped from his round helmet trimmed with gold about the eyes and on the nosepiece. His horse was powerful and well trained, plunging into battle without flinching.

Lae rode toward the king at full speed, her sword ready. He would be the first important Viking she killed today. She was ready for the beginning of a fight to the death when a warning shout caused her to turn to her left. The warning came soon enough for her to raise her shield and ward off a deathblow, but not soon enough for her to escape the force of a battle-ax. It split her shield and sent her tumbling from Tanton.

When she hit the ground, she clung desperately to her sword, holding it away from her. She rolled away from the source of danger while one of her men rode in and sliced her attacker through his helmet with a battle-ax. Lae was close enough to be showered with hot, spurting blood, but she had no time to think about her near death; she jumped up and looked for the king whom she wanted to kill.

He stood in front of her, waiting for her to get to her feet. Lae was sure that he was smirking. She swooped down and grabbed a dead Viking's shield while keeping an eye on the king. He advanced. She quickly took a stance, feet planted apart, sword held tightly in her right hand. Somewhere behind her she was aware of Tanton snorting and pawing the ground. He would not leave her.

The king was quick to raise his sword. Lae grasped her shield tighter and maneuvered it between his sword and her body. The blow from the sword made her shield vibrate, and it sent a tremor up her arm.

Lae retreated a few steps to maintain her balance, then inched forward, effectively blocking the king's thrusts from the right, the left, then the right again. She looked for an opening to thrust her sword into his gut, but he was too quick.

Sweat trickled down her back, and she had to blink to clear the water from her eyes. If she got out of this encounter alive, she would never think so highly of herself again. She could not imagine why she thought she could take on someone of this stature.

Thrust, parry, and slice. The clank of swords developed an odd rhythm. She shook the mesmerizing sounds from her head and consciously changed the rhythm of the fight.

The change caught her adversary off guard; he dropped his sword too low, and Lae hacked at his arm in a swift and powerful movement born of desperation. She sliced through his leather arm covering, and blood flowed like a river. It surprised them both so much they stopped fighting. Lae took deep gulps of air. Her lungs had never burned so much before.

There was not much time for rest. She was close enough to the king to see his eyes change from a look of amusement to one of hatred. She watched, fascinated, as he switched his sword to his left hand and raised it against her once more.

Unbalanced by fighting a left-handed soldier, Lae had to adjust her technique. His quick thrust was thwarted by her, but the next lightning movement sent her sword flying. She yelped and looked in the direction that it flew, sidestepping toward it, as the king, intent on her death, followed, stabbing at her.

She held her shield in front of each jab, but could not get the opportunity to retrieve her sword. She stood on the blade so that no one else would grab it. "St. Oswald, help your daughter in her time of need!" Her words brought laughter from the man who kept stabbing at her.

Lae did not know that help had come until she saw the king's eyes shift from her to somewhere behind her. Stan scuttled around her and swung at the king with his sword. The ring of metal against metal was followed by the king's cry as his sword was knocked from his hand. Lae took this moment to pick up her own sword. Never had it felt so good. She was ready to send her enemy to Valhalla when she heard him say what she thought was a prayer. He crumpled at her feet.

Stan pulled his sword from the body of the king. "Are you all right?" he shouted.

Lae nodded, unable to speak above the noise of the battle. She looked for Tanton and, seeing him, whistled. His ears pricked up and he trotted to her side. Stan helped her mount, and she saluted him. She was smiling behind her chain-mail mask, but he could not see her face.

It was easy to ride into another fight. Two of her men were outnumbered by a gang of Danes, so she rode one Viking down, smashing his skull inside a helmet that was too thin to withstand a war horse's hooves. She sliced into another Dane's neck when he looked up at her as she rode past. His chain-mail had parted, exposing mangled flesh.

She rode on, looking for more Vikings to slaughter. No longer did she fear death and no longer did she feel at a disadvantage. She looked for another king to vindicate herself, but she was never able to reach the one she saw across the field. She slashed her way toward him, but always he seemed to maintain the same distance. After one of her sword battles, she looked again for the king, but he was nowhere to be found.

Lae did not know how long the battle lasted, but all at once it seemed that only Mercians were on the field. What was left of the Viking armies broke rank and ran, leaving their dead behind. Some tried to carry the wounded, but they could not escape and were cut down.

Lae was ecstatic at the retreat of the Vikings. She shouted, "Take no prisoners! Take no one hostage! Death to all Vikings." She sat back in the saddle and watched as the wounded were quickly set upon and killed. It would be a fine story to share with Red. He would be pleased, indeed, at the Mercian success.

Lae did not think she would ever get clean. She slid down in the tub. "More hot water. I smell like the verjuice used in pickling."

She bent her legs and watched through half-closed eyes as the servant poured boiling water in the tub and swirled it around. "Red, I am too old to fight. My muscles ache. Even my bones hurt."

"I am surprised you had nothing more than blisters on your hands from the sword. I have been told that you did your share of killing today." Red talked to her from the bed where he reclined against a pile of pillows.

"I wanted to kill a king, but I failed at that. It was a good thing Stan came along, or I would not be here." Lae stretched one arm out of the water and lazily ran a sponge up and down her arm, making a white lather glove. She dropped the arm back under water and watched the soap dissipate. "We killed thousands of Vikings and King Agmund, King Gunter, and King Egil. Three kings, and I could not even kill one myself."

"This battle has been a great triumph for us. Mercia will not only be safe, but so will Wessex. Our lands have almost tripled in area because of this battle. You, my dear, have done better than if you had killed all three kings yourself. You have made our land safe, and the Vikings will be wary of us for a long time. For the first time in a decade, our people will know peace," Red said.

"There may be more battles," Lae said.

"Mayhap, but essentially, the wars are over."

"I was frightened. I have never been so frightened in all my life. I thought that king was going to kill me. I did not mind dying, but I did mind dying without having killed anyone of importance."

Red laughed. "Lae, you are a strange one. I am glad that we are on the same side. I have dispatched a messenger to Edward telling him the news. I told him of Stan's kills. . . ."

"How many?"

"His men say he killed at least twenty. I told Edward twenty or more. I told the messenger not to return unless he had word from Edward. I knew you would want to know what was happening in the southeast."

"You are so good to me, Red." Lae stretched. "Were you this tired after a battle? I seem to remember wanting to celebrate, not take a bath."

"Age slows one down. When one almost dies in a battle, it makes one sleepy."

"I would think that sleep would seem too much like death." Lae stood, reached for a linen cloth held by the servant and, wrapping herself in it, stepped from the tub. She shook her head when the servant wanted to put slippers on her feet. "You may go now." Lae waited for the door to close behind the servant before running across the room and climbing into bed with her husband. "I am going to build a monument to commemorate the Mercian victory at Tettenhall."

Red opened his arms as Lae burrowed into them like a sleepy child. He kissed her cheek. "A monument? What kind of monument do you want to build?"

"I am going to build a fort on the Penk River near the Bremesburh battle site. I want the peasants to know that we will always be nearby to protect them. It will not hurt the Vikings to know that we will be close by, either." Laughter rumbled from Red's chest, and Lae had to smile. "Will it not be an irritant to the Vikings to have a Mercian fort near their border?"

"That it will. When will you start this fort?" Red kissed Lae's throat.

"Red, please." Lae gently pulled away from her husband. She was afraid he had no strength for her. "After I sleep for two or three days, I will start making plans." Lae closed her eyes. "Would you hold me while I sleep? I am prone to nightmares, so if I have bad dreams, please awaken me."

"I am most happy to do that for my warrior. First, I have a favor to ask of you." Red pushed away the linen wrap, cupped a breast in his hand, leaned over and kissed her nipple.

Lae trembled with need and excitement. "Red, I am afraid for you." She rolled away from him.

"What good is life without love?" Red reached for Lae, enfolding her completely with his body. "I do not want to live if I cannot make love to my wife. I need memories for the long night that awaits me."

"Oh, Red." Lae grabbed him and pushed herself at him. She, too, needed memories. It would be a sweet gift from her husband made sweeter by its rarity.

Lae never knew anything could be as invigorating as a good battle followed by being bedded, so she was surprised to discover that she also had a passion for building. She sat in the great hall near the firepit, staring at the two men who stood in front of her. She had called for the best builders she could find, and when they finally arrived from Windlesora, she was shocked to discover how young they were.

"I thought you would be much older." Lae stared at the brown-haired, brown-eyed youth. "You are not the man for whom I sent." She turned to another man, who was older. "Who are you?"

"I am Carl. We are the sons of the man you wanted. Regretfully, he is too old to build anymore, but has taught us all that he knows. We have worked for him all our lives."

Lae shook her head. "I need someone who will build a sturdy fort that will last a century or more. Finding another builder will put us behind schedule. Winter will be on us before we know it."

"We are good builders. We can do whatever you please." Carl glanced at Robert. "My brother is excellent at getting men to do what he wants. I have sketched some drawings for you."

"I wanted someone with experience."

"We have much experience at the right hand of our father. He has sent us to you because he knows we are master builders." Carl stood quietly, hands clasped behind his back.

"I have no choice. If we are to have a fort built and manned before winter, then you must build it. Bring me your wax tablets. I would like to see the plans."

The two men bowed and backed away from her all the way to the door and opened a trunk that had been placed there. They seemed to be more energetic than when they had come in, and their conversation was animated. The men returned to her, each ladened with a half-dozen wooden pallets. They set the wooden frames on the floor around Lae on the side away from the firepit.

"Did you build the frames?"

"Yes, we did."

"They are built like fine furniture." Lae looked at the corners. They fit together so tightly that the wax had not had a chance to seep out before getting hard. "Your wax looks even, too. Where did you get such a level spot to make these?"

"We have a special table that is level. Our father always said that quality begins with the tools," Robert said. He twisted a stylus around in his fingers.

"Your father was right. I am impressed." Lae leaned over to see the wax forms better. "Shall we begin? Tell me about the drawings you have made."

Carl squatted in front of the wax trays and arranged them in order. "We tried to follow your specifications, with a few exceptions. We felt that the strength of the fort would be weakened if we used your plan exactly, so we changed it. If you approve the changes, then we will leave immediately for the site. We want to cut the trees as soon as possible."

For the next two hours, Lae was instructed in the fine art of building. When she was satisfied that the changes were satisfactory, she sent the men to the kitchen to stock up on food for themselves and the skilled workers they had brought with them. As the men rode out of the fortress toward the northwest, Lae returned to Red's chambers.

Red lay sleeping. His coloring was grayer than it had ever been. A tear slid down her cheek as she allowed herself to realize that, if Red lived past Christmas, it would be a small miracle. She had increased his medication so much that she was afraid to give him any more; he could die of its poisonous effects. She had wanted to send for an Arabian physician, but Stan had gently talked her out of it. The physician would not arrive in time.

Lae touched Red's hand. It was cool. She took a woolen cover from the end of the bed and laid it across him, covering his hands. She was frustrated because she could do no more for him. Lae sat in the chair next to his bed and worked on her embroidery. She had wanted to have a Christmas banquet, but now the idea seemed ludicrous. She glanced at Red. She would spend as much time with him as possible. She could not remember when he had not been a part of her life. She pushed thoughts of death from her and tried to recall happier times. She could not. Red stirred, and Lae leaned forward. He slept soundly once more, and she went back to her embroidery.

Many weeks passed with Lae next to Red's bed, soaking up his lucid moments like a beggar. She noticed that people who had known Red sensed, somehow, that he was gravely ill. Lae spent countless afternoons talking with guests while more often than not, Red slept through entire conversations. When he did awaken and was told who had been visiting, he was pleased.

Christmas passed in much the same way. Lae wondered what gift to give to Red in the name of the Christ child. She finally made him a new night tunic that was warmer than his present one. She doubled the material and lined it in soft silk that she had purchased at the small market square. Because Lundenburh's port was open to ships from many lands, Lae was able to order wonderful things.

Lae usually enjoyed choosing presents that the Lundenburh merchants brought for her to see, but this time the task was fraught with a bittersweet urgency. She purchased a new pair of shoes for Wyn and a fine gold ring for Stan. Edward was a problem, but she had bought a fine piece of wool and made him a new cloak. Christmas was melancholy, but Lae remembered to thank God for letting Red live through the holy day.

Every day, Lae still sat next to Red's bed, embroidering more than she had ever done in her life. She looked at the pile of material scattered at her feet and leaned back in the chair, letting her head fall back. She closed her eyes. A timid knock on the door startled her, for it was morning — not the usual time for visitors. She had sent the servants away so that she could be alone with Red.

She reluctantly pushed herself from the chair and opened the door. "Wyn, how good of you to come."

"I have to see Father."

Lae stepped aside. "Come in. He sleeps." Lae motioned to a chair. "Please sit down."

Arranging her skirts about her, Wyn settled into a chair next to her mother. "He will never get well, will he?"

"No."

"How much longer do you think he will live?"

Lae frowned. Wyn was not usually so concerned about her father's health. "Why do you ask?"

"I am his daughter."

"You have never shown compassion before. Why now?"

"You think I am a terrible person, do you not? Well, I view life differently now. Since my father has become sicker . . ." Wyn choked back a sob. She licked her lips, then continued. "Since my own father is near death, I have seen how tenuous life is." She looked at

Red. "He is my father and can never be replaced. I want to make peace with him before he dies. I have never been a good daughter."

Lae studied her daughter. She could see no falseness in her. "Do not worry whether you were a good daughter. Your father never said anything unfavorable about you. He loves you."

"He is alone in his love for me."

"Wyn, do not say such things." Lae started to tell her daughter that she loved her, but the words would not come. "What is the weather outside?"

"The weather? You ask about the weather as if to change the subject to something that is safe." Wyn twisted her ring around her finger. "It snows."

"Snows? How much?"

"Not much." Wyn sounded disgusted. "It is past the Epiphany. One can expect frost or snow."

"Spring will come."

"Without Father."

Lae started to scold her daughter, but thought better of it when she saw her face. Wyn was distressed.

"I have some things to tend to, Wyn. I would not trust anyone else to watch your father for me. Would you stay here for an hour or so while I go to the kitchen?" The smile from Wyn was proof to Lae that she had been right: Wyn needed to help.

"I will be happy to. Go and tend to the kitchen." Wyn leaned forward and looked at her father. "Why do not you send him some broth? It would be good for him."

Lae started to tell her that Red had not eaten for two days, but she held back the words. "As you wish."

Her walk to the kitchen through the timbered fortress was met with smiles. Lae was aware that she created a flurry of excitement, but she assumed it was because she had been with Red for the better part of three months. Gifts to her servants had been given to them on Christmas Day by Stan and Wyn. She had spent the entire time with Red convinced each day that he would not live through it.

Lae returned the smiles of her servants, asked about husbands, wives, and children as she led a servant with a tray up the wooden staircase to their chamber.

A second servant opened the door for Lae when the bottom of the door was kicked. Lae sighed at the intrusion of the servants again, but smiled at the young girl who had fixed the fire in her absence. "Set the tray with the broth on the table beside the bed. Wyn, how is your father?"

"He stirs as if to awaken, but does not. Why?"

"It is an effort for him to do anything. He is not the strong man I married. His body has forsaken him, but his mind is still young." She grinned a silly lopsided grin at the memory of the last time they had made love.

"Mother, his eyes have opened."

Lae pushed the servant girl out of the way. "You may go now. We wish to be alone with our lord." She stood next to Wyn. "Good morning, Red."

"Do I see two lovely angels? Am I in heaven already?"

"Father, you should not jest about such things. Are you hungry? Mother has brought you some broth."

Lae could see that Red was going to refuse the broth. "I know that you will want some. It was Wyn's idea." She watched Red struggle to sit. "Here, let me help you."

"I will help, too," Wyn said.

Lae held Red upright while Wyn arranged his pillows. When Red was in a sitting position, Wyn climbed onto the huge bed and sat next to him. "Hand me the tray. I will feed you, Father."

"She is persistent. I would not argue with her, Red."

"I can tell she is your daughter, Lae."

Wyn glanced at her mother, an embarrassed smile on her face. "I am not sure I am worthy of that comparison."

"Having my wife and daughter nurse me has given life to these old bones. No, Wyn, do not feed me. I can lift a spoon from bowl to lips."

Lae watched in amazement as Red consumed the entire bowl of soup. His hand was unsteady, but he did not spill much on the cloth that Wyn had tucked under his chin. Lae took the tray, placed it outside the door and hurried back to sit on the bed with Wyn and Red.

The day passed quickly with the three of them laughing, talking seriously, and reading aloud. Lae was surprised to find that Wyn read well and was more of a scholar than she had realized. She was not as learned as Lae, but she was young yet. Given time, she could be well educated.

Evening came and Lae could see that Red was happy but tired. He refused more food when Wyn offered it. Lae felt sorry for Wyn. "Wyn, tomorrow you may return. I think that your father needs rest now."

Wyn kissed her father on the cheek and climbed down from the bed. "It is with reluctance that I leave. I shall return tomorrow with your breakfast."

"I will get fat with no exercise and all the food you try to force on me."

"Good night, Father, and sleep peacefully." Wyn blew a kiss to her father from the door, slipped out, and closed it quietly.

Lae patted Red on the cheek. "It is time for sleep, Red. I need to get into my night-kirtle. I will read to you until you sleep, if you would like." She lit the tapers in the tripod at the head of the bed and the candles on the table.

"Read to me if you want, but I think that in two words I will be asleep. I am tired."

Dressed in her night clothes, Lae placed another log on the fire. When she was satisfied with the fire, she crawled into bed with Red and leaned over the book that lay at the end of the bed. "Would you like me to read from Bede?"

"Anything will do. Take away one of these pillows, would you?"

"Of course." Lae removed a pillow, throwing it at the end of the bed. As Red moved down and closed his eyes, she began to read aloud. In a few minutes she stopped, aware that Red's breathing was regular, although shallow.

She glanced at the notched candle clock, an invention of her father's, and saw that it was nine. She giggled at the memory of her father and his obsession with time. Lae leaned over and kissed Red on the forehead, closed the book, and blew out the candles on the table. She lay down beside him and fell asleep.

Startled, Lae opened her eyes. It was morning. Something had awakened her. She rolled over to look at Red. He was so still that she could not see the rising or falling of his chest. His hand clutched his night tunic at the throat.

Lae sat up. "Red, are you in pain?" She expected no response; she had merely spoken to break the silence of the room. She placed her hand on his and noted how cold it was. Lae closed her eyes and

laid her head against his chest. She knew there would be no heartbeat. She wanted to pretend that he was asleep. Reality would come
later.

He would be buried at Gleawanceaster, with St. Oswald. There,
he would wait for her. There, he would be safe from the Vikings.
Her king, her husband, was dead. Lae felt deserted. The tears surged
against her eyelids, and she cried for the life that was over — both
Red's and hers.

The councilmen were waiting to see Lae. She adjusted her
tunic. Out of habit, she turned so that Red could tell her how pretty
she looked. The empty bed startled her, as it had every time she
looked at it in the last month. Of course, she told herself, Red had
occupied that bed since their marriage nearly twenty-five years ago.
No wonder she still expected him to be there. Lae bit her lip to
hold back the tears. It would not do to greet the council with a
splotchy face streaked by tears.

As she walked down the stairs to the great hall, Lae thought
about the funeral. It had been spectacular. As the entourage traveled
across the country to the burial site, the peasants had lined the
route. Lae had not only been touched by their grief, but she had
wondered how far they had had to travel to see their lord one final
time.

There were a dozen men waiting for her in the great hall. They
stood in a circle, backs to the firepit, warming themselves. As soon
as she entered, the men bowed. She wondered what they wanted.
Mayhap they felt it would be better if Stan or Edward took over
Mercia. If they felt she could not rule, then they would have a war
to contend with. She would rule Mercia as she had while Red was
ill.

Lae stopped before the group of gentlemen and waited for them
to speak. A gray-haired man stepped forward, their spokesman, no
doubt. Lae recognized him from his many conferences with her
husband. He was a distant cousin, a minor nobleman.

Lae extended her hand. "Aelfgar of Lundenburh. It is a pleasure to see you. I had expected to see you before Candlemas, but the
weather was brutal at that time."

"My lady." Aelfgar kissed her hand. "It is good to see you looking well after your ordeal."

"Thank you. Never had I fought such a battle as that of the death of my husband." Lae gestured toward the table covered with a cloth and food and drink. "Shall we sit and eat? I have taken the liberty of preparing food. I know that some of the gentlemen have ridden a long distance." Lae allowed herself to be escorted to the table and seated in the place that had usually been reserved for Red. It was interesting to her that she was considered a replacement for him, even if only at the dinner table.

"We have come to discuss matters of state with you, my lady." Aelfgar gestured for the other men to sit. He put a cloth on his lap, broke a chunk of bread and buttered it. "We are aware that you have been successful in controlling Mercia."

"You have kept it safe from the Vikings, for the most part," one of the men said.

"Your expertise at warfare has not gone unnoticed," a third man said.

Lae looked around the table at each man in turn. Something was not quite right. "Stop pushing words at me. If you have come here to ask me to step down from the throne, you are wasting your time and mine. I will not step down."

Lae was surprised at the chorus of voices that spoke in protest.

"We want nothing of the kind," Aelfgar said.

"Then what do you want?" Lae laid her eating knife beside her plate. She had a habit of stabbing the table when she was angry, and she did not want to startle these men.

Aelfgar cleared his throat. "It is a delicate matter that we need to discuss."

"I am sometimes impatient because I have difficulty containing my curiosity." Lae picked up her knife and stabbed a piece of meat. She did not feel like eating, but she had to stab something. "Speak."

"Since our Lord Aethelred died, it has come to our attention that you are no longer as young as you once were." Aelfgar stumbled over his choice of words.

Lae stabbed another piece of meat. She would not eat it, but she would feed it to those blasted dogs that always lurked near the table. "We all grow older."

"You have just one heir, a daughter — Princess Aelfwyn."

"I seem to recall that." Lae could not resist. She stabbed her knife into the table with a tremendous force and let it stay there, quivering.

"We feel that she is . . . that she is unsuited to follow in your footsteps." Aelfgar's words tumbled out so fast that they fell over each other. His face was red.

Lae felt her eyes narrow. She glared at Aelfgar of Lundenburh. "How so?"

Aelfgar took a deep breath. "She is unpredictable. She has a terrible temper and does not appear to . . ."

"Princess Aelfwyn has been trained by me to take over the government of Mercia after her father and I have both died. She has been by my side at all important functions." Lae did not want these men to know that she had already discovered the same things about her daughter.

"Has she been allowed to make any policy decisions?" Aelfgar asked.

"Been allowed?"

"You have put Prince Aethelstan in charge of many things. Have you put Princess Aelfwyn in charge of anything?"

Lae wanted to remain angry at this elder, but what he said was true. She had never allowed Wyn to make any decisions. Why? Lae had to answer the question truthfully. It was because she did not trust her own daughter. She could be — was — self-serving and cruel. The death of her father had not changed her much. The woman was as the little girl had been — spoiled and arrogant.

Lae stared at Aelfgar. She did not want to agree with him. She hoped she made them uncomfortable, for she did not want to be bothered with their counseling. She watched each one squirm in turn, then she spoke to Aelfgar. "This meeting is ended. I will not tolerate unfounded charges against the next ruler of Mercia." Lae stood.

"My lady, please. For the good of our country. For our people. You have done so much for us. You have lead us away from war and toward peace. Can you not rule with your mind rather than your heart?"

"Your words drip honey."

"My words are truly spoken."

"We have reared Aelfwyn to be a ruler."

"Does she meet your high standards?"

Lae jerked the imbedded knife from the table top. Pieces of linen clung to the blade. She sheathed it. "You are right. I have never put Princess Aelfwyn in charge of anything because she cannot rule in a just manner."

Aelfgar's sigh of relief was audible. "Do you agree that Prince Aethelstan or King Edward would be a better choice to rule Mercia?"

"I would choose King Edward, if he lives past me, for he has proven his leadership. Prince Aethelstan is good but still young. The years ahead will be turbulent. A strong hand is needed. I concede that Princess Aelfwyn will not rule. She cannot lead an army, but worse, she cannot control her temper. I will make the proper arrangements to prevent her from succeeding me. King Edward will unite Mercia and Wessex."

"I leave you to your meal. I no longer care for the company. Gentlemen, stay and eat. Most of you have traveled a great distance. You may stay the night." Lae marched across the room to the steps that led to her chambers.

She finally sent word to Stan to come in from the stables to talk with her, and he appeared at the door to the great hall moments later. The winter wind whipped across the floor, sending a rustling through the reeds that covered the planks and stirring the sparks in the firepit. Lae sat again at the table, staring at the places that had been vacated by the councilmen less than an hour before. By the time Stan came up behind her and kissed her cheek, a decision had been made.

"How are you today?" Stan sat down at the table and grabbed a piece of meat. "I am starved."

"You are always starved. I am surprised you are not as fat as the cook's wife."

"I work hard. I ride hard. I love . . . I work." Stan blushed.

Lae laughed at him. "I know you must have a woman or two or three hidden away somewhere. I have not called you in here to talk of women, though you should be thinking of a wife."

Stan stopped eating. He frowned. "I thought that I was to marry Wyn."

"She is not a good match for you, Stan. You two hate each other. It is better to have someone to love. Besides, Wyn cannot rule effectively if you must be gone for a period of time fighting the Vikings. I have decided that Wyn is not to rule Mercia after I am dead."

"Let us not talk of death. We have had one death too many this last month." Stan put his head in his hands. "I have felt an emptiness like that after the death of my mother."

"Suffer not, Stan. Put thoughts of death aside. We have to discuss your future."

"Lae, I must disagree with you about marrying Wyn. That is not what was planned by your father or your husband."

"My father did not see Wyn as a grown woman. I see her faults as clearly as Red did. He had changed his mind about Wyn ruling Mercia, but I was slower to change mine. If Mercia and Wessex are to remain strong, they need each other. Wyn would antagonize you and your father until Mercia and Wessex were fighting each other. The Vikings would attack both and take both. For the good of the people, Wyn must never rule."

"Do you not think that I could control her?"

"Would you want to waste all your energy trying to control someone who had power?"

"No."

"There is something else. I would like to see you marry someone you love. It makes the nights much more pleasant." Lae enjoyed Stan's shocked look, and she patted his hand. "If I should die suddenly, make certain that you take control of Mercia if your father cannot."

"You want me to marry for love?"

"I do. Your father was happiest when Egwinna lived. He did not marry her, but he should have."

"I pledge my protection of Mercia from Wyn. Should you not write a letter for me regarding your decision to prevent civil war?"

"The councilmen were here to entreat me to remove Wyn from consideration. However, it would be best that my will be written for all to see. Mercia and Wessex must be preserved."

BOOK III

916 a.d. — 918 a.d.

chapter

XVIII

hy must I stay at Tamoworthig?" Wyn folded her arms across her chest and scowled at Lae. "Of all the forts you have built, why must we live in this place that even God has forsaken?"

Lae looked up from the table where she was writing and brushed a strand of hair from her eyes. She tried to hold down the piece of vellum she was using, but it curled, making the ink run. "It is beautiful. I have always loved this area. That is one of the reasons I had this fort built here."

"Forts, forts! Is that all you care about? How many forts have you built? How many years have you wasted building forts?"

Lae picked up a pumice stone and began to erase the errant line of ink from the vellum. "Forts are necessary. I have had nine forts built in the last five years. Edward is building his seventh one now. It should be finished soon."

"It has been the most boring five years of my life. Ever since Father died, we have done nothing but move farther and farther away from civilization." Wyn stomped over to a window and leaned on the sill. "There is nothing to see out there." She turned abruptly, catching her sleeve on a splinter. She jerked free, her face registering disgust.

"See? This place is not even built properly. I want to go back to Lundenburh."

"Lundenburh was hardly civilization. A hundred huts, a small marketplace, the docks, and our fortress do not denote civilization."

"The marketplace was exciting."

Lae blew erasure crumbs from the vellum. "I like being at Tamoworthig. It gives the Vikings something to think about."

"It gives me nothing to think about." Wyn looked at the tear in her sleeve. "My tunic is ruined. There is not even a place to shop for a new tunic."

"You have plenty of tunics."

"I like this one best."

Lae sighed. She blew on a newly penned word until the ink was dry. Holding the vellum in place, she looked at Wyn. "We will not move back to Lundenburh."

Wyn turned away from her mother and stared out the window again. "I might as well be dead. You have succeeded in burying me in this awful place."

"Would you like to go visiting?"

Wyn whirled around. "Where?"

"I could allow you to go to Wessex to visit your Uncle Edward's wife."

"Please. She is always pregnant and surrounded by disgusting little children. How many does she have now? Eight? Nine?"

"She has eight children."

Wyn giggled. "She drops them like a brood mare."

"Wyn, do not be disrespectful. It is important for Edward to have many children to insure that his line continues."

"Why did not you do the same? Did not you want your line to continue?" Wyn flung her words at Lae like tiny spears.

"My line has continued. I have you." Lae tried to concentrate on writing, but she could not. She had not discussed succession to the Mercian throne with Wyn since her daughter had foolishly run away. Lae had not told anyone other than Stan the gist of the conversation she had had with the council more than five years ago. When the time came, she would confide in Edward as she had Stan. She was taking a chance. If she died suddenly, Stan would prevent Wyn from becoming queen, but she did not want her daughter to know that for certain. It would be best to catch Wyn off guard.

"Can you think of any place you would like to go?" Lae put the vellum aside once more.

"I would like to go to Ireland. King Niall would allow me to visit."

Lae's breath caught in her throat. "Ireland?" Her mind raced. Would Wyn never give her a moment's peace about an innocent game of chess? Lae looked into Wyn's eyes. "Why Ireland?"

"I need to be entertained. It seems that you were entertained very well by King Niall." Wyn pretended to study the rent in her sleeve.

"If you think that you can anger me with your juvenile attempts, you are mistaken. King Niall and I had nothing more than admiration for one another. You have tried to make a romance where none was to be found. I loved your father far more than I could ever have loved anyone else. I do not have to justify or explain anything to you, but it seems to have been seething in your heart."

"You have an answer for everything. I suppose you do not want me to go to Ireland?"

"No, I will not allow you to go. You would try to embarrass me." Lae went back to her writing, but her hand was shaking too much to form the letters.

"I would try to get King Niall to marry me."

"Marry you? Do not be absurd. He has a wife." Lae refused to give up on the writing. She formed a few more words carefully. "Whatever made you say such a thing?"

"To relieve my boredom. What do you expect? You bring me to this abominable place. Why do you hide me?"

"I do not hide you."

"Why will not you allow me to live somewhere else?"

"Enough! I will not waste time bantering with you any longer. I have to write to Stan. I want confirmation that the Vikings of Bedanford and Hamtun have submitted to his rule. Go to your own rooms and find something to do." Lae saw the frown on Wyn's face, but it did not hide the hurt in her eyes. Lae felt guilty about the harshness of her words. She tried to speak in a softer voice. "Why do not you do some embroidery? You do beautiful work. It is much finer than mine."

"I have enough embroidery to make tents for a thousand soldiers."

The picture that Lae saw of a field of embroidered tents made her laugh. "Wyn, you can be very entertaining."

A knock on the door startled Lae, and she saw that Wyn had also been surprised. It was not the servants; Lae had sent them away to do the washing and to make soap.

Lae reached for her dagger, hidden in the sleeve of her tunic. She nodded to Wyn, who was waiting for her mother's signal. They were both aware that they lived on the border of Viking territory. Vikings might knock in deceit.

Wyn opened the door to a messenger that they both knew as Edward's. Lae took her hand off her dagger. Rand was a faithful soldier to Edward and had been for years.

"Come in. Lady Aethelflaed is there." Wyn gestured toward her mother.

"Has anything happened to King Edward?" Lae asked.

"No, my lady. King Edward is well. He sent me because the message is important."

"Continue."

"I am to tell you that the fort at Maldon has been finished and is occupied by soldiers. However, more important is the news that the Welsh King of Brycheiniog has set upon a Mercian Abbot, Egbert, and slain him and his companions."

"What? How dare he?" Lae jumped up so quickly that her chair fell back, making a thud as it hit the floor. "That Welsh dog will pay for his stupidity. He broke the treaty he signed with Mercia." Lae paced back and forth. "I will send Stan to deal with him." She faced Rand. "Tell me what happened."

"The good man and five of his monks left the monastery with food and medicine for some villagers. They had but one hunting knife among them. The Welsh King and his men crossed the border into Mercia, set upon Abbot Egbert and the monks, and in a short time slew them."

"How do we know who committed this atrocity?"

"They were in sight of the village. The villagers identified the men as Welsh because of their clothing and the royal crest. There is no question as to who the murderers were."

"Abbot Egbert was a kind and compassionate man. Why does God allow a good man to die before his time?" Lae saw a look of shock on Rand's face and bit her lower lip to keep more blasphemy from spilling out. She turned her rage into a plan. "In the morning, you will ride to Bedanford to Prince Aethelstan. I will have a note ready for him. Now you must eat and rest. Take a new horse if you need to. I want the prince to ride against the Welsh dog. He will be taught to heel."

Wyn cleared her throat. "Why do not you ride against the Welsh king?"

"It would be foolish for me to leave here now. We are beginning to subdue the Vikings, but they could resist us at any time, in any place. If I left, I feel certain that Tamoworthig would be attacked. No Mercian fortress must be attacked at this point." Lae started to pick up her chair, but Rand rushed over and lifted it for her. She smiled her thanks. "Wyn, get a servant to show Rand where he can sleep, then take him to the kitchen. We have dinner in the evening, just after sundown. Please join us in the great hall if you are not sleeping."

"It would be a privilege, my lady." Rand bowed.

Wyn snapped her fingers and a servant led him from the room. She followed close behind, to Lae's relief. Lae turned her attention back to the message she had been writing to Edward. She had more to say to him now. Next, she would write to Stan. Lae looked out the window. It was still early in the afternoon. She would have time to write to them both before lighting candles. She had noticed that each year she required more light in order to see. Her silver-blonde hair was becoming more silver with age; still, with forty-five summers behind her, the mirror showed no lines in her face, a trait inherited from her mother. She was glad she looked young and had her figure. It was probably the daily rides and exercises with the sword, battle-ax, and spear that kept her in shape. Lae chuckled at her vanity and went back to her letter writing.

Fall and winter passed quietly after Stan captured the Welsh court that included the Queen, all her ladies-in-waiting, and a few knights. The Welsh king, humiliated and angry, paid Stan an enormous ransom. The men who actually did the murders had escaped and so it was a bitter-sweet victory.

One morning while walking in Tamoworthig's garden, Lae was amazed to see tender shoots of spring flowers pushing through the earth. It was early yet, April being barely at the end of its first week.

Lae pulled her woolen cloak tighter around her shoulders. The sun was warm, but the wind was chilling. She waited for Edward to arrive.

The sound of horses alerted her, and Lae walked quickly across the inner bailey toward the gate. She reached the gate as Edward, as handsome and strong as ever, rode through at the head of thirty men. He waved to Lae and dropped down from his horse, handing the reins to a groom.

"Lae! It is good to see you again." He swooped her up and swung her around.

"Put me down. Is that any way to treat the leader of the Mercians?" Lae pummeled him about the head, laughing as Edward tried to ward off her blows. "Put me down, or I will wrestle you to the earth and embarrass you before your men."

Edward lowered Lae to the ground. "You always were a tough woman. I am surprised the Vikings have not gone by now."

Linking her arm through Edward's, Lae led him toward the garden. "Let us walk outside for awhile. The weather is so nice today, I hate to go inside."

Lae leaned against Edward. It was good to have him near. "I have something I want to discuss with you. It is about Vikings, of course. Edward, I think you can attack several of their fortresses at the same time and beat them. Their weaknesses have become our strengths, and their strengths have become our strengths."

"Let me guess. You want me to launch a strong offensive against them by midsummer."

Lae studied her brother carefully. "Who could have told you that? I have kept my ideas to myself."

Edward laughed. "Who trained me to fight? Was it not the same father that trained you? Did you not reinforce that training with lessons of your own? We think alike, you and I."

"Where would you attack, my clever brother?"

"Are you testing me?"

"Yes."

Edward sighed. "Father used to always test us. You have already built Tamoworthig and Staethford and before that Bremesburh on Penk. Then there is Scergeat, Bridgenorth . . ."

"Edward, you sound like a talking map. Stop." Lae waved her hand. "We have other things to discuss."

"Eadesbyrig, Waeringwic . . ."

"Edward! I have built nine forts to your five."

"Seven."

"There are five sites."

"But I built two forts at Heorotford and two at Buccingaham," Edward said.

Lae shrugged. "I am still ahead."

"Not for long."

"Enough. So? Where would you mount your offensive?"

"Colneceaster, to block incoming supplies from across the Narrow Sea; Temesanford, because it is close to Bedanford, and those Danes have already been conquered and converted, and they have sworn fealty to Mercia."

"Where else?"

"Where else? Is not that enough?"

"You have enough men. A third offensive would send them into a frenzy. It would spread their army so thin that it would snap like a worn thread." Lae gripped his arm tighter.

"We are close to winning, Edward. I can sense it." The elation she felt was greater than any she ever had before a battle. "A third attack, Edward, and I will mount a fourth."

"Yes, it will work." Edward walked without speaking for a few minutes. "Tofeceaster is on the border of Mercia. I want to build a fort there." Edward ran his hand down the handle of his sword. "It is time to rout those Vikings out of there."

"Good. That is where I would have gone had you chosen another place."

"Where do you plan to attack?"

"I will take Deoraby. It lies a mere twenty miles north of Tamoworthig and should have no one left to guard it. All the men will be out fighting you. Between the two of us, we can drive a wedge between the eastern and western factions."

Edward put his arm around her shoulder, and they continued walking. "I have a message for you from the enemy."

"You do? From whom?"

"I happened to meet with Eiric. We were exchanging prisoners. He said to tell you that he has never forgotten you." Edward cleared his throat. "What did he mean?"

Lae winced. Her past was always haunting the present. "He speaks of the time his sister, Olenka, had to heal my broken arm. He is trying to play on my sympathies. He thinks that will weaken us. Pay no attention to his words."

"Then it is set. We shall attack. Can you be ready in two months?"

"I have been ready for years, Edward. I am ready now. It will not take many men to wrest Deoraby from the enemy. You will have the most difficult part."

"I shall have Stan lead part of the attack. He has become a fine warrior, has he not?" Edward's smile was that of a proud father. "He is the strongest of my two sons."

"That he is. The others are but young. Mayhap in time Edwin will be strong."

Edward shook his head. "Their mother makes him weak by her coddling." Edward walked the full length of the garden without speaking. "I never knew how much I would miss Egwinna. Thank goodness Stan was born of that union. Father saw my son's greatness even when he was a child."

Lae stopped by the wicker pen that held dozens of fowl, scratching and peeping. "Rebirth comes with spring. Already we have chicks."

"Is there food? I am starved, and seeing those chicks reminds me of your wonderful cook. Are you going to feed me, or do I starve?"

"Edward, you still have the appetite of a young boy. If you eat like one, you will get fat." Lae poked him in the stomach. "I detect fat under that tunic already."

"You are saying that so I will not eat. Lead me to the great hall and feed me. I will demand it as guest of host."

"Come then, pig. We will celebrate your being here." Lae grabbed her brother's arm and squeezed it. She loved having him near her.

The summer day was still, hot, and humid. It was especially muggy by the Trent River where Lae and her army had stopped. Insects buzzed about Lae's head, and she wished that she did not have to wear chain-mail. She fanned herself with a small piece of parchment map as she studied the walled town that was Deoraby.

Next to her Archer sat astride his old horse. Her grizzled lieutenant was not as tall and straight as he used to be. She had tried to persuade him to stay at the fortress, but he politely refused, and she was glad. Lae enjoyed his company. He was a link to her past. "Archer, do you see anyone? I see only two guards."

Archer rose in his stirrups. "There are two guards by the gates. Are those the ones you see?"

"Yes."

"That is all. You said Deoraby would be poorly manned." Archer sat. He slapped at his face to get rid of the troublesome insects.

"Good. They are more stupid than we thought. It could be a trap, but I do not think so." Lae patted Maximilian's neck to calm him. The horse snorted his thanks and pranced from hoof to hoof. She pulled back on the reins when he bumped into Archer's mount.

"How does your new horse do?" Archer asked.

"He is young and never tried in battle, but he has been well trained." Lae watched Maximilian's ear twitch. "I miss Tanton dearly."

Lae clenched her teeth to keep tears from sliding unbidden down her cheek. She remembered that the snow had been coming down at a tremendous rate. The groom had reported that Tanton had not returned to the stable from the field. Together, they had gone out to find her horse. Walking across the fields with the groom, they had found Tanton leaning against a tree. He had been too cold to walk.

Lae remembered sending the groom back for a wagon of straw, blankets, and wood to build a fire, foregoing the custom of slitting the jugular. She had not the heart.

Lae spent the next twenty hours with Tanton in the snow. They made him a bed of straw and he half lay, half fell into it. Lae leaned against the tree, Tanton's head in her lap, the two of them covered with blankets. The groom kept the fire blazing until more of the servants from the stable came to help. There was nothing she could have done. Tanton was old. When his last breath came, ragged and shallow, Lae was relieved that the suffering was over, but she had grieved as if Tanton had been a brother instead of a horse. Even at the last, she had felt the bond between horse and rider.

Maximilian snorted and brought Lae to the present. She petted his neck. "It is time to attack. We will slide out of the woods quietly, then race up the hill toward the walled town." Lae put her helmet on carefully, glad for once that she had worn a heavier cowl. She arranged the weighty chain-mail across her shoulders and adjusted her sword out of habit. It had become a ritual before battle. She could no more stop the movement than she could stop time.

"We are ready," Archer said.

With her arm raised in its familiar signal, Lae dropped it as she kneed Maximilian in the ribs. The army surged forward, running through the few feet of forest, splashing across a small tributary, and up the hundred foot rampart. Arrows flew past Lae's head, but she paid no attention as she raced toward the gates. She would keep the guards occupied while the battering ram was brought into place. The gates would not last long.

Flaming arrows from her army flew into the timbered fort and stuck there, doing little damage other than instilling terror in the enemy. As Lae's army got closer, their arrows soared over the walls. The smell of burning thatched roofs was soon followed by towers of black smoke billowing over the walls.

Lae turned around to check the pace of the battering ram. It was being pulled at a steady rate by four oxen. The gates would be opened one way or another. Riding along the wall, but not close enough to be in danger, Lae looked for an opening or a weak spot. Seeing none, she turned Maximilian around and headed back toward the gate. The rhythmic thud, thud, thud told her the battering ram was in use. She reached the gate just as it splintered, and she was able to ride through with the army.

The first Viking who tried to attack her fell beneath her sword. Lae left him in the dirt, his blood pooling beneath him. The next soldier backed away from her, threw down his sword and ran. She grinned beneath her hot helmet. He had probably been taught that women warriors were evil.

The fight was no fight. It was over within an hour. Lae removed her helmet, removed her cowl, and shook her hair loose. She draped the cowl around her shoulders as she asked for the man in charge. Four of her own men brought him to her.

Lae was startled to see that the commander of the fort looked as if he had not yet grown a beard. He stood before Lae, his expression a mixture of forced pride and fear. Lae pitied him. He did not have the experience to protect the fort against an army such as hers. "Where are the rest of your soldiers?" Lae asked.

"I do not wish to say." The young man's eyes were defiant.

"It is no great secret that they are out fighting. I was merely wondering why you were left in charge with so few men to keep the fort. For all the good it did, you might as well have taken all the men and left the women in charge." Lae was aware of the chuckling from her ranks. She had not meant to ridicule the boy. "It is customary at times like these for the vanquished to submit to the rule of the conqueror. Since you are the commanding officer, I ask for your sword as this token."

"I will never submit."

Lae blinked at his response. There were always problems when dealing with the young. They did not know how to surrender gracefully. They did not even know when they had no hope. "It will be no disgrace to surrender to save your people. You will be treated well and mayhap exchanged for prisoners."

The young man stood straight, shoulders back. His eyes were filled with hatred. "I will never surrender to a woman."

"Oh, for the grace of God! Another misguided Viking. Archer, where do they breed these poor souls?" Lae felt like shaking the young man for his stupidity.

Archer laughed aloud. He leaned down from his horse and looked the soldier straight in the eye. "You had better not make this woman angry. When she is in armor she fights like the lioness who protects her cubs. It is the female of the species who has the sharpest of claws."

"We will take you as a prisoner without surrender if it makes you feel more like a soldier. All your men, the few that I see, will be held prisoners as well." Lae turned to Archer. "See that we leave enough soldiers to guard them. Leave men to rebuild and hold this fort. I claim it for Mercia. The women and children are not to be harmed."

"It will be taken care of, my lady," Archer said.

"I will start the ride back to Tamoworthig with my own unit. I want to send a message to Edward, and I also want to find out how well his campaigns have gone."

"You will have to hurry to get there before dark, my lady."

"I have the energy of a thousand women today. I shall be home well before dark." Lae patted Archer on the arm. "Thank you for your concern. I will see you in a few days when all is taken care of here." Lae turned Maximilian around and rode through the gates. She guided Maximilian at an angle down the ramparts so that he would not stumble. The horse handled well, though young and somewhat awkward.

The ride along the river through the forest was cool and more pleasant than the ride had been in the heat of the day. Lae shifted her helmet from her right arm to her left. She wished she did not have to keep it so close, but they were still in enemy territory, and she did not want it in the supply wagon.

Lae glanced back over her shoulder at the men who followed. They were laughing and joking amongst themselves as they marched. Although her mounted soldiers rode close to her, she felt alone. Without Red, Stan, or Edward, there was no one with whom to discuss strategy.

Lae missed Red. Often in the middle of the night, she swore she could hear him calling her name. She would sit up and look at his side of the bed, but he was not there. She had requested that candles be kept lighted at night. If he did return from the other side to be with her, she wanted to be able to see him. She did not really think that Red could come back from the dead, but there was no way to be sure.

The timbers of Tamoworthig appeared on the horizon. The thought of a hot bath seemed so pleasant to Lae that she spurred Maximilian on. He shot forward with a little jump-step, and she almost lost her seat. She righted herself quickly, gained control and gave him his head. Maximilian laid his ears back and ran flat out. Lae bent down as far over his neck as she could, although the helmet she held in the crook of her left arm hampered her movement.

The horse felt good to her as he ran, but he was not as smooth as he would be when he was older. She did miss Tanton, but Maximilian was a good replacement.

The wind felt cool as it blew her hair away from her face and dried the perspiration that dotted her forehead. As rider and horse came to a shallow stream, Lae let Maximilian clatter through. The water splashed up, soaking Lae's tunic, but she did not care. The horse's strides were so long that he raced up the bank in three paces. At the top he stumbled and flung Lae from his back.

Lae landed on her side, with her helmet under her, the wind knocked from her. She felt as if she would never breathe again. A vise held her chest, and she could not move. Her head hurt. She was aware of Maximilian's hot breath on her face. He nickered. She could not answer him. The sky disappeared and after that she remembered nothing.

When Lae awoke, she was in bed. Her tongue felt dry and swollen, and she was burning hot with the worst fever she had ever had. She turned her head to see who sat next to her bed, and the movement sent pain shooting through her back and ribs. She closed her eyes and took a breath. It hurt. Suddenly, she remembered that she had fallen on the helmet.

"Are you awake, Mother?" Wyn asked.

"I am, but I wish I were not."

Wyn laid a cool cloth on Lae's forehead. "You have been unconscious for two days."

"Two days?"

"I sent for a physician. He gave me some medicine for the pain, and you are to take it as soon as you are conscious. It will make you sleep, but I think that is best." Wyn slid her hand under Lae's shoulders.

"Wait, I want water. I am so thirsty."

"It is here." Wyn put the medicine aside and took a cup from the bedside table. She lifted her mother and helped her to drink. "Is that enough?"

"No." Wyn gave her more water. "You are a good nurse," Lae whispered. "Thank you." She hated being dependent on anyone, and it was all she could do not to push her daughter away. For the first time, she realized what Red had expressed to her nearly everyday during his illness. This illness was not so difficult to bear as the dependency on someone else.

Wyn lowered Lae carefully. "I was so frightened when they brought you in. I thought you were dead."

"I feel wretched." Lae noticed that her words were slurred, but as sleep swept over her, she no longer cared.

Lae was surprised that she did not recover easily. She had never been so ill before. It was many weeks before her strength returned, and even then Wyn rarely allowed her to walk in the garden. Lae could smell fall in the air. She felt cheated out of part of her life; she had slept right through most of the summer.

Lae sat on a stool near the garden. The vegetables were almost gone, and winter would soon be covering the earth with snow. Lae usually did not mind winter, but this year she had had too little summer. Mayhap that explained her stiffness. She was sitting in the sun, kicking a clod of dirt, when Wyn's shadow fell across her lap. Lae looked up. "What is it? More medicine?"

"In a way." Wyn held up a tri-folded piece of vellum. "It is a message from Uncle Edward."

Lae took the vellum and noted that the seal was indeed Edward's. She had not heard from him in more than two weeks, and she was worried. Lae ran her finger under the flap. The letter popped open and she read it quickly. Smiling, she looked at Wyn. "Do you wish to hear what Edward has written?"

"You know I am not terribly interested in wars, but please go ahead." Wyn clasped her hands behind her back and pursed her lips.

"Edward writes that he has successfully taken Temesanford." Lae looked up at Wyn. "That means that he has split the Viking's resistance. He goes on to say that Stan was vital to holding off the Vikings at Maldon and has repelled their attack." Lae laid the vellum on her lap. "Wyn, this is important. It means that soon our long fight with the Vikings will be over."

"I am happy for you, but it means nothing to me." Wyn stifled a yawn and turned away from Lae. "Your entire life has been focused on those disgusting Vikings. I could not care that much about who has what lands or which people are servants to us. Egwinna tried to explain to me why you thought it was important. She tried to tell me that it was for all our sakes that you were always gone. Running here and there. Fighting this group of Danes or another."

"It is been that way for years, neither of us understanding the other." Lae held out her hand. "Help me to my chambers. I feel the stiffness attacking me again."

Wyn helped Lae to her feet. "It is time for your medicine anyway. You walked farther today. I think you have been outside longer, too."

"I wonder how many days before I will be able to ride? I hate this." Lae forced herself to ignore the pain in her left side as she stood. "Is Maximilian still being trained?"

"I saw to that. The groom has been working with him twice as long as any other horse."

"Thank you. Maximilian is a good horse. He stood over me after I had fallen, I remember."

"I was told that the horse neighed all the way home while you were carried on the litter."

"Horses can be friends, especially when both horse and rider have gone through battles together and have escaped death."

"Mother, you have always been sentimental about your horses. To my way of thinking a horse is a simple-minded brute that eats all day long. I never had any particular fondness for horses."

Lae waved her hand. "Enough talk. I must rest." She did not want Wyn to see the pain in her eyes.

Lae allowed Wyn to place her in bed. It would have been just as easy for Lae to get into bed by herself, but Wyn seemed to have a strange need to nurse her.

Spring had come again. Lae was walking around the walls of the outer bailey, glad to be healthy, happy to be alive. The winter had disappeared in dreams and pain, medicine and short wakefulness. She barely remembered Christmas or Easter. Those holidays were merely a collection of colors for her; people were nameless and faceless; events had no sequence.

Lae resolved not to think about the lost time. She would get on with her life by building her strength until she could ride again. With that thought in mind, she walked toward the stable, as she had done every day for the past month.

Maximilian's nickering interrupted Lae's musing. She hung over the half-door to the stable where the huge war horse was tied. A groom brushed him with long strokes. Maximilian flicked his ears and gazed at her with soft, brown eyes. He switched the flies away with his tail, slapping the groom in the process. Maximilian stood delicately on three feet while his left forefoot was held aloft by the groom and cleaned. When he nickered again, Lae crossed to him and laid her hand against his muzzle. He searched her palm for a treat. He snorted when none appeared, raised his head, and looked at her.

"I have spoiled him, my lady. He expects each visitor to bring him a gift. He is the king of horses in this stable." The groom dropped the forefoot and ran his large, angular hands gently up the horse's foreleg.

"Is he injured?"

"Two days ago he picked up a stone. He is fine." The young man patted Maximilian on the shoulder, then shoved a strand of curly brown hair from his eyes. "He is ready to ride if you are."

Lae was shocked at the suggestion. She had not considered riding Maximilian today or even tomorrow. "Is he easy to handle?"

"I trained him so well that a child could ride him," the groom said.

Lae looked at the groom. He had the features of an ancient Roman with crooked nose and square jaw. She could not place him. "Excuse me, but I can not remember your name."

"I am Thomas, son of the blacksmith called Rhys. My older brother used to groom the horses. This winter King Edward borrowed him to help train other grooms." Thomas held his head higher. "I have been chosen by my father to take the place of my brother. I have done well by your horse. Princess Wyn promised my death would be swift if I did not do a proper job. I have been working with Maximilian since you bought him. He is a fine horse."

Lae looked down at her riding tunic. It was odd to her that she had put it on without dwelling on it. Mayhap God had given her a sign. "Thomas, saddle him up. He needs to become accustomed to me once more. I will ride." Lae strode toward the door, calling back over her shoulder, "I shall await you in the courtyard."

The sun was shining, and it was a perfect day for riding. Lae mounted the horse with little difficulty, although she had to strain to lift her leg high enough to clear Maximilian's back. Thomas walked the stallion around the outer bailey, talking all the while about the finer points of controlling the horse.

"Do you think I could take him on my own around the yard?"

Thomas blushed and stammered. "Why yes, my lady. He is your horse. I did not mean to be impertinent."

"You were not impertinent, Thomas. You are a natural teacher. You should be very proud of that gift. I will be careful." Thomas let go of the bridle as if it were fresh from the blacksmith's fire. He stepped aside, and she rode past him toward the gate.

Trotting past the wagon shed, the blacksmith shop, and the brew house, she was assaulted by strong smells. She had been inside for so long that she had forgotten the odor of new wood, hot metal, and fermentation. The servants and laborers stopped what they were doing and stared at her. The ones who had known her since she was a young bride had the nerve to bow. She waved in return, thankful for their gestures of welcome. It was good to be out of bed and out of her chambers, and it was especially good to be able to ride. The freedom was glorious. Lae slapped the reins lightly against Maximilian's neck as she had been instructed, and with his head held high, she rode to the gate. She motioned for the guards to open the gate. When they hesitated, she frowned. Was she not mistress of her own fortress any longer?

"Why do you hesitate?" She had to speak carefully, for she did not want them to notice her annoyance.

"We were instructed by King Edward not to let you ride alone." The guard shifted from foot to foot.

"I understand your concern and King Edward's, but I am quite well. I judge myself to be capable of riding outside the walls."

The men opened the gates. She wondered what other instructions Edward had given. She must have been sicker than she thought, for Edward would never have presumed to take over her duties.

Lae rode along the river in front of the fortress until she came to a small tributary. Maximilian handled easily, and riding him was a joy. When they came to an open field tended by a sheep herder at the far end with his ewes and lambs, Lae waved at him. It took a moment for the boy to wave back, but he finally did. Lae stayed away from the sheep, for they were foolish creatures and frightened easily.

She put Maximilian through his paces, reversing, traversing, and changing gaits. He was smooth and quick to respond. Although she was not tired, she decided to turn back toward the fortress. Wyn would wonder where she had gone. Lae ignored the pain in her left side.

Dinner that evening was especially good. The ride had helped Lae's appetite. She ate like the cook's wife, starting with the lamb that had been wrapped with bacon and roasted on the spit. Lae devoured the early spring onions so rapidly that one of the servants had to make three trips to the kitchen. Lae surprised herself when she ate a turnip. It was pithy from having been in storage all winter, but to her it tasted fine. She hardly spoke to anyone at the head table because she was so busy eating. Once, when she glanced up from buttering a portion of her bread trencher, she saw Wyn frowning at her. Lae raised her piece of trencher in salute to her daughter and said, "Wyn, I never knew this dark bread could taste so good. I may not want to give any away to the beggars at the gates."

"Mother!" Wyn's eyes shifted from one guest to another to see if they had heard Lae.

Lae reached for her bowl of mead, her third in the last hour. She held up the bowl. "I want you to know, Wyn, that I feel good, and this mead is good. It makes my head have its own music." Lae shouted to her lieutenant at the table below hers. "Archer, does it ever make your head sing?"

"Many times, my lady, especially after a battle." Archer's mouth twitched and he hid a half smile with his hand. "It could give you an aching in the head if you consume too much."

"I refuse to let my head ache. I have had enough pain this past winter to last a lifetime." Lae held up the bowl once more. "Here is to no more pain."

"I will toast that, my lady." Archer held up his bowl and drank with Lae.

The door to the great hall burst open, and the candles in the wall sconces flickered. Thomas, the groom, came running in. He dodged the dogs that begged for scraps, ran between servants clutching at trays of food, and slid to a stop in front of Lae. "My lady! My lady! The Vikings are coming! They float down the River Trent from the north. They will be here in two days or less."

At the mention of the enemy, Lae jumped up, knocking over the bowl. Its sticky contents oozed from the container and spread across the table. "How do you know this?"

"I was outside the walls riding before the darkness fell, when a farmer came up to me on his cart horse. He was exhausted, for he had ridden the night through and today as well." Thomas talked so fast that his words ran together. He took a deep breath. "I rode back here as fast as I could. The man follows."

"When he arrives, feed him well, then bring him to my chambers. I will want to get more details from him before I let him sleep. Are you sure this man is not counterfeit?"

"He gave me the name of a relative of mine who knows him. I think he is a good Mercian farmer." Thomas twisted the sleeve of his tunic in his hands. "He said there are a hundred Vikings in large boats. They slide through the river like demons. He said they do not speak like the Vikings from Northumbria, and he thinks they might have been sent by the witches."

"Thank you, Thomas. Take some sustenance, then get all the horses ready. Tomorrow we will stop the Vikings once again. You may be dismissed." Lae turned to Archer, her mind working quickly and clearly, which surprised her, given the amount of mead she had drunk. "Get the men ready. We will ride at dawn, heading north along the Trent River. We should intercept them about midday."

"Mother, are you well?" Wyn asked.

"I am ready for battle, and I feel like a girl again." Lae picked up her overturned bowl. With the drop of mead still in it, she proposed a toast. "Here is to another Mercian victory. Here is to freedom for our people for all times."

The Vikings rowed their forty-foot, shallow-bottomed boats to shore. Lae and her army hid quietly in the forest, waiting. The sun shone brightly on the polished wood of the beautifully crafted ships. The curved bow was graceful with geometric designs and dancing animals laced through the carved scrolls. She wondered how such artistic people could be so murderous. These devils would do no murdering here. Tamoworthig's people would be safe.

Lae watched, hearing nothing from her own army, but listened to the Vikings talk amongst themselves as they beached the boats. Orders rang out from an old man who was wrapped in woolen robes even though it was a warm spring day. He seemed to be ailing, but brushed away a younger man's attempt to help him walk. Lae nodded in understanding. Too often the young underestimated the strength and determination of the old. Mayhap that was only fair, since often the old underestimated the knowledge of the young.

A second vessel slid into view, hardly breaking the surface of the water. Lae stared at the contents of that boat. Horses! At least thirty. They were planning to ride the rest of the way to

Tamoworthig. She would not allow that. Lae leaned over to Archer. "We wait until the boat is at the shore and the men are busy, then we ride down and take them before they have a chance to mount."

"Yes, my lady. A good plan."

Lae's gaze fastened on the boat and the men. Judging the distance carefully, she waited, then rode swiftly from the forest across the meadow, her army behind her. The Mercians were on the Vikings in a matter of seconds, and Lae slew the first two Danes she came upon. In spite of her long convalescence, she still had enough dexterity to fight.

The screams from the Vikings made Lae's ears ring. She turned around in time to see her army cutting a path through the enemy. She searched for the old man, but could not see him. Had he been killed already? Lae wheeled Maximilian to the right just in time to see the robes of the old man as he disappeared into the woods. She raced after him, wary, because he would be shrewd. She rode back and forth amongst the trees, stopping now and then to listen. She could hear nothing and see nothing; it was as if the fiend had taken to the air.

Lae rode out of the woods and across the meadow, allowing Maximilian to pick his way between the bodies. She was glad to see so few Mercians downed. The skirmish was over. She rode over to Archer. "Where are the rest of the Vikings?"

"They have disappeared into the north woods. They hide like the hart."

"They hide like the hare. They are not noble enough to be compared to the hart." Lae stared at the woods. "How large an area do you guess the woods cover?"

"It is small. No more than ten acres. Why?"

"I want to flush the Viking rabbits. First, we surround the woods on three sides, then . . ."

"Forgive me, my lady, but we have fewer than a hundred men left. The forest is too vast to surround." Archer looked at the woods. "The trees are young. Probably they have overgrown an abandoned farm."

"We will cut them down from this end and drive the Vikings toward the north where the rest of the army will be waiting." Lae pulled Maximilian around and rode toward one of her lieutenants. "Have you carpenters in the infantry? With axes?"

"Always, my lady, in case we have to build quick protection."

"Good. Gather them together and cut down the woods between the Vikings and their boats. Send the rest of the men to Archer and me. Do it quickly." Lae noted the man's astonished look.

She rode back to Archer. "You are to lead a detachment up the river side of the woods. I will take another group up the far side. We will force the Vikings out of hiding. The woods will be smaller after our carpenters cut part of it down."

Archer raised his eyebrows. "A strange offensive, but one that could work. Will not the Vikings be surprised?" He saluted Lae and rode off to claim a faction of the army.

Lae took thirty-two men with her as Archer had done. The rest of the men filled the air with the noise of chopping. Lae heard the sound of trees falling behind her as if a storm were raging through the forest. She would teach the Vikings that they could no longer sneak into Mercian territory. They were no longer tolerable, even in land they used to claim.

Coming around the far side of the woods with her army, Lae saw Archer with the other men waiting for her. At Lae's signal, both groups spread out like a comb and rode through the woods, flushing the Danish foot soldiers. When the Vikings reached the edge of the woods, they discovered they had no protection and could not get to their boats without being seen. Drawing their swords, they turned to face the Mercian army.

When the battle was over, Lae rode through the bodies of the dead Vikings. She looked intently at each of their faces. Archer rode beside her.

Finally, he asked, "What is it that you wish to find?"

"I am looking for their king. I cannot find the old man who wore the crown and shouted orders."

"That is so; he is not here." Archer rode beside her as they checked each body. "He has disappeared."

"I am going to check the woods. Mayhap he is hiding under a log." Lae turned Maximilian toward the few trees that remained standing.

Archer rode beside her, frowning. "I do not understand why their leader did not lead them."

They rode in silence, the only noise coming from the snapping of twigs as the horses moved through the trees like shadows. Lae could not read the signs on the ground because of all the activity that had taken place in the last few hours. She rode on, continually scanning the ground anyway.

Maximilian snorted and halted, tossing his head and pawing the ground. Lae patted him on the neck. "It is all right, boy. Calm down. There is nothing here." It was then that she saw the old man. He sat on the ground, leaning against a tree. Lae stared at him for a moment, unable to comprehend why he had been left behind. "Archer, look." Lae pointed.

"It is their king. I see no blood. He lives. See, his hand just tightened on the sword."

Lae dismounted, drew her sword and advanced toward the white-haired man. He was thin, with blue-veined skin that stretched tightly over arthritic bones. He held a sword in one knobby hand. It wavered.

Lae stopped out of range of the sword. "Who are you? Why do you sit in the woods like a child?"

"I am dying, but in dying I refuse to allow a Mercian to have the satisfaction of sending my soul to Valhalla. I will get there on my own. Because of this battle, I am assured a place of honor."

Archer dismounted and stood next to Lae. He did not draw his sword. "You have to die in battle to go to Valhalla. Is not that the way of your people?"

"I intend to fool the gods. If I die with my sword in hand on a field of battle, then Valhalla is open to me." The old man coughed. His frail frame shook so hard Lae was afraid he would fall apart.

"Who are you? From whence come you?" Lae asked.

"I am King Oittir of the lands where summer has little darkness and the water runs cold. My men and I have traveled a long way to find a war for me." The old man coughed. "Are there any of my men still living?"

Lae shook her head. "No."

"I shall have a good army with me in Valhalla."

"Archer, what shall we do with this old soldier?"

"Leave him to the wolves."

"I cannot do that. Even if the Vikings are inhuman, I am not."

King Oittir coughed. When he was finished, he lay back against the tree. "I have but a few minutes left." His watery eyes blinked as he stared at Lae. "Are you the Lady of the Mercians?"

"I am she."

"I thought so," King Oittir said. "Your name has come to mean death to the Vikings. We frighten our children into behaving by invoking your name." His eyes crinkled as he alternately laughed and coughed.

"I am not flattered."

"You should be. It puts you in the same category as your witches."

Archer laughed aloud so long and hard that he had to wipe tears from his eyes. "You have a good wit about you, sire."

"Thank you." King Oittir let his sword drop with a soft thud into the leaves, dirt, and moss. "I no longer have the strength to hold it. Would you bury it with me?"

Lae sheathed her sword. "I will bury you with your men and your sword. I will face you north so that you may see your homeland."

"Thank you." King Oittir closed his eyes and exhaled. He never inhaled.

Lae dispatched a burying party to put all the Vikings to rest. She stood next to Archer and watched the burials. "I have found a few interesting Vikings in my time, but he was one of the most interesting. Sometimes, Archer, I wish that we did not have to fight. I would have liked to have known King Oittir better."

"The ways of man are strange. We tear up our own land to save it. We cut down trees to cut down men. Why do we do this? All for a piece of earth."

"All for a piece of earth that will not mean a thing after we are dead. I have further plans for this piece of earth, Archer, and it involves the Scots."

"The Scots, my lady?"

"Yes." Lae tugged at Archer's sleeve. "Come, old friend. I will explain on the way. Let us go home. We have an army to feed."

"I am always glad to follow you, but to follow you home is best."

chapter

XIX

RCHER STOOD BEFORE THE FIREPIT as he faced Lae. "The noblemen from Scotland are here, my lady. They have brought the heathens with them."

"Those heathens were called Picts by the Romans and since I know no other name for them, I shall call them the same. They are important to my plan." Lae smiled to soften the harshness of her words. She was nervous, but that was no reason to be short with Archer. She looked across the room at the thrones she had had placed on the dais. It looked imposing with its heavy, carved wooden legs and arms. The huge back had the seal of Mercia carved in the oak. It had darkened with age. It was exactly what she needed to impress her guests. To the right of her throne she had placed one almost as large for Wyn and to her left, a similar throne had been set there for Stan.

"When the visitors are ready, bring them here? I will be waiting." Archer looked puzzled, then shrugged as he left. He was a good soldier, but he did not understand the finer points of diplomacy.

"Go tell Prince Aethelstan and Princess Aelfwyn that I am ready for them," Lae told a servant, and returned to the dais. She climbed it, then settled herself into the cushions on her throne. She twisted the wide cuff of her sleeve around and around in her fingers. How barbaric were these men from Scotland?

It was a great compliment to Lae that the Scottish delegation had come and a good sign, mayhap, that the Picts had also accepted her invitation. After her victory on the Tyne River against King Oittir and his Viking army, she had decided the time was right to tighten the noose on the Danes. She moved rapidly through the northern land, gathering it up for Mercia. The Scots would be the northern half of a vise that would squeeze the Vikings into submission.

She looked out the window at the rainy sky. It had rained for three days in a row, and she was restless. She had to convince the wily Scots to join her. Her message must have intrigued them.

A rustling from the stairway interrupted her thoughts, and Stan and Wyn approached. Wyn looked beautiful in a saffron-colored tunic over a blue under-kirtle. Her sleeves were trimmed with elaborately embroidered ribbons. A girdle of braided blue encircled her waist. The entire outfit enhanced her black hair and gray eyes. Lae sighed. Beneath the soft beauty was a hard heart.

Stan escorted Wyn to the throne, and as he seated himself he asked, "Have you seen them yet?"

Lae shook her head. "I wanted them to get settled first. We need their alliance badly."

Wyn leaned over and whispered, "You will get it, Mother."

Stan nudged Lae. "They must have settled in quickly. Look, they come."

Lae knew that the Scots were rough looking, but she was not prepared for what she saw. Four burly men came stomping into the room, plaids flying. Their hair was unkempt, and their clothing stained with sweat.

However, compared to the Picts who accompanied them, the Scots looked tame. Lae tried not to show her shock at the painted Picts who stared up at her. They were naked from the waist up and covered with blue dye. She had heard they only colored themselves blue for battle. Did they expect to fight? If so, who? Lae ignored the gasp from Wyn. It had been a tactical error to have placed herself on a throne. Lae knew it by the grim expression on the face of the oldest Scottish chief. Lae did not look away from him as he stared at her. Instead, she stood, walked across the dais and descended the steps, holding out her hand in what she hoped would be taken as a greeting.

"Welcome to Mercia. I am happy that you have come." Lae let the big man encase her fingers with his oak-hard hand. He gripped it so firmly that she thought she would screech. It was not the pain that was unbearable, but the thought that he would damage her sword hand that had her worried. She was shocked when he kissed her hand, his rough whiskers stabbing into her skin.

"Please, come with me to the firepit. It is more comfortable there. The dampness permeates the entire fortress on rainy days, especially in the spring."

"That would be most kind, my lady."

Lae was surprised at the smoothness of the voice that addressed her in good Anglo-Saxon. She looked into the man's blue eyes. Intelligent, but wary. "You are Cam Sron?"

"That I am. The king has sent me to speak with you." Cam Sron bowed awkwardly.

Lae pointed to the chairs next to the firepit. "You may sit."

"After you, my lady." Cam Sron bowed again like a child practicing a new game.

"Thank you." Lae sat in her favorite chair next to the firepit and arranged her skirts to warm her ankles. She waited as Cam Sron and his three silent companions eased themselves into her brocaded chairs. "What of them?" She nodded toward the Picts.

"They have little use for fancy chairs. They stand," Cam Sron said.

Lae snapped her fingers and two servants stepped up to her immediately. "Please tell your Lord Aethelstan and Lady Aelfwyn to join us. Also, bring us a goodly amount of our best wine for our guests."

Lae turned back to the men, trying to ignore the blue bodies of the Picts. She did not know their language, so she spoke her own. She addressed the Pict whom she thought was dominant. "I hope your journey went well and that you suffered no trouble with the Vikings."

Cam Sron shouted at the blue man, then spoke to Lae. "He does not understand your language. He has refused to learn it because he says it makes him sound like a barking dog."

Lae wanted to laugh, but she was afraid that she would insult the men. "I am sorry that I am ignorant of his tongue. Please tell him I would like to learn it if he will teach me." Lae watched as Cam Sron translated for her. The Pict's eyes lit up, and he smiled at her. She smiled in return.

"He said to tell you that he would be honored to teach the Lady of the Mercians because she is gracious and beautiful." Cam Sron whispered a warning. "You must watch out for Gar, my lady. He will want to marry you and take you back to the northern lands."

Lae's mouth dropped open. She clamped it shut, embarrassed that she had let the mask of diplomacy slip. "I know not what to say."

"I will tell him that you have a man already. It will be better that way." Cam Sron's eyes crinkled with laughter.

Lae leaned forward and whispered to Cam Sron, "Are you teasing me?"

"Mayhap."

Lae was not certain how to respond, but she was saved from embarrassment by the arrival of Stan and Wyn. She motioned them to sit. "I present to you my nephew, Prince Aethelstan, who will rule Wessex after his father, Edward. My daughter, Princess Aelfwyn, who is to rule Mercia." Lae cleared her throat. She had told this necessary lie so many times in the last few years that it slid off her tongue easily.

"It is my pleasure to meet you," Wyn said. She stared at Cam Sron, then at the Picts.

Lae watched her closely. What was Wyn up to now? She was not usually so gracious. "Wyn, would you be so kind as to serve the wine? The servants bring it now." Even after many years, Lae could not tolerate seeing red wine in silver, and so she had to depend on Wyn to serve in her stead. Lae could tell from Wyn's frown that her natural aversion to serving anyone was still strong in her.

"I might spill it."

"Nonsense. You will do fine. Cam Sron, I think you know why I have asked you here." Cam Sron took a chalice of wine from Wyn. He did not seem to notice that a dark rivulet of wine ran down his hand. "I know you would like a treaty of peace. You want us to help you fight the Vikings."

Stan leaned forward, his arm resting on his knee. "We would like to insure peace for this entire island."

Lae was forced to take a chalice of wine from Wyn whose glee at her mother's consternation was obvious. Lae was relieved that Wyn did not embarrass her further by spilling wine on her new white tunic. "It is true that we would like to form a lasting friendship with you, our neighbors to the north," Lae said.

"I have questions." Cam Sron drained wine from his chalice in one swallow. "How do we know that you will honor such a treaty?"

"My word is law," Lae said. "I have never broken a treaty that was honored by the other side."

"Why do you need us to fight the Vikings? Are you weak?" Cam Sron stared at her through slitted eyes.

"We do not need you to fight the Vikings. I have fought King Oittir and defeated him. I have taken many Viking forts. The Vikings of Ligoraceaster have come under my sword and Ligoraceaster is mine. One hundred miles north of here is the fortress called Eoforwic. You know it well, I believe. The leader of the those Danes have submitted to my power." Lae pretended to take a sip of wine and stared back at Cam Sron through her own half-closed eyes. "We do not need you. I am offering Scotland the protection of the Mercian army against the Vikings." Lae let the insult settle. Cam Sron's face reddened and he squirmed in his chair. She almost had him.

Cam Sron set his chalice on the floor next to his chair and folded his arms across his chest. "Why should we want your protection?"

Lae leaned forward and whispered loudly so that her words would sound eerie to the superstitious Scot. "I am the strength. Join a winning army, my army, or eventually you and your people will die."

"You cannot frighten me."

"Cam Sron, you have a choice. You may choose Mercia, or you may choose death for your people. The Vikings have already killed your people time and time again as they move north. The Danes love to slaughter your friends, the Picts. Mercia fights Vikings and kills them. Mercia always wins. Wessex always wins. Our God protects us." Lae sat back in her chair and waited before speaking again. "Cam Sron, the Vikings will be a part of the past, but not a part of the future."

Cam Sron pulled at a strand of unruly hair, twisting it around his finger. Leaning toward his companions, he spoke rapidly in a language that Lae could not follow.

He gestured wildly, pointing to the north and then pointing at Lae. His companions frowned and argued in return.

Lae was too astonished at their unruly actions to be amused. Even Wyn stared at their guests. Stan was very still, rubbing his thumb against his belt where his sword was usually attached.

Turning suddenly and slapping his hands against his thighs, Cam Sron said, "Done. We see the wisdom of a treaty with Mercia. We will seal the documents. Where are they?"

"We will have them written as we speak the words. That way, your voice and those of the Picts will be in the document. We will attend to that on the morrow."

"Good." Cam Sron picked up his chalice. "A toast."

Lae, Wyn, and Stan held up their chalices to the men who sat with them. "A toast, please," Lae said.

"Here is to a gallant lady and a true warrior. May our countries remain friends until the end of the world. *Slainte mLath!*"

With relief, Lae watched chalices click together as the newfound friends toasted to the death of the Vikings. The blue Picts smiled at her, their teeth a startling white in contrast to their sky-colored faces. Cam Sron and his companions laughed easily, for the thick wine had taken effect. Lae smiled with Cam Sron. He was more of a gentleman than she had expected, and it would be foolish to underestimate his abilities in diplomacy or war. Lae found that this had been one of the most interesting meetings she had ever conducted. She was content, for she could see the end of the war with the Vikings.

The Scots and the Picts stayed for the five days it took to write the documents. Lae was glad when they left, for although she enjoyed learning the ways of her new allies, she did not feel as well as she should have. As soon as they left, she was struck with a fever that raced through her body and raged for more than a week. The pain in her left side had flared up at the same time.

For the fourth night, Lae awakened and called for her servants to come and change the sheets soaked with perspiration. After they had put her back to bed, she called for them to bring her more blankets. She was chilled to the bone, and her teeth clacked together with the sound of horses' hoofs on a wooden bridge. She wished that Wyn were here, but she was in her own suite of rooms.

For the next three days and nights, Wyn stayed with her, but exhaustion caught up with her daughter at last, and she needed rest. Lae did not want her to get sick. Lae felt weak. She had not felt this weak since last year when she had fallen off Maximilian. Lae took a deep breath, but stopped midway because of the pain in her side. For some reason, she was wide awake. She had asked that Edward be sent a message requesting him to visit her. Although she was not ready to die, she was certain that the time had come.

Lae glanced at the candle clock. It was just past midnight — the lonely time of night when one searched one's soul for company. She did not want to search her soul. What day was it? The twelfth day of June, the year of our Lord, nine hundred and eighteen. No saints had a feast on this day. A good day to die.

Lae closed her eyes and tried to picture her mother, her father, her husband, and dear Egwinna. Their faces were clear in her mind. Lae would see them soon, for she felt the surge of energy that came to people before death called.

Lae wanted water, but she was too weak to reach for the glass. She cried out, and a servant was beside her instantly, offering her water. Lae drank deeply, but her thirst would not leave. Finally, tiring, she quit drinking, but clasped the servant's hand. "Send for Prince Aethelstan. Quickly."

She must have dozed because the next thing she knew, Stan stood by her. She smiled at him. "Stan, I have but a few minutes to live. I must tell you something to convey to Edward."

Stan's intake of breath was audible. "You cannot be serious. You will recover. You did before. The physician has left many medicines for you. I have sent for an Arabian physician who resides in Lundenburh."

"I cannot waste my breath arguing. The medicines will not stop this illness." Lae rested for a moment before continuing. "You have always been like a son to me. I have loved you as much as I did Wyn, mayhap more. I must remind you of a decision that was made by me several years ago."

"It can wait for my father, can it not?" Stan wiped a tear from the corner of his eye.

"Do not grieve, Stan. I go to be with your mother, my parents, and my beloved Red. God calls me, for my work on earth is done.

The Vikings are almost eradicated." Lae stopped speaking, for her breath would not come.

"Lae?" Stan's voice cracked.

Gathering what was left of her strength, Lae continued. "You and your father will finish the Danes, and Wessex and Mercia will be united under Edward, then you."

"What about Wyn?"

"Stan, she was not meant to be queen."

Lae swallowed to rid herself of the dryness in her mouth. "I have failed with Wyn. I have been able to control the Vikings, but never Wyn. Worse than any battle with the Danes was a battle with Wyn."

"I will marry her if you wish."

"Wyn would not marry you. I have decreed that neither Wyn nor any husband she may bed nor any issue of that union shall have claim to the Mercian throne." The pain in her left side was a fire that consumed her.

Lae stared at the candle clock. It was melting faster, taking her life's breath with it. "The strength of this entire island depends on Edward's controlling Mercia as well as Wessex. The future must be secured here and now. Promise me that you will tell Edward to take Mercia. Promise me."

Stan cleared his throat. "I promise, my lady. I promise."

"It is imperative that you do something else for me."

"I shall." Tears streamed down Stan's face. "I shall do anything for you."

"Take my name from the Anglo-Saxon Chronicles."

"Take your name from King Aelfred's history? Why?"

"It is important that my memory die with me. I do not want Wyn to have any claim to the Mercian throne because of my conquests. Take my name out of history."

"I cannot. You must have your place in the Chronicles. God knows that you have earned it. Your brother, Aethelweard, has continued Aelfred's chronicles. Your history is there."

"Do not defy me! Do as I say!" Lae was surprised at the sharpness of her words.

"I shall. I shall do anything that you ask. I love you as much as I loved my own mother." Tears streamed down Stan's cheeks.

"Egwinna. I will see Egwinna, too." Lae smiled. "Would you also send a message to Eiric who resides in the northern sections now? Tell him that in another time, another place, we could have been friends. Send a message to King Niall of Ireland." Lae smiled. "Tell him to honor Edward as he has honored me."

Stan leaned over and kissed Lae's cheek. "I promise."

"Send for Edith to reside with you. She can leave the convent, for she will be safe now. Find her a kind man for a husband."

"I promise."

Lae seized Stan's hand and held it against her cheek. "It is the sunset of my life. I have seen many sunrises, and I have flown to the heavens. I have no regrets. Bury me in Gleawanceaster with my husband and St. Oswald."

"It will be done."

"Red calls to me." Lae closed her eyes.